THE HEALER

THE HEALER

GREG HOLLINGSHEAD

A Phyllis Bruce Book
Harper*Flamingo*Canada

The names of those who have my gratitude in respect of this book: Ronald Burwash, Mark Czarnecki, my son David, Bernice Eisenstein, Dick Hebdige, Laura Jofre, Norm Mackie, Anne McDermid, Chris Rechner, and, as ever, my wife Rosa Spricer. I am particularly indebted to my editor, Phyllis Bruce.

I thank the Canada Council for financial assistance, and I thank the University of Alberta for the time provided by a McCalla Research Professorship.

First edition

Canadian Cataloguing in Publication Data

Hollingshead, Greg, 1947–
The healer

"A Phyllis Bruce book."
ISBN 0-00-225516-2

I. Title.

PS8565.O624H42 1998   C813'.54   C98-931389-1
PR9199.3.H64H42 1998

98 99 00 01 02 03 HC 10 9 8 7 6 5 4 3 2 1

Printed and bound in the United States

For Dick

For there is a dim glimmering of light yet un-put-out in men; let them walk, let them walk, that the darkness overtake them not.

— St. Augustine, *Confessions*

SHEEP'S CLOTHING

Timothy Wakelin, age thirty-two, pale features handsome or weak, it was hard to tell, fine dark hair thinning, widower food stains down the front of his blue cotton turtleneck, sat, dismayed and receiving looks, along a rear wall in the single chair at a table for two in the Grant Gemboree, a bus-stop café in the mining town of Grant. It was lunchtime on a hot weekday in late June. Outside, through layers of smoke, blue and enfolded, pickup trucks slowly passed. Inside, the place was jammed. Everybody knew everybody else, and everybody except the stranger had a cigarette going. A din of talk, shouts, horseplay. Clattering cutlery and banging dishes. The name tag of the waitress—not Wakelin's own waitress but the one who had taken away the other chair from his table—said Ardis, and he was watching her closely because he knew that this was the name of the healer's mother, and it did not strike him as a common name, unless it was common around here. Ardis was a tall woman, five-eight (Wakelin guessed) in flat heels. In adolescence she must have enjoyed the attractiveness of a cherub or an animal cub. Wakelin saw cheeks once rosy with new powers, but those powers, with the booze and the cigarettes, in middle age were swollen with disappointment, the cheeks pouchy, the bleached hair pinned up like straw, eyes dark-ringed and guarded.

She did not look like the mother of a saint.

Two other things Wakelin noticed. One, makeup intended to cover an area of bruising down the left side of Ardis's face. Two, the red-rimmed eyes of a dog—an old black Lab lying by the door, dewlaps outspread on the

3

grime—that followed her everywhere as she wove and squeezed through the press of diners.

Wakelin's lunch was just awful. Eggs of crumbling yolk and rubber-white albumen on a carbon laminate, dank toast, coffee a rusted knife-edge of heartburn, thin and without taste. A breakfast something like a story about a healer, something like a saint's life. Of dubious provenance. The dog's breakfast of narratives. Hearsay, exaggeration, wishful thinking, local legend. Followed now through a confusion of smoke and opinion, in a place for locals, a meetinghouse of initiates, with the blanket of the familiar draped soft all round. Cozy as heaven, old as hell.

The healer's name was Caroline Troyer. All her twenty years lived in this uranium town of thirty-three hundred people, a five-hour drive northeast of the city. From the articles already done on her, most of them published over the past year, confections too credulous not to be cynical, Wakelin had learned enough to expect some kind of saint, fanatic and pathetic in equal proportions. Of course, he was up here as a journalist, for the story. A journalist impersonating someone looking for a piece of country property. Impersonating himself, actually, from last summer, a year after Jane died, when he was roaming the Canadian Shield doing just that, looking for property, until he asked himself why he wanted to live in the country— what he thought he'd find up here, what he thought he'd do, how he'd make it from breakfast to bedtime—and couldn't think of an answer. Not a good one. Anyway, it was his own former intentions he was here in the name of. Former intentions now false pretences. These were his drawn line. All he proposed to bring to this and to take away was enough truth to make the thing fly. He would not purposely distort, he would do an honest, writerly job in the time allotted. Three to four thousand words for a major-circulation woman's magazine, whatever he wanted. Whatever he could come up with that would pass for new information, a fresh angle, a little insight, and failing all else a worldly, yet sensitive, last word.

Wakelin was watching a small old man ease in the front door. It was a difficult arrival, the movements halting and inexact. This was more than age. There was or had been illness. The palsy, the ravaged breathing, the trousers on heavy suspenders swaying clown-style, a gabardine barrel.

Across the room Wakelin's own waitress, whose name was Gail, glanced toward the old man as he approached from the door and shouted, "Hey there, Frank!"

Gail was a beautiful young woman with the luminous skin of an angel, a bad permanent, and something of a stoop. Also a poor clothes sense. A blue polyester gypsy blouse with ruffles, grey flannel slacks, and on her feet running shoes of convolved rubber extrusion in purple and lime.

A minute later, skull shining through his yellowing hair, Old Frank was being helped by Gail into the chair at the small table adjacent to Wakelin's.

"Everybody's hungry today," Old Frank said. His dentures, fingers, and nails were yellow too, and they seemed to be his biggest and strongest components.

"The usual, Frank?" Gail shouted, though she was right beside him.

The old fingers were groping the shirt pocket.

"The usual, Frank?"

Old Frank's teeth clacked. "Everybody's hungry today."

"I know," Gail said, turning her head as if to look around but not using her eyes. "It's unreal. The usual?"

"That'll be right."

Gail went away.

Old Frank was fumbling open a pack of Export "A." Three cigarettes spilled to the table. It was some time before he got one of them picked up, but when he did, Wakelin was right there with a match.

"Hi." The match flared. "Tim Wakelin."

Confusion in the old eyes until the flame had narrowed them to the task at hand, which when completed it was Wakelin who narrowed them next. "Reporter?"

"Not me," Wakelin replied and went on shaking out the match. "Up to look for a piece of country property."

Old Frank seemed to consider this. Then he said, "Sure as hell won't find much around here," and looked sharply at Wakelin to see how he would take the disappointment.

"Well, I'll tell you," Wakelin said, and leaned forward, confiding. "The only thing I haven't seen much of around here so far is a lack of For Sale signs."

Old Frank turned swiftly away. Whether stung by such insolence or stumped for a comeback, Wakelin did not have a chance to discover, because Gail was already right there, setting before Old Frank a platter of fried eggs and toast with bacon in a charred and twisted stack.

"You're looking for property," she told Wakelin, "you talk to Ross Troyer."

Ross Troyer, *yes*. Father of the healer.

"Ross Troyer Realty," Wakelin agreed, nodding. "I've been seeing the signs."

"You've been seeing the signs, have you," Gail said. She was making sure Old Frank had everything he needed. This done, she toted Wakelin's bill and slapped it down next to his plate. Then she stood and looked at him.

Wakelin looked back. He wanted to reach up and square those shoulders. In the shower, with both hands, he wanted to straighten that terrible permanent. Later, in front of a bonfire he would make of those slacks, blouse, runners, socks, underpants, and bra, he wanted to nuzzle and bite every part of her. He tried to think of something to tell her, besides this. He squirmed for his wallet. She seemed to shake her head. He froze. She did not move. He resolved to say something, anything.

"Pay at the cash," Gail said from the corner of her mouth and walked away.

After that, Wakelin spent some time sideways in his chair, holding the bill and his wallet, facing Old Frank's hair-dense right ear as the old man chewed in the tentative, reactive way of the dentured, for whom all food is now laced with tinfoil.

"So what's the story?" Wakelin said.

"*Eh?*" The head swung round. A column of yolk down the chin was a yellow thermometer. Delicate skin had formed on the bulb, which creased as the jaws with their electric dentures, their numb mouthparts, continued to chew.

"A reporter," Wakelin said, more loudly, "on what story?"

The Grant Gemboree noise level might have fallen slightly when he said these words.

Again Old Frank turned away. This time Wakelin did not know whether he had heard or not. Or, if he had, what.

Gail was back. "You got some egg on your chin there, Frank!" she shouted. Old Frank's fork clattered to his plate and both hands went scrabbling for a serviette. She helped him release one from the powerful dispenser and wiped his chin for him.

"Lying scum-suckers," Old Frank commented as she did this.

"What was that, Frank?" she shouted.

But she had finished wiping, and Old Frank was chewing again. She looked at Wakelin. Whether querying or accusatory, he did not know. There was no expression on her alabaster face.

"I'm leaving, I'm leaving," Wakelin said lightly.

She shrugged and glanced away as she removed a pack of Player's Mild from the side pocket of her flannels. "Too late," she said and fired one up. "Rush is over."

Old Frank was looking at Wakelin. "Had a cancer on my lung. Size and shape of a small grapefruit. Son-of-a-bitch doctors threw up their hands and walked away."

"I'm sorry," Wakelin said.

"Crushing other organs. Throwing off clots like a pinwheel."

"God."

Old Frank held Wakelin's eye. "Seventeenth of last month she shows up at my place. I'm at the kitchen table, there. No knock. She just walks in—"

"Who's this?" Wakelin asked, and before he could stop himself, "Caroline Troyer?" Quickly he glanced to Gail, but she had already turned to look significantly at Ardis, who stood directly behind her holding a coffeepot in her right hand and in her left hand the chair she had taken earlier from Wakelin's table. Ardis lowered the chair until its front legs rested on the floor. Gazing at Wakelin from around the chair was the black Lab, which had got to its feet. Gail's eyes came back to Wakelin. Ardis's had never left him.

Old Frank had butted out his cigarette. Now he was rattling his knife and fork onto his plate. He pushed it across to Wakelin's table and drew his coffee mug in tighter to his chest. This was how he had been sitting at his kitchen table. "Not dark yet. No lights on. Never heard her come in."

"Caroline would knock," Gail mouthed above Old Frank's head to Wakelin, nodding, mock-assuring, pointing to her ear. "He wouldn't hear."

"First I seen the light," Frank said. "Then I seen her."

"What kind of light was it, Frank?" Gail said, and Wakelin thought of a child asking to hear a favourite part.

"Soft firefly glow," Old Frank stated. He must have said this many times. It came out like one word. Softfireflyglow. "She was lit up in herself. That's the only way to say it. Call me crazy, I know what I saw."

"You're crazy, Frank," somebody said from across the room, not unkindly, and it struck Wakelin that the entire Grant Gemboree was listening. Even the old cook, a wizened dissolute man with shiny skin and a ponytail in a hairnet, had come out of the kitchen to lean against the cash and smoke. The story must have been spinning off apocrypha for a month, and now here was Wakelin himself the occasion of a new authoritative telling. He couldn't believe his luck.

"She sits down at the table there. She takes me by the hands and she looks me straight in the face." The old man stopped speaking. He sat and blinked.

"Did she say anything, Frank?" Gail asked, prompting, leaning past him to crush her cigarette in his ashtray.

"Not with words, she didn't."

Again Old Frank did not continue. He took a small dry lump of tissue from his pocket and with shaking hands opened it and blew his nose.

"Is that when you cried, Frank?" Gail asked at his ear.

"Didn't cry," the old man said with surprising force. "Nobody cried." He half-turned to Gail. "Stand behind me! Put your hands on my shoulders!"

Gail positioned herself behind Frank and did as she was told. He had leaned slightly forward in his chair.

"Now move them down my back—No, *hell!* not that way! Not thumbs together! The other—That's right—Stop right there—Left on top of right. Not so much pressure. And *hold it.*" From his leaning position Old Frank surveyed the room. "Whole lung went hot-cold right through. Like Vicks

VapoRub. Then she done the left one. Same thing. A couple minutes each lung, no more. I never felt anything like it in my life. The girl has power in the palms of her hands. She beamed that power inside there the way you'd go in with a storm light."

Again Old Frank did not continue.

"And then what?" From the healer's mother.

Old Frank looked at Ardis. "That's all she needed. Next ultrasound, cancer's the size of one of them mandarins you see at Christmas. This last one"—he snapped his fingers—"clean as a whistle."

There was quiet in the Grant Gemboree. The coffeemaker hissing and spluttering.

Gail lifted her hands away from the old back.

"So what do you think happened, Frank?" someone asked.

"I'll tell you what happened. Caroline Troyer give this body the knowledge to do what it had to do. She showed it how things were with it, and that's all it needed to know."

No one said anything. The dog yawned. Gail was back at Frank's ear. "Tell the rest, Frank," she said. "Now that you got everybody's undivided attention."

"You do it," Old Frank said. "I wasn't there. I stayed inside the house."

It was Ardis Troyer who told the rest, and she told it directly to Wakelin. "What happened," she said, "this wasn't the first time Caroline went out to heal, and when she come out of Frank's a crowd was waiting at the side door. It was dark, and either it was the light from the kitchen—"

"Kitchen light weren't on," Old Frank said.

"—or she still had the glow on her. The ones waiting didn't know whether to run up and touch the hem of her garment or cry out to God where they stood. Well, she didn't give them the chance. She told them to get the hell on home, and when nobody budged she pushed through them and started back to town herself. By that time half of them were on their knees. The ones that weren't, they clutched at her, but she struck their hands off and kept moving, with everybody trailing behind.

"By the time she gets to the main street she's got over sixty people in tow, and this is the last straw. She turns on the stairs out front of our place and she tells them she's finished with healing. You lay the hands of life on people left and right, and what do they do? Treat it like no more than their due, and heaven forbid anybody try to tell them they owe a goddamn thing to a living soul."

"You weren't there, Ardis," someone put in from a table by the door, a man with blow-dried hair and Culligan stitched on his shirt. "The wife wasn't out to Frank's, she only heard what Caroline said on your steps. All Caroline said was, 'It's not me and it's not you. Go home. There won't be any more of this.' It was about a dozen people, by the way, fifteen at the most, half of them kids, and half of them there to horse around. If there was a glow on her out at Frank's, Doreen never saw it. When people ask her she doesn't say there was or wasn't, she just says she never saw it herself. People don't glow, Ardis. They only seem to sometimes."

Old Frank might have contributed something on the glow question, but he was engaged in retrieving his plate from Wakelin's table and had stopped listening, or couldn't hear. Ardis chose neither to accept nor to refuse the correction. While Culligan was speaking, her eyes remained on Wakelin, and when Culligan finished saying what he had to say, it was Wakelin she pointed her chin at. "Think you got enough yet?"

"Enough—?"

"You're a reporter, aren't you?"

"No—" He cleared his throat. "I'm not, actually. I'm looking for a country place."

"Well, isn't that a convenient coincidence."

"What do you mean?"

"Country place, my ass. Ignorant hick superstition is what you're looking for."

Wakelin did a helpless shrug. "Not at all—"

"Well, she's had it up to here. She's quit healing, and she's quit talking to reporters for free. Interview's going to cost you five hundred an hour."

"What?" Wakelin could only say.

There was a pause then, and Wakelin, though he was genuinely amazed,

10

was also conscious of the amazed expression staying longer on his face than it would have were he being candid about his motives. And then the black Lab was swinging its head to see how to back up. Gail too was stepping away. Ardis lifted the chair. As she replaced it at Wakelin's table she said, "This is for whoever it is you're working for." She did not wink as she said this. There was no twinkle from those hooded eyes.

Wakelin smiled, nervously, a little confused, and Old Frank's head came around. "Only trouble is," Old Frank said, "he don't know if it's Jesus or the Devil."

"That's right, Frank," Ardis said, and she passed on, refilling cups.

Wakelin stared at his bill. As he did so the Grant Gemboree noise level made a rapid return to its former level. Finally Wakelin was able to take in what he owed: $2.99.

Why, it was nothing at all.

Gail was back. "So anyways," she shouted, "Frank's Caroline Troyer's biggest fan, and no wonder, eh? Aren't you, Frank?"

Old Frank had pushed away his plate. "I guess I would be that," he acknowledged.

Gail stepped closer, gazing down upon the old skull. "Too bad she stopped, eh? She could still help a few more poor souls around here if she wanted to, I guess."

"She never stopped," Old Frank declared. "Nobody could stop that. I won't be the last one that gets their health set to rights by that one."

"Hey, maybe not, eh?" Gail said hopefully.

Old Frank's head had come around once more to Wakelin. "It's not every young lass can heal a man," he said.

"No, it's not," Wakelin agreed.

But Old Frank had already turned back to Gail, indicating his plate. "Could you throw this in the microwave, darlin'? In all the excitement the cocksucker went cold on me."

11

The establishment known in Grant as the Troyer Building was of ancient frame construction in brown shingle-brick pressed up against the heaved narrow sidewalk of the main street. Unlike most of the other buildings on the main street of Grant, it was not false-fronted but an actual two-storey, with a gable, separated from the shoebox IDA Drugs by a broad wooden staircase roofed and set back from the street and rising into darkness. Wakelin stepped into the shadows there. Immediately at his right hand was a dusty window covered on the inside with some kind of perforated board, the regimented holes shining sickly. Stepping deeper, he sighted up the staircase. At the top was a landing and to the right of that a door, which from his research he knew opened into the Troyer home, an apartment on the second floor. Was it from these stairs that Caroline Troyer had addressed a crowd of between twelve and sixty, speaking words of disputable import? It smelled like a urinal in here.

Wakelin walked back out into the sun and stood on the curb and looked up at the building. From the articles he had read he knew that the attic gable window was hers. Above it, in the apex, an oval plaque: Erected 1919. Lower down, at the second-storey level, two windows, larger. Sun-damaged brown drapes, their falls crushed by furniture against the sills. On the ground floor, the family enterprises. To the right of the single entrance from the street, one window only, no sign on the glass. Beneath that, in a row along the sidewalk and leaning at different angles against the front of the building, seven marble headstones. To the left of the door, where the window had been, a rectangle of shingle-brick a deeper shade of brown. Above the door a shingle, brown lettering on beige, divided left and right by a double slash. To the left of the slash, Crooked Hand's Fine Jewellery and Tackle. To the right, Ross Troyer Realty.

The door was a full two steps above the level of the sidewalk. The steps were concrete, eroded to settings of polished stones. As Wakelin placed his foot on the lower step he was moved to reach over and lay his right hand flat against the ink-blank centre of the nearest marble headstone. A surface glassy and warm in the sun. Other stones were salmon and sand-colour. One was black. All with lapidary margins of maple leaves, lilies, Scotch thistles. Leaning across, Wakelin could also see, along the inside sill of the window, in a gap created by a shortfall of amber cellophane creased and bubbled against the pane, a row of bleached Polaroids, and he leaned farther to study those pale images, of frame cottages, aluminum-sided bungalows, waterfront lots and woodlots, all prices neatly inscribed in faded ballpoint across the bottom margins, and when he had finished this scrutiny he saw, higher up the glass, an octagonal silver sticker, lifting away around the edges: Monuments Sold Here. And he thought, Well, for your long-last home you've got your aluminum siding, and before it needs replacing you'll be wanting the marble. For your long, last home.

He closed his eyes. From a public speaker down the street Roy Orbison was singing "Running Scared" in a voice undersea and pure as bel canto on an old seventy-eight. At Wakelin's back, two pickups idled at a light. Overhead, a squirrel on a phone cable was turning one of last year's acorns into a hail of shells, the fragments clicking and bouncing on the sidewalk. The sun was hot against the right side of Wakelin's face and against the back of his hand on the headstone. He could smell the exhaust from the street, he could smell the scorched sugar fanblast from a doughnut shop somewhere. And he knew that he was right here, that he was nowhere but where he was.

Wakelin lifted his hand from the stone and straightened up. The door was dirty matte white, boot-scuffed along the bottom, an aura of grease around the knob.

Three to four thousand words. Anything he wanted to write on Caroline Troyer he could write. His editor, a buzz-cut beauty, was being kind to him because his wife had died only twenty-two months earlier. Try that again. His editor was being kind to him instead of sleeping with him. She was being kind, and she was being not dumb. She knew there would be three of them in the bed. The healing story he could take to a book if there was a book in it, though that did not seem likely. He was not here to do a hick superstition story. He was not here to put Caroline Troyer down. A little cultural anthropology for the instruction and delight of the readers of a national woman's magazine. Allow them to make up their own minds. Of course he was here to do a hick superstition story. Of course he was here to put Caroline Troyer down. He didn't intend to demonstrate she could heal, did he? Attention-seeking daughter of dysfunction. That was his understanding when the stories on her had first started to appear, that was his understanding after he had gone through the files, and that was his understanding driving up here. And if she had stopped healing, or pretending or thinking she was healing, then that was new, nobody to his knowledge had written about that yet, and maybe that could be his story. But it seemed that his predecessors, callous impatient hacks, had betrayed whatever small trust they'd once enjoyed in local hearts, and if he himself hoped to uncover a story in this picked-over patch of glacial outwash, then he would need to continue being a guy just looking for country property. Would need to keep his sheep's clothing buttoned up a while longer yet.

Or so Wakelin assumed as he climbed the steps of the Troyer Building. Grasped the warm, cheap brass knob. Leaned into the door.

Through the display board at her left hand, from directly the other side of it, Caroline Troyer could feel the man's unease and the pull of his curiosity as he stepped deeper in to study the stairs to the apartment. She waited to hear if he would climb them, and when he did not she slipped off her stool behind the counter and crossed to the front window, beyond the door. There she waited again, until she saw his face, the face of a child, crinkled and ambered by the cellophane, craning into the frame as he studied the pictures, not idly and not as a buyer but in the more abstracted manner of someone working to assemble an understanding. And she saw his eyes close as he seemed to listen. Or maybe it was the warmth of the sun against his face that was causing him to hesitate this way, one hand, she imagined, flat on a gravestone—but she could see the print of fatigue, the habit of obliquity in the set of the mouth. And she saw a man, though not old, already half turned to the past. His energy accordingly devoted, his suffering consequent.

She walked back to her place behind the counter, and there she watched herself try to believe that this was not another one here for a story.

Country bells jangled over Wakelin's head. Sunlight widened across linoleum and partway up an oak desk, narrowed and was gone. Commotion in darkness. On the desk an electric fan revolved its swollen cage toward him, a robot head, the rock-weighted papers in its swath agitating so violently that surely they would fly up and blow around at any time. He moved forward, blinded by the sudden diminishment of light: fluorescent tubes flickering from a stipple ceiling, an arborite sheen off walls of nicotine pine, knots like black gouts. At the rear, above the desk, certificates of qualification. Photographs in black frames. Groups of men in shirtsleeves and jackets, shaking each other's hands. The fan swung away, and multicoloured plastic streamers across a back doorway took up the dance.

Wakelin moved right, to a cork wall tacked with more Polaroids of cabins among leafless birches in thin sunlight. Small cottages separated by gravel roads from steel-coloured water. Slope-porched red-brick farmhouses, narrow and spruce-darkened. Rural properties. He returned to the desk and smartly, with the flat of his palm, whacked a desk bell.

"Here," she said.

"Aaah!" Wakelin cried, and as the surprise kept lifting him higher into the air and the embarrassment came flushing up into his face he knew again what a floater he was, and already as he settled back into his shoes he was turning, too fast, and he could feel his whole body clamouring for balance.

That it was Caroline Troyer he knew from a picture in her high school yearbook, reproduced in more than one of the articles. *If there was a glow on her I couldn't see it, and then she smiled.* The story was already writing itself in his head, a shameful dodge, the corruption of a good journalist, and it wasn't even partly true, she was a long way from smiling and yet he could see it right away, a quality of light about her, and if *light* was too much, then maybe *calm focus* would do. No one, anyway, who glimpsed this young woman would fail to look a second time. She was sitting on a stool behind a display counter along the street wall, next to the door he had just come through. Her hair was straight and dark, cropped at the livid jaw, and she wore a weed-coloured cardigan unbuttoned over a white T-shirt. Broad shoulders. For the sake of the story he wanted her to be beautiful, but he couldn't tell at first if she was or wasn't, and he thought she must be one of those who are either very beautiful or very plain, in some moods and attitudes one and some the other, except that when she is plain you are not sure, and when she is beautiful you have no doubt. A certain rawness or youth in the bones of the face. But not the eyes. No failure of clarity or maturity or definition there. At first he thought they were raging, but moving closer he saw they were simply in a state of full attention. Eyes beholding an accident. No emotion as yet. The accident continuing to unfold.

"I didn't see you there," Wakelin said. He was standing across the display case from her. He reached over. "Hi. Tim Wakelin."

She did not take or, for that matter, look at the hand. He might have been holding out something vile or dangerous he had found lying in the street. He looked down and saw the hand now following through with a feigned casual gesture toward the contents of the case. Well, there was one problem right there.

He pretended to study the contents of the case. An assortment of jewellery and tackle, as the shingle had promised. Many lures and brooches. Many intricately beaded and feathered earrings and dry flies. "Nice work," he said, knowing nothing about such things. The pieces were certainly beautiful enough. "Yours?"

She shook her head, scarcely. Still watching him.

"But you're the . . . daughter?" he said.

"He's not here."

Wakelin nodded. A bad question. To his right, her left, a sheet of perforated white pressboard arrayed with rods and other fishing gear. Bolted over a window. He peered down into the case. "Local artist?"

"Bachelor Crooked Hand."

Again Wakelin nodded. It was possible he had not stopped nodding. "He's good," he said. "Mr. Crooked Hand knows his stuff. He is local, then?"

She hooked the hair over her left ear. "Friend of my father's." This last word a hard one for her to say apparently. You could hear the wince in it.

"I thought they looked native," Wakelin said.

She made no reply.

"Listen," Wakelin said. "I'm looking for a place in the country. Could you—?"

"It's him does the properties. He's in in the mornings or I can tell you where he's at."

So. The father.

Not quite the order of things Wakelin had had in mind. But then, neither was she. None of that pleading presumption you get from the serious neurotics.

The Grant Fairgrounds were five minutes north and east of the town, on a tabletop cuesta that towered like Eden above the working fields. As the lane wound upward, the plume of red dust in the rearview swelled and rose and moved out through the planted pines. Wakelin slowed at a rusted gate, standing open. The peeling white fences of the grounds were swamped in their decay by milkweed and field grass. It was evident that this year's Grant Fair would not be some weekend soon. Now on Wakelin's right was a long, low sag-roofed building, like stables. At the chained doors of a larger, more barnlike structure, he turned left and drove down into the thistle-and-dirt bed of a racetrack and up out of it, crossed a patchy barren of dandelion and gravel, and descended into the track bed on the far side of the oval. A hundred metres down the stretch to his right, he saw weather-blackened white bleachers. Immediately ahead, a graffitied exhibition hall in cream-yellow slate, where a shining red tow truck stood majestic amidst a few battered pickups.

From inside the exhibition hall, the sound of hammering. Wakelin left his car alongside one of the lesser vehicles and passed through great standing wooden doors into the echoing space. The building had a mansard roof and gables, and the green light came tilting down in long shafts from the ancient mossy windows. At the far end, in a haze of dust, two kneeling carpenters were hammering away at what looked like the raw skeleton of a low platform. Two other men stood nearby, their figures large in the particulate blur. As Wakelin came up to them, the shorter, stockier man glanced at him past the other's shoulder. He was First Nations, wearing workboots and soiled coveralls unzipped to the navel. To Wakelin's eye there was no hair on his head or body whatsoever. Not eyebrows, not belly hair. His head and face and chest had a pinguid smoothness, the skin like a latex bodysuit from which the trapped and lashless eyes gazed sadly forth.

Bachelor Crooked Hand, Wakelin thought. It's got to be.

When one of the carpenters looked over at Wakelin, the other, taller man, the one speaking, turned to see who or what had caught the carpenter's attention. But only briefly, too briefly for Wakelin to see his eyes, which required the merest glance to discover the utter lack of significance of this arrival. And so Wakelin found himself standing waiting for the man to finish telling a story, a rural incident, in which a child's head had been sawed off in front of its mother, except that the sawer had got either the wrong child or the wrong mother, and this would be the lawyer's plea: diminished guilt by reason of mistaken identity. Not so much grief caused as otherwise, your Honour.

Lawyers, fuck 'em, Wakelin thought. And then he wondered what the teller was pretending to think: that a stranger would show up in an empty exhibition hall in out-of-season fairgrounds where nameless construction was under way and just stand around being pointedly ignored while eavesdropping on a leisurely recounting of some grisly local horror? And then he saw a look pass between the two carpenters and one of them glanced over, and that did it. He stepped forward.

"Excuse me," he said.

The man stopped talking. The native considered Wakelin once more.

"I'm looking for Ross Troyer," Wakelin said.

Now the other turned to face him. He was taller and older and better dressed than either his companion or Wakelin. He wore a collarless stitch-striped blue shirt with dress jeans and loafers. His face was handsome like a child's, large and mild, and he wore his hair long and combed back in waves, like a movie star's, except that there was something terrible about his eyes. It was as if they had been lobbed in on a dare from a distance of several feet, or as if it just happened to be human sockets they had landed in, it could as easily have been a wolf's. The irises were milk-green, paler than the circle of the sun-beat face and paler still at their inside than their outside rims, a circumstance causing an impression of concavity, which in turn caused the pupils to appear to protrude, like rods. Rods that swelled and contracted, swelled and contracted, until they had got Wakelin just right. Then they stopped moving.

The man said nothing at all, just drilled Wakelin, just skewered him.

"Are you Ross Troyer?" Wakelin said.

In reply, heavy lids lowered slowly over the terrible eyes. Lifted once more.

"I'm Ross Troyer," the other, hairless man said.

"Oh, really?" Wakelin cried and turned, so surprised he behaved like someone startled. "I thought you were—" Holding out his hand.

The hairless man's hands remained in the pockets of his coveralls. He just looked at Wakelin. Face of iron, acid-pocked iron.

"What do you want?" the first man said, any impatience he might have felt at his companion's little trick directed clean at Wakelin.

Turning back to him, Wakelin said stupidly, "You're Ross Troyer?" and then, "I'm looking for some country property. Something—"

"You talked to her?" Troyer said quickly, a glance at his friend.

"Yes, I—"

"What'd she say?"

"She told me to talk to you."

Troyer nodded. He seemed to wait.

And so Wakelin talked to him. He said what he had planned to say, the same thing he had said with fanatic earnestness to every realtor he had spoken to when he was up in this area last summer, in his hot hand the money Jane had left him, when he truly was looking for a place in the country. Or thought he was. Three months off and on, spring to fall, he had searched. Nothing. Until one airless September night in a cricketing motel room, not so far from here actually, he had leaned into the half-unsilvered mirror above the cigarette-burn scalloped dresser top and asked himself what exactly he thought he was going to do in the country. Get in touch with his grief? Commune with the chipmunks? Hang himself from a tall oak tree? When no answer came from the glass, he drove back to the city where he would rid his mind of all thought of sylvan redemption. Or try to.

The word Wakelin had used most often in his statement to realtors last summer when describing what he was looking for in a piece of property was *silence*. He used this word again now in his statement to Ross Troyer. Silence. Country silence. No neighbours, no traffic. No highway over the next hill. He told Ross Troyer that he had been searching for silence since early spring. He asked him if he realized how hard it is to find silence in the city. He told him how in his search for silence he had crossed and recrossed half the southern Shield, that he was serious, that he could pay cash. He told him exactly how much he could afford to pay (though he could afford a little more than what he said, because he still had the money from Jane). He did not tell Ross Troyer (and did not know himself) if he was talking about silence because silence was still, or ever had been, of genuine value to him, or because last summer he had talked about it so often that he was starting to believe in it himself, or because in the pressure of the moment he was mouthing bits of last summer's speeches, and really this was nothing but words. Repeats, at that. Old words. He didn't believe in silence and never had. And he did not tell Ross Troyer that the sole reason he was here—conscious reason—was to find a way to talk to his daughter in order to get enough new material on her healing activities, or on her having given them up, so that he could go back to the city and write the story and so move on to the next and after that the next, and all this talk about silence was really just a symptom of a private fantasy of respite from the mechanical round of the life of a man who had lost its compass when he lost his wife.

After Wakelin finished talking there was a pause while Troyer fixed him with his pupils before he said, "You're not going to find much for that kind of money."

"Yeah," Wakelin replied wearily. He had heard this many times.

"Of course, if you could see your way to coming in a little higher—"

But Troyer was already shrugging, and in the tired casual voice of one advising a fool he added, "Drop by the office tomorrow. I can show you what I've got." And he turned upon Wakelin a look that might have been intended to say he was sorry not to be able to be more encouraging, but what the look actually said was, Now you get the hell out of my sight.

Wakelin glanced across at the hairless man to see if he might offer some sort of foil for this sentiment, but everything about the look he received from that quarter made it clear that it was not for one such as Wakelin to know how it was inside that balaclava of flesh.

Wakelin walked down the echoing hall and out into the bright heat of the afternoon. He knew he could climb into his car and be back in the city by dinnertime. He knew he could just write off this whole gig. Flop down in front of the tube in time for the ten o'clock news. Wake up tomorrow and start on something quick and clean and over with by the end of the week. Something without all this northern history. This cast of the repressed.

Except that as he drove south, approaching Grant, with every conscious intention of passing through and keeping going, he turned in suddenly at a motel called the Birches. There the grass had been trimmed to the bases of the slender white trunks of those trees and made a green carpet to the river. There, owing to the fine summer weather, all the tired woman on the desk had available was a cabin out back. "Sounds good to me," Wakelin said, and a few minutes later he was unlocking the door of a mock-log shack hardly big enough for a double bed, a small hot space smelling of mould spores, Pine-Sol, and cigarettes. Tens of thousands of cigarettes, from the decades when every holiday traveller smoked and the scenery when viewed at all was viewed asquint.

Wakelin was in the trance that goes with doing the opposite of what you'd intended, when everything has to be thought about because nothing now is going to be easier than to start making mistakes. You are off-track, which is to say you are divided against yourself, and who better qualified to fuck you up? For ventilation's sake Wakelin left both the door and the one small window of his hot shack wide open, took off his shoes and socks, and shuffled down the carpet of grass to the river in its narrow channel.

Divided or not, he was not, it seemed, ready to give up on this story, and not because things were going so well. All he had for tomorrow was a pretext for reentering the Troyer Building. To learn what her father had to sell him. Mind you, given the general tenor of his welcome around here, this could be considered a significant achievement for one day. Tomorrow morning he'd be waiting out front when she opened for business, her father would still be upstairs shaving, and this time she would talk to him.

Not likely.

So why was he still here?

For a chance, like a believer, to touch the hem of her garment?

Wakelin looked to the water, sliding with a constant force. So swift, so black. Universal magnet for despair. He sat down. Not one for rash acts or anything like that, but a single move could undo that favourite little idea about himself forever.

Something not kosher between the father and the daughter. Not to this day, maybe, but once. He could feel it. Something.

Was this what was keeping him here? The story behind the story?

The shore opposite was talus at the foot of a height of black rock with the disshevelled appearance of igneous toothpaste squeezed a hundred feet out of the earth and fallen back on itself with a great weight. The cliff was barely in shadow, but the shadow was headed this way, across that spill of rock. Wakelin lay down on the grass where he sat, an arm over his eyes. He was hardly sleeping these days. Compensated by being half asleep most of the day and dozing at any time. There on the grass he fell asleep and dreamed that he was back in the city, in the summer night. At that small hour when the commotion stumbles to rest, when the roar of human commerce subsides to a broken peace, when at any moment you are liable to be jolted upright by a mufflerless acceleration, by a window slammed shut against a drunk bellowing in the street, by cats yowling and hissing in the grey backyards of the morning.

In the city Wakelin slept with a pillow over his ear, a feather buffer, but for some reason the pillow made the fear worse, and most nights he woke afraid, sometimes with a cry or a shout, sometimes crouched by the bed, toes gripping the fibre mat, no idea why, no particular memory of a particular dream, just the fear. This had been going on so long and was so familiar and at the same time so fresh a condition that Wakelin had all but forgotten it had been no different when Jane was alive, that it had not started with losing her. With Jane, when he bolted up in terror, he had trained himself to pass straight into the follow-through, pillow in hand, a comforter pulled from the hall closet as he passed, and he was on the futon in the living room, already working at getting back to sleep, rocking his hips in a steady rhythm, something he could not do in the same bed with Jane, who felt every shift, heard every sound. If so much as the pattern of Wakelin's breathing changed, she was wide awake. *What's wrong?* she would whisper, and she would be talking to him.

Nothing, Love. Nothing's wrong. Nothing at all.

What was wrong? He blamed the city, he still blamed the city, but he knew the city was not it. Not really. Sometimes when Wakelin slept it was as if the sweet flow of his dreaming were a supersaturated solution the faintest *ping* could crystallize to terror. As he slept, his mind would pass out through the pillow pressed against his ear, and it would range across the ambient field until when the moment was ripe it would pluck one sound and swell it to a chime. *Ping! Time for your fear, Tim!* This was how it happened on the riverbank behind the Birches. In the distance somewhere, all but beyond auditory range, probably, the slam of a screen door exploded like a gunshot inside his head, and it was a detonation of sorrow, a bullet of fear and longing. He sat up on the grass in the shadow of the black cliff, and the blue sky above him was perhaps not cold but it looked cold. He got to his feet shivering, the arm lately over his eyes now numb and useless, brushing himself off with the other, and walked stiffly back to his mock shack, which had retained the heat of the day with the same shabby tenacity it had retained the cigarette smoke of its occupants and the spores of the mould in the carpet and the cheap curtains, and he curled up on the warm bed with a gentle rocking of his hips, and he was grateful for that warmth now.

Caroline Troyer was sitting behind Crooked Hand's counter. She was reading. Something was bothering her, and as she went on reading she half-thought it must be the man who had just been in looking for property (so he said), how his half-turn to the past and the habits of blindness and deception cultivated by that in him had muddied and compromised his nature, but then she realized that it was not him, at least not only him, but her own immediate state of intending to do something she wasn't doing. Of knowing there was something but not knowing what it was. Like knowing something is there before you turn your head. Before you recognize it, it's there as a husk, as the ghost of itself, waiting to be known. And then the sun had reached the cellophaned window, and the office did not get hotter, not yet, but the patch of bright amber light on the linoleum at the corner of her eye caused her, even as she continued to read, to think of heat, and that was how she remembered that she'd been meaning to plug in the fan, which she had unplugged when she went upstairs for lunch, right after the man had come in, and that's what it was she wasn't doing.

Now it seemed to her there must be a way to act that would not, like this, like him, be confused, half hidden to yourself, half backward-turned, your timing always that little bit late. And she decided to see if it would be possible to know the right time to get up and go over and plug in the fan. She knew she could just do it. Decide to do it, then get down off her stool and walk over and do it. But it seemed to her that that would only be acting according to an idea of what she should do. Acting to fit an idea of acting.

26

And she wondered if there could be some other way to do it. So she sat up straight and she waited, and before she knew it she was springing up to go and do it. But instead she sat down again, because it seemed to her that doing it that way, without thinking, was even more mechanical than doing it according to some idea. So she waited. Again she sprang up to do it, and again she sat down and waited.

And then it happened. She saw when to get up and go and plug in the fan, and in the exact same action of seeing it she got down off the stool and walked over and she plugged in the fan. And this was another kind of action altogether, a third kind, completely different from the other two. It was a harmony, a grace of movement, and she wondered if a person's whole life could be this way. And how this would be different from the other ways. How it might change how she was able to know. Whether she could live in order to act out of seeing and not according to an old reflex or the last idea. And she knew that it would be easy to think you were doing it when you were not, believing in it as an idea but not doing it. Or doing it in love with the person you wanted to be. But the thing was, she knew that she knew this, and she knew that she didn't have to stop there, because she understood that knowing this was also part of what she could see, and all she had to do was to try to find out how far this thing was possible to be done.

In this way, moment by moment, not gradually but all at once, at each moment, she would empty herself, if she could, she would empty herself of the slave.

Ross Troyer leaned across the seat and opened the passenger door for his daughter Caroline, who climbed up and pulled hard at the door but not hard enough for the door to engage. It was an old truck.

He raked his fingers through his hair, observing in the rearview the effect of doing so upon the lie of it.

"Door's not shut," he said.

She tried it again.

"Who got in?" he murmured, his old joke. His eyes had left the rearview. She was clicking into her seat belt.

His hand went lightly to the handle of the knife in the sheath at his left side, as it often did. Then his hand went to the ignition. "Better wind down that window."

She wound down the window.

He eased the truck along the narrow alley, and when he reached the street he nosed out cautiously beyond the parked cars. They left the main street by the north bridge. Passed the Birches Motel (where Wakelin lay in his hot shack out back, watching TV) and next to the Birches the new six-unit white-brick plaza. Two more minutes and they were beyond the built-up area, into farmland. In the distance to the north and east the fairgrounds in their elevation. This was just after six in the evening. The sun was pale and it would not set for nearly three hours. It was only just summer, but there had already been more heat than rain, and the trees and the crops though green were not lush. Caroline Troyer sat with her hands loose in her lap and her head tilted slightly, the way her father often held his, but her expression betrayed none of his facetiousness, only the affliction that was often there too in his, her eyes downcast upon the toes of her boots set evenly upon the floor of the cab.

This was farm country close to that part of the Shield where on three different occasions, over two billion years, alpine ranges had pushed up, all now eroded to fault escarpments and low domes of granite wrapped and separated by the forested sag and swell of the shreds of sedimentary gneisses. Where in this area the roots of those ranges lay exposed was a short distance to the north, beyond hills of clay and gravel and wooded outcrops and Precambrian erratics now ploughed around for oats and corn. Where the grade was steepest it was girdled by high faceted walls in olive and black and pink, for the roadway had been blasted out of the batholith for the pleasure men take in linearity achieved by the effective placement of dynamite. As the truck climbed toward this channel, Caroline Troyer's eyes remained lowered.

"You're okay?" he said.

She nodded. Not looking up, she added, "Why?"

"You seem depressed."

"I was dry," she said, and looked away out the window where a sign read, Rock Collecting Along this Highway Is Dangerous and Unlawful.

"Dry," he said.

"Dry in my heart."

"Would this be why you've been hiding your light under a bushel? Or because?"

She made no answer.

The truck was losing speed with the steepness of the grade.

"Why did you stop the healing, anyway?" he asked her. "Your mother could have sworn you had a good thing going there. I think she expected you'd take it on the road."

She looked at him.

He smiled. "Tears of the world a constant quantity? Or its gratitude?"

She looked away again. "I don't like crowds."

"Me neither. But there's money in them. As your mother has pointed out to you many times." He put his face close to hers and said in a waggish voice, "But do you listen?"

She didn't say anything.

"So what are you going to do?"

"I don't know."

"You don't know. I don't suppose you ever heard the expression, 'When a woman has nothing to do she buys a pig'? Pig comes along looking for country property, she marries him. Gives her mother a nice city porker to sit on. Distributes the weight a little."

She was still looking away. After a while she said quietly, "What do I need with somebody else's body to look after?"

He laughed at this, pleased, a soft crowing, and pounded the heels of his hands lightly against the wheel. And then he said, "Healer sick of healing speaks."

"We're not talking about healing."

"No."

After a pause he said, "Still, you could. What if marriage is the next thing to do, as you will know in your bones? The next thing's enough for most people. They sit around on their ass until all other options exhaust themselves, and then they do it. Circle closes. What's so wrong with the next thing? Without it, what have you got? Doubts, littleness"—he hunched at the wheel, making himself small—"laziness, putting off, closing down, that's the person, tiny and scared. The next thing, now, that's the larger wisdom."

"It's no wisdom," she said.

He didn't say anything, and then he touched her knee, and when she looked at him he mouthed, "That's my girl."

She scowled and turned away.

They had reached the crown of the highest height of highway in that high country, where rocks amber and olive lined the channel the road had been laid in, great angular blocks so heavily demarcated one from the next it was as if they had been placed in that stepped array by giant masons. Just beyond the crest of the road, where the rock went into terraces, tilted terraces, a sign saying Ross Troyer Realty stood at the foot of a sandy drive that cut back hard to the right and climbed one such angled terrace to where a tall black tar-paper house with a patchwork tin roof stood untended in long grass, invisible from the road. Windows paneless. Troyer nosed the truck up to the north wall of the house and turned off the engine.

Crickets and cicadas. The hot engine ticking.

Caroline Troyer got out of the truck and walked to a window and looked in while her father removed a rifle from a chest in the box. The smell from the house was the smell of bats and mice and the defecations of larger creatures in a hot space. A nothing room slow to lighten after the brightness of the evening. Curling linoleum. Torn wallpaper and squatter litter. She stepped back and looked up. Nests of cliff swallows high up under the water-stained eaves.

She walked to the west corner and looked along there. The front door was halfway down, three feet from the tops of the weeds. There were no steps. She walked back to the east corner and down that wall past coal-cellar stairs under a sheet of melt-sagged plywood; a gas stove, controls gutted; and small corroded items of automobile and appliance it was necessary to step around until she came to the south wall and sloping away from there an open area of rock and stubbled grass where not so long ago children had played. A rusty swing set. In the dust by her foot a warped red plastic shovel bleached to pinkness. From here the land continued to fall away to the east and south where the dark river twisted and turned through the village in the anguish of human propinquity until the peace of fields permitted serenity once more. Along the south wall of the house was an old sofa slumped by the elements upon its frame and springs. It looked soaking, but it was hard and crumbly to the touch like something mummified, and upon it hung the miasma of manured dog. In the middle of that wall a door had swung open. It creaked in an imperceptible breeze. The steps to it were concrete blocks sunk at an angle. She glanced at that door and turned away. A clothesline, a bare wire, had been strung from a hook in the side of the house to a jack pine with a russet crown. Something hung from the wire. She went over. From its rear foot by a string a chipmunk, headless.

The string was knotted to the line. She worked at the knot to undo it, drawing back her face from the dessicant stink. Jumped when he said, "What are you doing?"

"Throwing this away."

"Good. You're learning. Your anxious homebuyer, they do love an omen."

"Why?" she asked, meaning the desecration.

He shrugged. "Somebody needed a head?"

She ignored this. "Why couldn't they just feed it or give it a name?"

"Probably they did. First." He smiled.

He had his hunting knife out, to cut the knot, but she got it undone before he could do that and threw the small carcass down the slope, into the longer grass.

"How can you sell a place like this?" she said.

It was a moral question, or more accurately, an accusation, though that was not how he heard it.

"For the view." Which he indicated. Then the house. "This'll come down."

"What do you tell them about water?"

"I tell them around here it's three-quarters water. Rock and water. Two billion years of rock and ice and water. Cool it down, rock and ice. Warm it up, rock and water."

She just looked at him.

He stepped closer. "Listen to me. People buying a house are buying their own dreams. Same as healing. They'll be healed as much as they want to be healed, and they'll buy what they want to buy. You don't want people to believe you can heal, you don't want to sell them back their dreams, that's fine. Just don't let me ever hear anybody say I stood in your way."

He turned and she followed him, followed his shirt, the perspiration in a stain at the spine, around the house and through the old scrap and long grass to where the rock surfaced grey and smooth and level with the curve of the land and the eye rose from it to a sky like a luminous bowl of fine-sanded glass. Beyond the clearing of rock was a rail fence on which stood a pair of riddled cans, Coke and beer. Troyer walked over and picked up three others, also riddled, a Cott's, a green one probably ginger ale, and a Diet Coke, and placed them at spaced intervals along the rail. He walked back to where she stood waiting and handed her the rifle.

She checked the breech, placed the rifle firmly against her shoulder, aiming. Fired. The Diet Coke popped into the air as the echo of the report came off the house behind them. When she fired a second time the beer can behaved in exactly the same way. A third time and the Cott's can too was gone. The Coke can was not hit dead centre, and it flew off obliquely. The ginger ale was as the others. She lowered the rifle. A breeze thrashed delicately the leaves of a cluster of yellow birches just beyond the fence. The sound was the sound of running water.

"You're getting there," he said and sadly smiled.

Rubbing her shoulder, she turned to look at him.

"You know," he said, "we should go camping again some time. Just the two of us. How long has it been? Twelve years?"

The pain in her eyes must have been what he was after.

"No, eh?" he said mildly and again he stepped closer. "Anyway, you'll remember what I've always told you." He laid the tip of his right index finger against the centre of his chest. "*Bang*, right? Anybody tries anything with you?"

Her eyes stayed with his. "That's about you," she said. "What you'd do. Now what about everything else?"

But he had already turned away and was walking back toward the fence and failed to see the movement of her hand to indicate not only the grove beyond but also everything around them, the house and the seventy and more years of isolation and suffering and blundering clutches at freedom it had known, and the entry into its history that selling it would constitute, and the squeamishness of such a consideration, and this primeval rock the house stood on, and the land to the south, all the contention and folly and sorrow of the town down there, the contention and folly and sorrow of her own heart, of everything physical, everything human.

"What else?" he said. He was stooping for cans. When she didn't answer he looked around and made a grin using an economy of face muscles in a ritual they had not had between them since she was a girl of nine or ten. "What do I care about everything else? Is it going to snap you out of this phase? Is it going to give me back my precious angel?"

"I'm not talking about everything else for me. I'm not talking about any phase. I'm not talking about precious angels."

He set the cans along the rail and walked back to where she stood. "I'd say we're both dry," he said. "I'd say we've both been dry for too long." He took back the rifle. From his pocket he drew a .32 handgun, which he passed over to her and stepped back facing the cans.

She was not so accurate with the handgun, missing two cans altogether on the first try and hitting directly only one.

As he moved forward once more to restore the cans to the railing, she sank to her haunches in a single effortless movement, her elbows on her knees and her arms locked straight, the gun lax in her hand.

"I was taking the clothes out of the dryer yesterday," she said. "Folding them and dropping them in the basket. When they landed they made a funny sound."

He looked around at her. He was holding a can. "Funny sound," he said.

"A crackly popping. Somewhere between a crackle and a pop."

"Don't forget the snap. I always carry a good big pocketful. It's bulky, but it's light. I admit it tends to clog the machine."

"I thought it might be static, from the heat," she said, "but it wasn't crackly enough. It didn't sound enough like static."

"Huh."

"What was it?"

"Don't ask me," he said. "I know it looks like I'm busy setting up cans here, but really I'm just putting in time until you tell me what it was."

"It was suds that came back out the drain where the washer empties, right next to the clothesbasket. I didn't notice them against the light-coloured lino, there. I had my eyes on the clothes dropping. Well, the air pushed out by the clothes as they landed was passing through the mesh of the basket and popping the suds. It was the suds popping I was hearing, and it sounded almost electric but not really."

"Well, well," he said.

She looked up at him. "It didn't sound like suds when they pop. I know what suds popping sounds like. Or I thought I did. This was more crackly. I was thinking I was hearing something electric, so it wasn't the same sound."

"Not the same sound, no," he said.

She was looking up at him in an attitude of imploring, but that was not what she was doing. The look was to say that this was for him. For his benefit. That she knew what she knew, fugitive and inconsequential and perhaps dreary or trivial to another as it might be, but it didn't matter, because she also knew that it would operate to the degree of its significance, and if it were not significant, then it would not last, it would make no difference, it would not operate at all.

"It was like eating a cherry," she said, "when you think you're eating a grape. It's not the same as eating a cherry when you're expecting a cherry. It's a strange cherry."

"You're a strange cherry," he said. "A strange cherry with too little on her mind."

And then she seemed to have to will herself to continue. For a long time now it had been difficult for her to talk to him at all, let alone about anything that mattered to her. This was hard work, and the only thing that made it possible at all was how much it did matter to her. "I'm not saying everything's in a person's mind or that nothing's ever the same the next time, I'm saying a person can be wide open to how much it is and it isn't the same the next time. You don't have to hold on to believing things are a certain way any more than you have to act according to some idea of what you should do. It's only going to wear you down. Well, today I stopped. All that's gone, I let it go, and it doesn't matter, or maybe it's the only thing to do. The energy's back, it's gathering. It turns out it never stopped. And I'm still here. I'm saying it's not the end of the world."

She had lowered her head and was scraping at the dirt with the barrel of the gun. Now she looked up. "Or maybe it is the end. But if it is, it's the beginning too. Every moment."

His face was averted. "I thought you said you were dry," he murmured.

"Not any more."

Now he came down beside her, squatting too. Her head was bowed again. He looked to the west, where the sun was making a blaze out of a new tin roof on the other side of the sunken highway. If there was more to say about the bubbles, she didn't say it, only went on scraping with the gun. He looked back at her, at the top of her head.

"Whew," he said. "For a moment there I thought you were going to tell me you saw God in the suds. Fell to your knees and licked out the drain."

She rose up off her haunches and started for the truck. He came after her and placed a hand on her arm, and she turned with the gun in both hands and raised it until the end of the barrel came up to the point directly in the centre of his chest.

"Don't ever, ever do this," he said.

"I know what happened," she said. "But I don't understand what it's done to me. It's obvious it's done something, and then there's all this energy, and it's not ordinary, it's not like any other kind. I don't know what's happening, I have no idea, and I don't want to pretend to myself that I do. I need to find out so I can know what to do next. Not just the next thing, but what needs to be done. It's like there's been a disaster to the land. The question is, What's growing here now?"

"Lower the gun."

She did not lower the gun.

He took a breath. Exhaled. At that moment he too must have recognized the extraordinariness of her talking to him, for he seemed to resolve to go along. He rocked back on his heels. "So what is? Growing here now?"

"I'm telling you I don't know. I have to find out for myself."

"Nothing new about that. 'Caro'ine do it by se'f.' That's your problem."

"Then I'll find that out too. Why aren't I allowed to know what I can know? Why can't a person know a thing unless everybody else is right there to say, 'Okay, fine, we're all ready, you can go ahead and know that now.' What if other people haven't had the same kinds of things happen to them? Good or bad, I'm not talking about only bad—"

"People keep each other on track. That's how they move ahead. This is the problem since you quit school."

"I quit school because I wasn't learning anything in school."

"You're learning now? What? How special you are? The powers available to the true believer?"

"What do I believe?" she cried. "Tell me what I believe! Tell me right now!"

He ignored this. "And you quit healing because you couldn't—what? Deserve it? Or heal?"

"It's the energy heals," she said. "The energy's got nothing to do with deserving or not deserving."

"Of course it does. Whatever you happen to think about it. You just don't want to see your own part in this. In anything. Nothing new about that either. Look, Caroline. Anybody can be a saint if they never leave their own room. At least when you were laying hands on people you were getting out of the house. You're too old for this. You're too smart. It's time to come back to reality. It's time to remember who you are."

She lowered the gun. "Who I am is fog," she said. "Who I am is poison gas."

He looked at her, and then he performed one of his unexpected acts. Brought his hands up to press the heels against his eyes. For a full minute he stood like that, still facing her, heels pressing, and then he took them away and his eyes were red and hollow and wet. He blinked. "Just don't leave me, Precious Angel," he said in a soft voice, almost a lisp. "I'm begging you. Don't do it."

She watched him as he said this. And then she said, "This isn't begging, it's warning."

She turned and walked back to the truck.

When Ross Troyer spoke in the kitchen his voice caused the heat duct that fed his daughter's room overhead to resonate. Caroline would know her parents were arguing by the quality of the sound from the duct. Her father did not have to raise his voice, all he had to do was speak long enough each time for the duct to resonate. She would know he was not talking on the phone because the phone was directly below her bed, in the front sitting room, next to her mother's hand. She would know her parents were arguing because it was only when they argued that her father addressed more than one or two words to her mother at one time. If Caroline were to crouch by the register, as she used to do when she was a child, she could hear what he was saying, and if she were to lie flat on the floor and press her ear to the register, as she used to do until the burden of knowing came to outweigh the secret strength of it, she could hear as well what her mother was saying, all the way from the front sitting room, which was separated from the kitchen by the dining area, less a room than a space between the kitchen and the front room. There her mother, the dog at her feet, would be watching TV or reading a magazine or doing a crossword puzzle, a tumbler of vermouth on the coffee table in front of her, while in the kitchen her father, who did not drink, would be cleaning his rifle or going through real estate listings, and Caroline would know that he was listening to her mother as he had always listened to her, now listening and now not listening, in a way that to judge from his intermittent responses had done nothing over three decades to diminish the irritating effect of her words. Sooner or later the duct would start to resonate.

It was resonating tonight, but Caroline did not get off her bed, where she had been writing (the small black notebook now slack in her hand, the ballpoint pen capped and fallen to the bedspread alongside her knee), but listened only to the pure sign of her parents' arguing as she had listened to it not as a child crouched at the register who understood the words or most of them but earlier, as an infant on her back, her limbs waving in air to its inflections, her muscles drinking its rhythms, that she might be informed by, and so survive, and in surviving one day react against and in reacting echo and so recreate the world of her parents' emotions. Now, twenty years later, loath, she was sitting upright on her bed, where she could hear echoing inside her the legacy of that infant thirst: the tone and rhythm and tenor of the old wrangle, of the voices that moved without ceasing. And all of it—not only her parents' passion but the turmoil it caused at the depths of her own muscles, her own being—was no less physical and familiar than the traffic noise and the rest of the low constant din from the street or than the full moon visible through the window like a halogen floodlamp behind speeding clouds. And she continued to listen to the rasp of the curtains in the night breezes and to the sound of her own breathing deeper and slower. And the other, the interior and past, was contained within the ground of these immediate sights and sounds, soothed by them, slowed and quieted though not silenced, held by them in an embrace of perception that calmed and so enabled the discovery of grace even in that.

In the front room Ardis Troyer had been drinking Bright's President vermouth with ice while snapping through the pages of *Chatelaine*. She had been doing this for some time, every once in a while leaning forward to take a sip of her drink, but then she closed the magazine on her lap and sat like that, with her hands folded upon it. Reached for her drink. Drained it. Set down the tumbler with alcoholic care, though she was not drunk. Cleared her throat. Keeper, the black Lab, who lay with his chin on his foreleg, opened his eyes to look at her but was not roused to lift his head. She began to speak, at first almost wistfully but with increasing force and in a tone of amazed grievance concerning matters financial as they pertained to old plans of household acquisition and renovation too long in abeyance. Expectations cancelled, prolongations of waiting endured, not without bitterness.

These were old beads, slick with handling, and it would be remarkable if her husband listened at all.

When she spoke next, the connection at first obscure, the subject was her fellow waitress Gail Poot's sister-in-law Bertie, who recently with the help of her husband Wilf had set herself up in the electrolysis business.

"Hair removal," Ross Troyer said from the kitchen.

"That's right. Unsightly body hair. Also spider veins. Spider veins is same equipment, different course."

She reached for her glass. "Gail says people still think it hurts. Bertie told her it takes a little practice to get the depth right, that's all. You get the depth right and they don't feel a thing. A mild discomfort. Bertie's better at it than most of them. She can already do thirty an hour."

"Not customers she can't."

"Customers? *Hairs.*"

"Christ."

"Bertie says the people act just like patients. They respect you and they're grateful. They never dreamed this would be possible in their lifetime. What more could you ask? I think it would be a wonderful opportunity. In hard times people look to their appearance."

He was studying a real estate listing.

"When it's all they've got," Ardis said.

"Who's Bertie?"

"Gail Poot's sister-in-law."

"Gail Poot isn't married."

"No, but June is, and Dave's brother Wilf married Bertie."

"Dave's an asshole."

"I have no doubt that Dave is. Unfortunately we're not talking about Dave. Any more than we're talking about Gail or June or how in hell they're related."

"They're half-sisters."

"Ross, she could take the course."

"What course?"

As he said this his chair scraped. Keeper looked around. She could see from where she sat that her husband was rising to his feet, and she was about to ask him, as long as he was up—but he passed from view, and she heard the back door open. She closed her mouth.

Night air blew cooler from the kitchen. Keeper got up, though with difficulty, and went to see. His toenails clicked across the linoleum of the dining area toward the kitchen.

Ardis felt for the remote. The screen flashed and came on. A jet-lagged-looking man in a foreign suit and brass-coloured hairpiece was standing in a studio audience pulling a silk rope of scarlet and blue from the cleavage of an obese woman looking up at him with a fight-or-flight expression, possibly an admixture of gratitude. Ardis watched this feat at once absently and in an attitude of calculation, as one who though with weightier matters on her mind would solve the illusion. When she heard a scuff on the fire escape she switched off the TV.

She looked to the kitchen. "You could at least shut the door after you when you wander out without a word."

He was leaning a rifle against the wall by the table.

"Keep leaving those in the truck and the next we know some ten-year-old'll be lying dead in the street."

He was clearing the table.

Keeper returned from the kitchen to circle next to the coffee table, preparing to lie down once more.

"But anyways," she said.

He was laying the rifle upon the empty table.

"Handsome? As long as you're up—?"

A few minutes later he came into the front room carrying a bottle of vermouth by the neck. Keeper looked around. Her husband stopped at the coffee table, extending his free fist, palm-downward, over the tumbler. As he did this, she gazed at the back of that hand, a fervent scrutiny. Reached out to stroke the hairs along the clench-smooth skin of it. A tentative caress. At the first touch of her finger the fist released. Two ice cubes clattered into the tumbler. The other fist came forward to pour.

"Thank you, lover," she said and then quickly, "Why can't you clean that thing in here? Shouting back and forth like a couple of fishwives."

He was returning to the kitchen and made no answer.

She took a deep breath and told him everything she had learned from Gail Poot. Where the course was offered, how many weeks, how many hours a day of classes, the cost. She told him what Gail had reported the necessary equipment had set back Wilf and Bertie, and she told him the dimensions of the space in the Belmount Mall they had rented and how Wilf had done all the necessary carpentry and wiring and even a certain amount of the plumbing to get her started. What the space had cost per square foot. How long the lease.

This was information with a real estate component, and he seemed to listen. When she had finished telling him everything she knew, he cleared his throat and said, "No."

"Don't tell me Alex Connor wouldn't give you a good rate," she cried immediately, prepared for this. "She can pay us back. If she stays on here, she contributes for once in her life like anybody else. It's not like we don't need the money."

"No."

A silence fell.

"I honestly don't know any more," Ardis said quietly, "why I bother."

This admission drew no reply.

"I guess a person lives around here long enough," she continued, snapping the pages of her magazine, "she just gives up. Who wants to go on slamming their head against the same wall?"

And this question drew no answer.

After a few minutes Ardis said, "I'll tell you one thing. No woman not a complete monster who's ever been through the living hell of a child is not going to look out for her, it doesn't matter how useless she's turned out, and when men grow tits maybe they can start to understand that."

Neither did this assertion elicit any sort of response.

"You know what I'd like to know?" Ardis said. "Why in God's name she'd stop the healing."

In the kitchen the fridge started up, and shortly after, in the manner of a man who, even as he begins to speak, is extricating, with the greatest reluctance, his attention from something incomparably more interesting, he said, "This assumes she started."

"Get off it, Ross!" Ardis cried. "These weren't no-name strangers! And even if it was only the ones ignorant enough to have the faith, the point is it was her they were ready to put it in. She's the one that's got what it takes to bring people so far on side all she has to do is touch them with her baby finger and they tip over into perfect health. And don't tell me that's not a rarer gift than anything these pill-pushers are up to these days, with their tainted blood and their antigoddamnbiotics. Doctors are nothing any more but a bunch of little Chinese and Jews fresh out of the cradle who think they know everything, when in fact they're stumbling around in the dark like everybody else."

She stopped and looked to the kitchen. He was rubbing his face.

"Why'd she stop?" Ardis said.

The hands continued rubbing and then they fell away. "Just as well," he said.

Another short silence, and Ardis said, "I honestly don't understand how even you could say something that ignorant. Your daughter has the halt and lame picking up their beds and walking out to meet the new dawn, and you sit there and say it's just as well if she doesn't."

He did not deny that this was what he had said.

"You know what I think?" she asked him.

"I do. You keep me constantly informed."

"I think she's up there having the same nervous breakdown she's been having for the past month, and the reason is, you don't turn power like that off and on like a kitchen tap. I say she hasn't got the first clue in hell what she's sitting on."

"Not if it's not her ass."

"I can't talk to you."

There was a pause.

"Look," he said. "If she's up there thinking twice about getting herself canonized, it'll be the first healthy sign out of her in twelve years."

Ardis had moved on. "You know what she needs? An agent. All right. She was a, shall we say, unusual child with less than zero social skills and an overactive imagination. She flames out in high school, she's got no aptitude for real estate, she hasn't had a date in five years, and who am I kidding, she's not going to be happy doing moustaches and bikini lines. But for Christ sake, Ross, look what she's capable of! These reporters sniffing around here all winter. The world's interested, if you aren't. All she needs is some outside direction."

"She's got it. He lives in the sky and his take is one hundred per cent."

Ardis was holding up the *Chatelaine*, rattling its pages to get his attention.

"Why isn't there anything on her in here, for instance? We're just scraping the surface. Play our cards right and our little Two-shoes could be bigger than Jesus and the Beatles put together. These TV evangelists make fortunes, and they're charlatans, every last horny bugger. I know. I watch those shows. The real thing does not come along every week, and when it does, believe me, the hunger's there. It's a market that never dies."

"You know what?" he said. "I don't want to hear any more about this."

"No, I'm sure you goddamn don't," Ardis said quickly. "And for the life of me, I can't imagine why that should come as no surprise."

And pages of *Chatelaine* began to snap again, like little whips.

But of course nothing had been concluded, for it was not necessary for Ardis Troyer to know the reason she bothered in order for her to continue to do so, and slowly, with the persistence of fire, or life, the argument resumed, its participants ever more voluble and repetitive, luxuriant each in their refusal to yield, appearing never to progress but always progressing, like a dance or a sport or other human activity constantly on its way to repose, if never conclusion. And though patterns were retraced they were not on that account the same, informed as they were by histories of their own recurrence. Meanwhile overhead the high winds of the lower atmosphere had stripped all clouds from the face of the moon, allowing the light from the sun that reflected off that spheroid mass of dust and rock to brighten the air and the floor and the foot of the bed in the attic room where Caroline Troyer could see it by the translucence of her eyelids as she listened to the commotion from the street now generally waning but more raucous when it did erupt and the now gentler scrape of the curtains. And always the insistent resonance of the duct as her father made his stands on behalf of his version of her and of her few conceivable futures and of his own need, in response to her mother's stands on behalf of her version and her need. And none of this was the same. None of it, ever. Because none of it was as it had been the last time, for there had been no last time, not really, and even were it all as old as that four-and-a-half-billion-year-old satellite lit by a star only slightly older, it would still be in the perceiving of it constantly new, because the perceiving was informed by the energy that all of it had come from and was still coming from and still falling back into, and that energy did not dance to time's music but time to its.

Next morning, in the sudden sunless dark of the Troyer Realty office, Wakelin practically collided with Caroline Troyer, who was standing, for no visible reason, in a state of apparent complete idleness, in the centre of the floor. As he fell back he saw how tall she was, as tall as her mother, though not her father, and at least as tall as himself. A tall young woman wearing the same weed-coloured cardigan she had worn yesterday, this time with a cotton blouse buttoned to the neck. A plain skirt. She was not old, just dressed old. Old or schoolgirl. Unadorned even by the jewellery she sold. Big hands, hanging at her sides. Sober of mien.

"Sorry," Wakelin said and added quickly, "Is he here?" He glanced around anxiously. He could see now but was not taking anything in.

She shook her head.

"You're expecting him though," Wakelin said in a tone caught uneasily between apprehensive and coaxing.

She seemed to notice. Then she said, "Truck's out back, but I haven't seen him."

"Listen, he told me to come in today! I stayed over, at the Birches!"

She was still standing directly in front of him. Watching him. This ongoing accident his presence.

"What time did he tell you?" she said.

"He didn't. But you said he was in in the mornings."

"Well, he never mentioned anything to me."

"So what am I supposed to do?"

"You could see what they got over to Mahan and try back here around eleven. If he comes in, I'll try and catch him."

"How far's Mahan?"

"Twenty-five minutes. Pringle Realty 2000. Ask for Merle."

"Hell," Wakelin said and did a petulant knee-flex. He lowered his face a moment. When he brought it up he said, "Listen. You don't want to go for coffee, do you? Or I could—What do you take? It's just"—he put his hands to his face—"I really need to stay awake." But these last words, being specious, echoed inwardly as noise and misgiving. "No?" he said, before she could respond. "That's okay, I'll just wait." He plunked down on the nearest chair and looked up at her. Made a smile.

She turned to face him head-on once more. "What kind of property?" she said.

Swiftly Wakelin rose to make a short version of the speech he had made for her father and Bachelor Crooked Hand.

"Silence," she said dubiously when he had finished. "You get far enough back in the bush you'll have silence. In winter, anyways. Middle of the night. But daytime and evenings there'll be the snow machines. And the chainsaws. Sound travels in the cold. On the lakes as soon as the ice is out there'll be outboards, and jet skis."

"Okay," he said. "Fine. It doesn't have to be on water. No 250 Evinrudes. No neighbour kids drunk on the next dock doing loon calls at two a.m. But also nothing next to an airfield. Or on a highway. Or a snowmobile run. Or an ATV route. Or railroad tracks. I don't want to wake up to the five-fifteen. Or a lumber mill. Or a log sorting area. Or a firing range. No artillery. Nothing like that. Silence. A basic ground of silence. The wind in the firs. The snowflakes crashing down."

"Why?" she said.

Wakelin opened his mouth. Shut it. Would, if it killed him, for once here, answer honestly, sort of. Leaven the guile. "I need to hear myself think. I've got a few . . . personal matters to sort out. I need peace. A little peace and quiet in my life."

She nodded.

Wakelin followed Caroline Troyer through the plastic streamers and down a corridor of leaning headstones and realty signs and other clutter, umbral and glaring, toward the white glow of a screen door that opened directly into a chain-link bare-earth compound in eye-stabbing sunshine. There he climbed into the baking cab of a primer-grey Ford pickup, a smell of road dust, French fries, engine oil, the dashboard vinyl gaping dirty foam padding, an extensive crack system networking down the windshield like fork lightning. It was the kind of truck in which you would not be too surprised to see a rod come melting up through the hood.

"So how far to the first property?" he asked as she steered the rattling vehicle down a narrow alleyway, a grey board wall to the left, concrete block to the right. An inch to spare.

"Twenty minutes."

"Practically to Mahan."

"Mahan's east."

As they came out between parked cars and pulled onto the street, Wakelin saw Bachelor Crooked Hand. He was leaning into a sidewalk phone next to the Stedman's, in a corner of the parking lot across the street. He was speaking into the mouthpiece, toy-sized in the meat of his grasp, and as he did this he was looking straight in through the windshield of the truck at Wakelin.

"What does that guy do?" Wakelin asked, the gaze following him as Caroline made the turn. "Besides make lures and brooches?"

"That's his," she replied, indicating the red tow truck rising behind Crooked Hand like an image on a billboard, the shining grille rippling in the heat. The same tow truck Wakelin had seen parked outside the exhibition hall at the fairgrounds. "Nights he drives the ambulance," she added.

"Busy man," Wakelin said. He had twisted in his seat to look out the rear window of the cab. The eyes were still on him. Quickly Wakelin turned back around in his seat. "I met him yesterday, with your father. Well, not *met*, exactly."

She didn't say anything.

In two minutes they were moving out of Grant, a rhythmic bump from the left rear wheel like a bulge in a bicycle tire, a pulse accelerating. The Birches Motel came up on the right, and from his present unforeseen vantage Wakelin watched with improbable nostalgia his home of last night pass like something from a parallel life. A glimpse too of the person as recently as this morning he had been when there, as alien and spectral as the friend of a friend in an anecdote told in a dream. As a matter of fact, in the confidence that sometimes in the pursuit of a story, good faith can drive out the bad, he had not yet checked out. A small white-brick plaza then, and on that same, east side, beyond a spreading oak and under a blue *H*, the district hospital, clapboard ranch-style, like a retirement home. Past that and to the north and east, on their elevation, the fairgrounds.

"Maybe your dad's back up at the exhibition hall," Wakelin suggested.

If Caroline Troyer agreed that this might be the case, she did not acknowledge as much to Wakelin.

"Of course, we've got the truck, so how would he—" and Wakelin thought, Stop talking right now. You don't know a thing about it.

"What are they building up there?" he said next, for conversation.

"I don't know," she said. "I haven't been up. He's on council."

Wakelin nodded.

Pale fields rolling; sun-bleached barns on distant hillsides, like mock-ups; blue sky. Ahead a grey-black swell of the Shield. Through the window at his back the sun shone hot on Wakelin's shoulders under his shirt. The truck after his little car felt spacious and high up off the road. She drove with the seat all the way back to accommodate her long legs, and she moved in a way that seemed to take possession of the vehicle and the road.

"So tell me more about these properties," Wakelin said.

"One's a two-storey frame with a view, the other's a sixteen-acre farm run to bush. A two-storey five-bedroom brick."

Wakelin waited. "That's a lot of bedrooms," he said finally. "I could sleep around."

Silence followed here. And then, though of course he knew what it was, Wakelin said, "Can I ask you your name?"

"Caroline."

"Tim." He reached over. At first all his hand got was a glance, but he left it there, stubborn in the air between them, and finally her own came off the wheel and briefly, firmly, he grasped it. A strong hand as big as it looked. If this was the hand of a healer, it was no shaking hysteric's. Or so Wakelin decided. As it returned to the wheel, his own returned to his right knee in an image of his left hand, thumbs in parallel. He had always liked sitting this way. He also liked the heat of the sun at his back. He closed his eyes. Maybe they could ride like this forever. He looked at the side of her face. Would this be a good time to broach the subject of healing? Just kind of segue into it? But how?

"Will I love these properties?" he asked instead.

She gave him a scant wordless look, and Wakelin thought, One thing about these country salespeople, they do not stoop to charm or flattery. Nor do they lay down a pitch. It is almost as if they were reluctant to sell.

The truck was labouring ever more slowly toward a chiselled slot in the horizon, a blue tab.

"Anyway, it's nice to meet you, Caroline," Wakelin said.

Just past the summit of the long climb was a Troyer Realty For Sale sign, at the foot of a gravel drive that cut back steeply to the top of the rock wall. They had passed other such signs on the way, nailed to fences and trees. This one had a diagonal of tape across one corner saying Reduced, and this time Caroline swung in. They mounted a gravel slope to a tar-paper house with black window frames. She pulled the truck right up into the shadow of it and turned off the engine.

"Needs a few panes," Wakelin mentioned, crushing a mosquito against his temple as they stepped forward. The place suggested a rural bomb-site. "What'd they—blow out?"

She didn't say anything.

"Where's the front door?" he asked next. Looking around for it in every direction including away from the house altogether, he saw riddled pop cans on a rail fence. "Somebody's been doing some target practice," he called to her as he stumbled after her down the side of the house among scattered appliances and automotive parts to a slope of rock and brown grass. At the foot of the brown grass, a dead spruce with a russet crown.

"You're right," Wakelin said, fanning at blackflies. "It's a wonderful view. Is that really Grant down there?"

The river was a flung sash. Above the town, corrugations of rapids. He walked over to a clothesline. In the spirit of a prospective car buyer kicking a tire, he tested the spring of it. Looked back around at the house.

Last summer one of the realtors Wakelin consulted had spoken to him of the paramount importance of a straight ridgepole. He was a squat guy with frizzy no-colour hair and the breath of a cat. Your first line of defence, he kept saying with fierce, tooth-sucking emotion.

"Roof seems okay," Wakelin now observed. "What are they asking?"

She told him.

Wakelin was astounded but too cunning to let on. "How much land?" he asked calmly.

"Two acres."

Now he could hardly contain himself. "Not bad," he murmured, practically stroking his jaw. "Not bad at all." He ventured a glance at her then, and she was looking at him as if he were insane. "Of course it needs a little work," he added quickly. "A new door, for one thing. From this angle that one looks kind of warped. And windows. Can you see a single intact pane? I can't."

She had started for the house.

"Could we look inside?" Wakelin called.

It was a dreary warren of scat-littered open-lathed cubicles remarkably unventilated considering the amount of window glass scattered across the floors. Wakelin kept crunching over to the light and gazing off into the distance. Anyhow, it was a great view. He was a menace to his own livelihood, wasn't he, to be so impressionable? When even a place like this could have him forgetting he was not here to buy property.

"Those are hydro lines, right?" he said, pointing out a window at wires with insulation frayed and rotting. "Or would that be phone?"

"There's no phone."

"And heat?"

"Oil."

She was looking at him, waiting, he imagined, for more questions. "They deliver up here, do they?" he said.

"It needs a proper well."

"For *oil*?"

She waited.

"Oh, right, of course," he said, nodding. "That might be fun. Could I dowse?"

She turned away.

When they were out in the fresh air again, same blackflies—must have waited—he asked, "So is there in fact a front door?" but he was already sighing. "Look," he said. "I'm afraid upstairs I heard a car go by. Two cars. I appreciate the highway's at the bottom of that channel so you don't actually see it, and I guess windowpanes would make the place more sound-proof, but, I mean"—vaguely he looked to where he imagined the highway—"it's right there." When he turned back, she was walking away.

"Hey, where are you going?"

The second property was fifty miles north and east. Wakelin looked again to the side of her face. Where was she taking him? To the land where all foolishness is exploded? He tried to get her to talk, not about healing necessarily, about anything, small talk, but the driver's preroga-tive being silence he soon gave up, though grateful. He was not enjoying the sound of himself with her. A tenor of wheedling. Persona of a ditz. A pale little voice from a box-inside-a-box of ignorance feigned and igno-rance real. Where was the affable lettered fellow with the easy laugh and the endearing stammer who should have had the story by now? *A* story. *Some* story. Was it her country authenticity throwing him or only some-thing that passed for it, a dark reflector of his own devious passing, and here at the wheel of this truck was a natural power demon, an old-world witch, the sort of woman that people can't stop themselves submitting their bodies to?

After forty minutes down a rolling corridor of black spruce, the asphalt acceded to washboard. A government sign said Highway Improvement Project and Caution: Unsurfaced Road. Ten minutes later a propped sign with a red-rag flag above it said Slow for Highway Workers, but there was no equipment and no road crew, just the hanging dust of vanished speedsters. Asphalt again and soon after, Coppice, a truck-stop hamlet on a black river in a valley more a shallow dip in the rock than a valley. Caroline Troyer pulled in for gas at a Shell station where the man on the pumps was a study in black faded to the landscape. Mafic attire. Black shirt, black jeans, black boots, all like the rock here weathered to grey. Receding black hair greying, combed straight back. A lean hollow-chested man with the complexion of late Auden and the non-rotational spine of an old farmer. The faded black shirt he wore open at the neck, a square of peach-coloured plastic mesh at his throat, and when he leaned down to Caroline's window his fingers fiddled up under the mesh and his voice came out electronic and raw.

"How are you folks t'day."

"Orest Pereki," she said.

Now he looked at her more closely.

"Caroline Troyer," she said.

"So it is," the voice said, the fingers up under the mesh. "How's your dad?"

The service station had a restaurant with peach curtains punched out in that same plastic mesh. Wakelin said he needed to stop for lunch, he was ravenous. He knew that if he didn't get her talking soon he had no story. It would be two wasted days. "On me," he said. "Please."

For a mile or so the highway had run parallel to a hydro power line, and now in three columns the giant pylons stalked the horizon like skeletons of Martian war machines. When Wakelin and Caroline were seated inside by the window, she parted the curtain of mesh and indicated the man dressed like rock. "Orest used to be cut sprayman for Hydro," she said.

Wakelin considered this, and then he said, "Defoliant? Orest should sue."

She was still looking out the window. "He'd need money to sue."

"Not necessarily," but that sounded fairly unlikely. Wakelin considered adding something like, Too late for a healing, I guess, a case like that. Or, Kind of raises the larger issue of why people get sick, doesn't it?

But he didn't. Instead he ordered the club on brown, toasted, with fries. Caroline Troyer, the egg salad on white. They both chose medium Cokes. A point of connection, Wakelin felt. Over lunch he got down to work. He started by asking her if she liked living in the country.

"I don't."

"Why not?"

"I live in town."

"Right. How's town?"

She shrugged her shoulders. They really were very broad. A fine head on them, too. "I never lived anyplace else."

Wakelin shifted in his seat. "Tell me. What do you think to yourself when somebody shows up from the city looking for a piece of country property?"

"I don't think anything. It's always him takes them out."

"Hey. I'm honoured."

Gravely she studied his eyes, perhaps to discover there a finer intelligence than could be inferred from his words.

Wakelin persisted. "But why me?"

"He told you to come in when he wouldn't be there."

"Because he didn't like my face."

She did not deny this, instead said, "It would be him we saw Bachelor Crooked Hand talking to."

"He set this up?"

"No. But Bachelor would tell him what he saw."

"Why? Your father wants you or he doesn't want you to take people out?"

"He doesn't know if he wants me to or not."

"But you don't. Want to. Normally."

"My parents, they think I should have a career."

"And you don't agree, particularly? But it doesn't have to be this one, does it?" She didn't say anything.

"Doesn't a person have to lie to sell houses?" Wakelin asked next.

"You don't have to lie. You show them a bad one and then you show them a good one. That's what he does."

Wakelin sat back, disarmed. It was a long time since he had been with anyone like this. Childhood. This was innocence. Candour, no strings. A source of alarm. How could he not pity it? Not seek, despite himself, in juicy small increments, to wisen it up? Not sooner or later with one half-unwitting word or gesture finish it off? How could he trust himself?

He asked her, "So will you do this again?"

"No."

"Your decision has nothing to do with me, right?" He grinned. "I mean, this isn't personal?"

No expression marked the honest beauty of her face. No hostility, no amusement, no tightening of the skin around the eyes, nothing. Only watching.

"Tell me," Wakelin said, leaning forward with great calm, scrambling to keep this going. "How do you know Orest?"

A flicker. Just that. A shadow. "My father, he used to bring me up here in the summers, when I was little. We'd camp. Down the cut a ways— Look, we have to go."

"Just you and him?"

She nodded. Eyes downcast. Making no move to leave, and, like her, Wakelin sat watching her weigh and turn the truck keys in her fingers. And he was thinking, Jesus Christ, I can't even tell if what I'm feeling right now is compassion or desire. Who's supposed to be the emotional illiterate at this table, again?

Without raising her eyes, she said, "There's Wakelins out around Avery Lake."

"Bow legs and bad hearts?"

Quickly she glanced up.

"They'll be the impostors. Awful thorns in our sides."

She looked away.

And then it was more brutal of him still, but the waitress was standing right there, looking at him. He ordered pumpkin pie and coffee. "Two seconds, I promise," he told Caroline Troyer. "I just can't seem to stay awake today." He let his lids droop and hated himself all over again from the beginning.

When his order came he paused with a forkful of pie and said, "So what do you want your career to be?"

"I don't know."

"Did you ever think about joining the Church?"

He might have pricked her with a pin. "Why would I do that?"

"Only a suggestion. Exercise your faith—"

"What faith?"

"You don't have to have faith—"

"Why would I want to have faith?"

"Beats despair?"

She was sliding along her bench to leave.

"Listen," Wakelin said. "I was a really nosy kid. I tried hard to keep it clean, but—"

She was halfway to the door.

As he put down money to cover the bill, Wakelin thought, A faith healer hostile to faith. Hmm.

Or was that former faith healer?

Christ, I don't have a thing here.

The rest of the afternoon they spent lost on gravel roads among hill farms. A quality in that region of confinement and reduction in scale. Limited horizons. The soil thin and stony. Sourest of podzol, a smear of humus. Frost-free days few in number. Land not intended, not in any millennium of this climate era, to be farmed. Goats and chickens and bug-bitten kids with bare feet standing at the bottoms of lanes, kids who didn't see many trucks they didn't know, who would pause amidst their play to watch, from first sighting to last, this latest unfamiliar vehicle pass, and as Wakelin waved and the kids just stared and continued staring even as the dust-roll

enfolded them, two words kept coming to his mind: *Isolation. Suffering.*
On many stretches, poplars dustily crowded the road like elephantine
weeds. A land of escarps and gravelish moraine. Bulrush swamp. Fields of
chicory the colour of blue sky. Signs bad or non-existent, they kept getting
lost. They would find themselves on roads that turned out to be private
lanes or that ended at checkerboards now signposts for dumped garbage or
that petered out to tractor ruts across rocky till.

At a stream that passed under the road through an exposed and grader-
battered culvert with bedspring grates, Caroline Troyer pulled over and
took a crushed litre milk carton from under the seat and walked down to
the water reshaping it. Wakelin got out to stretch his legs and watch her
squat by the water to fill this container, her skirt bunched between her
knees, her hair swung forward hiding the pale sombreness of her face, and
his spirit travelled down the embankment to embrace her in her lowly task.
The blackflies at this spot still thought it was May. He tried to have the
hood popped all ready for her, but he couldn't figure out how. She returned
and did it herself amidst a furnace blast of heat off the engine. She balanced
the hood on its slender rod, then used a rag to loosen the rad cap—"Um,
please be really, really careful doing that," said Wakelin, who had stepped
back—and refilled the carton by means of two more trips to the stream.

It was almost six by the time they found the place, on a stretch where the
ditch-grass and aspens were powdered white from the road, a stately red-brick
farmhouse with a wraparound porch. The day had diminished to a silent white
haze of late-day heat, but inside, where grain sheaves in white-plaster relief
bordered the high creamy ceilings and the burnished linoleum shone in the
slanting light, the air was cool and commotionous. The whole place smelled
of baking bread, and Wakelin, as he stood alongside Caroline Troyer in the
front hall before an osteoporosal old woman with upraised eyes, was aware of
strange stirrings, ghostly and expansive rustlings, as of bread rising in remote
corners. A man with a nine-inch lift on his right boot dragged it into the front
hall and spoke passionately concerning the R20 insulation he had had installed
the previous spring at great expense, and yet a seventh as much had been saved
already on heating fuel this winter past. As the man spoke, behind him in a

kind of sunroom Wakelin could see beings moving like outsized children or sleepwalkers, and overhead he could hear as well the footfalls of uncertain dreamers. The whole house in a movement of habitation. The man dragged away his elevator boot, and the old woman explained that though the farm had been their life, leaving it would be nothing compared to losing the children, who would be scattered and lost, even one to another.

"Why do you have to sell?" Caroline Troyer asked the woman, and Wakelin looked at her, though he had been wondering exactly the same thing.

The woman sighed and said because they had no money left, and with the latest round of cuts to foster care—

She led them to that sunroom, where the man had returned to reading a story to the six or seven hydrocephalics gathered around him, possibly listening, possibly not, a few others musing at a low table spread with puzzles and books. When the woman entered with visitors, the children crowded forward in shy excitement.

Back at the truck Wakelin exclaimed, "I'll take it! And the nice old couple and the kids, too!"

"It's too cheap," Caroline said. "It should have sold."

"After two years of looking!" cried Wakelin, overlooking the year he had put the whole thing aside as a bad idea. He was ready to buy. Was this or was this not textbook serendipity? "I can't believe my luck! I'll be the new landed gentry!"

"It's too cheap," Caroline said again.

"Maybe the kids spook people," Wakelin suggested hopefully.

And then she turned the other way out the drive and it was right there, a gravel pit so vast the trucks at the bottom looked like Dinky Toys.

"The listing should have said something," Caroline said.

"Listen," Wakelin told her. "People can adapt to anything. They'll walk around with an open sore for years. Before you know it, you're dressing it in your sleep. Besides, a pit is more an absence than an actual—"

Here a gravel truck roared by and the whole world turned white.

"You never said what he looked like," Ardis Troyer observed as she sat with her husband at the table in the dining area, their evening meal of grilled pork chops and boiled potatoes and carrots in front of them, their daughter's drying in the oven. Ardis's dog Keeper lay under the table, against her foot.

He glanced up. "What?"

"What he looked like."

He turned away.

Ardis put down her fork like something fragile. "The only reason I ask, Ross, it doesn't seem to have occurred to you that at least your daughter's showing a little initiative for once. Venturing out into the world like a functioning adult female of the species."

"There's nothing functioning about seven hours to show a few properties."

"No?" Ardis smiled. She picked up her fork. "How old was he?"

"I don't know."

"Approximately."

"No idea. Thirty."

"Handsome?"

"What? How should I know?"

"You saw him! You talked to him, Ross! Ross, listen to me. Something about this mystery stranger has inspired your holier-than-the-Christ hermit daughter to get up off her skinny arse and drive him out to show him seven hours' worth of properties. That's the miracle unfolding as we

61

speak, and it's beyond me why you aren't showing a little more interest or enthusiasm, something."

When her husband did not respond, Ardis sat for a moment watching him, perhaps waiting to see if he was only taking his time. Waiting, she sipped her vermouth. As she set down her glass she murmured, "Of course with our luck he'll be a serial killer." Again she waited, and then she said, "Not that after seven straight hours of her anybody wouldn't be." She looked at him. "What properties?"

He shook his head.

In a musing tone she said, "It's a long ways if she took it on herself to show him them two A-frames up by Biddesfirth."

"It's not seven hours."

"Not any more." She was looking at her watch. "It's eight." She was thinking again. "Of course there's meals. If she didn't eat lunch, she'd need dinner. You know how hypo she gets. Candlelight at the Coach House maybe?"

His eyes came up to consider her.

"Ross, relax. Eat something, for God's sake. Stop looking like somebody just rammed a hot poker up your arse. It's not even dark yet. I'm sure she'll phone when she comes to one. She's fine. Exploring life, we should hope."

His eyes had gone to the kitchen, to the clock over the stove. Now they came away from there.

Ardis resumed eating. After a minute she asked, "How tall was he?"

"I don't know."

"Well, when you talked to him," she said in a lilt of exasperation, "were you looking up, or down, or what?"

He gazed at her with incredulous loathing.

She had thought of something. "He didn't have dark hair, did he? Fine and straight—?"

"I don't remember." He looked away. "Maybe."

"A blue turtleneck? Stained?"

"A dark turtleneck. I don't know about stained."

She clapped her hands. "I talked to him yesterday! At the restaurant! He's looking for property!"

"He's not looking for property. He's another reporter."

Ardis was musing. "Maybe. That's what I thought. But eight hours, Ross. Eight hours. You know yourself she won't give reporters the time of day any more. You practically have to—Well well well. It does seem like she got lost, all right. Lost in a truck ceiling. Just like the rest of them around here after all. A little slow to sort her ass from the heavenly bodies, but—" Ardis sat back in an attitude of relief. A moment later she leaned forward with her eyes googled and waggling her hands at the sides of her face. "Feelings! Funny feelings! *Whooo!* Must be from on high!"

"The reason she took him out," he said carefully, his attention upon his plate, the food untouched, "I wasn't there."

"So you claim. But there's nothing very new about that, is there, Ross? It's never got her to take them out before."

"I know what she's thinking," he said in an ordinary voice, although it no longer seemed to be his wife he was addressing. "I'm not fooled."

"Look on the bright side," Ardis said. "Even as we speak she's out there solving our problem. Either she's got off her rear end to sell property or she's on her back arranging things another way—*What are you doing?*"

He was holding his dinner plate in his right hand, touching the rim of it to his left arm just below the shoulder. He was doing this casually, with his head tilted downward and to the side as if to regard the plate, and yet his attention seemed upon some object more remote.

Ardis's hand went to her heart. She was silent now, and watched in a freeze of dismay as the plate moved swiftly rightward across his chest, his right arm extending, fingers releasing so that the plate sailed like a Frisbee through the doorway and across the space of the kitchen to explode against the oven door. There a gob of mashed potato adhered a moment to the Pyrex of the oven window before it fell away to leave a white pucker, and Ardis understood that the pucker appeared at that moment as white as it did only because the Pyrex was carbon-fouled inside a double pane, owing to an engineering flaw in that so-called quality stove, they get a reputation and the next thing you know immigrants working for chicken feed are asleep on their feet throwing together any old crap, and who pays—? She was on her feet. "*Ross, honey, don't!*"

He now held his bread-and-butter plate in that same hand, the rim of it just brushing his left arm midway between the elbow and shoulder as if to indicate something there, and she looked to it hopeful, but his arm moved swiftly back, extending as before, and the wrist flicked, the fingers releasing, and that plate too travelled through the air, to smash against the hall-entrance door frame and scatter down the length of the hall to the front door.

"She doesn't fool me," he said again, quietly. "I know her." And then he put his hands over his face and sat in silence.

Ardis lowered herself into her chair. It was as if she had been struck a blow to the stomach. She had no breath.

When he brought his hands away he was calm. "I'll clean that up," he said. "And clear the table." He pushed his chair back and with his hands on his knees, elbows spread, peered beneath the table at her stockinged feet, which were drawn together under her chair. The dog was still under there, and it looked out at him with frightened eyes. "Don't walk." He stood up. "I'll get your shoes. You put the dog out and go straight to the room and wait for me there. Have the gear ready. You know I don't like that kind of talk."

"Oh, Ross," Ardis said, and sighed. Sighed so profoundly she could hardly speak. "I can talk a lot more like this than this, than, than, than—"

"No more. That's enough. Where's your fucking shoes?"

"My fucking shoes," Ardis sighed and seemed about to faint in her chair at the table where she sat.

Wakelin and Caroline Troyer were back on the unpaved stretch, fifteen minutes into the washboard dance, when that rhythmic bump from the rear became enfolded by a sound more flubby and catastrophic. A flat tire.

Wakelin felt this was a job for himself, but he was too slow. Crouching beside her on the shoulder amidst blasts of dust and flying stones from the big trucks, he watched her forearms cord and soften as she loosened wheelnuts, one after the other. The nuts had seized, but she possessed the necessary strength, or more accurately the confidence of the strength and therefore she had the strength. What was this if not faith? Wakelin, extending the hubcap as a tray for wheelnuts, was tempted to make this point out loud, but when she took his tray and set it on the ground at her feet he remained silent, just continued to watch her hands and forearms, fighting an impulse now to reach out and touch them, to trace the perfection of blue veins in the backs of her hands as they worked, a desire that struck him as being exactly as creepy and inappropriate as it would strike her. But he knew that, he understood that, and was grateful to his genes, to his upbringing, to something, to be able to squat here in a state of as-good-as perfect control, blameless as your perfect gentleman, and just watch, while reflecting in a removed and dispassionate way upon the stubbornness of the physical world. And at that moment it came to Wakelin that paramount in a life in the country would be the physical problems, the small humiliations by intractable materiality, the cold-sweat stand-offs, and maybe he should think some more about this country-property thing.

The problem was, with a physical problem you really did have a problem. A physical problem was another order altogether from those issuing from the usual obstacles and defeats of money, work, and other people. When you had done all you could do and still something physical did not work, then it did not work. It was not like a magazine story, infinitely malleable given thought enough and time. Unless your name was Uri Geller and your physical problem was a shortage of bent spoons, you were not going to solve it by mind alone. When you had a problem writing a magazine piece you could always sleep on it, a fresh start. With a physical problem you could sleep on it as much as you wanted, it wouldn't make any difference. For Wakelin, a fresh start in the physical world consisted of driving to Canadian Tire and throwing himself on the mercy of the first clerk who bothered to toss him a glance. It was buying a new one and paying extra to have somebody come around and set it up.

Caroline Troyer was speaking to him, telling him to fetch rocks for under the wheels on the passenger's side, she'd be jacking on a grade.

Wakelin jumped up and jogged around the front of the truck and skidded down off the shoulder for two big rocks and clambered back up with one in each hand. They were bigger than they needed to be, the weight of ten-pin bowling balls, and twice he fell, embedding an elbow in the soft gravel, but he made it and jammed them in. "Done," he said, squatting once more at her side, game as a puppet.

Now she unbolted the spare from under the bed and located the axle and positioned the jack and jacked the truck and removed the blown tire and lifted on the spare and tightened the nuts partway and unjacked the truck until the ground held the tire, and tightened the nuts the rest of the way and unjacked the truck until it came down fully onto its springs and the jack was loose enough to free it from under the axle and threw the blown tire into the bed. And this entire procedure Wakelin followed helplessly ever one step behind, not quite keeping out of her way, his thoughts lapsed to overexposure, his mind bleached, the small interior voice stuck meaningless back there with *What was this if not faith?* stuck and repeating. And the world as manifest on that dirt shoulder in that corridor of spruce and fir under the deepening blue of evening, a cooler breeze from the forest margin fragrant with fungus and conifer in mitigation of the vaporous gritty pall of dust and diesel upon that stripped road surface, the world rose up on its old elbows aggrieved, and seeing it that way Wakelin felt a need for redemption, or something like it, a need undiminished by his utter ignorance concerning what redemption could be or how to get it. Why it should be necessary at all.

And then she was taking the jack out of his hands (dismantling it as she did so) and the socket wrench, and this hardware she replaced behind the seat while he struggled to fit the hubcap back on, but after one glance she repositioned it and kicked it on herself. And so much further unnerved was he by the short sharp efficiency of this action in the midst of all that personal chagrin, all that despair of old helplessness, that he had climbed into the cab and buckled himself in before he realized that she herself was not getting in but walking around the back of the truck to kick away the rocks he had placed under the tires, except then when he glanced around, she was just standing there looking at them.

He struggled out of his seat belt and threw open his door. "I can do that!" he called. "I'm sorry, I completely forgot—" He jumped down.

"You put them at the backs of the tires," she said.

Wakelin was not sure if this statement was descriptive or prescriptive. He checked the rocks. "Right," he said.

She was walking back to the driver's door.

Wakelin continued to stare at the rocks. Something was wrong, but what? And then he saw that he had wedged them under the upslope side of the tires, and a hot wavefront travelled his neck and cheeks and climbed his temples, and though there was no need at all he kicked away the rocks and did so with some energy.

They were on the road again. A few minutes later back on asphalt, moving once more down a corridor of spruce and fir, and that rear bump had not gone away.

Roused from his mortified flush, Wakelin looked over.

Her eyes were fixed down the road. "It's the good tire blew," she said.

It's always this, Caroline Troyer reflected. The main thing about thought: move away. From anything it lights on. It doesn't matter what it is. Like a fire or a Slinky, move away and start up again some place else. Move away and do it different. Do it as it should be. As things like this used to be. When they were better. Or if it seems to be a good thing it's lit on, then do it as precious. Out of reach. Or better: do it sacred. That's right, sacred, needing defending. Or do it lost forever, at any time now. That's always a good one.

Now in memory, she is standing in her windbreaker and cap and rubber boots before her father in the yard, where blank gravestones lean among winter weeds along the chain link. It is a hard bright morning. The air is cool, the sun hot. He kneels on a foam pallet before a glassy stone, a drill in his hand. He is wearing sound mufflers, a dust mask, goggles. He switches off the drill. He pulls the mask and goggles down around his neck but not the mufflers, and the fine salmon dusting of marble leaves naked white goggles around his eyes.

I'm going up the hill, she says.

You should.

I'll be back to make lunch.

I'd appreciate it.

And in memory she is climbing through the sumacs and among the pines above the war memorial and following the rising path along the ridge. Where the rock is exposed it is warm from the sun and the snow is granular and has been quick to recede. The air is cool in the shade where the snow lies deep yet in places, and the path is muddy but not where the shade now falls or has fallen upon it today.

Her destination is not the highest part of the ridge but almost. It is a sloped clearing several yards in diameter below, but not visible from, the path, south-facing, where no immediate green is visible as yet except the mosses and conifers. Neither is rock visible, but scratch for ten seconds and there it is. The clearing is surrounded by young hemlock and balsam. Higher up, above the path, a white pine. The clearing is sheltered and warm on days when few are. It is a place where animals bring their kill or perhaps are themselves killed here, for it is scattered with the intricate bones of small birds and mice and voles, and the skeletons of squirrels, and even a few of the vertebrae and what remains of the forelegs of a fawn, all bleached to the chalk whiteness of bone.

This is her sanctuary. No people come here. In this place it is possible to believe that no one knows where she is. Here she kicks off her rubber boots and spreads her white legs. At her feet is a screen of chokecherry and dogwood thick enough, even unleafed, to cancel the town. A brown creeper darts pecking through the winter stalks. Eastward the white meridial pain of the spring sun. South, the undulant bluish grey and lime-green horizon of forested hills. She can hear a killdeer, she can hear a Canada jay. A squirrel gone squirrelly at her trespass. She can hear the ravens, from the bluff on the other side of the summit, up in arms as ever, and she can hear the wind that moves through the white pine above her, a tunnel of soft roaring. And she feels smaller breezes on her face and arms, smells the insolate fragrance of the mosses, and as her fingers sift the pulpy till, her thoughts do not recede but slow and quiet to a sequence of resistances in her skull, small catches, palpable in their sucession.

To go to that place is to wake from thoughts inspired by the dream of freedom that are not freedom.

She is not free now, only remembering her secret place on the ridge as she drives her father's truck through the dusk listening to a man so reactive to himself, so blind, that a properly intuitive choice such as where he will spend his solitude is perplexed, impulsive, in the end will be the result practically of chance; that the nature of his relationship with a woman he lost nearly two years ago is no less complicated a mystery for him tonight than it was on the day he lost her, his suffering hardly diminished, his life snagged, twisting on that loss. And five minutes after she has delivered this lost soul to his car, she will stand before another baffled devious sufferer, her father, whose pain instead of a maundering aggrieved soliloquy will issue in old rage, because he is the one who long ago laid claim to the unpredictable, and how dare she by similar behaviour presume?

She should phone. Where on this stretch has she seen a phone?

Her passenger rambles on. First they sell you their version, done out in the way they imagine resembles your own, and then they sell you what they have come to sell you. This is why to hear him you would almost think his disappointment was a small huddled sadness and not a wail of self-pity and flailing rage at the one lost.

One of her headaches is starting. She attends to the pain as to distant thunder, and then she attends to herself thinking about her father's rage, and that is when she notices a cast to this thinking, a cast familiar yet difficult to discern because obscured by its subject, or rather by his nature, by his own cast. And that is when she understands that these thoughts, although hers, although old catches in old succession, are kinetic with other energy that is not simply her own old emotion. And she understands that this other energy is not her own anticipation arising out of past experience. And she knows that it is another's, that it derives from some other site that is finding repercussion here.

And that site is the rage of her father.

And that site is active and it is active now.

"Did you get them?" Wakelin asked when Caroline Troyer returned to the truck. He knew she hadn't because the whole time she was in the phone booth he had watched her lips.

"There's no answer."

"So they're out. Aren't we almost there?" Why was she shaking?

"Forty minutes."

"And there you'll be. Large as life. Obviously they're not worried."

Half an hour before she pulled over to call he had started telling her about Jane. The feeling he had as he did this, indulged himself shamelessly, was similar to the one on those occasions, always with women, he would lay himself wide open. Sometimes in arousal, sometimes in sorrow. Like a dog on its back, lolling, thighs splayed. A guttural freedom. Here I am, grovelling in my display. Rub or scratch as you will, only be careful. I bite. He had got talking about silence, and the next thing he knew he was talking about Jane.

Now they were back on the road, and he wondered if he should try to make himself a little clearer. He'd been practically free-associating. You meet a stranger who herself has a predilection for silence and she could almost do for a shrink. If this were California, he could tell her everything. She might even be interested. You don't get out much and when you do you take in all you can. Sustenance for those long afternoons behind the jewellery-and-tackle counter.

But she was not a shrink and this was not California and she was not

72

interested, and it was time to tell her the truth: That he was here for a story. Didn't she know stories can heal? Yeah, right. And then he'd tell her another one: That he intended to write it whether she talked to him or not. So she really should talk to him. Make sure he got everything straight. The truth as it had been crying out to be told.

Except, this was not how he worked at all. None of his behaviour with this woman was how anybody in their right mind would behave who had spent more than two minutes in her company. What was going on here? Was it her throwing him? You grow up outside the pale of ordinary behaviour and what does this do to how a stranger will see himself through your eyes? Or had he always been this way, and with her he could see it?

Wakelin looked out the window. In the night it was impossible to know or imagine this as the same highway they had travelled in daytime. Its margins—grass or sandbank or grey-bouldered swale (canting phone poles anchored in corrugated buckets of rocks)—walled both sides by forest featureless as clipped hedges, except here and there a young birch or aspen arced into the cut, ice-bowed from last winter, a slender gleam in the dusk. Where a house or cabin or trailer or inhabited school bus was set in a niche in the barrier of trees, the yellow emanation from its windows afforded presence beyond any available to that dwelling place shabby and unremarkable in sunlight.

No, this wasn't California. In the night it could be, but it wasn't.

Sometimes Jane used to sleep as badly as he did. Wander the flat alone. He'd find her flipping through a magazine. Making tea. He'd come upon her in a pool of lamplight writing a letter, and she would look up at him as if he were somehow familiar.

When Wakelin was scared everything scared him. All it had to do was exist. It was a great apartment, great location, but when Jane died he moved. Could not have stayed on there another day alone. Not with every piece of furniture, every physical surface looming out of the muck of the city night to ask how long he intended to go on counting on his own private version of how things were. As opposed to how they were in fact. To ask if he was ready yet to appreciate what a failure of respect for the world-as-it-was his daylight, lamplight, thoughtlight distraction constituted, had always constituted. And how much the world resented him for it. To ask if he hadn't tried to make his love for Jane a refuge from that resentment, and now that she was gone, if this clinging to her memory wasn't a clinging to that refuge? Because weren't his relations with the world shabbier than ever? Shabbier and with thinner and poorer excuses as the days passed.

"Do you ever wake up afraid?" Wakelin asked Caroline Troyer.

Her eyes came around. "I'm afraid now."

"What? Why on earth? Because we're late?"

She shook her head. Turned back to the road. "He's beating her," she said quietly. At least that's what Wakelin thought she said.

"Pardon? *Beating? Who?*" He watched her, waiting for more.

"Meeting?" he tried. When she still said nothing he said, "I don't mean with a bad dream."

"I don't dream."

"Oh, sure you do. Everybody dreams. You just don't remember. You'd go nuts if—"

"I stopped."

"Really," Wakelin said. He was embarrassed for her and let it go. Did not want her to think he thought she was nuts.

When he bolted up in the night, it would be with the understanding, say, that folly breeds. That compartments, the walls between compartments, break down. Or he would know that it is possible to be torn into small pieces and scattered by love and yet still, and yet still somehow to go on. He would know that with a certain person it is not their body, not their waking or sleeping presence, it is their whole existence you crave, every molecule at every moment. And your need for this person is like the need of a child for the entirety of its parent's being, and your doom is the child's, never to be satisfied. It is not that the beloved is beyond compare (though Jane was), it is that they are what you lack. What you will always lack. You give yourself without restriction, you let it all go, unashamed, without limits, you fall in love, you fall and fall and there is only the falling. You have spent the first half of your life walking the edge of the precipice, and now you are spending the second half of your life falling. This is not a matter of superiority—oh, she was too good for him, too intelligent, too beautiful—it is not that, not exactly (though she was), or who took the initiative in love and who didn't. It is something else. It is who is capable of love and who is not. And it is something more. It is, If I ever hoped to be, it was with you. It is, I am nothing now.

Once again, rock walls. Suddenly, on the left, at the foot of a gravel drive, a sign: Ross Troyer Realty. A strip of tape diagonal across one corner: Reduced.

"By the elements," Wakelin said. "The wind and the rain. Does it seem to you too like about a week since we looked at that place?"

A question the silence in its wake caused Wakelin when he reviewed it, which he soon did, to hear as purely rhetorical.

They were descending the long hill to the valley floor, where the lights of Grant flickered in an irregular grid. Another northern enterprise discouraged early. The asphalt was levelling. In ten minutes they would pass the hospital, the small white plaza, the Birches Motel. There was already more traffic. Highway's empty, you pass no intersections, and suddenly . . . Where do all the cars come from?

"Grant actually seems more like a farming than a mining—" Wakelin began idly.

She was craning forward, and when he glanced over he saw that she was peering down the darkness of the far shoulder. He looked too and saw it, a lit form. And then she was braking, hard. A dog. It veered in front of oncoming headlights and came at full gallop straight up this lane. She pulled to the shoulder. Seconds later two great front paws slammed against her window. Sharp yelping barks. Eyes of alarm. The black Lab's, from the restaurant, her mother's dog. Foaming and wheezing. Too old for this. Caroline got out and squatted before it. The creature could not decide whether to sit or stand. It could not decide whether to nose under her skirt—she pushed its muzzle aside—or bark in her face. And then she was leading it to the rear of the truck, but when she dropped the tailgate it refused to jump up. Wakelin's door opened.

"Move over."

"Please," he said.

They were on the road again. Wakelin was wedged between her and the dog, his legs pressed over to make room for the gearshift, the dog whining and panting halitotic at his ear.

When his daughter's late for dinner he beats the dog? What the hell is going on here?

"He beat the dog?" Wakelin asked Caroline Troyer.

"No."

"What is it, then? What's happening?"

She didn't answer.

The dog woofed anxiously at Wakelin's ear.

"Oh, be quiet," Wakelin said.

The last time he had been in a vehicle with a dog in a state like this it was just him and the dog, Luc, an Irish setter, his and Jane's—well, Jane's dog long before it was his—and on that occasion things had not gone well at all.

It had been a Saturday morning in September, twenty-two months ago. An hour earlier Luc had been pacing the hall, his nails clicking on the hardwood. *Click click click click.* Every few minutes he would come out to Wakelin, who was on the deck trying to read the paper, and talk to him from deep in his throat in a yeowrly-reowrly voice until Wakelin said, Okay Luc, let's go, and Luc went dancing backwards.

Woof! Woof!

When Wakelin tried to go inside, Luc scrambled through the sliding door at the same time and they both stumbled into the living room.

What is the matter with you?

To Luc's chagrin Wakelin stopped to restore the futon bed to a sofa. Luc waited impatient, then returned to pace the hall. *Click click click click.* As Wakelin folded the eiderdown Luc stood at the near end of the hall watching him, tail going so hard that both walls were thumping.

Woof!

Quiet, Luc. She's trying to sleep.

Before they left the flat, Wakelin checked on Jane. He had to press Luc to the wall with his knee to keep him out. The room smelled of old sleep. Hot morning sun on dusty curtains. She was curled on her side, very still. Skin clammy. Either softly sleeping or pretending. Home from the hospital following another attempt. Veins stitched shut once more. Outside the door Luc barked. Wakelin straightened the sheets and got out of there. Never had been much of a nurse. Lacked the necessary steadiness and courage of hand, eye, stomach, voice, heart. Whatever it took to be a nurse, Wakelin lacked it. Not at all good with blood, pain, morbid symptoms of any kind, really. Could hardly bear to visit the sickroom of his own mate in his own apartment.

Normally Luc would hit the stairs like a whippet sprung from a trap. Today he stood on the landing and barked down at Wakelin until Wakelin went back up and got him. He practically had to be wrestled into the car.

They crossed the viaduct, Luc in the front seat with his head in the wind, and then they cut back down into the parkland along the river. When Wakelin got out of the car Luc came willingly enough, but when Wakelin started along the path Luc did not, as he usually did, take off sniffing and irrigating trees and barrelling after squirrels. Instead he stayed several doleful paces behind, just creeping along, until Wakelin looked back. Then Luc would wag and bark.

For a while Wakelin tried. The afternoon would be hot but the air was not hot yet and it was good to be outside. There were few people on the path. White-haired couples passing him from both directions, really swinging their arms. Kids swooping wide on bikes.

He looked around. Luc barked and started back to the car as if Wakelin had just had a terrific idea.

After half an hour Wakelin gave up. At the car he said, You could at least have peed. ·

But Luc was already in the front seat, looking to Wakelin to wind down the window.

And so they drove up out of the river valley and came back across the viaduct.

And here in the truck with Caroline Troyer, Wakelin remembered how on the drive back from that walk with Luc he was blaming the city. You're driving in your car in the city. You've taken the dog to the park and now you're driving back. You've just watched yourself get into the car with the dog and wind down the window and start the engine and drive up out of the ravine to street level and now you're asking yourself what it is you can't see past. You're not suddenly a stranger to yourself, you are who you are. But that's it. It's like a wall. Sometimes you think the problem is the city. In the city you've got the buildings and the streets. You've got the people and the things on these streets and on other streets and inside these buildings and inside other buildings, but that's it. And then you think, The city's the city. Why blame the city? The wall is not made out of bricks and asphalt any more than it's made out of fear. It goes with fear, that's all. It's the wall between you and the world ever since you were a kid. The wall between you and things when things aren't as they should be. *My wife isn't doing so well, and neither is the marriage. I guess I'm just really anxious.* When you were a kid you didn't call it anxious, you called it afraid. *Well, isn't everybody afraid? Isn't being half afraid most of the time a good qualification for being human, and some people just happen to be more neurotic about their fear than others, meaning they have or they take more time to worry about it?* Maybe. But let's say you've tried a hundred things and nothing's changed. So you decide the problem may not be the city but it will go away if you move to the country. So you move to the country. But of course the country's the country, and that's it. The country isn't as it should be either, not that this comes as much of a surprise. *Yes, but then I'll know, won't I? That the problem wasn't the city. That I didn't want to live in the country after all, I never did. The only thing I really ever wanted to do was run. Run from the city, run from the country. Grab my princess and run.*

Don't fence me in, Wakelin told Luc.

Luc looked around and whined.

Oh, be quiet.

"What's going on?" Wakelin now asked, giving the black Lab a shove. "Calm down! Why's he so overwrought?"

From Caroline Troyer no answer.

Wakelin looked at his watch. Thank Christ he'd soon be climbing out of this insane truck. A short drive to the Birches to pick up his stuff and goodbye Village of Grant. Back in the city—speaking of living in the city—by midnight. Wake up tomorrow, a fresh start, as formerly intended. Two days shot, advance to return, expenses in the three figures, what can you do. Top Freelance Tim Wakelin Says: Cut Your Losses.

The town speed limit sign whipped past, and Wakelin was back on that Saturday morning in September twenty-two months ago.

He had made it nearly to the west end of the viaduct and was starting to slow for the first of the four turns that would bring him back to the flat, when Luc, standing on the front seat in such a way as to thrust his head as far as possible out the window, his anus consequently not ten inches from the side of Wakelin's head, farted, wetly.

Wakelin now seemed to hear Luc's wet fart in present time, and then he heard it again and knew the sound had come from the throat of Caroline Troyer and thought, Good lord, she's horking. A country spitter. Give the woman a lump of clay and she'll restore sight to the sightless. He waited for her window to go down, and when this did not happen he turned to see her face cachectic in the dashlight, the mute jaw working. He looked to the road—nothing. Her hands were lifting away from the wheel. He grabbed at it. The truck swerved, the black Lab fell heavily against him, panting, a rope of slobber, and Caroline Troyer was pressed back in her seat, hands protecting her face as if from a beating, her body rigid. She was standing on the gas.

"What?" Wakelin cried. "What is it? *What?*"

A rattling in her throat. Divine epilepsy, oh Jesus, God help us all.

Ahead the heavy-mesh tailgate, the rusted bumper, of a Japanese pickup, swelling fast. Three or four pairs of headlights oncoming. Maybe there was time to pass, but Wakelin hit the shoulder, that runnelled surface, at eighty-five miles an hour. The truck went into radical shimmying, and when he tried to swing it back to the pavement it fishtailed, ploughing diagonally, and he understood that they could go over, the rear wheels catch on a culvert, a rut, on anything, and they would be in air, bucking and twisting in a weightless eternity punctuated by impacts diversified, demolitional—

And as the world beyond the truck transformed to pure contingency and Wakelin's mind went riffling through its infinite catalogue of ways to die, part of it flashed back to that Saturday morning, to that wet fart, upon which, with words to the effect, You had your chance, Luc! Now *don't start!* he had struck Luc's flank a fateful blow, fateful and precipitative, for without warning (unless all events and reflections of that morning could be construed warnings, unless this long skid to probable death twenty-two months later was also a warning) there was loosed from the depths of Luc's bowels a discharge (which Wakelin from the corner of his eye actually witnessed from a sphincteral convulsion explode into the air and yet—one hand on the wheel, the other still returning to it inertial from striking—was too slow to deflect), a discharge so propulsive in force, a projectile mass of such velocity, that the car swerved with the shock of it even as Luc glanced around apologetic before the immediate release of a sequel even more horrific, a fecal deluge of hot jaundice-yellow foulness, essence of ordure from a firehose sulphurous, wet and thick and of an unspeakable stench, burning against Wakelin's skin like pestilential waste from some fulminant pit of Hell, stinging his right eyeball and clogging his right nostril and entering the follicles of his scalp and the pores of his face and neck and into his mouth musky and acerbate and sweet, as frantically he wiped at his face with the fresh shit heavy on the back of his right hand, blinded, the wheel gone slippery as he continued the turn, and whether this was in a childlike bid to undo the moment by denial, or out of a more urbane reluctance to draw the attention of his fellow citizens at so awkward a juncture in his affairs, or whether from a reluctance more rational, since to stop could well have been fatal, Wakelin would never know, only that the turn was wider than it would have been had he been able to see, wide enough even for entry to a lane of oncoming traffic and for his left eye though burning and blear to become witness to the peeling away of vehicles left and right until his own had gone into its own slow slide, which no sooner had it come to an end than Luc's head snapped in as a grey steel barrier (the side panel of a Canpar van) slammed them broadside, and they were in motion again, until hit a second time, hard, like a rebuke for inattention, at the rear, from the other direction, and this time they went accelerating in a slow pinwheel that was quickly crumpled as in a fist by a double collision with what Wakelin, in a crystal hail of niblets, could only imagine as two vehicles parked at five-minute meters while their drivers rushed in to do some last-minute shopping for the weekend.

But now the car had stopped moving, and silence arched like a rainbow, and the understanding arose that there would be no more collisions at this time, and Wakelin opened his door and stepped out, and Luc was right there, so eager to be at Wakelin's side that he nearly knocked him down, and as Wakelin clutched at the open door of his car, one hand sliding greased along the top of it in a brown smear, he raised the other to assure or perhaps bless any who might have stepped forward out of concern for his welfare, and several witnesses to the accident were in fact just then approaching to offer what assistance they might, but the one who reached him first, a four-square fellow with a face kindly as flannel, thinking perhaps he had discovered in Wakelin a being in whose veins flowed not blood but some reeky fecal fluid, fell back in revulsion and terror, and Wakelin might have been trying to assure him otherwise, but at that moment he did not recognize the language that he himself spoke, so animal was it, a language of pure emotion, and he wondered if this might be older unhappiness than he had lately known—and yet his mouth was closed and his throat still. His eyes shit-stinging, not half tearing enough. His breast numb and without fear. And as an animal devoid of appropriate discursive understanding will attempt to deflect attention from itself as it stands before you dumb and accountless and lamely wagging, by glancing away, Wakelin glanced away, and immediately his one good eye fell on Luc, and it had been Luc all along! Howling next to him in the street, long wolfish howling, keen and unearthly, taking a few short positioning steps before howling again. Howling like some wild creature that has never known the corruption of human company. Or perhaps known it to its inexpressible sorrow. Howling as if his wretched, animal heart would break. For the dog knew. Luc knew. If his master didn't. . . .

But that was twenty-two months ago. Now Wakelin had somehow got his leg extended across the shins of Caroline Troyer and his foot jammed onto the brake as simultaneously he yanked the gearshift into roaring neutral, and the three of them careened at last to rocking stasis like stunned patrons of some incredibly violent sideshow ride abruptly finished.

Headlights beaming across the pavement, dust entering those beams in a slow cloud, the engine roaring.

Wakelin looked at Caroline Troyer. Her head was pushed high into the rear corner of the cab, her hands cupped at her eyes. Her sight, it seemed, all she had need to protect. He gripped her wrists. With difficulty—there was tremendous strength in them—he pulled down her hands. What he glimpsed then in the light of high beams from the rearview were eyes locked on a horror invisible. Slowly he released his grip. The hands came up once more.

The roaring engine was set to explode. He switched it off and immediately a good dozen vehicles passed in quick series as if nothing had happened here. He leaned around the dog and got the passenger door open. Outside, a silence of crickets.

"Come on, boy. Out! Let's *go!*"

But the Lab only barked in Wakelin's face, and when he pushed at its chest it went instantly confidential, uttering a deep-throat don't-fuck-with-me-man growl. So Wakelin squeezed around it—already it was back panting, ignoring him, looking to Caroline Troyer—and fell out of the truck, for there was no ground out there, only space and soft gravel, and he rolled and slid for quite a while. This was more than a ditch. But in time he stopped, on rock, and crawled sliding back up, to grab hold of the truck and haul himself around the back of it to the driver's door, which he got open.

The Lab was licking Caroline Troyer's face as if trying to close her eyes with its tongue, from the bottom up. Wakelin struggled to move her over on the seat so he could drive. But her knees would not unlock, and he could not get her legs to fold over the gearshift. Casting around then, he saw, like a vision, practically across the highway, the blue *H*.

"We got lucky," he told her, his voice shaking. "Hospital's right here." He pulled her out of the truck. She was keening, a strangled moan, her hands back at her face, but when he supported her arm and drew her forward, her feet moved. The black Lab was close at her side. There was no traffic. To the right, the lights of the town; to the left, darkness. One foot in front of the other.

They had made it to the opposite shoulder and were starting toward the top of the lane to the hospital when Wakelin heard the crunch of tires on gravel and looked around to see the truck rolling slowly backwards. The driver's door standing open. The progress of the vehicle was constant and inexorable, and then it might have picked up a little speed. The Lab looked at Wakelin and said "Woof" with the inflection dogs use when they mean, *Do something*. The left front fender lifted, and like a sinking barge the truck keeled upward and descended from sight.

The shiftings and slidings of thousands of small stones. After that, the languorous crumpling of an old truck rolling over on rock.

Wakelin was trembling. He was also soaking wet. At least this time it wasn't shit. He turned to Caroline Troyer. Her hands had come away from her face. She was not in her eyes. "I *am* doing something," he said. His voice was not in control. He held her firmly. Slowly they walked.

COUNTRY PROPERTY

From the moment Timothy Wakelin pushed through the doors of Grant Memorial Hospital supporting Caroline Troyer in his arms, all attention was on her, and it seemed like a good time to leave. He was stopped at Reception. There, without objection, he provided his driver's licence, failing only to mention that the address and phone number the receptionist was taking from it and putting into her computer were from before, when he lived with Jane, in the great apartment. Then he kept going. Walked back out the doors he had brought Caroline Troyer through. Before the receptionist could ask him to do something about the dog barking and whining at the door of the examination room. He walked out and kept going. Down the lane to the highway and down the highway to Grant. Got his car from the Royal Bank parking lot—untowed, unticketed; ah, the merciful sweet slack of small-town life—picked up his bag at the Birches, and by quarter to midnight was accelerating south, headed for the city. Drove for hours, feeling like a bastard, but tell him, somebody, please, what should he have done? The polite thing? Stayed at the Birches overnight and checked on her in the morning? Was he his sister's keeper? Or a freelance with no story who didn't get paid when he didn't work? I delivered her safe into the hands of trained medical people who have probably known her forever and obviously cared about her. I saved her life, for God's sake. The dog wasn't about to take the wheel. Why shouldn't this be enough? Why am I feeling like a total shit? Surely not for walking away when all I could do with a story on this would be more damage? She's better off clear of me. I'm a fucking parasite in the matter.

Still. He could have stayed over and checked on her in the morning. He could at least have done that, he'd already paid for the room. There was more to her than he'd gone up there expecting to find. She'd more than survived, that one.

And what about himself? He did need to see her again, didn't he? He couldn't ever not see her again, right?

But how could he? What good could he be with innocence like that? illness like that?

And remind him: Who was it responsible for the demolition of the Troyer Realty vehicle? And who was it who'd provided that false information back there?

Christ, Wakelin thought. I'm not just a cad, I'm a felon. I can't go back now.

Possibly not, but on the outskirts of the great metropolis he took an exit that brought him into the parking lot of a mall. That he should do this did not surprise him, except that he did not know why. In other circumstances it might have been for the all-night Shoppers Drug: a little gimcrack dazzle after the long dark. After so much sitting, stretch his legs. A bag of chips and a pop, leaf through the magazines. See how his latest article looked on this particular rack. But instead of pulling up to the door—there were no other cars, it was four in the morning—he continued the turn, and when this did not surprise him either, he wondered what now possibly could, and when at the service road he found himself exiting in the wrong direction, now the right direction, he knew that he was going back, not to Grant necessarily, for not knowing how he could possibly go back to Grant he was not yet ready to know he could be, but north, he was definitely going back north, and when he was still not surprised to know this, he knew that something had changed. Your ears pop and you can hear again, and mostly what you hear, at first, anyway, is the silence.

It was a class of turn something like that unintended one into the Birches Motel the other day, except this time it wasn't a story he was making the turn for, it was silence, country silence.

This is what Wakelin told himself as he drove back past the malls, the smaller ones like the one he had just turned around in and the giant ones set back like fortresses in asphalt seas. And he drove past the high-rises in their desolate groupings and past the detached three-bedroom developments pressing up against the steel-weave highway barriers. And he drove through the landscape of industry in the sombre incandescence of early morning, and on past the unchosen spaghetti intersections with thoroughfares east and west across the top of the city until, beyond the last exit before farmland, in the day-bright of an all-night driving range, he pulled to the shoulder and turned off the engine and sat in a silence structured by whacked golf balls (for even at four in the morning will be those out to improve their swing) and structured too by blasts from occasional shock waves from the big trucks.

And there by the side of the highway Wakelin felt that he was not one for the world as it is, not really, and he remembered how when he was sixteen and seventeen he used to imagine that he and his true love, when he found her, would make a new world, and the old one, so disappointing, so dedicated to the overturn of all best intentions, would be as nothing, cast aside, unworthy. And young Wakelin, still floundering, would catch glimpses across the frontier of time to the land where he and his true love would dwell, and he would watch them as they went about the rational absurd lives of ideal beings, and his heart would swell. And then he met Jane, and everything was as he had foreseen, immediate deliverance from all lack and compromise, everything complete and in focus. With only this problem: Jane kept breaking down. You could say it was her, you could say it was him, you could say it was the marriage. If it was the marriage, it must have been the perfect match of it that she couldn't bear, and maybe this would be because she couldn't bear to lose it, and surely she would lose it, because she was not worthy (who could be? except she was, Jane was), and sooner or later in the course of her incapacitation the point would come up, out of nowhere, received wisdom, that perhaps the best thing would be for them to separate, this love was somehow, fantastically, killing her, a potion obscurely wrong for her blood, but of course he could not bear to do that, and she could not bear to let him go, and slowly she would come around, and life would be wonderful again, and then she would break down again, and all would be as before, except this time it was surely the end, but he would fight it, this was the one thing from which he would never walk away, in which he refused to fail to believe, this woman was the bride of his life and his love for her was its redemption, and she fought it too, was a courageous fighter, more courageous than himself in many ways, and like him she believed in love and in the love they had, and it would not be the end after all. By no means.

Because everything would happen as before.

And nothing and everything since those days had changed for Wakelin, and those days were gone. And it had always seemed that there was something their disappearance should have done for him, as in the way of moving him along somehow, of making him a, you know, better person, or maybe just more mature, which he supposed would be the same thing, but for the life of him he had never been able to discover what this was. What it was he was supposed to have learned.

Later Wakelin did not know how long he sat on the shoulder in the light of the all-night driving range before he pulled back onto the highway and continued north. It could have been five minutes, it could have been an hour. What time does the sun first come over the trees at the end of June two hours south of the southern-most edge of the visible Shield in that part of the country? Five? Five-thirty? Pretty early. A fine hour to be on the road, unless, of course, you haven't slept in twenty-four hours and are running on pure nervous despair, in which case you would be far better off still sharing the wheel of a runaway pickup with a seizuring daughter of God.

The remote percussive beat of a helicopter.

Caroline Troyer threw back the bedclothes, swung her feet to the floor. A small ward of the Grant Memorial Hospital, eight beds. Various snoring. Her clothes had been laundered and folded over a chair. She put them on. Searched for Timothy Wakelin in the men's ward and the four double rooms of the opposite wing. He was not here. By the time she started down the main corridor the big blades were directly overhead. Except for the sleepers, now stirring, there was no one in the building, not even at Reception, where the swivel chair behind the counter had been pushed back at an angle, a pink cardigan pressed to the oval backrest in intricate creases.

Outside, the black machine hung clamorous. The lights on its underbelly as it manoeuvred against the surging sky swept in corrective arcs to light in flashes a concrete pad beyond the great oak. The ambulance was there, its rear doors open. The staff, all four— Eunice Bragg, from Reception, hugging herself; Dr. Li; and a nurse and orderly she did not know— were standing by a gurney watching the machine position itself in air. And then she saw the ambulance driver leaning against the side of that vehicle half hidden by one of its rear doors, and this was Bachelor Crooked Hand, in his night whites.

She passed under the oak and moved down the margin of the drive. In the beating air no one saw her approach. At the gurney she could have reached over and touched the shoulder of Dr. Li. The sheet was starkly lit by the aircraft lights, the shadows swinging. As she approached she saw the sheet pulled high, but the white over the eyes and the lower face was bandages, the mouth a black hole. The darkness of the upper head was not shadow but contusion. When she leaned close, the sheet heaved at the chest, and over the racket of the helicopter now descending Ardis Troyer made a sound, unintelligible, a speaking groan, an exhalation of cabbage and iron.

She cupped her hands above her mother's face.

From the black mouth no sound.

She kept her hands where they were. The helicopter was settling. Her mother seemed to speak. She leaned closer, her forehead touching the backs of her wrists, and then Keeper was rounding the gurney already barking and Bachelor Crooked Hand made a reach for her from behind the ambulance door, but she had stepped away.

She hit the front doors of the hospital at a run. Skirted three old women in housecoats, startled dreamers. Slammed out the fire exit into a circle of scythed and flattened grass around a picnic table. Started across the soaked dark field. A few minutes later, slowing, she heard the helicopter lift off, carrying her mother. Panting, shoes drenched, she watched it rise beyond the building and cant southwest for the medical facilities of Besborough, a sound like muffled gunshots receding, and then it was two lights on the horizon, and the sky was foreground, three-dimensional. Radiation drapery in magnetic wind. She stood to watch it billow and revolve, and then she moved on.

The night was cooler than the day but not cold. No moon. The northern lights illuminated the sky but not travellers below, and yet the fields were full of scurryings and lumbering dashes. Many tonight had destinations in that tumultuous darkness.

When she came to the river in its channel she followed it south and the slow curve of it westward. At the Birches she checked the cars. She had seen what Wakelin drove. He was not here either. She walked along the lower floodlands of the river properties, some groomed lawn to the water, trellised or flamingoed, some grown wild and still litter-snagged from last year's flood, until she came to the bridge. There she climbed the earth embankment to the highway. A pickup passed her wide. To the east a bright arch of orange and white like the tip of a luminous Creamsicle or the dark curtain of sky lifted on a better world. She walked until the sidewalk started and the highway became main street. From two blocks away she could see the small crowd of people. Police cars. She turned up an alley and took the path along the back fences to the bottom of the lane by her parents' building. From there she could see the kitchen light on. At 3:45 in the morning.

Someone spoke. Three people she hadn't seen until this moment were pressed against the chain link, also looking up at the kitchen light.

She continued down the fences. From the ditch alongside grew blackberry bushes, and she emerged onto Prospect Street with legs bleeding as if scarified in a ritual or game. At Prospect she turned east. A third cruiser was parked in front of the police station, a small orange-brick building like something Masonic. Too few windows, and what there were, narrow with tinted glass. The rear of the building was featureless but for a steel handleless door and two vertical slits. She stood and looked at those slits.

Later she returned through the blackberry prickles with no less difficulty along that path to the rear of her parents' building, where the kitchen light had been turned off, or seemed to have been, the sun now reflecting red off the glass. There were no gawkers in the lane.

She must have left her keys in the truck. Could remember nothing more. From under a rock at an outside corner of the compound she removed a rusted set. On the gate a red police tag said, This Property Has Been Secured by Order of Police. No Trespassing. She unlocked the gate. Climbed the fire escape to the kitchen door and let herself in. Mounted to her room and lay down on top of the covers. Her window was open. She heard voices from the street, not what they discussed but their tenor, solemn and a little urgent with discussion. She also heard morning sounds of the building unaffected by human developments. A soothing ground. The fridge. The starlings under the eaves. First traffic. She listened and the listening mitigated the retraction of listening that had come with the fear.

A short time later she changed into jeans and a cotton shirt and was washing at the bathroom sink. As she rinsed she glanced up and saw shining in the mirror the face of the creature. Mammalian, human, watching. Careless of any imagined uniqueness or normalcy to that other face, the one not in the glass.

Considered it. The dark eyes circled black with shock and fatigue. The pupils enlarged like those of the damaged or mad or drugged or over-loving. The pale skin raw and thin at the bone, contours of the skull discernible. The long straight nose, the lips sullen somehow, the upper lip almost protuberant so you would think it pursed. The line of the jaw, the imprint of contortion in the muscles of the face only now beginning to fade. Communication received.

The creature in the mirror bared its white teeth.

The eyes regarding.

The face lowered once more to the water in these cupped hands.

She went along the hall to their room. The door was barred with yellow tape: No Entry by Order Chief of Police. But unlocked.

The marital chamber. Small-windowed, north-facing, ever dim. Flowered walls. The caved-spring bed with the wood-print metal headboard. When she was small the weight of her sleeping father made a steep unclimbable slope to the rim of the mattress. Orange-crate bedtables surfaced and edged by her mother in white satin twenty years ago. White satin sun-yellowed since. Pink rayon skirts. The bedclothes had been taken away. Both scatter rugs. Bare lino. The closet door open. Rings bolted to the wall. Blood down the wallpaper in a faint spray.

By mid-morning Wakelin, back in Shield country, was checking into the Little Sister River Motel unit farthest from the highway. The Little Sister River Motel had been built on a gravelled white ledge of green-ribboned amazonite that ran not six feet above the pelting stream. There, worried about Caroline Troyer, he tried a phone call to the hospital in Grant, but the receptionist—not the one from last night—could or would not tell him anything except that she had no Troyer in her computer list of admittances from yesterday. When Wakelin told her that was impossible and to check again, she replied that she had already checked again, and when he said she couldn't have, she hadn't had time, she wanted to know his name and his relationship to Caroline Troyer, and suddenly he felt very tired and replaced the handset in the receiver. After that he lay in the heat, diagonal on the short bed, listening to the river, and when he closed his eyes he was back in an old dream that he knew very well because he had been back in it many times. It was the one he had been having the night he woke to learn that his life with Jane was not always going to be as he had hoped or imagined.

In the dream he is on a liner on that stretch of the Great Lakes that is rapids for a hundred days. He is stumbling the decks in fog, searching, he has forgotten for whom or for what, when he comes upon a woman in a fog-coloured robe, reclined in some kind of deckchair.

Jane?

They say you forget most thoroughly the faces of the ones you love, well, the dreamer doesn't know the face of his own wife. He studies the lines of the mouth, and it's her mouth, all right. At least he thinks so, he thinks it is. But the eyes of this woman are blood-red saucers, like setting suns. He is looking again to the mouth, when the lips part.

Woof!

The scrape of her wooden tail across the loose iron slats of the deckchair is what wakes him, the clanking of her iron bracelets against the—

Woof!

Where's Jane? Wakelin, awake then, awake for real, said to Luc, who was right there. Intent on him. Tags clanking the bedtable. Tail going. Muzzle tilted.

Wakelin fell back, patting the bunched covers next to him. Looked to Luc, who would know.

Luc's muzzle was tilted steep to bark. Woof. *Do something.* The balloon of dewlaps, Woof, and collapse. *Do something.* The balloon of dewlaps, Woof, and collapse.

Quiet, Wakelin said. His voice hoarse, a sleeper's. Where is she?

Luc barked. Woof. A high, frightened bark. *Do something.* Wagged, whacking the blinds. And then Luc walked backwards fast, nails clicking on the hardwood, and when he reached the foot of the bed he wheeled in the narrow passage, and there, incredibly, he slipped, scrabbling, and fell against the dresser and from there heavily to the floor, with a startled, human cry. Scrambled up wildly and kept on. At the door he stopped and turned once more. Muzzle tilted, tilting steeper to bark. Woof. *Do something.*

Luc was gone. Down the hall, nails clicking. Wakelin was wearing only the T-shirt he slept in. Why was it so cold? Why was the floor so cold on his feet? No light from the bathroom, none from the living room.

The living room was still colder. The door to the deck had been left open. The outside light was not on. When Wakelin stepped out, Luc was already out there. He backed away whining, in his anxiety lifting his rear legs high, like a horse.

As one in a dream—it had to be a dream, this was still that dream, please, his own fear, *please,* private and containable, without correlative—Wakelin moved forward. The dog was approaching again, now in a state of advanced animal pleading. Muzzle tilted. Tilting steeper to bark.

Just shut up, Luc, Wakelin whispered. Please.

It had been cold in the living room but it was colder on the deck. Deck of a flat, not a liner. Not a Great Lakes liner on rapids for a hundred days. Not a dream.

Wakelin was very afraid. Bowels melting. Jane? *Janey—?*

She was on her hands and knees, in her silk dressing gown, which had fallen open. She was too white. Her head was down, her hair fallen to touch the deck. Her hands and knees were sticky with blood, her hair was trailing in the blood. She was bunting the iron table like a wind-up toy that had met with an obstruction.

As he reached out to touch her bare arm his hand shook so—it was very cold. As he reached out to touch her bare arm—a siren somewhere, wailing. As he leaned forward to touch her arm—

What is it, what have you—?

He was helpless here, powerless to save her, he could do nothing about all this blood. Nothing. He could call an ambulance, and at the hospital they would bind her wounds and pump her out and dose her, but there was nothing he could do, he was caught, paralysed, his love that forgave—that could perfect, that could forget, that could redeem—anything, poisoning her, and there was nothing that he could do.

And the one who shot up wide awake in the morning sunlight in the unit of the Little Sister River Motel farthest from the highway was, incredibly, the same one from that night, and everything was different, it was not even night, and nothing had changed.

By early afternoon, Caroline Troyer was sitting in a waiting area on the fifth floor of the Besborough District Hospital, a smell like insulin in a bottle, windows on two walls, at her back the commercial downtown. Prewar warehouses and trash-blown alleyways. Across from her an old woman sat in disarray, a tube in each nostril, smoking a cigarette. As the old woman smoked she stared at Caroline. When she had finished the cigarette she crushed it under the heel of her slipper, then seemed to lapse into temporary sleep. Eventually she struggled to stand. Caroline went over to help. Without looking up, the woman waved her away. Caroline returned to her seat. When she looked over, the old woman had gained her feet. On stiff bone legs she shuffled away, pushing ahead of her the cylinder of oxygen, swinging on its rack.

Alone then with the heat of the sun against the back of her head, she dozed as she had not done on the bus. No one told her when her mother came out of surgery, but later she stepped in front of an exasperated-looking doctor moving fast down the corridor.

"She's one lucky lady," he told her. "Listen, there could be some perceptual problems. Focus, depth, that kind of thing. It was quite a fall."

"Where is she?"

"You know what? Why don't you let her rest a little bit? Come see her tomorrow."

Her mother lay in a large ward with a beige plastic curtain around the bed. The bandages were different, lesser. She was on an IV drip. Caroline held her hands at her mother's face. After midnight an orderly wheeled in a cot. Caroline dragged the thin mattress off the springs and lay on the floor. Listening to her mother's labouring breath. Every few hours she got up to hold her hands over her mother's face. Like a child, warming them. Like an old woman, bestowing the blessing of her sorrowing love upon a sleeping child.

When Wakelin woke it was dusk. At the Little Sister River Motel office he found a bottle of grape pop at the bottom of a cooler so cold that when he opened the cap the contents emerged in a blanched snake of purple slush. The pop and a bag of chips he carried back to his room. There he waited for the pop to melt. He had plenty of time. The pop and chips themselves had already waited this long, being first cousins to the ones he had failed to pick up last night at the Shoppers Drug. Wakelin drank the pop as it melted, and ate the chips, watching TV.

And then he turned off the TV and stared at the ceiling for quite a while. Dirty yellow water stains in those old mineral fibre ceiling tiles, with the holes. Distinctly edged, like coastlines. Got up and washed the salt and grease off his fingers. Went out to the car and from the trunk took a denim bag with a drawstring, about the size of a large handbag. Lay down on the bed and opened the bag.

Soon, in memory, he was back a month after Jane's death in the empty flat where they had lived for three years, and it turned out his home with her when stripped of habitation was nothing but a few rooms at the top of some stairs. A floor in a house. A way of life is everything, it is a whole world, and then it goes.

He had brought Luc back with him, driven out to the suburbs to pick him up at Jane's brother's, knew immediately he should not have. The dog was too happy. The closer they got to the house, the happier Luc became. By the time they were parking in back like old times he was rapturous, barking inside the car. The stairs he took in four bounds. Now he was sniffing along the baseboards, tail brisking. Once uncannily in tune with her, now that she was gone, a complete fool. The *click click click click* of Luc's claws against the hardwood were detonations on the emptied air, and death was just a trick that humans could play.

Wakelin himself was shuffling through in mental blindness for what he had missed in the exhaustion of last night's trips down to the U-Haul. He knew he wasn't really seeing anything. He tried, but it was all like the future, perspectiveless, flattened to nothing. Wakelin was mostly the past these days, mostly her. Eating breakfast this morning he had found himself spreading jam on his toast one small section at a time. This had been her method. Wandering the flat he noticed he was running his fingers through his hair the way she did, puffing out exasperated and despairing through loose lips in that French way, as if this would bring her back.

Absently checking, he was opening and closing the set of oak drawers built into the bedroom wall—it was an old house—and the bottom one was still full of her things. A lost cache of her. Wakelin crouched over the drawer and inhaled. He removed the drawer altogether and set it in the centre of the bare floor and knelt over it, sifting through it like a thief through a casket of silks. He burrowed with both hands to the bottom and lifted the contents—camisoles, stockings, scarves—and these treasures were not smooth the way her skin had been smooth, they were smooth like silk, but they smelled sweetly of her body and her perfumes.

Luc came clicking in to see. Wakelin was sobbing. Luc sniffed the drawer, then sat and watched Wakelin, who after a while curled up on his side and went on weeping.

The sobs grew spaced and eventually they stopped. Luc had left again. *Click click click click* down the hall. Wakelin lay quietly, breath still catching, sighting along the floor, a foreshortening of dust.

At some point Wakelin got up off the floor and went back to the space that had been the living room. Placed his forehead against the glass door to the deck, where he had found her, that first time she tried. Outside was winter's tricolour: white snow, black trees, grey sky. Land of death. Drifts had hardened on the deck. The barbecue was frozen in, another item he had forgotten in the move. Clearly Wakelin was no longer the guy who had lived here with a barbecue and a peerless fragile wife. For how outlandish a contraption did a barbecue seem to him now.

When Wakelin turned back to the room Luc was sitting in the kitchen doorway, eagerly, tail thumping.

Mark not feed you all week?

Wakelin checked the fridge. Nothing. An earthenware bowl of recongealed butter like a hippie candle. Left over from a dinner party cancelled owing to a mood crash of the hostess. Why not? Wakelin placed the bowl on the floor, then went to the kitchen sink and rinsed his face and chest with cold water. When he turned back, dripping, towelless, Luc was looking at him anxiously. Sniffed the butter in a pointed way and looked at him again.

Well, go on. You love butter. You've killed for less.

Luc wagged fretfully.

Ah, you're a fickle animal. Wakelin lifted the bowl and sniffed. I take everything back. And bowl in hand he moved toward the green garbage bag slumped on the counter.

But this caused Luc to bark, so Wakelin returned the bowl to the floor.

And that was how he came to watch a dog eat a bowl of lemon butter. Luc's desperate muzzle puckering so powerfully after each essay that Wakelin's own salivary glands were starting to jet. By the time Luc was halfway done he was looking to Wakelin for mercy, but Wakelin just kept making big disclaiming gestures and saying, Look, it's not my fault, and, It's your own free choice, and Luc would duck his head grimly to the bowl, until in a kind of strangled whinny his muzzle would corkscrew upward, dewlaps crinkled, and Wakelin could see the lemon butter caked in his teeth, and Luc's head would roll in the air, wincing and pursing and whimpering, and then it would dip for more.

Suddenly a key in the front door, swiftly effectual. A guy with a studio tan and a muscled neck capped by a small skull pushed in carrying an enormous cardboard box. When he saw Wakelin doubled up against the kitchen counter his movements slowed right down.

What the hell's going on here?

Dog's—Wakelin wiped tears from his eyes—dog's eating lemon butter.

Who are you?

Wakelin told him. He indicated Luc. Dog's mine. Or used to be. I gave him to my brother-in-law. I'm divesting. Let me give you a hand with that box—

How'd you get in here?

From the counter Wakelin held up a key.

Muscleneck moved on. In the living room he set down the box and went about a tour of inspection. Of the empty spaces. Of plaster scarred by the rages of a desperate woman. Of a desolated widower's dustbunnies.

The glass door slid, and Muscleneck stepped out onto the deck.

Sober now, Wakelin squatted to watch Luc persist with the lemon butter. How am I ever going to part with a sick fool like you? He reached out to rub the dog's neck, but Luc froze and growled as he always did when he was touched while eating, and then his whole face tugged sideways in a splendid grimace of sourness.

Muscleneck was back, from behind, to announce his findings. This place is a pigsty.

When Wakelin rose and turned, Muscleneck was standing there holding the frozen, snow-caked barbecue, which he now pushed at him. Wakelin looked at the contraption, and then he looked at Muscleneck. A young man with a studio tan and moving-day halitosis.

Yeah, I know, Wakelin said. And it used to be so clean and neat, too.

Well, you take your fucking barbecue and get out of my apartment.

Actually, I think I'll wait here while my dog finishes his lemon butter.

I said, get out of my apartment.

Wakelin smiled a slow, sad what-can-you-do smile. He looked around at Luc. What do you think of that, boy? Feel up to sicking him?

The last thing Wakelin saw before he hit the fridge was Luc glance up and wag. Wakelin's rage was the rage of the bereaved, but Muscleneck was a bodybuilder and his was steroidal. At first Luc was torn between finishing the lemon butter and barking at Wakelin's being bounced around the kitchen like a junkie thief, and then he got booted out too. The door slammed and Wakelin and Luc recovered their balance on the landing.

Don't you just hate Polo Sport? Wakelin asked Luc.

The door opened, and Muscleneck kicked out the barbecue, which fell onto Luc, who scrambled out from under it with a panicky yelp.

Wakelin was lifting the barbecue when a sari-clad young woman holding a computer monitor in her arms appeared on the lower landing. She hesitated.

Hi, Wakelin said.

Behind Wakelin the door opened and Muscleneck said, Sita, wait right there until he's gone.

Sita was peering nervously over the top of her monitor at Luc, who had descended the stairs and was sniffing at her, making strange, chops-licking faces.

Ron, it is becoming a little bit heavy, Sita said quietly.

Now Ron muscled past Wakelin and descended to relieve Sita of the monitor. Wakelin watched to make sure he offered no injury to Luc, who was growling at him. Sita followed Ron up the stairs with a shy glance for Wakelin as she passed into the flat. Ron kicked the door shut with his foot. Luc barked from the lower landing.

Ron and Sita's van was parked out front. Briefly Wakelin considered smashing a floor lamp or kicking in a speaker, but this seemed an unworthy impulse, and anyway, he'd have to put down the barbecue. He called Luc, who had his head thrust in the side door of the van, wagging hard. They took the alley that led to the back of the house, where he was parked. Wakelin knew he was forgetting something, but he thought it must be his failure to do damage to Ron and Sita's possessions. He had the barbecue, which he got into the trunk. And then he had backed out of his old parking spot and was about to drive away, put this entire nasty little encounter behind him, when he saw Ron on the deck with the drawer balanced on the railing.

Hey, you forgot your underwear!

No, please, Wakelin whispered. He was getting out of the car.

Ron tipped the drawer, and like party favours, Jane's things—stockings, garters, scarves, panties, bras—floated down onto the bare earth and crusted snow of the parking lot.

Wakelin advanced to gather them all up and did not once lift his eyes. Refused Young Muscleneck Ron the satisfaction of his tears. One black pair of pantyhose had wafted as far as the windshield. From inside the car Luc was barking at it.

Out on the street Wakelin managed a furrow an inch deep and possibly three feet in length down the body and door on the driver's side of Ron and Sita's van, and did so in a manner that engaged the right corner only of the Honda's front bumper, did not even crack the turn-signal lens, though this was a chance he had taken.

Good revenge, he told Luc as they sped away. Too bad though. Sita seemed kind of nice.

Luc wasn't listening. His paw had slipped from the dashboard when they hit the van. Now he had it in place again and was back scouring his gums.

It was Jane's things in the denim bag. Wakelin took them with him when he travelled, because their scent and the touch of them against his face was on some nights the only drug that made sleep possible. And so it was in that unit at the far end of the Little Sister River Motel, nosing garments that had touched the skin of his wife, eased by her fragrance, that Wakelin found sleep until the first light. The sun was still behind the trees when he got back into his car, to peer out through the bug-juice-glazed windshield and make sure that whatever he did he got the lane he wanted, the one signed Region of 10,000 Lakes. The one signed North.

It was dusk, a fine drizzle, when Caroline Troyer came down off the steps of the Besborough bus into the parking lot and started along the main street of Grant. This the night following the one she had spent at the Besborough District Hospital with her mother Ardis.

A pickup truck slowed when the driver saw who it was. Returned to speed when she looked around.

She did not go to the front door but took the alley. The chain-link gate stood open, the police tape was gone. She looked up.

The kitchen light was on.

Immediately she dropped to her haunches. The drizzle was now a light rain. She squatted there for several minutes, gazing up at the kitchen window. Watching it perhaps, though what she was likely to see through the closed curtains could tell her no more than what she already knew. Which was that, unaccountably, he was back here. No longer in custody.

Meaning that she had nowhere to go.

For some time she considered her situation. When she had finished doing this, she looked around her in the manner of one who has come to a decision and is now about to act, and then she came up to her full height and walked away.

At the street she turned north. Passed the Gemboree, the bus parked out front, the driver visible inside at the counter, drinking coffee. Continued beyond the end of the sidewalk and over the bridge and kept walking. She was not far out of town when night fell absolutely, and for a short time there was no light. She walked on, her only illumination the occasional headlights of passing vehicles. Just beyond the bridge a car slowed and came up behind her. When the roof-light flashed red she knew it was the cruiser and who it was: Elvin Hryniuk. His window whirred down.

"Hey, Caroline! You're all wet!"

She put a hand to her hair. It was plastered against her skull. She ducked to see him. "I'm just going out to the hospital," she said.

"What's wrong? Get in."

She got in. When he didn't pull back onto the highway right away she looked over at him.

"Hi," he said.

"Hi."

"I guess you know they took her down to Besborough. She was only out here at first, eh?"

She nodded. "Why didn't Justice Bob have him held?"

"He did. Detention order. But today Judge Walter Heinrichs come through and let him out." Now Hryniuk was pulling onto the road. "Even Al Parks said it wasn't like he killed her, and I guess for once the judge agreed with the prosecutor. Or maybe he had no choice."

For a short time Elvin didn't say anything. And then he said, "You're all right, yourself?"

She nodded.

The entrance to the hospital was approaching. He took a flashlight from the glove compartment and passed it to her. "Shine it down there." He had done a U-turn and was pulling alongside the edge of the shoulder opposite.

It was the truck, at the bottom of the gully. On its wheels, but the driver's door was twisted on its hinges, and the roof was caved in.

"How'd it get down there?" she said.

"You know we never got a chance to charge the reporter guy, eh? Eunice said he told them you took an epileptic seizure. Would that be right?"

"No."

"I didn't believe it. Hey, Caroline, listen. If there's anything—A place to stay. My aunt's. Anything. I mean it, eh?" He was leaning across the seat as she got out. "Do you want me to wait for you?"

"It's okay." She slammed the door.

Elvin Hryniuk waited until she was inside the building and then he pulled away.

The first thing Eunice Bragg on Reception said when she saw her was, "Why didn't you tell us? You had us worried half to death! At least until Barb figured to call down to Besborough." And then she said, "Why are you so wet? I thought I heard a car."

"Where's the guy that was with me?" Caroline said.

Eunice shrugged. "Who knows. The first time I looked around he was gone."

Caroline turned and started for the door.

"Hey Caroline! I got an address—"

Caroline turned back.

Eunice was looking at her screen. "Of course, it's totally confidential."

Caroline wiped at her forehead with the underside of her wrist.

Eunice told her the address, and a phone number. "Kind of cute, eh? Sort of."

Caroline turned.

"Wakelin," Eunice said. "Timothy Wakelin. W-A-K-E-L-I-N."

Caroline nodded. She was at the door.

"Hey, Caroline, write it all down! You're going to forget it!"

"I won't forget it."

In the plaza convenience on the way back to town she bought a bag of peanuts, a chocolate bar, and a carton of milk. By the time she reached the Gemboree it was closed and the bus had returned to Besborough. She continued down the street and took an alley and from there climbed the rise of land above the war memorial. The rain had stopped, and it was not cold, but her clothes were damp. In her place on the slope under the pine she ate the peanuts and drank the milk. For some time she sat and watched the night above the town, yellowed by the lights.

Later she broke off a dozen hemlock boughs and piled them in the small clearing and stood and looked at them. A few minutes later she climbed the hill above the path to a bowl of rock bottomed with needles of pine and balsam. The forest canopy was thicker there, and the needles were dry, or dry enough. She returned to the clearing for the boughs. It was past midnight by the time she had got them and others arranged over her and was settled into the needles in the rock bowl. It was not cold but she was shivering. There were a few mosquitoes. She fell asleep.

He came later in the night. A twig snapped. From the upper canopy no flashlight beam was reflected, but this was not a deer. He would not switch on the light until he had stepped down into the clearing, which she had not known he knew about. And why not? she wondered. Why hadn't she known that he would know about it?

When he did step down she knew the fresh stumps of the branches she had broken off would show up practically fluorescent in the beam of his flashlight.

She heard him come up out of the clearing to the path, and she knew that he was playing the beam along the ground. She heard him walk back down the path a short way. Return and walk a short way farther on. And return. She saw the top of the pile of boughs above her flash briefly, and then she heard his footsteps, coming through the undergrowth toward her. And stop. Again the beam swept the top of the pile of boughs in the unmerciful persistence of its searching. And again he came forward. Halted. Silence. The flashlight clicked off. She knew that if he were close enough, with or without the flashlight, as the early light came on, he would be able to see her through the branches. And if he had not come close enough to see her, then a rock hollow filled with fresh-cut boughs would be enough. Her bed was not going to be mistaken by him for anything created by nature. She knew that except for the flashlight and a preparedness to do what was necessary, he would be unarmed. She also knew that like a bear he was capable of waiting the two or three hours it would take, until her breathing grew heavy or, as was more likely, the trembling became uncontrollable.

For a long time it was as if he had gone. But then he seemed to turn and go back down to the path. Seemed to.

She waited.

And then she knew that he had indeed gone away, and that she should have run when she had a chance, because she did not have much of one now. He was coming back, with Keeper, on a leash. She did not understand the leash. Judging from the light, it was less than an hour to dawn. She heard a dry rustle and then she saw the outline of her father's head above the horizon of her pit against the pearly fissures in the canopy. She did not know what he was waiting for. She was hearing, beyond the choking breath of Keeper, another sort of rasp or rustle and could not place it, and then she heard what it was. He was standing where he had stopped, calling to her in a soundless whisper. Monotonous and febrile. *Precious*, he was saying. *Precious Angel.* Her limbs froze. And then he was approaching again, and the gasps of the old dog grew louder, because of course it too knew exactly where she was. But Keeper was being held back, to Keeper's frustration, and above her, not six feet from where she lay, he began to bark.

And then she heard the click and marvelled. The gunshot, so close, so loud, jolted her. The barking ended abruptly. In one movement she rolled to her knees and stood, throwing off the boughs as she sprang back to leap from the pit, but the needles were deep and they slid away under her and she went down. Already he was into the boughs, already lunging as she threw herself upwards, and then he had her right ankle in one hand. She rolled to her side and with her free foot kicked out at his face with her boot. Again and again. Even so, he held on, his head tucked down into his chest still gripping as she kicked, until he made a grab for her free leg to stop it, and she jerked free her held ankle and threw herself leftward around the curve of the pit, scrambling. She heard the gasps of his breathing, she felt him lunge once more, his fingers claw down the backs of her jeans, and then he had her again, by one cuff, but now she aimed a kick directly at that hand. The fingers did not let go but slipped, and before they could grip again she was on her knees, out of the pit, and then she was stumbling uphill, staggering, and fell hard, onto a sharp dead stalk thick as a man's thumb, and this broke against her collarbone, a sickening pain. She heard his breath, his footsteps, and she was up again, moving through the undergrowth, stumbling, panting, crashing on, still faster and more recklessly, for she would go down if her legs did not match the rate of the forward falling of her body, and several times she did go down, and each time she scrambled up and staggered on, in too great alarm to know how close behind her he was.

And then she knew that he was not there and remembered that it was a long time since she had become too strong and fast to be caught on foot by him.

She crossed the northern edge of the rise in the early dawn. Beyond there she came to a path that curved down a hardwood slope and crossed a field in fallow to a gravel road that met the highway south of town. At the highway she waited in the ditch, and when the seven-thirty bus appeared she waved it down.

As she paid, the driver looked at the bloody tear in her shirt from the thumb-thick stalk.

"I fell," she said.

He looked away.

She made her way down the aisle. The other passengers were watching her, and for an instant she knew that he could be among them.

On the bus she slept.

He was waiting for her in Besborough. She saw him through the grit-streaked window of the terminal café, his swollen face lifting from some unhappy consideration to study the bus as it pulled in. She slipped into the aisle. When the door opened she jumped down into diesel heat, and he was right there, the damaged face mild, the eyes calm, coming in fast. She threw herself left, scraped along the bug-encrusted grille, and another bus was right there, pulling alongside, the doors already open. "*Hey!*" the driver shouted as she squeezed between the two vehicles and ran until she was out into the glare, horns blasting, and when she looked back the bus entrance was a great square of darkness. She did not stop running until she had rounded the far corner of a ruined storehouse or factory, where she leaned against the urine-baked wall, her hands on her knees, looking out at a scatter of corroded drums and tanks and flipped iron reservoirs and heaved for breath.

Over the next hour she moved south through the warehouse back lanes of East Besborough, where cats basked and stalked and the weeds pushed up through the crumbled asphalt. By noon she was standing on a concrete boulevard between a mall service road and a four-lane highway at a point where the road widened to a bus stop. She did not know what he would be driving, but she believed that if necessary she could make it to the mall. And then a man in some kind of shining black sports car convertible stopped for her. The man wore a blue silk shirt, and his nose was so narrow and pitched at such an angle that it seemed to her a miracle that anything so thin, so fragile, could have passed through the world this long intact.

The first thing the man said after he had reentered the flow of traffic by accelerating with skin-pressing speed was, "You ever meditate?"

She shook her head.

"You should. Organize yourself." He indicated her collarbone. "What's that blood?"

"I fell."

The man's name was Donny. Meditation he described as lining up a deal, in resonance. "You start with the baseline oscillators, one at a time: aorta, heart sounds, standing waves in the ventricles, kundalini current. That's four. Step five, you polarize the sensory cortex. This sets up a field in both hemispheres, and it pulsates in rhythm with the rest. Get all five in sync and you're in sync with the magnetic field of the Earth."

She looked at him.

"*Don't* look at me like that!" he shouted. "I know what I'm talking about!

Try it. *Om mane padme om.* From the diaphragm. Watch your breathing. Concentrate on the sound."

Donny chanted this mantra as he drove ninety miles an hour down the highway. "Come on. Do it with me."

They chanted together until Donny had to take a call on his speakerphone concerning an acquaintance who had left undone some things he ought to have done. This wouldn't have been so bad, but the guy had also done a few things he ought not to have done. It seemed there was no health in him.

"Have Sam pay him a visit," Donny kept saying. "No, no, no. Forget that. Call Sam. Just call Sam. Do you hear what I'm saying to you? Do you hear me? Do you hear me?"

On the expressway that ran across the top of the city the traffic had come to a complete stop. They resumed chanting. A few people in other cars glanced over and made comments, always to each other. There was a certain amount of distracted smiling but, all in all, little reaction.

And then they were off the main expressway onto a smaller one, and in a few minutes, still chanting, they were downtown. Donny broke off chanting to ask her where she wanted out. She had no idea. She had been to the city, of course, but knew only the principal streets and was vague on their relative locations. She told him the name of the street she had been given at the hospital. "That's west," Donny said. "I can set you down a lot closer than this."

As she was getting out of the car Donny told her how close he was to synchronization with the Earth. "This far, sweetheart," he said, holding up his thumb and forefinger. "This far."

He waved goodbye as he pulled back into traffic.

She was standing on a broad sidewalk with many people passing her wearing bright-coloured clothing. To her left, a large young man wearing an earring, his head shaved, was rummaging through the contents of a garbage bin. Every once in a while he straightened and barbarously, with obscene relish, his belly hanging down in a great swaying slab, stuffed food into his mouth or drained a can of pop. She was still watching him, when suddenly, like a man rushing from a burning building, he pushed past her on his way to the next bin. And then she too was part of the flow, watching the faces of people hurrying toward her with their clean hair and neutral eyes, while her own image came back at her outlandish from every window and expanse of mirrored glass. Moving low and empty, a tired hunter, out of her ground. Most of the people she approached ignored her. Many said "Sorry" or, stranger still, "Not today." She learned to ask quickly, but she found that those who did take the time to stop and listen to her question were often uncertain even of the name of the street they were hurrying along, their relationship to the city vexed and private, and she wondered if they found the many reflections of themselves in the glass that was everywhere a reassurance or a torment. Or if they noticed them at all.

The street was not west, as Donny had asserted, but close to the ravine. Two blocks this side of it, twenty east of where he had let her off. She had walked and asked, walked and asked, until she was ready to faint. But she found it. A mansion, divided into flats. There was no Wakelin among the names alongside the buzzers, but on the second floor a deeply muscled, crew-cut man in a tank top and satin boxers said, "Wait." When he came back he pushed a wedge of mail at her and added, "Tell him I burned anything personal, including the special deliveries, and he can go fuck himself." He was about to close the door when he looked at her for the first time. He shook his head and closed the door.

The mail was for Timothy Wakelin. From the postmarks, it went back more than a year. She left it on the floor beside the door.

That night she slept in the ravine, where she had gone in the late afternoon for the quiet and for escape from the heat of the concrete and glass. There, in a fouled and bare-worn rubble area, a settlement of human burrows where the embankment met the underside of the viaduct, she found a refrigerator carton, which she dragged to a cluster of poplars in crushed grass. In the night someone tried to take her cardboard. She felt it sliding away and held on tight. The interloper displayed little strength or will. Soon stumbled away. All this without words.

In the early morning, people walking their dogs passed a few feet from where she lay. The dogs who were off their leashes snuffled in under the cardboard and dashed on. Others barked madly or strained until they were choked by their collars.

She walked up out of the ravine. It was already hot. Rush-hour traffic had stalled both ways across the bridge. At a phone booth she tried the number Eunice had given her at the hospital and got an answering machine, not his. She called the operator, who gave her a different number but wouldn't tell her the address. When she called the number she got an answering machine that was overloaded with messages or had broken down. For five minutes it played fragments and repetitions of interleaved messages for Timothy Wakelin, and then it cut off. She tried again, and it did the same thing. And here she was at a further broken remove, hearing only the wreckage of voices of those who would also count on this man.

At a fast-food place she bought a chicken sandwich and ate it sitting on a bench by a fountain in a concrete square. She watched the people there, the tramps and the old ones. The young mothers and the babysitters with one eye on their charges while talking to each other or reading magazines, and her mind as she sat on after she had finished eating, her hands slack on the table on either side of her waxed sandwich wrapper splashed with white dressing, was the space in which these people continued arriving at their own particular form and were held there not frozen or finished but went on in their perfection unfolding.

And then she rose and walked again, deeper into downtown, moving with the human radar for bus terminals.

By noon she was headed north, gazing out at the small suburban industries, one after the other, that lined the highway corridor, from the window of a bus with Besborough lettered on the scroll over the shining windshield.

The idea Wakelin had come full circle on, the renewed object of his search, was silence. Evening crickets. He'd decided that last year he had given up too soon. Whoever told him the right property would be easy to find? Easy or hard, this was something he had to do. First find your quiet place. He didn't think he was stalling. Having done his usual cut and run, now stalling. And if he was, then this would be because he wasn't ready to go back to his life. Besides, if it was this hot up north, what was it like in the city? He was enjoying thinking about that.

What did Caroline Troyer have to do with his turnaround at the mall? Well, he still believed that by keeping his itchy typing fingers away from her he was doing her a bigger favour than any other he was capable of. What kind of positive contribution could he possibly make there? She'd been fucked over enough in her life. That much he was sure of. She didn't need it from him. But still, but still. He shouldn't have left. He really shouldn't have. And he only wished he could go back and start again. Wished he could drop down before her and say, Okay, I'm ready. I wasn't before. Wrong auspices, phony pretext. All now given over, and I am wide open. Go ahead. Heal me. Or fail to, that's okay too. We can take it from here.

As it was, he'd called his editor and told her he couldn't do the story. When she sounded actively relieved he remembered he'd had to talk her into it. Why up there? she'd kept saying. Why *this* story?

Well, maybe why this story had been that old promise of silence. Originating impulse as false pretence. Ironic, eh?

116

And so, like last summer, in realtors' offices in villages in townships he had never heard of, Wakelin would make his little speech about silence to a dull incredulous stare, then drive out to poke around properties that thirteen thousand years ago were still a mile under ice. In country that even the Algonquins had only ever passed through on their way to the Ottawa or Georgian Bay, or in winter hunted out from the shores of the biggest lakes. Country where the topsoil stretches so thin it gapes to expose bedrock in rough grey patches like the abraded backs of buried whales. An old farmer nudged Wakelin's arm and indicated one such patch. "That there's a little bit of Canada, showin' through." And in the houses Wakelin would follow another exhausted woman with a child on her hip picking up before her as she went, apologizing for the mess, while he apologized for being any trouble, when what he meant was for hating this much having to spend even five minutes inside the piss-and-cooked-cabbage poverty of her home. And at night he'd sit naked in the heat—what was the story with this heat, anyway? and right through the night, too (the whole point of nights up here was supposed to be they cooled down), and for weeks now—in the heat of another mouldering motel room on a vinyl chair directly in front of a TV set from the days before remotes, playing three-station roulette (one CBC, one in which all action took place in a raging snowstorm, one French), lifting now one sticky buttock and now the other to cool it or to fart.

Ross Troyer Realty signs were scattered through the larger area Wakelin searched, and they drew his car like a tongue to a swollen gum. In his fatigue, by the end of each day, he was doing U-turns at the sight of them. There was the tenderness around Troyer's demolished truck, but there was also something to do with Caroline Troyer that was more like an ache, and Wakelin's inability to understand the nature of that one did not make it go away.

Like Ross Troyer, most country realtors did not deign to drive out with Wakelin. Whether this was because they were lazy, or because their commissions on such minor sales would not have covered their fuel costs, or because they did not like the cut of his jib, Wakelin did not know. But he began to count himself lucky if they stirred themselves to provide directions for how to get there. After a lost back-roads drive—Say, did I miss a turn?—through heat-moired fields of knapweed and paintbrush he would pull up at a barren tar-paper enterprise so deeply informed by craziness and suffering it was all he could do to gather the strength to climb out of the car. Whether abandoned in stumbling defeat to colonies of milkweed and aspens or inhabited by suspicious adults and mosquito-ravaged kids with bad coughs and cigarette burns it did not matter to Wakelin, he could not have lived there if Century 21 paid him to.

Driving the back roads Wakelin saw a lot of ruined homesteads. Places where long ago hard-working people had been brought to their knees by a land that could not deliver. What hell it must have been not to know for sure, to pray it had been just a bad year—"Steady on, dearest. Tell the children not to worry"—then two, then three bad years, and now the terrible see-saw from comfort in God's loving hands to the sweet pain of punishment deserved—"We're all sinners in this life, woman"—while the cruel impassive land endures, taking on all human projections, all human folly, all just-so stories—whether it's How the North Wind Came to the Forest, or I go to prepare a place for you—all of it together just one more flicker of summer lightning in the long sky to solar extinction. Ah, but those homesteaders. Wakelin saw ruins of houses built directly beside malarial swamps, on the alluvial floodplains of coursing rivers, on desperate shelterless headlands, and he understood that the sepia wash of pioneer antiquity is just another illusion. When has hardship ever been a guarantor of courage or wisdom or virtue? And if deprivation and suffering and failure make character, then the real question is why pretend the character of this country is not as bitter and wretched and unforgiving as the experiences that formed it?

At the end of that first week Wakelin came upon a tall brick farmhouse on a gentle slope shaded by oaks, on sale for perhaps a quarter its value, no gravel pit within ten miles. As soon as he got out of the car the silence was right there, filling his ears. But back in the nearest town it seemed the farm had already been sold, the old woman had already accepted an offer.

Two days later he happened to drive past again and noticed something familiar about the car in the driveway. Next time through town he made a few inquiries, and it turned out the proud new owner was not the realtor exactly but his brother-in-law. Three days after that, Wakelin, still searching, drove past again, and the house, with a shining brass number and matching brass mailbox, was back on the market, for six times what the son of a bitch had paid. Wakelin could hear him with the old woman now: "Usual rule of thumb, Mrs. Langstaff, is a thousand a year, let's see, forty-seven years, make that fifty, comes to fifty plus thirty-five hundred, make that fifty-five, now isn't appreciation a wonderful thing? So we ask sixty-one and maybe you'll take fifty-nine, see how you're feeling on the day the offer comes in, and it's going to, believe me, Mrs. Langstaff, no sleepless nights on this one." He looks around as if appraisingly. "This certainly is a beautiful home you have here, Mrs. Langstaff. A bit worse for wear and in need of quite a lot of work but real old-time charming." So his brother-in-law's offer comes in at $57,500, the old woman is cheated out of somewhere around $200,000, her nest egg is slow death in a trailer, and it's just another day in this great land, darkness falls, the snow comes down, and it's a good life if you have no mercy.

One night, from his motel room, possibly after a few beers, Wakelin made a second call to the hospital in Grant to ask after Caroline Troyer. He was hoping to get the receptionist on duty the night he brought her in, and he did.

"You haven't seen her?" she said immediately, to his surprise. "Neither has anybody else around here since she went looking for you."

She told him if he was worried about Caroline Troyer, then he should call the police station. She gave him the number.

"Hello, this is Timothy Wakelin—"

"Hey, Mr. Wakelin! How are you doin'?" It was Officer Elvin Hryniuk. "No, I guess you wouldn't know me. I missed you at the hospital there. But you haven't forgotten you need to respond to the statement of claim before we can get you into court?"

Statement of claim? Wakelin didn't understand.

Hryniuk explained that the statement of claim would have been sent to the address he'd given the hospital. He must have signed for it or it wouldn't have been delivered.

Muscleneck, Wakelin thought. Muscleneck signed for it and threw it away.

He asked what the claim was for.

Hryniuk told him for the cost of Ross Troyer's truck.

Wakelin thought fast. "But it wasn't me driving! Did Caroline Troyer say it was?"

"Well, not to me she didn't. I don't think she knows how the damage was done."

"Neither does her father! He wasn't there!"

"You better make sure you tell them that in court. In your own interest, eh? Like if it wasn't you who left the parking brake off, say. But first you better come in and make your response. Unless you want it to go straight to assessment."

"Assessment."

"That's right. Of damages."

"Look. Has anybody talked to Caroline Troyer?"

"Sure. I talked to her. Last week."

"She's around, then—?"

"Oh, someplace."

"At home?"

"I don't think you'll find her at home, no."

"But she's okay?"

"As far as I know she is. If she wasn't, I'd do something about it. If I knew where to look."

"So she'll be there on the twelfth?"

"That's up to her, I guess. She kind of follows her own lights, that one."

Wakelin didn't say anything.

"Okay, Mr. Wakelin, so you'll drop in some—?"

"Please," Wakelin said. "If you're talking to her—"

"That's not all that—"

"But if you are—"

"It's honestly not all that likely I'll see her, Mr. Wakelin. I kind of give myself away with her. A man can only embarrass himself so often, and then he starts to feel like a damn fool."

"But if you do."

"Do what?"

"See her."

Hryniuk didn't say anything. And then he said, "So we'll see you soon then, eh?"

The realtor's name was Clarice Heinrichs, and she was taking Wakelin out early one morning in her white convertible Stingray to show him a property on a lake otherwise uninhabited. Clarice wore a skirt of brushed rayon the colour of heavy cream, it matched her ankle-strap sandals, and she had it hiked up for driving, above the knees, which shone dully in the gloom under the dash like small articulated gold helmets. Wakelin could see the oiled muscles of Clarice's calves stretch and go taut as her gold feet in those sandals braked and accelerated. When not tied back, as it was now for the drive, Clarice's hair too was a gold helmet, non-flyaway, and her features in its frame were handsome and clear.

"I love my car," Clarice said, accelerating into a curve.

"I feel that."

"I only use the Olds when I'm taking out couples and families."

"Huh."

"A sports car for somebody in real estate, not to mention country real estate, has got to be a weakness."

"I should think so."

She looked at him. "You're making fun of me."

"Nonsense."

"And here I am trying to do my job."

"I know. It's an unfair advantage and I'm taking it."

"Well, stop it."

The property was twelve miles down the hydro cut from Coppice. As they passed the Shell station, Wakelin checked the pumps for Orest, and there he was, doing a windshield. The customer had got out of his car and was leaning against the fender to talk. Orest's left hand was fiddling up under the mesh at his throat, but his head was turned away from the customer, and his eyes were on Wakelin.

The road into the bush from Coppice passed through the extensive operations of a sawmill, but once it crossed a red-coloured stream it became a winding washboard through low hills of mixed forest recently and haphazardly logged. About five miles in, a Kenworth truck rose over a crest like a juggernaut from out of the earth. "Fucking loggers," Clarice muttered, swerving clear. They entered its dust roll, a soft powder. A few minutes later they emerged climbing into the grassland of the cut-line, where the dust from the logging truck was still moving down it in a slow beige cloud. Here the road took to swinging back and forth in no regular way among a triple column of electrical pylons. At any one time on this side of the car or the other were the skeletal planted feet of a massive grey-steel tower with a small plaque bolted to one of the feet saying Danger: 220,000 Volts. Everything else in the cut was low to the ground: great rocks black or cinnamon, like bears; disintegrated stumps cedar-red or weather-bleached to bone; deciduous shrubs and upstart conifers chemically altered to intricate sculptures in darkness and rust.

"This is where Orest was sprayman," Wakelin said.

"Who?"

A mile down the cut the road veered left and disappeared into the bush. Clarice did not take that, the loggers' current thoroughfare, but kept to the cut, her route apparently cross-country, to follow no visible path up an incline of quartz-veined rock, which levelled and in time gave way to gravel and dust and field grass that went scraping and whispering along the undercarriage. And then the land fell sharply away, and just there Clarice pulled off and drove right up alongside a pylon and cut the engine. Overhead the cables buzzed under their burden of dew like high-voltage cicadas. Wakelin glanced up uneasily.

Clarice had climbed onto her doorsill and was pointing down the hood. "See where the road swings back left again, along the trees?"

The road was little more than a track. From here it swung hard right. After descending through the forest it skirted the hummocky marshland visible straight ahead and below, then came back into the cut to move back and forth among the pylons as before, until it sank down deeper, to where Clarice was pointing.

"Right there," she said, "beyond those trees—you can't see it—that's where you'll put your boat in."

"My boat," Wakelin said.

"You can borrow my husband's canoe, but really you need an outboard. Today we go in through the woods."

"Corvette, Stingray. Why these names if it can't even float?"

Wakelin too was standing on his doorsill gazing down the cut, that great swath through the dips and swells and shadows and layerings of the forest canopy, a swath that made the rock-bed angles and softer drift of the land itself simply green where it was not fireweed mauve. And then, below and to the left, just visible through the trees, reaching in not quite as far as the cut, Wakelin could see a third order of alternative to rock, and it was more like something simulated, a perfect fitted insert of blue: the lake. Cardinalis Lake.

"Crown land," Clarice said. "The place I'm taking you to see predates the legislation. For some reason it never got grandfathered in."

"The government has seventy-four ways to take your property," Wakelin said.

"You'll want to be thinking," Clarice said, "about four-wheel drive."

"Boat," Wakelin said. "Motor. Four-wheel drive. The seller's going to have to accept an offer of a dollar ninety-eight."

"Nobody maintains this road," Clarice said, stepping down from her doorsill, "except the various logging companies that own rights down here, and they'll let it go for ten years at a time. There's a law they can't clear-cut around lakes, by the way. Close your eyes."

She was rummaging in the trunk. When Wakelin peeked she was in a T-shirt and underpants, pulling on jeans. In a hardware store yesterday he had overheard the person on the cash, a hound-faced woman of middle age, say in a droll voice to the pretty teenager on the next register, "But I can't understand how you could go home without your shoes. Bra, panties . . . but shoes?" That little joke now made a synergy with this glimpse of Clarice, and Wakelin went a little faint.

Clarice put the windows and the roof up, that is to say, pressed the buttons and levers that performed these tasks, picked up her clipboard, and they set out. As they crossed to the wall of trees, the lightest of breezes was blowing, so light that Wakelin knew it only from the difference after he stepped through into air contained by an understorey of maple saplings.

"Selective cut through here a few years ago," Clarice said as she parted the slender dark stems and started down the slope. "Prime hardwood forest."

Wakelin followed. Not a spark of initiative. Just looking where he stepped.

After a while they were out of the maple saplings. A pileated woodpecker passed overhead like something out of the Mesozoic. It was a whole other world in here. Its own space, its own light. The grace of its own sufficiency. Not at all like what a passenger in a car imagines while a wall of forest is whipping past. A wall that when it is not a thin break insolently failing to hide a clear-cut is a sun-hungry barrier against what has got to be darkness and impenetrable chaos. But it is not that, it is not that at all.

Eventually they reached what Clarice referred to as a logging road. The logging road was overgrown with alders and ferns and raspberry and other bushes. Many bushes, many ferns.

Passage more difficult than under the trees and she calls this a road.

They did not follow the so-called road but crossed it at a diagonal to descend into shade once more. The ground, though rocky, levelled out, and Clarice, who Wakelin now noticed had also brought along an aerosol paint can, took to marking every fourth or fifth tree with a Day-Glo pink bull's-eye.

An hour later they came upon a tree bearing a Day-Glo pink bull's-eye.

"Walking in circles," Wakelin observed, palming a mosquito against his cheek, a dry satisfaction.

"Circle," Clarice murmured. She shook the can. It made a cushioned metal thunking.

"Don't get much for your money with these things, do you?" Wakelin said, meaning that they had got too much. Forest desecration, deadly fumes, ozone destruction, a clear, if circular, path for vandals to his conceivable future property.

"Let's just keep going downhill," Clarice said, pointing not downhill but in the direction of what sounded like a stream. "Seeks its own level, right?"

Wakelin followed Clarice downhill.

Once he thought he heard logging trucks.

Once Clarice looked over her shoulder and said, "I'm taking you to heaven."

Wakelin held his tongue.

The grade became steep and the trees first-growth, though that was not possible. If it were, he'd have a story here. The shards of glare below were water, Wakelin could smell it, the vapoury algal fragrance. And then they were standing on the shore. The water was clear and shallow, and it entered thocking and lapping in among the roots of young cedars where chickadees sang. The bright sand corrugations had black-grained crests and black siftings like tea leaves tracing their hollows. Wakelin, who was hot, wanted to take his shoes off and roll up his jeans and wade right in, but Clarice was following a deer path along the shore and he followed Clarice.

There was now little undergrowth, mostly fallen trunks on a heaved and springy carpet of russet needles. This was conifer forest, another order of universe from the beech-and-maple hardwood they had come through: darker, moister, quieter, softer, more acid. Resinous and still. Air of pitch, not mulch. The giant hemlock and pine in here were too big to hug and locate the alien touch of your own fingertips. Also unhuggable were the fluted columns of mist-clouded sunlight leaning stately from breaks in the crown of the canopy.

Over Clarice's shoulder Wakelin could now see a magnificent beech in full sunlight and beneath it the tin roof of a cabin of grey logs and behind the cabin, spreading up a mild slope from under that beech, an eruption of wildflowers. And then, hard to the right of where he and Clarice had reached now, among cedars, was another, smaller cabin in peeling plywood, built close to erosion-smooth and mostly buried pink and grey and green-lichened boulders at the water's edge, and around the little cabin and onto these Wakelin followed Clarice to place one foot on the high edge of a great dock heaved up sideways. Beyond the dock, a few inches of the edge of whose lower side was underwater, was the bay, breeze-marshalled in blue and silver ripples hustling eastward in endless succession. And two or three hundred yards across the bay was the other shore, more forest rising in a sanctuary wall.

"See that island in front of the cliff?" Clarice was pointing southeast.

Wakelin was aware only of her raised bare arm. The intimate hollow of her pit.

"You can't see it," she said, "but the channel to the main lake's to the left of that island. The cliff's on the main lake, which is around ten times the size of this bay."

"Doesn't feel like a bay," Wakelin replied surlily. "Feels like a big pond."

He looked at the island, a shuffle of conifer on low rock, and at the cliff of granite rising beyond it, and around at the plywood cabin just behind where they were standing, on its listing stilts of rocks. And then he looked back out at the bay.

"Foot of a wooded hill," Clarice said. "Southern exposure. Right on water." She paused. "And you know, I wouldn't be at all surprised if the seller agreed to take seven thousand less."

"Even so, that's an awful lot of money for a couple of shacks," Wakelin said without conviction. He glanced over to the log cabin. "Just look at that dry rot."

They toured.

A pretty spare set-up. Deal tables, wood chairs, iron beds thickly painted teapot-brown. Bare springs. Mattresses and bedding packed away from the mice in a metal-lined chest built into one corner of each cabin. In the larger cabin, a second chest for food. The interiors of both cabins were musty and spartan and somewhat dark. But then there was all this water, and that clearing out back, a flower garden in riot among the great boulders, hillocks of day lilies, poppies in a dozen shades from deep red to persimmon, and hollyhocks, there must have been a hundred hollyhocks, of all things. And columbine, and lupines, and pink lady's slippers. And right up to and all around the back of the cabin, a great bed of those green-veined tongues of lily of the valley. But mostly for Wakelin there was the beech, the wonderful ancient beech, with its muscular grey bark, branches uplifted toward the sun, rising high above the flowers and the boulders and the cabins, rising higher even than the birches that ringed the clearing back here.

That beech held Wakelin where he stood. He glanced around at Clarice, who was waiting for him, looking away, impatience in the very elegance of her posture. And he thought, I wish Caroline Troyer was here. She'd appreciate a tree like this.

And then he was back, balanced with Clarice on the dock at its terrific angle, crouched lowering his hand into the water, which was like glass on its way to silk. It was not cold at all. The deeper his arm went, the higher rose the tears. He did not want to embarrass himself. The breeze had died, and his arm leaving the water made ripples in the perfect surface. He could see the bottom clearly, ten feet down. Liquor bottles and what looked like rotten ten-gallon drums.

"A lot of work," he said. "A place like this."

Clarice was tapping the clipboard against her thigh.

"No electricity," Wakelin said. "No road."

"No phone," Clarice said. "No neighbours."

"How do I get the propane in?"

"Boat."

"Weren't those hundred-pound tanks I saw behind there?"

"Two-seventy-five loaded. Propane's a good gas. A tank should last you about three weeks. Assuming you run the fridge off it."

Wakelin looked up at her. "In the woods I heard logging trucks."

"Do you hear them now?"

Wakelin listened. He heard birdsong, in stereo, from the forum of the bay. He heard a jet somewhere, very high. Mostly, though, what he heard was the sound of blood coursing through the arteries in his head. He hadn't anticipated being this afraid. At the mere prospect. "Not really," he said diffidently. He had placed his hand flat on the warm dock. "How's a person supposed to get this thing floating?"

"Jack it and kick." Clarice squatted directly beside him. He could smell her, and she smelt clean and sweet, as if tramping a couple of hours through the forest had brought out the very best in her. When she spoke, it was straight into his ear. "This property is an acre freehold in a hundred thousand acres of crown land. You'll share this lake with fishermen and canoeists. Those anyway who come into the bay, which they won't do much after May because it's a trout lake and the bay's too shallow for trout once the water warms up and because there are campsites on the main lake but none on the bay. And since there's a four-horsepower limit, you won't have any jet skis. You said you wanted silence. You told me you'd given up on water. Well, Cardinalis is a fine lake, and your nearest neighbour's ten miles away. And I know it's been a beautiful summer and you're eager to get settled, so I'll tell you what. You can move in as soon as your offer's accepted. I know she's not going to mind, and if she does she's not going to know. What I suggest is you offer ten less, and when she asks for only five more because she never could figure out what the old boy saw in the place, give her three, and with the seven thousand difference buy a used four-wheel and a boat and motor."

"That'll be a pretty used four-wheel," Wakelin said. "Look," he added, "I'm going to need time to think about this. Sleep on it a while."

"Fine." Clarice rose to her feet. "Let's go."

"What, now? Already?"

On the drive back to Clarice's office in Bankhead, Wakelin told her he would possibly consider making an offer, but it would have to be twelve thousand less. She picked up her car phone without comment. By the time they reached the office a counteroffer was waiting. A request for seven thousand more.

Clarice Heinrichs was back late from showing a farmhouse to a couple from the city. The wife had completely fallen in love with the place, especially the sun porch, the one selling point of the dump, but while she and Clarice were in the kitchen going over some renovation ideas that were going to make all the difference, the sneaky-bastard husband disappeared, and when they stepped outside to think about where the herb garden should go, there he was, grimly stumping around on the roof. Clarice nearly climbed up there herself and threw him off. Now it was almost dark, and she was too tired and fed up to put the Olds in the garage. As she came around the house to the front door, her movement triggered the front floods, and someone was sitting in one of the patio chairs.

Her first thought: Rapist, where's my spray? Her second: Walter, off the bench a day early, he's forgotten his keys, will want to eat, I haven't shopped.

It was not a man.

She went over. She was shaking. "What the hell?" she said.

The young woman was sitting with her fists in the pockets of a torn windbreaker, her boots planted on the flagstones, looking up at her.

"I'm looking for a man named Wakelin," the woman said hoarsely. She cleared her throat. "You know where he's at?"

Clarice knew she ought to know who this woman was but she couldn't think. "Yes," she said. "I know where he's *at*. He's getting ready to move to a property I just sold him."

"Where's that?"

Clarice shook her head. "I'm sorry, I don't give out—"

Immediately the woman came up out of her chair. Clarice took a step back, for a moment thought she'd be swung at, but the woman kept her fists in her pockets, only brushed past—a stale menstrual odour, fragments of leaf in the matted hair—and disappeared into the glare of the floodlights.

Clarice went to the driveway to watch her as she crossed the service road and disappeared into the ditch and climbed the opposite bank to the shoulder of the highway, walking west, her hands in her pockets, head down.

"I know who that is," Clarice said. And then she said, "To hell with this," and got into the car.

When she came even with her, Caroline Troyer didn't look over. Clarice parked across the shoulder and got out. "Just hold on a minute," she said.

Caroline Troyer stopped, waiting. Her eyes flicked leftward.

"Where are you going?" Clarice said.

"Title office."

"You know what time it is, don't you?"

"It's open tomorrow."

A truck went by.

"Look," Clarice said. "Tomorrow morning, eight o'clock sharp, I'll drive you. But right now come back to the house and have something to eat and take a bath and get some sleep in a proper bed."

Caroline Troyer did not refuse, she just started around Clarice, who made a clutch at her, but she pulled away and kept going, down into the soft gravel of the shoulder and around the car.

Clarice skirted the car on the highway side. When she caught up to Caroline Troyer she grabbed her arm.

Caroline turned. She was looking at the hand on her arm.

Clarice withdrew the hand. "What the hell are you trying to prove?" she said.

A car went by. Caroline's face in its solemn filthy pallor was lit up by the headlights and then it returned to darkness. She moved away.

"God *damn* it!" Clarice cried, and again she came around in front of her. "Listen. Walter's not back until tomorrow night. If you won't sleep under his roof because he let your father out, you can pitch a tent in the back-yard. You're not going to have to thank me, you're not going to have to tell me anything, you're not going to have to say a single solitary word. Just come *on*!" And she waited while the woman stood like a jackass looking at her as if she were the lost one. A stupid lug of a country girl. The damage already so profound she would lumber to her doom with the dogged insistence of a domestic or herd animal that could not begin to grasp the forces in control of its life from insemination to slaughter. "God, I can't tell you how much I hate this country pride," Clarice said. "Will you just get in the goddamn car?"

Caroline Troyer took a step forward.

"Okay," Clarice said. "Okay." She was licking her lips.

Caroline started around her.

This time Clarice did not try to stop her. Instead she turned and shouted, "Walter had no choice! When Al Parks wants them out, all Walter can do is set the conditions! If he's violated the conditions, he goes back in!"

Caroline Troyer didn't answer, she kept on walking.

The brand-new Purley Township courthouse in Grant shared a triple-gabled powder-blue tin roof with the township office and the township library. The building stood at the southern edge of the village on a site freshly blasted out of an extrusion of gabbro the colour of charred aubergine. The building was bordered by browning cedars in beds of cork chips, and it was draped with a great hot bib of parking lot in gleaming asphalt of glycerine midnight with perfect white parking demarcations.

At his celebration lunch with Clarice in the restaurant across the street from her office in Bankhead, Wakelin had happened to mention his upcoming court appearance and, at her prompting, had provided a gloss on the circumstances that had given rise to it. Immediately Clarice reached into her purse and called him a lawyer. "Your judge'll be my husband, Walter," she said as she left a few minutes later to show a property. "That's not going to help or hinder you one way or another, but knowing his side of things makes me more cautious in these matters than you are, apparently. You'll like Duane."

The first thing Wakelin noticed about Duane Fehr, when they met the next day in Fehr's office in Bankhead, was his briefcase, which was dusty olive in colour, with serrated crossbands. Fehr explained he'd had it custom-made from the skin of an Eastern Cottonmouth he'd hit a few years ago while driving from Mississippi to Georgia. When Wakelin pulled up the day after that in front of the new courthouse in Grant, Fehr, a small man with pale red hair, was waiting for him, the briefcase bulging on the curb alongside him as if with a small mammal recently engorged.

They were still shaking hands when Fehr said grimly, "The Troyer girl never showed. Nobody around here that I've talked to's seen her since her mother first got admitted."

"Admitted," Wakelin said. "To what? Who? Ardis? The waitress? With the dog?"

Fehr's head tilted back and his mouth fell open as he cracked the tendons at the back of his neck, left side, then right side. He explained about Ardis.

"Christ," Wakelin said. "So that's who he was beating. I thought it was the dog."

"What?"

"Caroline Troyer knew already, when I was with her."

"How?"

"I don't know. Maybe she got through when she phoned. But I didn't think she—" Wakelin looked at Fehr. "And they let this guy walk around loose, suing people?"

Fehr took a step closer, glanced around. "Troyer's pleading his own case."

"Really? That's good, isn't it? For us?"

"Maybe. The judge we're up before—"

"Heinrichs."

"Right."

"Clarice's—"

"Right—let him out, but that doesn't mean anything. Heinrichs is okay. I freely admit to you I don't know what the hell's going on here. But I do think it would be a lot better for us if the daughter showed. Whatever she has to say about what did or didn't happen with the truck."

Inside, a full house, old-men regulars in the front row, everybody waiting for the judge to emerge from his chambers. Indeed, no Caroline Troyer. Her father was standing at the back wall with his hands in his pockets and his head bowed, his hair fallen forward. When he lifted his head to look around, Wakelin was surprised to see how scarred and beaten the face was, and he imagined Ardis putting up a fight. Troyer's scrutiny of the room was suggested more by the tilt of the large head than by the eyes, which were simply hard and strange, not exactly dead, more neutral. Scientific eyes.

Mocking in their refusal to be more than this. If at any time they focused upon Wakelin, he did not catch them at it. Next to Troyer, in the manner of a right-hand man or number-one son, was Bachelor Crooked Hand, whose tow truck Wakelin had seen parked out front in the lot, gleaming in the hot sun. Today Crooked Hand was wearing on his long torso a swamp-green sports jacket like a fungoid excrescence. Neither did Crooked Hand take any perceivable notice of Wakelin.

Officer Elvin Hryniuk crossed the room to pump Wakelin's hand. "Hey, nice to meet you!"

Hryniuk's complexion was highly coloured, in the manner of one who wears his emotions on his cheek.

Also there, suddenly, at Wakelin's elbow, wearing Banlon slacks and a baseball jacket that said Grant Diamonds across a big embroidered diamond on the back, was Gail, his waitress from the Gemboree Café.

"So why'd you go and total Ross's ve-hicle?" she said, poking him in the ribs.

"Gail, right?"

"Whoa! Hear that, Elvin? The man remembers my name!"

"All he had to do was think wind and lots of it," Hryniuk said, a simple joke that Wakelin took a while to get.

"Think there's time for a smoke?" Gail wondered, looking around after ducking her head to punch Hryniuk in the arm.

"Where's Caroline Troyer?" Wakelin asked them both. "Why isn't she here?"

Hryniuk only blushed crimson, but Gail said quickly, "Why should she be? Where were you for her?"

This caught Wakelin off guard, and when he said, "What do you mean—?" it was practically in a whine. And then everybody was standing up for the judge. Duane Fehr beckoned Wakelin over.

Heinrichs' entrance was one for the justice system. A man with the look and bearing of a high school principal or team coach, he manifested the sort of clear-headed good sense in whose company sophistry and irrelevance will echo ever tinnier until they are hollow nuisances only. Watching Heinrichs assume his place behind the bench, Wakelin remembered that it was this man's canoe his wife had promised to lend him. A promise from before the deal had closed, mind you, realtors with customers being like men with women, they'll say anything. Later it's as much as they can do to recognize you in the street. Wakelin wondered why a plain forthright man like this would marry such a person. And then he wondered if he might be wrong about one of them. Or both. And then he wondered if people were possibly more complicated than you gave them credit for when you wanted something from them.

Wakelin's case was fourth up. Preceding him were five teenagers charged with creating a disturbance at the Dunkin' Donuts in Sproule, a malcontent supplier who had driven his truck through the plate-glass window at Haworth Dairies, and a sad old man stopped on the sidewalk outside the Stedman's here in town with a pocketful of socks. After the old guy had been reproved at a pitch of toughness evidently—from their nods—acceptable to the old ones in the pit, Ross Troyer was invited to approach the bench and make his statement.

This Troyer did, and an unexpected statement it was. He began with an observation to the effect that a young man—I'm not that young, Wakelin thought—in the pride of his strength is too apt to be seduced by those women most proficient in the soft arts of recommending their own weakness, only to discover that what in anticipation was delight, in consummation is an immediate, loathesome burden, a clinging weight.

Who's he talking about? Wakelin wondered.

Of course it often enough happens, Troyer continued, that the young man who in this way has been early the dupe of his desire becomes its double dupe in that he finds himself yoked with its former object in that institution perhaps the best check upon it. I mean marriage.

This drew a laugh, albeit uneasy, or unsure.

Why, he's talking about himself, Wakelin realized.

Heinrichs looked irritated but did not rap his gavel, if he had one. "Mr. Troyer," he said, "please come to your point."

Troyer's point, or at least his next point, was that while those of a certain disposition will welcome that holy bond as the universal salve for their itch, those of another, confusing that itch with life, will aggravate it by transgressions of the familiar kind. Sordid and craven. But others, he said, will choose to move beyond yoke and transgression both, passing out from the petty vineyards of repute to that purer realm where the distance of desire has been vanquished, where desire is now a force out of all scale, free of appetite and season, a mutation of will—for what is will in its original but desire organized?—and not only sense but imagination incapable of keeping pace.

"Your last warning, Mr. Troyer," Judge Heinrichs said. "We have shown extraordinary patience here today. Out of respect to your standing in the community, the pressures upon you, and so forth. Our patience, however, is not limitless. This is a court of law, not a soapbox on some street corner."

Methodically, like a man sensing a matter rapidly begin to sort itself in darkness, Troyer seemed to look about him, as if to inquire of the room. Many, the old ones included, shifted in their seats, though these were new and well cushioned.

When Troyer continued he said that in the human realm the promise of transformation has always been freedom. This the achievement of the few. Imagination embarrassed and overwhelmed. Lagging, never to arrive, not really. That faculty outstripped, and all illusion thereby. And he said that some who have known such transformation have likened it to a clinging ride on a rocket of light, though some have called this light darkness in that it is a light that blinds. The name of the rocket is Power Absolute, and imagination can only hold on.

"All right, Mr. Troyer, we've heard enough. I'm afraid I'm going to have to ask you to sit down."

Troyer hesitated, but only for an instant. Then he returned to his seat. The scarred face, the terrible eyes without expression.

People coughed and blew their noses. To Fehr, Wakelin whispered, "What did he say?" but Fehr signalled him quiet with a hand he did not lift from the table in front of him.

The judge was saying that the complainant's having spoken nothing to the point, the court had no choice but to dismiss the case and adjourn for lunch, which it now did.

Troyer and Crooked Hand were gone before Wakelin had gathered himself to look around.

"So," Fehr said when they were back out on the chemical griddle of the parking lot. "That was sweet enough."

"What happened?" Wakelin said.

"Sounded to me like Troyer was under the impression it was him on trial. Either that or he felt like pretending as much. Weird, eh?"

"But why?"

"Change of mind? Eaten up by remorse after what he did to his wife?"

"But why bring me all the way down here?"

"Power Absolute? Last minute decision? Failed attempt to get his daughter to show? Didn't expect you to? Or just flipped right out?" Fehr cracked his neck, both sides, and added, "But we don't really know, do we? Here's exactly how much we know: Piss all." He reached for Wakelin's hand, saying, "And this is why, my friend, you must count yourself fortunate under heaven this day." Picking up his snakeskin briefcase, he added, "Look for my bill," and walked toward a rusted-out Mercedes sedan perhaps thirty years old. There he threw the briefcase into the back seat and with his hand on the door turned and said, "Family stuff, you know what I'm saying?"

Wakelin watched him get into the car.

Fehr rolled down the window. "The thing is," Fehr said, "when it comes to families, nobody knows anything. And if it's bad enough, they don't even know themselves."

After Fehr had driven away, Wakelin sat for a long time in his car in the extraordinary heat of the parking lot, rubbing his temples. When he smelled cigarette he looked up, and Gail, one eye closed against the smoke, was leaning against his door. In a careless tone, she said, "You know, she'll still be looking for you."

"Really?" Wakelin said, ingenuous as a child, though he knew immediately that this was true. Knew it for the same reason he had not been able to get her out of his mind.

"But why?" he asked Gail. "Why me?"

She knocked the ash off her cigarette. A gesture of remarkable fury for one so routine. "Why. You think she's got a lot of choice? Someplace else to go where he wouldn't find her in two hours?"

"So why don't they lock the fucker up?"

"Which fucker would this be, then?"

"What's going on here, Gail?"

"Tell me something. Would you die for her?"

"What? Look, I—"

"You don't have the first fucking clue about anything." She turned from him with one arm across her stomach and the elbow of the other pressing her hand against her hip and her head angled to smoke.

"So help me. Give me one clue."

She didn't say anything but seemed to consider, and without turning said in a voice half resignation, half defiance, "Fine. One and only. Caroline Troyer's got power coming out her ass. That's her big problem, not old Ross. Not any more. Ross is your problem."

"Ross seemed pretty out of it in there."

"Yeah, out of it like a wolverine."

"What kind of power?"

"Did you say problem, or did you really say power?" She flicked her cigarette far out across the tarmac and turned to him. "Listen. I got to get back to work. This pathetic crate actually goes, does it?"

"What happened about Ross Troyer's truck today?" Clarice Heinrichs asked her husband the night of Wakelin's court appearance. For once, she and Walter were both at home at the same time, eating a meal together.

"Why?" he asked. He was watching his plate, removing meat from the bone.

"I just sold the defendant a property. I got him Duane Fehr."

"I dismissed the case. Troyer wasn't making sense. Now, there's a man under a lot of pressure."

"Which came first, the pressure or hospitalizing his wife?"

He looked at her. "That's a different trial."

"Why didn't Al want him held?"

"Al didn't think it was necessary."

"Does Al think the daughter's safe at home?"

"The daughter. Is this the one who thinks she can heal?"

"You know she's been sleeping in the woods?"

"Who told you this?"

"Everybody knows it." Clarice did not want to compromise or confuse what she was after here by getting into her visit from Caroline Troyer. Or by dragging in Wakelin. But why not? Why not Wakelin? What, she wondered, is Wakelin to me now? And then she remembered: She'd promised him the canoe. Friday was completely booked, ten to seven. She'd have to take it out there early tomorrow, and if it wasn't one damn thing, it was another. And she'd have to take a change of clothes because she had people to meet in Sproule at two.

"Doesn't mean it's true," her husband had just said.

He was back eating. "You've got butter on your cheek," she said. "No. Other one."

Obediently, like a trained animal, he held his face before her. She wiped away the butter with her napkin.

"Well, could you talk to Al?" she said. "Because it is. True."

"No. I couldn't talk to Al. You know I couldn't talk to Al."

"Why not?"

"Because I'd be sacked."

"Call Al, Walter. Tomorrow. Nobody's going to sack you. Just pick up the phone."

"Clarice, I'm telling you I can't do it. We already reopened the bail hearing. Troyer's out until he violates the conditions. You know that."

She put down her fork. "So what does it take?"

"Is that a rhetorical question?"

"Walter, listen. Her father's just hospitalized her mother. Now he's back home and she's living in the woods. As a judge, you don't think there's something unfair about that situation? Suspicious? Unadvisable? That maybe Al made a mistake?"

"She can stay with a friend."

"Walter."

"Clarice. The only thing possible, and you'd have to do it, is have somebody suggest to him he volunteer for a mental health test."

"Volunteer? Do you actually think—"

"No, I don't. So when he ignores this advice, I could issue a mental health warrant. The police will then take him over to the psych ward at Highlands and put him through some tests."

"What a good idea."

"No, a crappy idea. In twenty-four hours he'll come out of there like a scalded snake."

"No. They'll hold him. You said he wasn't making sense. Christ, Walter.

He just about killed his wife."

"They won't hold him. They never hold them."

"You understand Troyer's not your normal wife-beater, don't you?"

"Doesn't mean they're going to hold him."

"But you don't know they won't."

"No, I don't. Not for absolute sure."

"So do it."

"Back up. We skipped a step. First, your somebody has to apply to have him examined."

"But when they do, you'll approve it."

"Probably. After I tell them the same thing I just told you. You're scalding a snake. Clarice, please don't pursue this. Whatever the situation, it'll be more complicated than some narrow feminist take."

"Jesus, Walter. What an annoying thing to say."

"You know what I mean. I'm just saying it. If she wants to come in—"

"Who?"

"I don't know. Who are we talking about? The daughter. The mother."

"Walter, the daughter's hiding in the bush and the mother's in hospital in Besborough."

"So who's going to make the application?"

"I'll make it."

"Another terrific idea. We can draw up the papers in the hot tub."

"Right. Well, who else was there today? Who heard him making no sense?"

"The usual hawk-eyed coots."

"But who'd be—"

"The Poot girl was there. Poot and the coots."

"Gail," Clarice said. "She worked with Ardis. I'll talk to her."

"It's a mistake, Clarice."

"If it's a mistake, I'll be the one making it. Not you, not Gail Poot. Me. And you'll sign the warrant?"

"Yeah. I'll sign the warrant. If you can get Gail Poot to say something to Troyer, then swear out an affidavit, I'll sign the warrant."

When at last the moon crested the horizon it was piebald cream and silver, half gone but vast. Caroline Troyer had been walking north in darkness. Now under the bright lunar horizon she climbed a wire fence into a field where the air was numinous. A homestead, she thought, from the weight of the despair and a certain tug of longing, undertow of regret. The house must have been just over there. Her own immediate destination tonight—preliminary to tomorrow's, Wakelin's cabins on Cardinalis Bay— was a weeping willow that had since grown up by the river, midway between the unvanquished homestead and the shuttle-track of the highway. In the river she rinsed her mouth and face and neck, and already she could feel the easement sometimes available from such a place, the way a sufferer will naturally find comfort in stage or screen tragedy however alien, if it is honest. After washing, she lay back, her knees bent, on the animal-flattened grass of the riverbank.

One of her headaches had come on as she was walking, and the pain of it now extended into her neck and shoulders and spine, a veil of blades. The voices—her own in particular—had all the while she walked been increasing in volume. They were now a racket of disordered force, a stick-ratcheted cage of dogs. But she listened to the river in its glinting darkness, and to the frogs that sang like small badly tuned instruments of wire and iron, and to the movement of the breezes through the willow, and to the pasture in the stately counterpoint of its cricketing, and to the dry wash-pasts of cars and trucks from the highway. And she also listened to those

143

voices each in the particular mechanism of its insistence. She listened to the anger in the realtor woman's the other night, now repeating, and she listened to a different anger, the one the realtor woman's even now provoked, older and larger and more familiar. Less a voice than a furious space of darkness. Her own. She listened to the city, its thin impatience, in the responses to her too-slow question. She listened to the distraction. She listened to the mantra chanted by the blade-nosed man in the car, now almost two weeks later still sounding, woven through her like a filament of tinsel. And after a while she heard the other anger again, the one the realtor woman's and her own in resonance with it had been drowning: her father's, not replayed or forecast but tuned to, emitted tonight at the frequency of his private desolation, a staticky hail of pain and rage, the signal tiny and remote, barely discernible amidst these sounds of nature and this homestead despair and all but cancelled by the raucousness of these more local movements of memory and imagination, these rattled dogs in their cage.

On the bank of the river she groped for balance, for the vertical axis, the tip of the bore, and when she had it she travelled inside. A task of listening sustained, the voices slowing until when they rose up, they rose up slow and discrete. And each as it climbed to view could be seen dragging traces of its own previous occurrences, and as she watched each it fell away, back into the field of sense, which itself was even now extending and deepening. And this was the truth of it now: that in this mind it had recurred and would recur again and doing so might be so witnessed and being witnessed fall away. And the voices that had slowed and gone discrete with listening also grew quieter, and yet the pain in her head and neck and spine did not diminish but intensified, seeming to draw into itself the energy of those voices. Eventually she crept in under the willow, but sleep meant only that the voices without recuperating that energy grew tenuous and wild. Because even in sleep the witnessing continued and so discovered that the wildness of the voices had assumed (as it sometimes did) the form of that pain and that pain had assumed the form of the wildness of her father's rage, which was no longer a signal staticky and remote but the tenor of all immediate contents of this receiving mind.

That night, several times in the hour of the first light of dawn, the pale moon still in the sky, she stood and parted the drapes of willow and walked deeper into the field among the dull souls of cattle still grazing from daytime like time-lapse blurs. In a voice of authority she called out to the one who had followed her here distraught and now stood in supplication, a female familiar, the mistress of this place perhaps, a hundred and fifty years later still caught. And yet this was not possible, because weirdly the woman came as a traveller from a greater distance than from that near site and also with eyes dark-ringed and a demeanour somehow contemporary if not thoroughly familiar, so familiar as to be unrecognizable, and also in a condition of whiteness the sleeper could and yet could not remember, as when in a dream it is imperative the eyes open, but this act the dreamer has no capacity to perform. More than this, the visitor shared a greater identity with that tenor of paternal rage than with the suffering of this place, and in a loud voice the sleeper called out hoarsely, "Go away! You have no right to come here! Now, go!"

Three times she returned to the willow and crawled back inside and curled up unrelieved by having acted however boldly. For, as also happens in dreams, her visitor had arrived with news to impart, in this case the particulars of the damage done as a result of the recent outrage committed against her person, details that the sleeper seemed already, in some form, to know but was now unable to hear, lest in her own weakness, her own incapacity, they be insupportable. Lest that outcome be more dreadful even than she feared. Than she feared she already knew. This, she now also knew, was not the first time the supplicant had come but had been travelling with her for days. This no initial declination. For though the sleeper already knew, at the same time she did not know and did not know at all times. And at no time could she choose to remember what it was that she knew, again and again forgetting as soon as she did remember, as again tonight she had forgotten to the extent even of refusing to accept that her follower could not possibly be the mistress of this place. For the sleeper in her reluctance to hear the full result of that assault was incapable even of knowing the identity of her follower, however intimate. And this condition of incapacity or refusal, inveterate in this matter, it seemed, was a crippling or buckle of energy in her mind, and that night there was little rest for either traveller in that restless place.

In the morning Caroline Troyer awoke ringed by the heads of cows, looking in at her. Backing away, bumping into one another, as she pushed through to go down to the stream.

By the time she reached the highway, the fitful herd lagging, her boots were soaked with dew. The pain in her head and neck was still there but had receded, taking with it all thought. Her mind scoured.

The truck that stopped was a farmer in a wool jacket who said nothing after "G'day" and by his silence and further lack of notice conveyed what portion of kindness and pity he had for her more effectively than by anything he could possibly have said, a fact that she understood and accepted without finding anything remarkable in it. He took her twenty-five miles north and two past the turn-off to his own destination to drop her at the hamlet of Coppice, and no more than she did he find anything remarkable in this.

In the stinking washroom of the Shell station she fastened her hair with a thick blue elastic she had picked up on the roadside, the kind more usual for securing stalks of broccoli, and washed her face and hands with pink metallic goo from a chipped plastic wall-mounted container. Dried herself under the blower.

Having no money, she could not eat in the restaurant. Orest Pereki was outside on the pumps. With his long gaze fixed upon her back, she started down the road that led to the forest and through the forest to the power line. The road was paved a short distance beyond the conical shelter for road sand, and next to it the firetruck and snowplough garage, and then the pavement ended. It was early yet. The air was clear, the sun a low white blaze above the trees. Twenty minutes out of the village the road climbed to higher ground as it passed through a lumberyard. She walked among piles of spruce and fir, skinny ragged logs in great stacks on a plateau of earth bulldozed out of a raw kame where a front-end loader with bowed pincers sorted. As she walked she looked down upon the shining metal of the planing shed and the gold cone of sawdust and the great stack pouring yellow smoke into the blue sky, and then she passed down a grade of rock and gravel over a stream flowing mud-red into the woods.

Wakelin had damn well better not lose the canoe, because it was not Clarice's to lend. It was Walter's, and though he never used it any more he would sometimes walk out to the shed just to look at it. His alter ego: the airiest most fragile thing. Translucent ruby fibreglass, frame of aluminum. Was it ever light. Long and shallow and wide. He had bought it in Rotterdam at the tail end of a nature kick. A canal-racing model. Keelless. No water displacement to speak of. For calm water use only. The lightest of breezes tugged at it like something moulded in cellophane. Lift your paddle in a cross-breeze and spin like a weathercock. The manufacturer had voided all standard warranties. In these rock lakes, what could be more impractical than so delicate a floater? Hardly used, and already the length of its underside was a weave of white scratches, a scatter of starburst points of impact.

Walter would never lend it. Not to his best friend.

Along here the shore of Cardinalis Lake fell away under a skein of inverted trunks. Gazing down through the interior of her reflection Clarice saw the eroded crowns of skeleton trees sunk criss-cross in the bottom darkness. Along the bank a sleepy raccoon kept pace, one eye on her. She passed a shallow cove of bleached logs. Bullfrogs sagging iridescent among bonsai spinneys performed slow blinks. A beaver surfaced by the bow pushing a roll of water before its block snout, did a twist and tail-slap and disappeared. Surfaced alongside the stern and did it again, that time made her jump.

On the near side of the island she steered among the great boulders, treacherous shadows, paint- and aluminum-scraped tips just below the surface. One rose at a distance in a small pink dome, a white gull its sole occupant. But now, when she looked, the gull had been crowded aside by seven mergansers, a mother and her six young as large almost as herself. The gull stood with water lapping its feet, its back rudely turned against the mergansers, watching her.

And then she was into Cardinalis Bay. Her arms and legs already aching. How long since she had done anything more physical than walked a property? How long since she had allowed her own time, once so precious, to be all-consumed by work? It wasn't Walter, was it? Walter was a duck, but that just made him a handier excuse.

He would be watching her by now. It was too late to do her face, and this light was merciless. She was squinting to see when he would step onto the dock, which he hadn't yet got off the rocks. A hopeless wreck of rotten lumber and waterlogged timber, it would probably go straight to the bottom. It frightened her sometimes what she was capable of selling. In middle age she finally finds something she has a talent for, and wouldn't you know it would be the next thing to whoring.

He sure was taking his time.

With difficulty on the steep-pitched surface of the dock she got out and tied the canoe. At least it was quiet here. On the other hand, why the hell shouldn't people be given a chance to pay the price they consider what they want to be worth? Put your money where your heart is.

Where was he? Straightening up the place. Hiding his skin magazines. A late sleeper.

He had to be here because she had passed his car parked at the top of the hill. Maybe he was out for a walk. Balanced there on the dock, she did her face. Real estate lady or bag lady, which will it be? Only a few microns of blush and eyeliner between her and Caroline Troyer the other night. Makeup and twenty years. Twenty years of little lies and a few great big ones. No wonder I married a judge. But who knows? Walter turfs me, I could wind up collecting bottles along the highway yet. On my good days.

She was coming around the front of the log cabin to the kitchen porch when she saw the gap where the east window should have been. She went up to it.

Her eyes took time to adjust. She saw the smashed panes in their smashed sashes lying on the floor. She saw the smashed window opposite. She saw the overturned table and chairs and space heater and scattered sections of stovepipe and broken bowl and scattered cutlery. She saw the bloody smear of feathers, flies buzzing. Then more feathers, grey or brown, and white, many white feathers. The smell of coal oil.

A grouse must have gone through the window. But then something went in after it.

Where was Tim Wakelin?

At right angles to the empty casing where she stood was the kitchen window, facing the lake. She cupped her hands to look in. The wood cook-stove on its side. A length of stovepipe dangling from a support wire. The sideboard fallen against the fridge, its contents in a pile on the floor. The garbage can upturned.

"Shit," Clarice whispered.

Behind the cabin, which was padlocked, she found the torn knapsack, splayed keys, scattered remains of groceries: empty plastic bags; a head of cabbage, unmauled; a plastic-mesh sack of onions. A propane tank on its side still attached to its regulator, the regulator ripped off the wall. As she leaned down to check that the gas was off she saw the punctures in the drained milk and drained cream and emptied cream-cheese and sour-cream containers and knew exactly what had made them.

"Tim! Tim Wakelin!"

This time she got an answer but it was not human. It was not even audible exactly, more a physical beating of the air, a succession of blows to the stomach, or the ear—decremental, accelerant—like a gigantic piece of furniture rocking to stasis on the floor of the morning. But after the first shock of the volume of it, Clarice knew what this was too—though it was too late in the year for mating rituals—and she started for the cedars. Passed an upturned wood chair. At the plywood cabin, the drumming faded now to a cochlear pulse, she saw the broken rear window stuffed with a grey blanket, and no sooner had she made out what it was than it moved and was ejected and dropped to the ground, and a naked man was squatting on the sill, then jumping out after it to reel and stagger back, his thin dark hair flyaway, flesh but for his neck and hands amazingly soft and pink and white, a long welling cut down the left side of his upper back from the jagged glass still in the window, rubbing his face to see what in God's name he had on his roof, and then she too saw it and had been right: a ruffed grouse, perched crossways at the centre of the dip in the ridgebeam, a bird in the saddle, and even as they both stared at the bird and the bird at them, it folded its wings and brought them down, in a quick short forward stroke, and then another, and another, each succeeding the last slowly at first but soon in a blur, and the entire little plywood cabin became once more the extraordinary instrument of the creature's bereaved and mateless drumming, the air hammering with what Clarice at that moment had no trouble at all understanding was grief and rage together making this muffled thunder of desire.

A road of gravel and dust. The lumber trucks roaring past whitened everything, and it seemed to Caroline Troyer that the dust might have been her own fear the way it paled the world. She was trembling now, all but stumbling. The air would no sooner clear than another truck roar past, rewhitening everything. She walked on. She was still passing through woods, perhaps half a mile before the power line, when she came to a small lane that forked climbing leftward, and she knew it, and took it, a long-grass centred track that dipped to the edge of a bog. There she crossed a clear stream on a broken corduroy of spruce poles and walked through a press of poplars and on down farther, to meet another lane or track that wound still farther downward through birches to a place that was only vaguely as she remembered it. Not a granite canyon like something out of a sound-stage western but a shallower saucer of rock, where fifty years ago a beaver dam had been dynamited to make another kind, in concrete. The space once opened up by beaver flooding now softly edged by maples, poplars, birches, with the grey rock and the silver-grey pylons of the power line more distant than in her memory. She saw too that what she remembered as bushes were now copses. That nothing of the rotted narrow dock that had once stood opposite the dam now remained but a few soft stumps under the clear water. The concrete dam itself not grand but low and dustily crumbling. The reservoir not an unfathomable darkness but a green-rock shallows.

She walked to the high ground at the top of the clearing above the reservoir. Here was where her father used to pitch the tent. The grass of the clearing had always been short. Deer-cropped. It was still short. The fire pit was right there. She was shaking. This site too was broadcasting, the hairs at the back of her neck and on her arms erect to receive, its frequency exactly the body's but the body, hunger- and exhaustion- and exposure-weakened, slipped yawning to the grass, molecules tumbling, shifting with a stony clicking like rocks striking underwater, and she was camped once more in the night with her father, by the low dam in the bowl of yellow birch and granite close to the hydro cut.

In daytime the pylons at the edge of the young girl's vision had seemed to hang like smoke against the pale August sky. Now, in the night, it was necessary to look straight at them if she would see them at all, skeletal darknesses among the stars, but with her father's powerful flashlight even at this distance from structures so tenuous she was able to bring forth grey substance where black nothing had been before.

There was no moon. The sky was clear as it was all that day and for as many days and nights as she and her father had been here, and there had been no rain in all that time, and longer. The river above the reservoir had dwindled to a creek that wandered its bed, lost. There was not enough water now to pass over the top of the dam. Earlier that day, in the heat of the sun, when she—a young girl—had walked out briefly upon the concrete and the dry-rotted timbers, she could neither feel nor see the water as it passed through this barrier, only hear its hollow gurgling as it moved beneath her invisible among the boulders boxed by these timbers and so down among the bases of still more boulders in their great spill of grey and black into the ravine below. But that was in daytime, and the dam, though it stood not far across the small reservoir from the dock where the girl in her nightgown now paced, was a distant pale strip in starlight, and the water as it filtered through and beyond the dam was only in the very deepest and most interior way audible at all.

The dock was narrow and listing. The dirt bikers who toured the gravel road that followed the cut had observed for years a tradition of driving their skeletal mud-encrusted machines out onto it and backing them off and driving them out onto it again and so had aggravated and skewed and here and there splintered and caved and all but demolished the structure, from whose edge the girl, who was five and knew this much concerning, but had no reason to give more thought to, the senseless pastimes of ignorant brutal men, shone the beam of her father's flashlight straight down into the water, through the mote-drifting darkness.

Day or night there was little breeze in that neglected place, and the water was clear. In sunshine it held the light, and along the shore the bottom revealed itself as one after the other luminous vignette of tannin transparency. But here in the night with her father's flashlight the girl could pierce the black water for other kinds of pictures. Tonight she shone it among the rocks near the shore and saw the trout minnows, synchronized dark slips of quick escape, and the tadpoles like bloated fleshy outgrowths of rock, immobile and intent. Also she saw a bloodsucker that clung to a sunken branch go long and beckon like a black frond and shrink again, and wait. But it was off the end of the dock, on the deeper bottom, that she saw for the first time the wax-white ragged chunk of fish flesh, a section of the central body—head, tail, guts gone—the tattered tips of the flesh smudged or blurred as if rotted there, waving gently in the small current. The water was perhaps six feet deep at that place, the sand-muck bottom a terrain of black and pearly gaping clamshells, half-buried algaed liquor bottles, and small dark rocks curious in their isolation, and then, bright at the centre of her beam, this chunk of fish, more curious still in its isolation, dead flesh unmeriting such vivid glowing.

Suddenly from beyond the edge of the light the girl became aware of a complex stir, ruby gleams of eyes, bony structures scuttling, the chunk of fish provender more enticing than darkness. And no sooner had the first to arrive, hoisting its claws, gripped the flesh to yank it in its own direction, than a second scurried forward objecting. A fierce grapple ensued, and the second, slowly and with tremendous effort, was pushed away, as meanwhile a third moved in for the prize, and a fourth came for that one. Now the girl swung the beam wide and saw how it was that other crayfish and still others waited in the outer darkness each for its chance, that the arrival in this place of this perfect white carrion (she had not noticed it in the day) was an occasion of great moment, and in how many other worlds of the universe were great occasions even now unfolding unknown?

As the girl watched, the combat proceeded, assuming many shapes. At times there were five crayfish inside the beam, all struggling, the meat ignored, the combatants pushing each other farther into the dark, while the ones who had just arrived from the deeper darkness, even as they made way for those ejected, calculated their own routes in. And yet none of those able to reach the prize held it for long. All were subject to the larger pattern of struggle, and if one dominated, soon enough it grew weary, compelled as it was to stave off all candidates. In this place loyalties were momentary, ally turned against ally with the vanquishment of the enemy nearest, so that outsiders were constantly coming to dominate, but they too grew weary, and so others, and this cycle of contention would surely continue until the sun rose to illuminate the bowl of the reservoir and there remained no more darkness from which fresh assailants might issue with cray-blood hot to engage.

Except then she saw them, though as soon as she did she knew that they had been there longer than she had, like thoughts before they are recognized as thoughts, cipherous and spectral. Even in her beam—mainly they skirted her beam—they were shadows, the two of them, on another scale, from another dimension, impervious to illumination, and they passed again and again above the foolish brawling of the abortive feast, high above the scuttering pinhead contenders. It was only when they descended, first one and then the other, that she knew how profound was their engagement, and soon after, by the whiskers and terrible white profile of the first as it came in from the side to seize the meat, she saw what they were. And next to the strength and bulk and ferocity of these great creatures the crayfish were nothing, dispersing like soft bones while frenzied as sharks the catfish worried the meat, their spines whipping, stirring up the bottom in clouds in which floated wisps of offal. The catfish operated in rapid turns, not quite in competition, nor quite in league, suddenly swimming off as one, done for now, a pause, and the crayfish moved in to resume their struggle, and not long after that the catfish were back high above, cruising.

The father came cautiously, for it was dark and he had no light, out onto the little jetty, naked. He was looking up at the stars with the interest of one who would know which, at this time of the night on this day of the month, would be where, and then he looked down at the girl, who was turned to watch him. His face was round like a moon, and as he tipped it over his crouching daughter his hair fell forward. She nestled into the broad cup of him, and together they watched the life in her beam.

After some time the father said, Crayfish are the scum of the earth.

Why are they?

They're worse than people. They'd wear peaked caps and drive pickups if they thought they could get away with it.

No they wouldn't.

You put a hundred crayfish in a bucket, he said. What have you got?

I don't know.

You've got a hundred crayfish in a bucket. Nothing's going to change. One tries to climb out, the others pull him back. Not catfish. Catfish are savvy. Catfish know who they are. They never did buy the *cat* part, you know.

It's the light makes the crays do it, the girl said. She was thinking how usually the beam was a physical thing, she could make them go anywhere she wanted, their little ruby eyes hated it so much. There was something unnatural, something ignoble, about their behaviour once they had spurred themselves into the light.

You're saying in the dark crayfish are creatures more worthy?

What?

They're better in the dark?

In the light they're confused, the girl said hopefully.

In the light, little one, we're all confused.

I'm not confused, the girl said, with a toss of her head.

Not now. One day.

No I won't.

Lost and confused like your old dad. Outside the nice clean bucket.

No you're not.

They watched. All below was as before.

I know! he said. We should call you Beam.

I don't want to be called Beam.

Why not?

It's not my name.

Ah, but consider the advantages. When the other one had to come back to the tent with her lost old dad, Beam could stay out here all night with her . . . beam.

I'm not Beam, she said. I'm Caroline. Anyways, Beam would be cold.

Indeed she would.

They watched. In the land of crayfish nothing changed.

So you're sure.

Yes.

You don't seem to mind it when I call you Precious Angel.

Precious Angel isn't my *name*!

So what is it?

It's just what you call me sometimes.

Ah. So that's different.

Yes.

Hm. Well, I suppose you know what this means.

She giggled. No. What?

And groaning like one in an anguish of physical exertion, he stood and reached down to lift her under the arms where she remained crouched and swung her gasping high and down onto his shoulders.

Now, shine the light. Or turn it off, so your old dad can see where he's going on this ramshackle structure we are out on here.

She shone the light.

She looked up. White sun. Unsteadily she rose to her feet. Kneeling to tie her boot, she kept losing her balance. Her hands shaking. The pain in her head, neck, spine was back as if it had never left. As if it would never leave.

She vacated the place climbing slowly, like someone old. Crossed the intersection with the lane that passed through the bog and connected to the road and followed instead this one she was on, to the cut and down the edge of the cut, where the land was level rock. Far ahead she could see a stretch of the logging road. By projecting rightward she could tell where it entered the cut, and so when the lane she was on returned to the woods she left it, stumbling constantly now, staggering almost, under a hotter sun, to cross the uneven rocky terrain to the road and the logging trucks or at least the hanging dust of them, but in time the truck route itself reentered the woods, and she continued on, to climb an unmaintained road scoured by the seasons to a white-swirled bed of midnight rock. Overhead the pylons hummed. As she crested the hill she came upon a young moose standing on long legs in the middle of the road. It had turned to watch her, and when it saw that she would keep on, it swung its head away and did its oblique cantering prance down the centre of the road. Eventually it moved off across a slope stained scarlet and ochre with hawkweed and disappeared into the forest.

Daisies lined where she stumbled. Her tongue was swollen, she could not swallow. She did not feel weak, but she was not steady. Pockets of collapse kept passing through her, hollow lacks. Except for the hum of the wires and for birdsong from the yellow-throats in the bushes along the road there was no sound. Only the scrape of her feet. More than once she fell. Lay in the road imagining a truck coming. Pushed herself up and went on. When she fell, her follower, in white, stood quietly at a distance, waiting. It was now very hot. Sky of cloudless blue. A red-tailed hawk swooped and hovered high above them.

She had seen the survey of the property in the title office, and so without coming upon his car she would have known where to enter the woods. The car was parked above where the cut dropped away to marsh and, somewhere beyond, the landing. From here, above the trees, she glimpsed the lake, a crucible of no simple colour. Silver or blue-grey. Glinting yellow-white. Now she left the power line to follow his trail downhill through the hardwood forest. Wondering why he would weave and circle. Why he would mark the trees with pink targets. Did he hate trees? She leaned against the ones he had marked, to rest. The other waited. The woods were hushed. A pileated woodpecker moaned and whined as it hunted insects. Looking up to see it she nearly fell. The woodpecker drilled at a dead maple with a sound like machine-gun fire. She moved on. Did not follow the stream downward but made her own path more directly to where she understood the property to be and so came to it not from the west, along the shore, but down the hill through the trees from the northeast.

If she had been well, she would have called out as she approached. You did not walk in unannounced on a person intent on their solitude. But she was now in that last stage of endurance when the body knows how little more is necessary and now begins, often foolishly, to rely on hope of human assistance. "Hello," she could only whisper. "We've come." At her right hand now the stinking ruin of a porcupine beech. She didn't need to look up. On her left, a log cabin. A propane tank bear-torn, it looked like, from its regulator, the east window of that cabin smashed. Why would he buy a ruin? She passed a wooden chair upturned near a rock. Why? Her next thought, He's here.

And then she saw the realtor woman, stooped before a small plywood cabin with a bowed roof, her back half-turned, and she saw the arms around the woman's waist, the arms of the naked man she was stooped over, her brass-coloured hair hanging forward, one hand on his shoulder, one stroking through the mess of his hair as he knelt, his face buried in her midriff, his skin paper-white where it was not cooked pink by the sun.

Her blood sank, heart falling, she must have stumbled then, because the vision skittered and swelled and flew up, the woman's head coming around, the brass hair swinging wide of the face as she turned to see, and before the bright curtains of darkness came down she spoke, her manner droll somehow, her lips moving hardly but readable: "Better put your pants on."

She heard the man's muffled "Wha—?" and though her own gaze now rested more clearly upon the gentle litter of hemlock needles and crumbled wood upraised upon the tide of blood from her nose, she saw the woman disengage from him, his face like a sleeper's move back from her belly to peer around her to see too, and it was him, her human destination, it was Wakelin.

"Looks like she's found you," the realtor woman said, and she started toward the fallen.

DAUGHTER OF GOD

Two days after his unsuccessful attempt to sue Timothy Wakelin for the cost of his truck, Ross Troyer was sitting with his friend Bachelor Crooked Hand in Crooked Hand's tow truck on the shoulder of the highway not far from the entrance to Grant Memorial Hospital. Below them, in a heavy rain, was the truck. Crooked Hand, who with an air of shrewd philosophical musing was smoking a rolled cigarette of tobacco and hashish, had just asked his companion if in his experience the physical world had ever in any respect offered to him personally a direct and concerted malevolence.

Troyer, stirring a little, observed that it might have. He asked Crooked Hand what sort of thing he had in mind.

"All things," Crooked Hand replied, answering a different question. "Familiar things, mainly."

"No," Troyer decided at last. "It never did. No." After a further stretch of time he asked Crooked Hand what he thought might be the reason for this malevolence.

"They hate you turning them familiar," Crooked Hand replied. "They think you're trying to suffocate them." He paused. "They could be right."

"You're talking about things, now."

"I am. Chair, tree, door. Pictures on the wall. Fucking hate it. Every once in a while I used to have to go through and destroy everything. Fucking wrath of God. Put them out of their misery. Start again. You always wondered why I did that, didn't you?"

"I see you as a vandal for the home."

"And a fine feeling it was, once. Possibly the finest. Boy in the china shop dreams of twenty minutes alone with a ten-pound sledgehammer. Now I have seen the light. Now I stand prepared to break the arm of a litterbug." Crooked Hand's head was fitted with sockets containing jellies less like eyes than apertures to red and yellow sky. Of course, he was not a sleeper and had not been for twenty years. He smiled, exposing perfect yellow teeth. Smiling, he coughed violently and wiped at tears.

The rain drummed on the roof of the truck. It dripped from the windshield seal, faulty since purchase, and splashed against the dashboard. Every once in a while it rounded the swell of the vinyl and streaked to the floor.

"What changed for you, then?" Troyer asked after a period of silence during which he seemed to be gathering his energy to inquire.

"When I was a kid," Crooked Hand said, "I needed to know where I stood with them. Animals, babies, tables, flowers, signs, walls. These things are not talkers. Later, thanks to your daughter—Caroline was the first one besides a trout to appreciate my dry flies—I got serious about that work, it's slow work, and it give me time to get acquainted with myself, and that's how I come to have a pretty good idea what their feelings are. Now I'm on their side one hundred per cent."

Troyer considered this. "What do they feel?" he asked finally.

"Loathing."

For a few minutes neither man spoke, Crooked Hand smiling his yellow smile as he gazed at the fragment of scorched paper between his finger stubs. Still smiling, he said, "Any news?"

"Not yet."

"Caroline know about her mother?"

There was no answer.

Crooked Hand glanced at the profile of his friend and said, "Did you ever visit her?"

"Who's this?"

Crooked Hand didn't answer.

"Not yet," Troyer said.

"Afraid she'd forgive you?"

Troyer's response to this question was to appear to suspend more pressing reflection.

"I did," Crooked Hand said. "I drove down there. Fucking Besborough."

Troyer didn't look at him. "I expected sooner or later you would. I guess you couldn't keep yourself away."

"I wanted to see if she needed anything."

"Did she?"

Crooked Hand shrugged. "If she did, she didn't say what it was."

"Did she mention it wasn't me who did her, it was the daughter?"

Crooked Hand turned to look at Troyer curiously, ready to smile.

Troyer's gaze continued directly ahead. "It was Caroline beat her up. She tell you that?"

Slowly all expression left the face of Bachelor Crooked Hand, though the change was itself highly expressive. "Get serious," he said. And then he didn't say anything. He scanned the cab ceiling. Finally he said, "This is something you'll say to Walter Heinrichs, Ross. Keep him on his toes. It's not what you say to me. I saw the damage. I know the score."

Troyer made no reply, and then he said, "No, you're the one I say it to. The one who's going to understand."

"Well, I don't." Crooked Hand considered further. "Caroline wouldn't do that," he concluded.

"She'd do anything. For example, she'd spend her days selling your featherwork."

"She'd do anything for you," Crooked Hand said.

"Not for years. Now it could be God at the wheel. Now it could be a reporter who claims he's looking for a home. Maybe he's already found one. Maybe I should check at the record office."

"Jesus Christ, Ross, I'm shaking here." Inwardly perhaps. Crooked Hand was sitting very still.

The rain drummed.

"Time to call her in," Troyer said.

"I guess you haven't all suffered enough."

"What if Christ lost a finger at carpentry?" Troyer said. "He couldn't walk away from the shop then, could he? Turn his back on his own family. His own profession."

"Yeah, well, she's no buzz saw, and you're no maimed fucking Son of God."

Saying this, Crooked Hand started the tow truck. For the next several minutes he manoeuvred it in line with the pickup according to increments of adjustment perceptible only to himself. When he was satisfied, he got out into an undiminished rain to place reflective markers on the pavement where the front fender now projected onto the highway. After that he skidded with the winch hooks down off the road and trudged across the rock to the pickup.

Troyer was sitting in the tow truck watching Crooked Hand as he worked to get the winch attached to the front axle, when the cruiser pulled into the rearview. By this time the rain had lessened, but Elvin Hryniuk seemed to wait for it to lessen further before he got out. When he did he waved to Crooked Hand, who was still on his knees. Crooked Hand waved back. Hryniuk came along the shoulder and stood at Troyer's window. Elvin Hryniuk was not a short man, but the size of Crooked Hand's truck was such that the top of his head came only halfway up the glass. Troyer wound down the window.

"Mr. Troyer, sir, I got a warrant here—well, not actually *here;* I left it back at the car—signed by Walter Heinrichs."

"Aw shit, Elvin, don't come out here and tell me that."

Hryniuk sniffed the air from the cab. "Bachelor smoking up again?"

"Not since I got in. What kind of warrant?"

Hryniuk flushed. "I think they just want you in for a few tests."

"What kind of tests?"

"Well, it doesn't say."

"You didn't look at the warrant?"

"Not really."

"So I guess you wouldn't know what act it's been issued under."

"No I wouldn't, Mr. Troyer."

"Why, Elvin, you must be one of these guys we hear about. Just doing their job."

"Yes sir."

"You know what my guess is? It'll be one of them warrants that get sent out from time to time under the Mental Health Act. It wouldn't be one of them, would it?"

"It might be."

"Because I already told Gail Poot I wasn't interested."

At the sound of this name, Hryniuk's eyes dropped to his feet, where he seemed to work to arrange a rock with his toe. When they came up they fixed on Troyer, and there was a quality in them like slyness. "I guess that's why he put out the warrant," he said, almost with a sigh.

Troyer made no response. And then he asked, "Who signed the application?"

Hryniuk blinked. "Judge Hein—"

"No. Heinrichs signed the *warrant*. Who signed the application? A man has a right to know who it is out there wants his head examined. If it's a conspiracy of women, say."

Hryniuk's cheeks were mottled bright red once more. "It doesn't say anything about who—"

"So you did look at it. But you couldn't tell from that what kind it was."

"Yeah, well, I *looked* at it—"

"Can you let us finish here, Elvin? Like a good man?"

Hryniuk studied his watch. Then he started back towards the cruiser, his head turned to watch Crooked Hand at the bottom of the slope. "Hey, Crook'!" he shouted. When Crooked Hand glanced up, Hryniuk made a toking gesture. Crooked Hand stared placidly.

A few minutes later Crooked Hand had got the winch attached and was climbing slowly back up to the shoulder with his mouth open to the rain, arms spread low, palms aimed forward like sensors. He climbed into the truck breathing hard and started the winch. The cable strummed. Smoothly the pickup came backwards, gouging through the soft gravel. It looked narrower than it should have. Somewhat oblique. Crushed. At the foot of the shoulder, the front end rose slightly and stopped. Crooked Hand got out to gather the road markers, which he stacked under one arm. He set them on the peg in the side of the truck, climbed back in and made a slow turn. The pickup came straight up the shoulder and followed in one tight movement.

The tow truck with its charge and its police escort did not stop until it came to the Troyer Building. Troyer got out and walked back to the cruiser, looking over his shoulder to see his pickup move away. When he turned and saw Hryniuk watching him he shook his head in a rueful manner. And then as he leaned down into Hryniuk's window, his eye was caught by his own image in the side mirror. He leaned lower and studied the glass.

"You know the problem, Elvin?"

"Which one is that?"

"We look in the mirror and we see these eyes looking back at us and we think, Why, there I am. The one and only, yet just like everybody else. Special, but normal."

"Why's that a problem?"

Troyer tapped his fingernail against the sideview. "You've heard of smoke and mirrors, Elvin? Well, this is mirrors." Now he pointed to his temple. "The whole time I'm right here. Inside this bone chamber you see before you. I'm not in any piece of mirror attached to your car. It doesn't matter how much time I spend looking in it. I'm still here inside this skull prison, this little soul palace. So is there another way out? That's the only real question. It's the one the boys down at the hotel are trying to answer every Saturday night, and it's the major issue facing mankind today."

"I guess I don't know what you're talking about," Hryniuk said. His cheeks glowed.

"No."

Hryniuk waited. A crackling from his radio.

"Few are special, Elvin. Everybody else is plain normal. Mirrors feed the lie."

"Special or not, Mr. Troyer, you better get in the car."

"I'm looking forward to that, Elvin. I welcome the chance to go into these matters with you more deeply. But I'll need a few things. I didn't want to mention it earlier—pride, I guess—but, you know, I've had a hunch for some time now this was coming. I've been boning up for these tests every chance I could get. How long did you say they'd take? Forty days? You're going to have to give me five minutes. Get my notes in order."

Hryniuk lifted his arm onto the back of the seat and craned around to check for a place to park. "Five minutes," he said, not looking at Troyer.

Slowly, after taking a long time in the better light to find his keys, Troyer entered the dark of the stairs to his second storey. Eight minutes later he was leaving by the kitchen fire escape, stroking the dog's head as he passed it on its stake in the yard. The fur was wet, for it was raining again. He was wearing his rain gear and sheathed at his waist his hunting knife, and he was carrying a .308 in a nylon case. He climbed the path behind the main street, through the pines beyond the war memorial upward to her little clearing. There he stood and watched the rain fall in brighter veils against its own falling grey against the sky.

He did not know about Crooked Hand's familiarity of the world, but he did know about the world's emptiness, which properly understood is the emptiness of the mirror. And he had taught himself how to enter that emptiness as a traveller, with eyes open. How to refuse all concession, indulge in no yearning, cast no pall of petty concern. For he was one of those unbounded, who had seen the back of the road and knew that the world's judgement was an old god's who could be circumvented, walked around and viewed from behind, and whose powers long ago had been revealed as old cunning and whose laws discarded as impositions upon the free mind. For this traveller had waked from the sleep of distance and loss. By this means he had entered the purer realm where what a man does is enough and complete in its own doing and all that is necessary to have been done.

Troyer turned and stepped back onto the path and continued along there through the dripping trees as the path climbed. Aware only of this movement upward, and all about him was that alert and tentative expansiveness of the one who has freed himself once more and now has only to choose at every moment the next thing to be done. Now this. Now this. Now this. Now this.

There were rain clouds the rest of that day but no rain. In the night it was cool with no wind, only the loon choirs and the porcupines at work in the trees, and Wakelin's sleep in the log cabin, amidst the chaos, even though he had nailed scrap plywood over the two smashed windows, was bear-haunted. Also afflicted-woman-haunted. At the first light he awoke. Dressed and went out. Listened at the window of the plywood cabin for the sound of her breathing. Silence now. No moaning. No crying out. The words *resting comfortably* came into his mind, and though little if any conscious meaning came with them he stepped away, onto the listing dock. The air was surprisingly cold. From the water a dense mist fleeted upward. He knelt and splashed his face, aware of an absence. Warmth? The far shore? Clarice? He looked around. The canoe. *Where was the canoe?* The paddles were here, laid neatly side by side at the end of the dock, but no canoe. It was how Clarice had arrived, right? And Wakelin could remember standing—dressed by that time—on the dock with the cord of the canoe in his hand, telling her he'd paddle her to the landing, and she'd said no, it was all right, she'd go through the woods. He had better see to Caroline Troyer.

Had he just dropped the cord then, in his confusion? But then how through the rest of that day could he not have noticed a missing canoe? All those trips out to pace the dock for a break from what was happening to Caroline Troyer. But he couldn't remember. The remainder of yesterday had a thumb over the lens, a space of light.

"Calm all night," he muttered now, peering into the whiteness. There was the constant impenetrable upflow, white into greyer white, but the air itself had no movement at all. At last it was going to rain, but it was not raining yet.

Canoe must be just out of sight, Wakelin told himself, but of course he did not know this. And once the day started so would the wind, and the canoe would be blown against the rocks, and after an hour or two of that it would have a hole rubbed in it and fill with water and sink and be lost, and he would not be able to get Caroline Troyer to a doctor as he had promised himself many times in the night he would do as soon as it was light.

During one of those breaks from the long vigil of yesterday, while looking for a mop to swab grouse blood, Wakelin had found, by the front door of the log cabin, in a scuffed and mouse-sticky plastic package, an inflatable plastic dinghy. Now he got it blown up. Pinpoint orange stars exploding in front of his eyes. He listened again at her window. Still silence. Excellent. Resting peacefully. Eased himself into the dinghy. Using an old paddle he had cracked in the night over the back of a porcupine that kept returning to stand on tiptoes to gnaw with remarkable resonance upon the sheet of plywood he had nailed up yesterday where the windowpane had been, the split blade still embedded with quills, he pushed off into the mist, into the wraiths still steaming upward. Among them he soon had the first of several experiences of seeing the canoe, but it was always a length of driftwood or a band of shoreline or water. By the time he had travelled the bay, the mist was all but vanished and he could see the entire surface. The canoe was nowhere in here.

Yesterday while Clarice staunched Caroline Troyer's nosebleed, Wakelin searched behind the main cabin among the leaves of lily of the valley for his keys, which took a long time to find, having been flung wide by the bear. By the time Wakelin returned with them, Clarice had Caroline Troyer sitting up. He unlocked the plywood cabin, and together they helped her to the bed. Wakelin was putting some clothes on when Clarice straightened from fixing a pillow under Caroline Troyer's head and said, "We should get her to a doctor."

"No doctor," Caroline whispered.

When she said this, Wakelin was gazing at the side of her face. Slowly she turned and looked at him, beseeching.

"She just tripped," he said. "It's a nosebleed. Let's let her rest."

"I don't know," Clarice said. She looked at Caroline Troyer, who met her eyes too.

"I'm not sick," Caroline said.

"Let's see how she does," Wakelin said.

"No," Clarice said, looking at her watch. "*You* see how she does. You've got the canoe, and I've got people to meet at two. Call me tomorrow and tell me you're both okay."

It must have been after that Clarice declined Wakelin's offer of a paddle to the landing and simply hiked off into the woods, leaving him suddenly alone with Caroline Troyer, who when he reentered the little cabin he discovered outstretched on her back, her arms at her sides, her chin tipped high, shaking. She was not cold. She was not asleep. At least, he could not wake her. She lay in her boots, shaking at a frequency he had never seen a body shake before. Too high and fast. He lifted her head and plumped the pillow and ran to get her a glass of water.

When he came back he stood over her and did not know what to do. He placed his palm against her forehead. It was not hot. The shaking had slowed a little. He wet her lips with the water. More water made her choke. He took off her runners, releasing the stink of her black feet. Already the ferric malodour of menses, and now this lumberjack fetor. He started to take off her windbreaker. Suddenly she was helping him, her spine arced in a grin of contortion, but it was something else, her body stricken in air. Slowly it settled. Arced once more. Slowly it settled. This went on.

After some time he left again, for a facecloth. When he came back her body was quieter. He got the windbreaker off. A greasy chino thing. Blood on her thin cotton shirt dried in a torn brown stain at the collarbone, her jeans soiled and ripped, had she been wrestling with animals? He undid her jeans. There was no belt. She was back twisting and turning. The blanket would not stay on. Did she need it? Keep her warm, Wakelin kept thinking. He fetched a pair of his socks and covered her filthy feet. Went away again for a basin of cold water—the propane was bear-disabled—and found a bar of soap and another cloth. Cleaned the dried blood from around her nose. This blood he could handle. Took off the socks and washed her feet in the water, which turned dark grey. Mosquitoes were coming in the window he had smashed to climb in here the night before last, his keys in the dark somewhere too close to the bear, which had returned at dusk to continue wrecking the other cabin while it searched for further courses to its breakfast of Wakelin's groceries. Under the little cabin Wakelin found a small stack of porcupine-chewed sheets of plywood. He nailed one over the broken window. Now it was even dimmer inside. He lit a candle. Sat on a wooden chair and watched over her in the jittering gloom. The day outside grey. A wind from the south. Not cold but inauspicious. Worse to come.

The night before, it was this, the plywood cabin, he had slept in, if that was sleep. All night the heavy enormous stumblings of animals against the walls, all night bears with grouse in their mouths wicking in through the blanket-stuffed window, crouching to leap onto the bed, their substance the sounds, all but tangible, of gnawing, loud and multiple and fierce, porcupines-in-the-trees gnawing in fact, but the dreamer did not know or kept forgetting this, and the pure bear-fear reduced him to the dizzy tickle in his own bowels, until the quavering duets of loons from the bay or the smug reiterative *hoo-hoo-hoo*-hootings and mental-breakdown cacklings of a barred owl woke him, and then he would sleep again, and bears with noodles of intestine jiggling from their jaws would wick in through the blanket and be back in the shape of those fierce gnawings until, in the pale dawn, the bats returned to roost in the ceiling—that was not a family of baby squirrels, Clarice, that was a hundred-strong bat colony—and out of the scurrying and screeching directly above, a new resonance came, not gnawings this time but a drumming, and Wakelin was now that intestine, swallowed, inside the belly of the bear, consumed by this larger resonance—

But that was a long time ago. That was this morning. No, it was yesterday morning. He had made a love-me-I-clasp-you-naked-on-my-knees bid for the affections of his lady realtor since then. Of course, all he had to do was look around to see that here dwelt a desperate submissive. To have been so easily sold at an inflated price this laughingstock of abandonment and decay. How many years ago had the old guy died, anyway? Squalid animal-chewed ruin. Mean shacks hardly substantial when first thrown up, now flimsy tinderboxes speeding back to loam. Everywhere was dry rot. Every-where was white-fungused lumber, pulp and mush. Rotten roofs, rotten porches, rotten steps, rotten dock.

And now, he supposed as he paddled the ridiculous plastic dinghy, in one of those unpreventable unconscious acts of revenge that are the signs of secret workings of a larger justice in the world, he had lost her canoe. Her husband the judge's canoe.

Sometimes yesterday Caroline Troyer's torso would fly to the vertical, slinging forward the head with eyes open but not for him. Settled back down in a float of bones. She was too tall for the bed. He padded the iron head-bar with an extra pillow. Sometimes it was the trunk of her body that rose in an arc from her heels and the back of her head, and she would stay like that so long, arrested so long in air, that he could swear she had lifted off, was hovering there, and it was also like levitation the way, when she fell, she fell so slowly. He could not wake her. She was not asleep. Sometimes her body tossed from side to side, abjuring everything, shouldering through. An underwater escape artist. That was how it seemed. She was not quaking or gnashing or foaming. This was not epilepsy as Wakelin had experienced that affliction in others. But he had witnessed his own body, when it saw danger before he did, act with fierce alien intelligence. This was more like that, only stretched out, a process of hours, like fever, or childbirth. The body suffer-ing for as long as the process would take. Sometimes she cried out. Her cries were not tamped dream-whimpers but ragged shouts of torment. Wakelin kept having to leave the cabin and pace outside until the shouts stopped or he had collected himself. Her pain was so sharp, so physical, so ongoing, so manifest. In emanation from her spine and neck, or so he imagined from the way she writhed. At certain moments it seemed to him that if she could have reached around and ripped out her spine, she would have, were her arms not useless by the terms of her condition.

This was not epilepsy but some other process. There was the force of her pain, the blind physical force of her suffering, that daunted and cowed and again and again drove him outside, but there was something else happening here inside this plywood shack, something as palpable as the odour of her, as the shouts of her anguish, some gathering of energy or power that was not a force in any ordinary physical sense known to Wakelin if it was physical at all and not capable in some other way of stirring a physical response in her, in him. He did not know what on earth was happening in here. What he was in the presence of. It was nothing he had even remotely known. He could see its effects on Caroline Troyer. Before him the wracking of this woman's body was a physical sign. He could sit here and watch it hale through her like the wind through a pair of lungs, causing them to breathe beyond the limits of their capacity. He could feel the blast of it, a blast regardful, a force field infinitely dimensional, articulating in a foreign tongue exquisite this woman's body, and articulating too, with the same amazed compassion, this accidental presence Wakelin, however unready or wrongly disposed he might be. However resisting. However out of phase. Body hairs on end. The sensation completely unrecognizable to him. The moment has opened up, undoing and pervading, and time and space is a wind roaring at the same time into and out of its own centre, which is not located in the brain or viscera of Caroline Troyer but everywhere, a wind that mounting intensifies its own stillness, a wind like a shining flame that does not waver and is not frozen and has no limit, a wind like the boundlessness of silence.

Five times yesterday, over a period Wakelin could not measure—time was not behaving like itself in here—he looked around to see a deer mouse walk straight up the veneer of the plywood wall with an infant in her mouth. Each trip another infant. This was the accommodation of a mother to that presence. Wakelin himself outwardly unaffected but overwhelmed. His molecules at such a pitch or density, locked to a channel of such habitual perversity, as to preserve him from immolation and transformation both, and yet at some terrible future cost, as of sorrow, or regret. Lifelong misgiving. Oh God, not more of that. Not the toll of another experience he could not begin to understand. For he was too stunned. That was it. He was stunned to wonder and dismay by what was happening in here. Words like *spiritual force* and *holy presence* kept rising to his mind, but only by their insistence did he notice them at all, for they had no more weight or meaning than jingles from the radio. This was not about what he could conceive. If the light in here was a firefly glow, it was some firefly. God's own, perhaps. Casting a light of mind, not eye. And that mind not Wakelin's, which was shadows in the light of this. All he could recognize with any certainty was his fear for her and how he might protect her body, and he was grateful, he was honoured, to be able to do what he could. At no time did she become feverish. But he needed to attend to her in whatever way this thing would allow. When he lifted her head and touched the damp cloth to the back of her neck he might as well have plugged the top of her spine into an open socket. Mostly he could only guard her head against the iron headbar; prevent her from throwing herself to the floor; wet her lips; press her nostrils when her nose bled, as it continued to do, off and on, all that day; replace the blanket.

Whatever this energy, it was not in itself hostile or negative, was not limited in that way, was in itself awesome not frightening, like some proximate intelligence too powerful, too subtle, too generous to fail to be sensitive. But also not to encompass death, and Wakelin was terrified that the body of Caroline Troyer would not be up to this. It did not seem to him that these were symptoms of a woman dying, but he feared that she could die from what this was. Her body, for all its stature and obvious, if now wasted, strength, would not have the stamina to undergo whatever process it was undergoing. Over and over that day he resolved to take her, as Clarice had so sensibly suggested, to a doctor, but when he tried to move her she jolted and writhed, and he understood that even if he could somehow get her into the canoe—he still thought he had a canoe, and maybe he still did—he would need to strap her down, and he could not imagine that she would not hurt herself if the seizuring resumed at even half the frequency and pitch it was now. This seizuring that was no medical symptom.

Many times he went outside, to pace, shaking, to rinse his face in the lake (how on at least one of those trips to the dock could he not have noticed the canoe? tied to the dock? not tied to the dock?), to nail plywood over the broken windows of the log cabin, to have something to eat.

That was another thing. There was not a lot of food. The bear, already inside the main cabin for the grouse when Wakelin arrived two days ago carrying his groceries through the woods, had eaten pretty well everything. While Wakelin waited five hours up the porcupine-stinking beech, the bear, a black bear, no grizzly but big, two hundred pounds at least, ate his groceries where Wakelin had dropped them, at the foot of the beech. High-fat items first: butter, cheese, cream. Fruit and vegetables with less relish, more batting around. After that, the skunky-cabbage fragrance of gas from around the valve inspired the animal to rock the propane tank until the copper line stretched like toffee and the regulator tore away from the wall and the tank fell onto its side. After an addict's fill of sniffing, the bear went back inside the log cabin to ransack and prowl. Every once in a while a fresh tremendous crash. Three times the bear returned to regard Wakelin with ursine concern, after which it would rise onto its hind legs and stretch languidly to claw bark at the twelve-foot mark, just short of Wakelin's lower foot, which he would retract with scrupulous care. Three times in all the bear swung away and went back to ransacking while Wakelin waited up the beech, every limb of which the sad tree he now had plenty of opportunity to observe was hopelessly porcupine-gnawed, leaves already yellowing. The whole doomed plant, it seemed to him then, an apt totem of his purchase. The dark, corrosive stench of porcupine urine a message for him on behalf of all the wildlife locals: Piss on this place.

And then the bear left for good, or seemed to, and Wakelin climbed in through the window of the log cabin carrying a plastic shopping bag containing a can of tuna, a jar of mayonnaise, and a bear-ignored head of lettuce and purple onion, to sit at the table in his trashed cabin and use dishes and utensils from his trashed kitchen to make himself a bear-reclaimed tuna salad. Even found salt and pepper.

From the table where he sat creating his salad, still shaking with fatigue and nerves from his wait up the beech, Wakelin could see, through the window that faced the bay, beyond the island at the bay's mouth, the cliff on the main lake. And as he worked in the day-warmed, dusty, bear-funky cabin, flies buzzing around the smear of grouse blood on the floor beside his chair, he started taking deeper breaths. It was quiet here. The wind had died. This overcast hush, a benediction. This fly-blown cabin, shelter after all. The bear had gone. Wakelin would eat. Later he would sleep. By the look of that sky, he would doze off to the sound of rain. When he woke it would be a new day, and he would walk out and drive back to Grant. Tomorrow he would find her, and he would talk to her honestly, directly, in the way she understood, and she would reply, and they would converse, back and forth, a meeting of minds, not an interview, for he would be doing this not for a story but to close this mysterious wound that had opened up inside him the night he delivered her to the Grant hospital and then just walked away. And on his way back here he would shop again for food. He would hike in without getting lost this time and make himself a hot meal, even better than this one taking shape before him, and after he had eaten he would crawl into bed and sleep the sleep of the dead in this blessing of silence. The next morning he would wake with his mind clear and he would get this place organized. On the deal table on the little screened porch he would place the old upright Underwood he had bought for twenty-five dollars in Bankhead yesterday, and this would be his work-place. Slowly, in these new surroundings, he would establish his old routine. He would move on with his life.

As Wakelin continued work on the tuna salad, he fell into longer and longer spells of staring at that darkening bluff of rock. At last his meal was ready. Pretty good for salvage, you had to admit. Before eating he leaned back for one more long gaze at the night-fallen cliff. A dry branch snapped. Wakelin looked to the empty frame of window hard on his left at the instant there rose into it the head and half the trunk of the bear, its giant paws resting on the sill. A customer with a serious grievance. The animal tilted its head and looked at Wakelin, behind whom a chair slammed to the floor.

The same chair Wakelin used a few seconds later to smash the west window, for his escape, all doors being still locked, his keys as yet on the ground somewhere out back, among hollyhocks. It was not that chair, which was no longer in his hands by the time he reached the plywood cabin, but a rock he clawed from out of the ground close by that he used to smash his next window, the one at the rear of that, the plywood cabin, in order to crawl in there while the bear stayed behind to eat his tuna salad before it smashed the bowl and overturned the table and recommenced ransacking.

The next day, seeing to Caroline Troyer, on one of his forays of reprieve out of the plywood cabin, Wakelin found a tin half full of rice left by the old man, but without propane he needed a wood fire to cook it. This got him clearing a space in his wrecked kitchen to put the cookstove and its pipes back together and light one. He would cook the rice. At the same time he heated water in a sticky grease-yellow aluminum kettle with tiny nuts and bolts screwed into the bottom where it had worn through. As Wakelin waited for the kettle he stood idly in the kitchen gazing at a mass of thick, flattened, greyish electrical cord in a tangle above the door, at a point not far from where it came in through the log wall from the generator to feed into the switchbox. There seemed to be an awful lot of it in an awful tangle, and then he saw the milk snake. It had twined its body in and around the grey cord, and it was resting there quietly, gazing back at him.

He washed her feet again, this time in warm water. Again the water turned dark. He heated more, and while it was heating he went through the clothes the old man had left pearled with mothballs in the chest in the log cabin. He came back to her carrying two towels and a shirt and a pair of the old man's jeans and a fresh basin of hot water. Working under the blanket until that proved cumbersome and all of a sudden idiotically prudish, he unbuttoned her shirt and got it off her, though with difficulty, and washed her upper body, the towel under her, rolling her onto her side to do her back, and either she was calmer now or the warmth of the water soothed her. Carefully he washed around the dark scab at her collarbone. When he washed her breasts and the nipples did not harden it seemed to him that he was doing no harm here but only what small good he was able.

With greater difficulty then, he got the old man's flannel shirt onto her and buttoned. He covered her and heated more water and started again. Got her jeans and stinking underwear off and washed her legs and lower body and between her legs, the water turning reddish from the blood dried there. He had to spread her legs a little to get her clean, but the body trusted him, and he did it and got her clean. After washing her feet a third time he pulled a pair of the old man's jeans onto her and covered her again with the blanket and sat back in his chair and closed his eyes, thinking, I've never properly taken care of anyone before. How did I come to be able to do this?

And then it was no lighter outside than in. Her seizures—that was not the word—had grown still slower and deeper. He leaned forward with his arms around her and his head on her breast and closed his eyes again. She smelled of naphthalene.

By the time Wakelin was eating a bowl of cold rice, the energy in the room had receded and she was moving in and out of tracts of snoring like the throaty snarling of dogfights in the night. Like any sleeper, except unwakable.

Then it was dark. The hairs on Wakelin's body had settled down. In his chair in the little cabin he could not keep his eyes open. From out of a great tin-lined chest he dragged a mattress and some blankets onto the springs of one of the beds in the log cabin. He did not know how long he had been there when he first heard her voice as a small child's, calling out for her mother, pleading and crying. From a place without succour. He went back to see to her, to mop her forehead though it was not hot and she clenched at his touch, and to sit over her until the cries subsided. Returned to his own bed. Later, dozing, he heard a shout from the wrong direction. Ran to her cabin. The door stood open, the bed was empty. Another shout. He found her in the grey light of the ruined garden, hair sleep-spiked. A tall young woman dreaming. Directing shouts of tear-streaming happiness at the wall of the forest. He took her trembling joyous arm and led her back to bed. She was stumbling. Her arm was not hot.

Who knows how much later it was when Wakelin staggered from his bed, heart pounding, at the sound of imperious praying? *O Lord, our precious God in Heaven.* A voice he did not know. Thinking now he was the one dreaming. *And us to Thy service in the name of Jesus Christ Almighty, our Holy Saviour.*

Wakelin was shaking when he entered the little cabin.

"What is it now?" the voice demanded.

"I—" Wakelin faltered.

"I told you I don't want supper today," another voice said softly, the voice of a girl.

"Oh, did you?" the other replied with heavy surprise. "And why would that be?"

Wakelin lowered himself into the chair by the bed. Both voices had come from the mouth of Caroline Troyer, her eyes now open though directed to objects or faces Wakelin could not see, the muscles, the cast of her face, wholly altering as the words passed from speaker to speaker, her arms unmoving at her sides, her body still and sunk.

"I want to see what it's like."

"What's like."

"Not eating a meal."

"So where are you going?" the other wanted to know, and Wakelin realized that it was Ardis.

"No place."

A long silence, the girl breathing. "Can I be excused?" she asked softly.

"Let me just tell you how much I need you dragging around here peckish and irritable all the rest of the one day I get to relax. Relax. That's a ripe one."

"I won't. I'll go out."

The expression on the face transformed to incredulity. "What did you just tell me a minute ago? You weren't going out!"

"I will if you want me to."

This assurance met with no response.

"Can I?"

Now Ardis cast a wan look at Wakelin. "She never quits. It's enough to make God weep." She spoke to the girl. "Well, I hate to be the one to break the news, but as you can see it's already in front of you. Getting cold."

The candle was guttering. Wakelin lit a new one. He sat back down.

Ardis seemed to be recounting news from church that morning. Her account was blurred, hardly audible. In the midst of it, she said lightly, "I see you're having no trouble shovelling it in."

There was a delay, a look of mortification on the face, and Caroline Troyer's voice when at last it emerged was very soft. "I didn't say I wouldn't be hungry." The eyes fell.

"What'd she say?" Ardis snapped at Wakelin, startling him. "You know what I can't get my head around? How anybody can be so lacking in routine sense. To *intend* to starve. As if the human body was not created to require nourishment."

Quickly, eagerly, the girl looked up. "There's a woman in India lives on air."

"There's a woman in India's got some ignorant Hindus fooled." Ardis seemed to be chewing. Shortly she stopped. "*Why?*" she demanded with renewed peevishness. "What in God's name are you out to prove? Or haven't you ever gone hungry? Is that the problem?"

"I just wanted to find out, if I could," the girl said, speaking more softly with each word, "how much I depend on meals."

Ardis directed a galled look at Wakelin. "How much she depends on meals. Just who the hell does she think she is? Pulling this holier-than-thou crap on working people she's hived off like a horseleech at the vein all her life? But you know the biggest farce about her? She's so predictable. I could have told you six months ago she'd pull a prank like this. Two years ago. You go down in flames at school, you refuse all offers from the nicest boys, as nice as they come anyways in this hick neck of the woods, loutish knuckle-draggers, you quit going to church—who needs God?—and what else is there left to do? Going off on one crackpot idea after the other. It's completely pathetic."

The face, which by the end of this speech had grown animate with disgust, resolved eventually to aggrieved resignation. "Honestly, I'm just so sick and tired and fed up with her. Not caring a fart in a windstorm about what the next person thinks or feels about anything. Day in and day out, sloping along in laziness and filth. Never an offer of help. Not once does she say, 'Is there anything I can help you with, Mother? Can I give you a hand with that?' Or: 'Why don't you go for a walk, Mother, while I take care of these dishes?' No. Any little thing you get you have to bow and scrape for. You'd think she was the goddamn Queen of Siam."

"I said I'd help," the girl pointed out hopelessly.

"Oh, yes," Ardis hissed. "Because you wanted something. I'm talking about Christian love. Something you obviously wouldn't understand. About thinking for once what the other person might need or want. I'm not talking about self-serving little deals."

Silence.

In a voice of bitter satisfaction Ardis said, "To hell with her. I give up."

Now a further silence, of several minutes, at the end of which Wakelin was caught off guard when suddenly the speaker twisted forward and shot him a vicious glare. "Where the Christ are *you* going?"

"Nowhere—" Wakelin whispered despite himself, at the same time as the face went impassive and the voice of Ross Troyer, bland and facetious, light as a breeze, said, "Out, why?"

Wakelin's plastic dinghy had two leaks, one of air from inside and one of water from below. Both were slow, but after forty-five minutes afloat he was kneeling in three inches of bilge, his craft sagging. Even so, foolishly, consciously reckless, he paddled hard for the narrow channel east of the island. He was tired now, and with every stroke he could feel the pull of the scar on his back. Ahead, on the main lake, there was mist yet, thinly rising. On his left as he came around the island, an arm of low granite, a blueberry point. He now had an escort of dragonflies in precise formation, like helicopter gunships. Beyond the point was a birch grove, hardly visible through the mist, and along the shore from that, the cliff, lost in whiteness.

If there was anybody, any early-morning fisherman out on this perfect great expanse, Wakelin could not hear or see him. No part of the lake surface belonged to himself, but a few days' residence and already he considered the bay his private property and out here public space. This morning its sole other users were wraiths. A concourse of the Heavenly City.

And then he saw the canoe.

It was like a mirage, a pure projection. With the mist and the buoyancy of it and the way the light reflected off the intervening band of glass, it seemed to float above, an ideal craft, its own image in the mind of its seeker, a figment of desire. But what greater and more subtle energy by far could direct it keelless through the mist on a night of absolute stillness, across a bay, down a narrow dog's-leg channel, and out into the perfect silent centre of the lake?

He was now approaching the canoe in his sinking dinghy, water to his waist. As he paddled, advancing too slowly, he made little waves, and the canoe rocked, but only slightly. It took him forever to cross the distance between himself and it, and by the time he was reaching out for the gunwale, water was chuting into the dinghy and suddenly he was lunging, his craft gone baggy around his legs, but he clung to the canoe, gripping with one hand his paddle, which kept banging against the side of it, the blows reporting off the cliff like gunshots. He feared the canoe would flip upside-down on top of him, but it was more stable than he expected, and then he lost all control in a tremulous falsetto scream of fright because Caroline Troyer was lying in the bottom of it, her head lifted and turned to speak to him, eyes waiting for him to discover them, her face whiter than the rising mist, a countenance of physical pain.

And in the gasping silence as Wakelin continued to clutch the side of the canoe while his womanlike scream circled again and again around the lake, she looked at him and said, "He's blinded her."

Ross Troyer slept under a maple among hay-smelling ferns near the riverbank. When the night was dark enough for his purpose he rose and made his way along the path there. Anticipating tonight no lovers or other strollers. It was still raining. The yellow windows of the low-eaved houses across the water he eyed warily. At the bridge he found that there was already no unsubmerged walkway between the concrete pile and the water. He waded it, but being clay the path was slick, and two or three times he slipped and nearly fell, cursing. Beyond the bridge he came to an old couple in macs, sitting on a bench provided by the township, watching the river. He saluted them as he passed, and they smiled back at this apparition in rubber rain gear in the delighted, slightly alarmed manner of people now tourists in their own lives.

That night he followed the river upstream. The Pardee its name. There was always now some kind of path, animal or human, along the margins of woods or cultivated fields. A good thing, because in the heat of escape he had brought with him no light of any kind save matches. Often in that streaming dark he proceeded by sound and feel alone. The sound mainly the sound of moving water, closest to silence when deepest. And then the water had risen over the path in more places than under the bridge, and he found it necessary at times to grope the slippery bank for a higher route. He had lived on this river all his life, and he never failed to be impressed by how fast it could rise. Of course the rain was hard and steady. In one night, an entire season's worth of rain.

By dawn or its dusky simulacrum he was north and west, into flatland once a marsh, four times in the past million years the bottom of a glacial lake, and on at least three occasions earlier the bottom of the sea. Currently drought-stunted farmland. There were trees, in clusters, but few near the river, and though the town of Grant was now eight hours behind him he proceeded, reluctant to be seen. He crossed a sodden field of desiccated cornstalks to a stand of aspen on a small rise, and there he lay and watched the light come on, which it hardly did. The rain continued to pour from the dun-coloured sky. In his rain gear he was not wet. He had brought no provisions along, had no such need. Only rested, having stopped, and stopping though he had seen no one as he came along the river, he now saw several. A pair of boys in jeans and soaked T-shirts with packs of cigarettes twisted at the shoulders. Wielding their boot heels ferociously to make cave-ins along the bank. A farmer out to see what the river was intending to do. Standing there for a long time, trying to judge the rate of its rising, no doubt thinking the following farmer thought: Three months of heat and drought and now a goddamn flood. Troyer took his rifle from its case and raised the sights to a spot at the back of the farmer's head, just below the capline. You're too familiar to me, he thought. Bang. There now. Out of your misery.

Troyer stayed where he was. He was neither uncomfortable nor bored. Now and then he slept. He was hungry, he supposed, but he had been hungry before and knew that as the time of each meal passed, so would pass the hunger. Anyway, hunger was simple. Enter into it. Forget all forward imagination of food. Hang back, inside that distance. Inside that hunger. That distance to actual food. Get serious, in other words. Get real.

She had taught him that, or something like it.

And what more appropriate wisdom on a mission to bring her back than the benefit of her own?

He could not believe this rain. It should have cleared by now. Even if it hadn't rained for three months. This downpour was now unusual. A portent perhaps. He waited until night, and then he moved on.

That night and the next he followed the river upstream where it did its slow whip through lacustrine farmland, followed it for thirty-five miles. At places it widened and went still and wild rice grew in it, even where it must have been six or more feet deep, and migratory waterfowl were there in their numbers. He could hear them in the dark. At times over those three days and nights the rain let up a little. Mostly it continued to pour down. The going, always in the dark, was difficult. To him it was likely that downstream the Pardee had by this time surpassed its banks. Below Grant this would be. Below Dennison. It happened all the time. Down there somewhere what in places up here was a sluiceway would already be a calm brown inexorable spreading lake.

In the early darkness of the third night he started to climb. He had crossed a glacial outwash to reach the mouth of the narrow ravine that eleven thousand years ago the Pardee as a minor glacial spillway first began to carve out of a faultline in the gneiss. He was not climbing rock but lesser sand and gravel banks from later times when the river ran merely five and not twenty feet higher than its present swollen level. He climbed because in the pitch dark, the rain still constant, it had seemed to him no longer advisable to be tracing this pelting death channel, which he could not see but only hear. So he climbed to a grassy ridge and walked along there. It struck him as he walked that the water in the darkness below was now running more quietly, and he wondered if he hadn't passed a flume where the detritus of the flood had created a constriction or blockage of some kind.

He walked until he came into sumac. There he stretched out on his back and waited for dawn.

It was the sound of frightened cattle that woke him. He sat up. The sound had come from below. There was no light. The rain was not so heavy but it had not stopped being rain. On the heels of his hands and feet, crablike, a rubber crab, he moved down out of the sumac, closer to the edge. He was still moving when something astonishing happened. A few hundred yards below, and it was no more, a ball of light travelled fifty feet across a surface of moving water. Upstream in the flash of it he glimpsed a barn, downstream a narrow clapboard farmhouse, water all around. In the next illumination—

the light travelling the same path—he could see, on the far side of the barn, close to it, a tree down on a hydro pole, or on the wire strung on that pole, weighing the pole obliquely, practically into the water.

The fireballs were travelling the wire.

Now he saw from inside or possibly from behind the barn a flickering light. He saw the beam of a flashlight sweep across an upstairs window and inside wall of the farmhouse. Another travelling ball of electricity, and this time he saw the light of it reflected in both front windows of the house. In the darkness then he could see the flickering from the barn reflected there too. Not clapboard, the narrow house wasn't clapboard but sheathed in battered aluminum siding. Battered and peeling. Sections missing to expose tar paper, itself peeling. He could see that the water was no more than halfway to the floor of the front porch. There was a car in the yard, an old Plymouth or Dodge. Water to the hubcaps. As for the barn, it had been built on an elevation possibly four feet higher than the ground the house stood on. People with their monkey heritage, sprightly climbers, had given advantage to those low phlegmatic grazers their cattle. The water had not reached the foundations of the barn. Suddenly the beam of the flash-light appeared on the farmhouse porch. A bolt travelled the wire, and he saw that the flashlight was in the hand of a tall woman in a white night-gown, and she could have been her. She wasn't but she could have been. The flashlight switched off and the next bolt from the wire showed her standing on the porch looking across at the barn and at the maybe thirty yards of two-foot-deep water. In the next flash she was turning away from this sight and in the next there was no one on the porch.

He could only think that the river had overflowed its banks this far up because, as he had surmised, some nest of flood debris had created a dam farther down, at a narrowing of the ravine. A blockage of flow he had passed unknowing in the night. He looked to the farmhouse and to the barn. The bolt might have been a Tourists Welcome sign, randomly flashing. Welcome to what? A floodplain-terrace subsistence farm nobody poor enough to be willing to work could afford to buy. Did not even own a truck.

These would be renters.

The fireballs along the wire had ended. Only darkness but for that light from the barn. The rain still coming down. And then the front door of the house opened and the flashlight came straight out. Straight down the porch steps and across the water, the beam slashed heavily by rain. He could see that the nightgown had been replaced by a man's shirt and she was wading hard against the current towards the slope to the barn, which slope she climbed to throw open the doors, causing a great white cloud of smoke to issue forth and the glow inside to brighten, and he understood that the flickering from inside was not a lantern or emergency lighting: The downed pole had started a fire. He saw her pull the shirt to her face against the smoke, and he saw that with the shirt she wore only underpants, underpants and high-top sneakers, and then he saw her go in.

He waited for a long time. Three minutes, anyway. She came out leading a cow by a rope. She led it down the slope and into the water. It didn't want to go, it was pulling back against the rope, but she was strong and went with it through the water all the way to the porch steps. The cow was reluctant to climb the steps, but she tugged and shouted at it in a loud, mannish voice, and eventually she got it into the house. Now in the light from the barn, the barn doors standing open, he could see that there were eight or nine cows outside, crowded before the slope, mooing and bellowing. She came back for another, and this time four others followed of their own accord, single file. All this time the water rising. He could see this from the way the cows stumbled sooner now against the porch steps, there being more of those steps concealed by water. The third and last time she came back there were two cows and one yearling calf remaining on the slope. The cattle inside the barn were screaming. She pushed past the three on the slope and tried to go into the barn, but the smoke overpowered her and she came out with her hands on her knees, choking. The two cows meanwhile, sorrowful and disgruntled at her neglect, had gone into the water, but once in they did not know where to go and wandered to the right (probably the direction they always went in, along the river), but the water was deeper there, and the current picked them up and swept them, slowly only at first, around and past the house, and he could hear them mooing as they sped away upon the flood.

Now she was leading the calf toward the house, and he could see the arduousness of her task. The water was above her waist, and the calf was floating and swung round past her, and though she kept a grip, the current seemed likely to snatch it as it had the others and pull her with it. But she held on and after great exertion she got the calf to the porch, now level with the water. A cow was standing with its head out the door of the farmhouse, bellowing encouragement. Another was standing on the porch silently watching. And then as she pulled the calf stumbling up the steps, the cow half out the door still bellowing, the one on the porch, stepping backwards, fell through in a sudden eruption of boards, its rear legs jammed astride struts. Piteously it cried out, its front hooves scrabbling. The woman pushed the other cow inside and got the calf in too. She closed the door on them both, and with the rope she had used for the calf she tried to haul the foundering cow out of the hole in the porch and could not. After much effort, nothing changing, he saw her kneel at the edge of the hole and examine the cow's rear legs. Even from this distance it appeared the left was broken. The question then was, Did she have a gun? It seemed that she did not, though this surprised him. A twenty-gauge surely, at least. But right away she turned from the cow back to the barn, and as she did so he became aware once more of the screams of the cattle still inside. A soundtrack of agony to this starklit scene.

The barn was glowing now like some great wooden lantern, every slat and rive and knothole a perfect delineation of light. The flames tonguing up over the tin eaves. The woman was halfway to it, the water mid-chest, her forearm across her eyes, slowed in her progress not only by the current but by the heat, when the structure exploded into pure flame, the wall nearest him erupting in a solid sheet of yellow, and vividly he saw her stagger back in the water, and even he on his prospect could feel the heat. The flames were so bright he looked down at himself, at the shadows of his rubber knees against the illumination of his rubber chest. He looked around and saw the range and extent of the sumac grove behind him. He looked below to the water and saw some of the cargo of the flood: tree branches, a surface and corner of some small outbuilding or shed, a drowned fawn, an oil drum, all eddying briefly before sweeping on. In the gravelly turf where he sat, the brightness made a ragged thin shadow of a seam that ran on either side of him and passed behind, and he moved back up beyond it and into the sumacs once more. The flames of the burning barn reflected off steam that now rose from the water all about it. They lit the rain and they lit the flood, which had reached the lower branches of trees that grew on the far slope of the ravine. They also lit the trees that had been torn from the earth or from shallow balance on rock and now churned revolving upon that roiling, fast-sliding surface.

For a long time he sat and gazed at the house and the burning barn. After an hour he could see that the water had reached the sills of the first-floor windows. He could see the force of it as it reared back foaming against itself and eddied wide at the corners. He was watching the Plymouth, the water now past the tops of the wheel wells, when slowly, as if someone had climbed into the driver's seat, the old car backed up, swung round, and entered the current. Accelerated past the house and was gone. And then, in the light of the burning barn, he saw a further remarkable sight. A wave of water perhaps two feet high, more like a low wall or step than a wave, its own flotsam-charged height behind it, came down the ravine. He saw it before it reached the farmhouse. The barn foundations deflected the force of it, but as it came through, the flood rose three-quarters up the front door of the farmhouse, halfway up the windows on the ground floor. He had not had time to wonder at this before the seam in the sod at his feet opened and everything the other side of it fell away with a great soft sigh of gravel parting from itself, a languid splash. In the light of the barn he saw a mighty wave with a solitary travelling peak of yellowish foam run temporary crosswise interference to the main surge of the flood and splash up almost to the eaves of the farmhouse.

"Lordy me," he whispered.

On heels of hands and feet he shifted higher still into the sumacs. There he imagined a weight of uprooted timber and other flood litter gathered upstream against the bridge at the power-line road, making a dam. He could not remember what kind of bridge it was up there, but he knew it was no culvert, and he imagined it giving way and a great dark wave of water and debris sweeping down the ravine taking everything not rooted fast in the shallow sediment.

He marvelled that the house had continued to hold. Surely at any moment the frame would shift and tip off its foundations and be borne away upon the flood.

She was wearing the nightgown again. She opened an upper window and also the other window on that side of the farmhouse that he could see. As she was opening the second window a cow stuck its head out the first and uttered a great moo into the night.

All this in the light, like day, of the burning barn. The sheets of the tin roof curling and crumpling and melting. The flaming walls beginning to buckle and cave.

He wondered if she had dragged that cow up the stairs or if it had climbed of its own accord. He wondered how many cows she had managed to drag or coax up and how many had been left swimming on the ground floor, bumping into floating furniture, into each other, the water rising, their muzzles lifted in the firelit darkness to rattle the brass-and-cut-glass chandelier. How well he knew these country interiors, though not so well when half filled with river water and cows. He wondered if in such a circumstance a cow would bite. If she would think, My sister offers necessary purchase, why should she be wanting to climb on me? He supposed that she would, that anything would.

After that the level of the flood as measurable against the side of the house receded slightly. To him it seemed that having withstood this much the wretched structure would survive, the narrowness of the front of it combined with the deflective upstream elevation of the barn a double advantage perhaps. Not without some disappointment he moved farther up into the sumacs, where as he slept all he had witnessed became previous fantastic dreams of brightness and dark, or memories of a faerie spectacle too outlandish for human eyes.

What woke him was the complete cessation of rain, but it was dark yet, the stone enclosure of the barn glowing ruby and beige in domes of rain-dimpled ash, like catalytic heaters just cooling, and he slept again. When he woke next it was early morning, an hour, he judged, to dawn. The sky was heavy, but nothing was falling out of it. He looked below and saw the river already shrunk to merely brimming its banks. That downstream obstruction too must have given way. He considered the scene. The barn's foundations held smoking ashes, now grey. Along the far wall among twisted sheets of tin he could see the carcasses of cows melted blue-black like slag. Smoking too, a darker smoke. He could see the unmarked small tract where, among muddy bent-looking pieces of farm machinery, the Plymouth must have been parked. He could see the house, its siding peeled back in narrow strips of metal that flapped a little in the breezes. The mud line halfway to the first-storey lintels.

It was a pleasure to be moving once more in daylight. He found a way around the newly sheer embankment and slid down to the smoothness of the ravine floor. Plodding through that sticky, puddled yellow silt he saw beer cans and pieces of plastic packaging and clumps of grass and other trash caught on bushes a short distance above his head. To his satisfaction—signs and portents everywhere it seemed—a spruce had come to rest across the raging channel a short distance downstream from the house. Carefully, stepping through mud-caked branches, he crossed the racing flood.

From the house, as he approached, no sound. From the barn the upwind stink of wet smoke, charred offal. The cow that had gone through the porch had drowned there, its carcass impossibly twisted in a drift of silt against the front wall of the house, the broken leg still caught. The screen door mud-plastered wide open against the wall. The front window smashed either by the animal in its thrashing whether living or dead or by something else. The front door stood open, the downstairs a sorry mess. It was a snapped-off fir that had come through that window, just short enough, once inside, to clear the sill. Three cows stood in the stinking muck, crowded by its branches into one half of the space. Flanks scored. Gazing bleakly. Two at him, one out the silted window on the river side. Two more lay drowned in a lacerated heap on a collapsed chesterfield against the downriver wall.

He climbed the stairs. A hognose snake had wrapped itself around the muddy banister. He poked at it with the gun but it just looked at him. She was not in her bed. The calf was down the narrow hall, eating wallpaper. When it saw Troyer it bowed its head to the floor and picked up something in its mouth. As if it were a pup and wanted him to play. Troyer stepped forward to take the thing. A small stuffed bear, of calf-chewed fur, losing straw. Black glass eyes. He pushed the calf aside and looked into the small room there. A low bed, no child. He slipped the bear into the pocket of his jacket.

In the first room, where the bed had been lain in, were two cows, one sitting, one standing. Both animals seemed to appraise him. He found her hunched in the nightgown, inside the closet. He lifted her chin with the tip of the barrel. She wasn't beautiful. She wasn't young either, particularly. Red-nosed. Complexion poor. A certain congenital weakness about the bones of the face. A thickness or heaviness through the eyes. The kind of woman's face that bore too strongly upon it the print of her father's, him being the kind of man you would not, if you could help it, have anything to do with at all.

Overcome by a shaking, her eyes flat with terror, lips silently going.

"Come out of there," Troyer said. "It's no occasion for prayer. There's no Devil, you know, just people, and if that's any consolation, we need to have a talk."

On the day after he had come upon Caroline Troyer in the canoe, Wakelin got lost again, trudging through the woods, the pack on his back like a boulder, the plastic handles of six enormously heavy bags of groceries from the IGA in Sproule cutting into his palms as he wandered in circles. The prickly flush of the conscious fool. Kept coming to the same Day-Glo-pink bull's-eyes and going into cursing. Worse, with both hands occupied by groceries, he could not swat at the mosquitoes and blackflies steadily gathering about his head. Don't ask him how there could be one living bug in this forest after little more precipitation than dew for three months. Do they somehow know it's been raining steadily and hard to the south for two days and the clouds are moving this way?

Not yesterday as promised but from Sproule today, Wakelin had called Clarice, at home and at her office, but she was not in at either place, so he told her answering machine at home and her voice mail at the office that Caroline Troyer was fine. Resting peacefully. He thanked Clarice for the canoe, which he assured her he was treating with terrific care and would return the day he found a secondhand boat and motor. After that, not knowing what more to say, he hung up.

He couldn't take these bugs any more. He stopped to apply the insect repellent he had picked up at the checkout. But when he reached down to lift the grocery bags the handles dissolved away to delicate spikes. This was how he came to leave his canned and bottled and dried supplies under a tree that he told himself he would find again with no trouble, it was so

195

distinctive, being completely dead, and repacked the knapsack with the rest of the food. What would not fit into the knapsack he carried in his arms. Meanwhile the only bugs repelled were four blackflies who descended from their orbits to burrow into his scalp. By the time he came to the brook, the one he thought he knew, or that looked like it, he was bug-crazed and staggering with exhaustion. Rivulets of blood were tickling his neck.

Not long after that, he was blindly into saplings, treading a carpet of maple leaves the colour of raw linen, when he heard a branch crack under a weight not his own and stopped to listen and so first, very distantly, heard the sound. Boat, he thought, but it was not a boat, and it was not a plane either, the sound was neither combustion nor jet, and it maintained its own insistent and multitudinous quality, like applause, the volume slowly increasing even as he stood and listened. He stumbled on. Now the upper canopy was tossing, and Wakelin understood that it was rain he was hearing, approaching at speed across the roof of the forest. Rising in pitch as it rose in volume.

He had come to an animal path through the saplings and was following that eastward. He heard the rain wall descend into the bay somewhere below, a new fullness to the sound. And then drops were landing all around him. He kept walking. Soon it was just hard rain. He came to another animal path. He was now out of the saplings into a clearing of brambles and rattlesnake fern. A log sorting area, once. So he imagined. He came upon a car seat. A restplace for the men. He wandered the periphery of the intractable flesh-snagging clearing until he came to a path he could imagine he remembered. It was a cold, driving rain. Already he was soaked. The knapsack repacked was even heavier, and his arms trembled under the weight of the groceries as he hugged them to himself. The path was streaming. He splashed down it, a rocky slope awash. In time, by making himself always take the steeper path downwards no matter what seemed like a better idea, he came to the lake and got himself oriented. He was east of his place, had nearly missed the bay altogether. Along the shore there the bear—or another—had been through, ripping apart stumps. A wide trail of sodden clumps and splinters of pale yellow vivid against the black amber needles of the forest floor. By the time he reached his dupe's purchase, his sloped patch of till-scant migmatite with shacks, the whole place, whether roof or ground, was sheeted with water coursing for the lake, water blocked and diverted by rocks and trees and fallen branches and temporary miniature dams of twigs and scraps of bark and leaves and needles of cedar and hemlock and all the other intricate disjecta that comprise the forest floor.

He set the groceries on the ground outside the plywood cabin and went in to check on Caroline Troyer. She was not there, her bed was made. Immediately panicking—he should not have left her, not even for food—he was casting around wildly when his eye was caught by the small window on the water side, and there she was, a spectre on the slope of the dock in the driving rain. The shock of her white gaunt frame fixed him as she stepped from what he could not see because of the slope but knew was a ring of old-man clothing. Swiftly she dropped to a squat and seemed to bring her hand to her face, tipped forward between her splayed knees, and he could not, did not, look away—rose on tiptoes, in fact—to see the lovely rear, the flash of thick dark nether hair, and with hardly any splash she was in.

Greatly anxious, he went to the dock. In slow motion she was swimming out.

"You're not strong enough!" he shouted. "You'll catch pneumonia!" He had no idea what he was saying. He had to hear the words to know what they were. Before he had left for Sproule this morning he got her to eat a little porridge he cooked using rolled oats he found in an unsmashed jar. Porridge with white sugar. No milk, the bear got the milk. When Caroline Troyer had lifted her head to speak to him from the bottom of the canoe yesterday morning the headache was already at full blast. To all appearances the worst kind of migraine, but she said she had them all the time (though never this bad) and they weren't migraines. Whatever they were, she could take only liquids all that day. After how many days of exposure and starvation and seizuring? She couldn't remember. There were a lot of things she couldn't remember.

She glanced around at him and kept swimming. A slow steady rate.

He felt agitated. In the pouring rain he paced the dock, examining loose boards, the luminous incursions of moss. The rain was a constant drilling upon the tin roof of the log cabin and the asphalt shingles of the plywood cabin and upon the dock itself and the rocks along the shore and upon the surface of the lake. A vertical driving force. He took off his own soaking clothes and sat on the edge of the dock with his legs in the water to the knees and should have been perhaps but was not prepared for what happened next. In the cold rain the lake felt warm. Mist was rising off it, though not blank white like yesterday morning but thin, tentative. It would disappear once the rain had cooled the surface. Meanwhile the warmth of the lake was a physical invitation, a tugging at Wakelin's head that said, Submerge, submerge. He could feel the pull, but he didn't move. Could not. He was fixed here. Instead, in place of his head, its contents, tears, welled and burst from his eyes and streamed down his face. If the head wouldn't come, the tears would. Or maybe his body was like that blanket he had stuffed in the broken window of the plywood cabin the other night, wicking bears: his body was wicking the lake, up his legs, genitals, stomach, chest, throat, and pouring it back out his eyes. This entire volume of water suddenly a reservoir of tears and Wakelin their sole syphon. Weeping for God only knew what. For everything. For Jane, for himself, for Caroline Troyer. For unhappy Ardis in her blindness. Weeping for us all. Universal emotion flooding up his body and gushing from his eyes.

Caroline Troyer had stopped to tread water. She was looking back at him.

He dropped his hands from his face. "Be careful out there!" he called, his voice catching in a sob. "You're in a weakened condition!" He sank to fresh weeping.

She was back at the dock.

"I'll close my eyes," he said, gasping convulsively by this time, like a child. "If you want to get out." He held his palms over the stinging. He had forgotten his own nakedness.

She didn't say anything.

Wakelin took away his hands. She was gripping the end of the dock next to him with both hers. Her fingers were white and spread at the tips in their press upon the streaming wood. Her hair was darker when wet, and it was swept back and finely shaped to her skull. She was looking up at him, breathing hard. Unsmiling and yet her face in its whiteness, in the absolute openness of its attention upon him, was radiant.

Wakelin could only shake his head as if she were asking something impossible, something that made everything seem just too hopelessly difficult. "Christ, I'm so glad you're alive," was all he could say. And then he went on weeping.

Already the mud was streaked and mottling to whites and darker yellows on the smashed porch and the drowned cow and the steps of the farmhouse when Ross Troyer descended to recross the river by the fallen spruce, the mud tips of its branches blanching. Beyond the river he skirted the cutbank, climbing leisurely as a hillwalker, and so proceeded along the edge of a higher forest of pine and maple under a grey sky, miasmal updrafts communicating the muck stink of the chaos below. Trees fallen heaped against trees, against boulders, boulders shifted. Disorder in the ravine. Higher paths needed.

A mile or so north of the farm he saw below him a rusted-out grey pickup on its nose in a birch grove. He felt in his rubber pocket for the stuffed bear. Impressed against the driver's window of the truck was a clownish face. Jack-in-the-box never more to be sprung. And then he saw the child, its shirt bunched at the armpits, stretched out in a bed of silt and water along the interior windshield. The yellow mud was inside there too, coating them both smooth as dolls. Her husband and son, he supposed. Racing back to save the farm. They'd had a truck after all. He saw the fishing rods, one long, one short, also caught among the birches, and he thought, There it is, the rest of the story. He looked into the face of the bear with its black eyes staring back at him. Here you thought you'd been set free, he said. Well, you haven't. And he put it back into his pocket.

Not far above the birch grove, not a quarter mile, he came to the bridge at the power line, and here the scene was pretty much as he had foreseen:

one concrete pile fallen oblique, the bank eroded wide, the span toppled, all but submerged, the other pile still upright, isolated in the fast brown water, a rotten stanchion, a crumbling snag for flotsam, mudline drying halfway up it, now like its fallen partner just another obstruction the river had needed to find a new way around.

Squatting, he gazed upon the forlorn spectacle of a bridge pile bereft of its span. After several minutes he avalanched down the gravel embankment. In the middle of the road, there he paused to survey the power-line cut. Pylons from grey horizon to grey horizon, their symmetry untroubled by these rains. Like the visible road in both directions, untroubled by pickup trucks racing down it. There would of course be more washouts than this, on this road and others, not apparent from here. The local boys' travels out restricted by the very same sites of disaster whetting their appetite for more.

He knew a little bit how the boys would be feeling. It was that power-line road running northeast he had come for. Now he stood in the road and asked himself why after that wall of water came through last night and he imagined this bridge out in exactly this way, he would cross back over and then go on intending to cross here. Was this the wonderful power of habit or of hope or a mind dark unto itself? Why, if he expected this, hadn't he stayed on the other side when he had the chance? Because the old itch from below, the old itch to slip a hand in where a skirt or a nightgown was concerned, had militated against a public stroll up the road there, that was why. And yet the only reason he had crossed in the first place had been the old intent to slip a hand in, and there it was, that nasty little twist of logic that events will manifest as soon as the hand has gone in for no better reason than the itch. It wasn't the pleasure of it, the pleasure was whatever pleasure is or may be construed as, it was the tyranny of the itch. There was what you had to do, and then there was the itch. Inflecting events with nasty twists and spreading darkness through the mind.

He followed the river beyond the power line into what in his view was Shield proper, more particularly, in that small section of it, five hundred square miles of hunt camps and logging tracts mostly unsurveyed bush, the ground just here slowly rising, the river channel once more narrowing, all the way to where the raging flow had not lately left its bed of rock. And yet through all that uncharted territory, though he walked until dusk, he found no feasible means to cross the Pardee.

And then the cloud cover passed and the night was cool in the understorey. No moon, stars in aggressive surfeit, decor from a spray can. At a bend in the river, under a great white pine whose crown, visible for five miles on his approach, he had estimated at twenty feet above the surrounding canopy, he kicked together a bed of needles and lay down. Beneath the great tree it came to him that without fire planes and firefighters this would once again be universal white pine forest, as in the days before the loggers, the days of two-hundred-foot white pines, because, growing taller than other trees, white pines draw lightning and so ignite, and igniting set the fires that provide the clear ground required by their own cones to germinate. With help in cracking open from the heat of the blaze.

To the unborn, a gift of fire.

Daddy, say it with flames.

He listened to the onrush of the river below and to the breezes rattling the long needles over his head, and these sounds together with the soughing of the wind made another like the sibilance of whispering, which as he dozed framed other truths less clear in the press of full daylight. Truths for which he had set aside a few minutes this morning to impress upon Our Lady of the Cows, preliminary to his devotions, though perhaps she knew them already; she didn't say. Truths the forest knew. The pines most clearly. Of course the pines had had three million centuries to undeceive themselves. Devastations sufficient unto the perfection of coniferous intelligence. Whereas the only advantage people had of time was the brevity of human life and its attendant promise of absolute exemption from seeing. Anything but that. You look away for seventy or eighty years, it's a way of life and one day it's over. What more could you have done? An eye sightless has finished with looking away. Compared to the truth, death is a small, grateful matter. Meanwhile, in order to create meaning when you have done everything you could to exclude its possibility, you assure yourself of allegiances when there are none. Of plans when there is no plan. Of order in the human realm when that realm is in chaos and always was. Of plots when no one has met or spoken and nothing has been determined. Of aliens at the gates when there is only one alien around here and the creature looking out its eyes is you.

You assure yourself that someone must know, when no one knows. When the ones in charge don't know. If they did, the world would not be run like a school yard by children with guns. The thinkers don't know. All the thinkers do is come up with more good reasons for why things should be different from how they are. Others disagree about particulars and methods and everybody's thinking and nothing changes. Where to look? What to do? The Church? The Church is the institutionalization of looking away. Nothing new about that. Somebody had to organize it. And each person's truth is a gathering of sparks thrown up by unexpected jolts and shifts of daily habit, which harden as they fly and are snatched from air and held and rubbed smooth by anxious numbering until fresh jolts send up new sparks, new fossils for rubbing. Soon themselves worn to relics of understanding, nameless and without meaning.

It had been like that for him, once. Her mother at twenty already a doll of pure reflex, a voluptuous mechanical, his belt the only language she understood. Each cut a heavier shadow, civilized once-nimble minds hardened by that discipline, eyes tranced, his locked by the seeing it, hers in a blur of coy weeping. And he would look at her and think, What have I done? It was like a joke: Truth from the mouth of that one would be as astonishing as an aria. But *she* was not like that. From that first moment in the hospital, that tiny blue-red god's face lifting away from the starched shoulder, those steady infant eyes of august regard. Her hand upraised. Was her hand upraised? He had dropped weeping to his knees in that sickly green corridor, to the alarm of the nurse, who fell back shielding the child.

His heart and soul on that blessed day transfigured by that absolute loving open hand of light.

And so too these truths even now this night under whispered conveyance by this tallest of trees, great truths, truths negative, refining fire, and as he slept he could feel it, deep in his brainstem, the subtlety of their conifer tongues working to temper, the vessel preparing, and one day from the mouth of this vessel would pour forth the living waters upon the famished earth, and the hand would reach forth to that other now outstretched from a quarter unworthy and that would be done which ought to have been done and darkness fall from intelligence once more.

This as he slept. New worlds of promise.

A warm night of steady rain. Walter Heinrichs would be watching TV in a motel room in Biddesfirth or Parksville or wherever equally remote he'd been sitting court today, and Clarice was at home, eating alone. Cold chicken breast and a salad. The radio had been on for the news. Now she turned it off.

She'd expected a reassuring message from Wakelin to set her mind at rest, but it had not. She was still trying to believe she would leave those two, in their respective states. It was not like her, and she could only think that she would not have done it had she not been so rattled by being come upon in that weird embrace. Come upon by her. Weird or pathetic didn't make it innocent, that embrace. Not seeing it through Caroline Troyer's eyes, it didn't.

But more than herself Clarice was worrying about tonight. Ross Troyer was still missing. In Bankhead they were saying he'd abducted his daughter. Having seen Caroline Troyer twice, both times later than anyone spreading the story, Clarice knew this was untrue. But tonight it seemed to her that in the complacency of her knowledge she had been slower than she should have been to realize that the abduction, or whatever, could be yet to come. That if Troyer—the son of a bitch knew every lake and bush road within fifty miles of Grant—were to turn up at Wakelin's cabins and something terrible happened, then who would have to spend the rest of her life knowing that she could have done something and didn't?

But she would do something. She would tell Walter. Tell him what? That Wakelin had just called and Caroline Troyer was at his cabins, and the police should understand that that was a possible destination for Troyer. If Walter didn't call tonight or tomorrow, she would tell him as soon as he got home. Which would be Thursday. The day after tomorrow. That would be soon enough. It would have to be. She couldn't call him. She had no idea where he was sitting this week. If he'd told her, she hadn't listened. But he usually called. If not tonight, then tomorrow. When he called, she would tell him. She would tell him first thing when he called.

It was still raining when Wakelin got the dock floating, levering mightily with a cudgel of yellow birch until the monster slid the last few inches of rock and settled floating, so massive that floating seemed a miracle comparable to the lift-off of a jetliner. With bright yellow nylon rope knotted to the iron rings at the ends of its two great timbers, the dock could be manoeuvred in water but slowly, in its own time. The same ropes, once Wakelin had got it positioned straight out, he secured to a pair of cedars by the shore, one on each side. For a long time then he walked around on his beautiful floater, experiencing the strange soft flex of the thing. It really was badly gone, a poor fabric of cupped and rotten and missing boards weathered to softness. But it was his and it was floating.

All this in the drumming rain. And then, also in the rain, with a dozen two-by-sixes he found in the shed at the back of the property, he built an access ramp from the rocks at the shore. He could see that his structure was a little skewed, but pounding in the last nail and shifting the thing around until it didn't wobble and walking back and forth on it many times gave him as much satisfaction as the writing of any piece for any magazine in recent memory, and on his way to check on Caroline Troyer he wondered if this was not the life for him after all.

She was sitting in the wooden chair in the plywood cabin, her hands flat on the deal table. She was still wearing the old man's wool shirt, the old man's jeans, and she was looking at Wakelin as he stepped in running with water. The clothes gave her the appearance of a young girl recuperating after a rescue from some extreme state of the elements. A quality of deliverance. The sober startled look of one back in a familiar place for the first time.

"It's floating," he said.

"I know."

"You watched?" The dumbness of this question reminded him that in his head he had done it all under her admiring gaze. "How's the pain?"

"Less now. Almost gone."

"Finally." He sat down on the bed, which she had made. But of course he was dripping wet. He sprang up.

She turned in her chair, reaching for his hands.

He looked down. Her fingers were as long as his own. No warmer. They held his lightly, easily. He could feel his attention moving to her touch, like a gaze to a fire. Such a simple thing. Why didn't everybody hold hands when they talked? Could it be because it would embarrass them half to death? Could it be for the same reason they couldn't live in peace?

"It comes from the outside," she said.

He understood that she did not mean the pain. It was bracketed by the pain but it was not the pain. The pain happened when it was on its way. Later the pain was the aftermath for a body used beyond the limits of its capacity. He knew it came from the outside, whatever that could mean now. Anyway, the body was the receiver, not the originator. All you needed to know this was to have been there. He couldn't write about this. It was too far outside the professional parameters of any magazine editor he had ever worked for, even the ones who paid in copies. It was strange, actually. To have had confirmed from so unanticipated a direction his decision not to write about her. Strange because it reminded him that his motivation for staying clear had not been pure at all, was a simple failure of compassion in compassion's guise. Whereas this was the real thing, the living fountainhead of that virtue. It was like being forgiven when you could not forgive yourself. Absolution from beyond. So strange. Such relief. Not to be another to submit her—and now this—to the scrutiny of a world that was always hungry for something this new, this old. But would have needed to be there. If it wasn't to read it all wrong. If it wasn't to read it in the usual dreary ways, medical, psychoanalytic, or religious.

The relief was also, he knew, not to have to push against the code of his profession. Not to have to risk going out there sounding like a believer.

But a believer in what?

"When it first comes," she said, "it comes from the left."

This was information Wakelin hardly took in. He was watching himself look down at his hands in hers. He was trying to tell if that energy in the air was back. Whether or not he was feeling it at this moment. Or only imagining it. Or remembering it.

And then he heard a voice—his own—saying, "From the left? Sounds a little sinister." And flushed hot.

Caroline Troyer was shaking her head, unamused. Hadn't got the stupid pun. Was not defensive. "It isn't sinister," she said. "That's what it's not."

"No, I realize—I didn't mean—"

"Can you feel it now?"

"*Yes.*" He sat down on the bed.

"Because we're talking about it," she said.

"Has it happened before?"

"Not like yesterday." She was looking at him. He tried to see her as struggling to put this into words for him, but all he could see was her eyes, searching a face. His own, he realized. What would she find?

"It's not me," she said.

He nodded. "What's going on?"

"I don't know."

It was all around them, that cataract of energy. Its aftermath. Roaring off her like an emanation.

"What's it want?" Wakelin said.

"It doesn't 'want.'"

"A better word?"

"Are you just asking questions?"

Not at all. They could hold your hands and they could search your face for a day and a night, but they couldn't make you talk to them. Not really.

Not even if they burned with holy fire could they make you talk to them. Not when you preferred to the truth, the wonderful guy you could be if only you did not have to be accountable to a whole world outside your own head.

"Where's it going, for you?" he said.

"I don't know."

"But it's changing?"

"It keeps going deeper."

"Into what?"

"Itself."

"How?"

She shook her head.

"Look," he said. "I'm sorry. I really am. You should just ignore me."

"Were you closed to her?"

"What? *Close?*"

"Closed."

"No. Not at all. I was wide open."

She looked at him.

"Why?" he asked.

Again she shook her head.

"I still am," he said. "That's my problem."

"What are you open to now?" she said.

Wakelin sighed. "Not much—" The tears were back. "Memories—?" When he gathered the courage to look at her she was glancing around at the air.

"It's going," she said.

"Yes—"

"I can cook and clean," she said. "I can hunt. You've got a gun?"

"No gun. You kill animals?" He was wiping his eyes.

"A hook and line? It's a trout lake?"

"Please, I said you could stay. You don't have to cook and clean. We can both cook and clean. When you're stronger. Here's the important question. Is he going to show up here?"

She let go of his hands. Immediately he jumped to his feet.

"If they don't change their minds about not holding him," she said. "If he finds out where I am. If he knows how to get here."

"*You* got here."

She didn't say anything.

"Look," Wakelin said. "I'm really happy you came to me. But why? Why me?"

She didn't hesitate. "You were the only stranger I knew."

Wakelin did not dare to hope she would smile. When she did, showing her wonderful teeth, the joy of it nearly buckled his knees. He was nodding again, wildly. He needed to do something. Take her in his arms—no. Be held by her, oh God yes, please, but then he'd start crying again. He was already crying again.

"What I mean," she said, reaching again for his hands as they frantically wiped at his eyes. "I could trust you."

Wakelin was amazed. "But how would you know that? *I* don't know that!"

"No," she said.

Then he didn't know what to say, lapsed instead of saying anything into gazing at her face, and as if to explain that murmured, "God, you're beautiful," and then was overcome by self-consciousness, could only drop his eyes in time to see her hands let go of his once more. "I'm sorry," he said.

She shook her head.

He sat back down on the bed.

"What's your father want?" he asked.

Her eyes had gone to the window. Now they came back. This time there was no smile. "What does anybody want," she said. "What he had."

How could she describe what was happening to her in any way of use to anybody else that would not be a betrayal? An act of contempt for her own experience? How could she describe to Wakelin or to anyone something that could not be contained by her understanding when it was not present, and when it was present could not be contained even by her body? When words were connected to images and ideas, and this was not. From books and church she knew the language so familiar it was like a substance in itself, needing nothing else. Now as she stumbled upon it from the other direction she could see what sincere speakers had intended it to mean and how wretchedly they had failed, and how other sincere speakers, who did not know, only hoped to know, knew only the words as modified by their own desire, the willed purity of sincere longing, how they had mocked and reduced it without intending to, and how the cynics and the users had twisted and corrupted those very same words and what a distance lay between such folly and what this was. The words were inadequate, old and finished, and none of them, not one, was worthy to carry the slightest hint of what this was.

But how to think about it? Not to rouse the dogs in their cage but to dispose the mind in a way that might discourage it from squandering in anticipation and useless longing its own small energy.

What has happened, what is happening, to this body?

Is there any possible understanding for what is happening that is not completely false?

What does she remember?

The longing. The journey. She remembers the pain. The usual, only worse.

She remembers the two of them, Wakelin on his knees before the realtor woman, his face in her stomach.

She remembers in herself, from long ago, the swoon of loving that way, in the imagination, abjectly.

She remembers falling.

She remembers blood like liquid iron. She remembers darkness.

She remembers a testing, from the left. A steady even pressure, implicit in the tentative increase, one question: How much, this time, can the body take? The answer: This time there will be no resistance. No limit. The question like heat-shrivelled foil melting and flowing away. No watcher. All thought in abeyance. Consumed. The kindled presence only. Flame of diamond. Intelligence self-informing through this body to the depths of its own depthless being. Destroying and creating and creating and destroying. Without difference.

Fire. Fire. Fire.

Light blazing. The amazement not the slave's but its own, at itself. The slave a momentary trick of hide-and-seek played by the light on itself. The slave the innocent continuing to believe, against all evidence, that good will be done. The slave the living scar of injury.

The secret is the seed of love. What happens if by some chance entry of light and heat into the heart the seedcase cracks? The energy released like energy atomic, out of all proportion to the tininess of the seed, and time and space are turned inside out and grow infinite and are no longer imagined to contain.

In the face of the injured one the world is muffled. Life through smeared glass. Eyes of spun gauze. Dainty cocoons.

Now the injured is cleansed of her face.

Mother, I love you.

The world is inside, no more this container. Perspective no more.

Father, I love you.

Yesterday she was walking east. Now she is walking west. Hands open. No. No. No.

Foolishness.
Foolishness.
Foolishness.

Ross Troyer did not discover a means to cross the Pardee River until almost to Jack Lake. This was late afternoon of the following day. His progress arduous. On the southwest bank of the river north and east of the power line had been no route of any kind save animal paths. The land rocky, complex with deadfall. Densely forested. Along the hot margin of the river the ferns and the boneset and the joe-pye weed grew thick, and so did high-bush cranberries, and he wished that he, like some African explorer, had a machete or, better, a gleaming young burrhead to hack out a path before him. As it was he spent hours together swarmed by deerflies, by rain-spurred mosquitoes and blackflies, crouched and crawling to squeeze down tunnels of underbrush, at best the mazy throughways of weasels and foxes. He would have followed some large-animal path more worthy of human passage, but the black rock here lay deeply fissured at a crosswise slant to the river.

In time he came to where blowdowns had recently occurred, many trees fallen, stony clotted yellow loam unrainwashed from amongst the veinous wheels of root. Water deep-pooled in the raw pocks. Maples and beeches mostly, fifty-year-old hardwoods toppled in their dozens by a ten-minute wind. Disorder in the forest. In one area farther upriver a gust like a blunt aerial cutting machine had sliced a stand of red spruce at five feet. Their trunks now issuing in generous bouquets of yellow splinters. These trees like most had fallen parallel to the water because the gusts had been channelled by the ravine, but one pine was toppled diagonal, and at last he found his means to cross. He walked that broad trunk as another might have walked a national-park footbridge, and long before he would reach its lower branches he climbed down to the stony shore opposite.

There he decided not to retrace the river to the power line but instead to use his compass to travel south. That way, if his calculation was correct, he would reach the power line at a point closer to where he wanted to be.

This in the late afternoon.

Passing at nightfall through a grove of larches he came upon a porcupine, its back turned, peering at him from around a swell of yellow-tipped quills. Out of his pocket he drew the flashlight he had picked up at the farmhouse, from the floor alongside her bed. Shining it down upon the head of the creature, he stepped around to face it. The gaze of the porcupine followed the white heaven of light and the creature did not turn again, even as he knelt before it and unlocked the breach and levelled the rifle alongside the flashlight, the barrel parallel to the beam. In the strong illumination he could see the gummy baleful eyes of the animal and he could hear the hard clatter of its yellow teeth in the helplessness of its terror, and he understood that the great love the hunter feels for his prey is nothing more than misbegotten pity or as likely some kind of autonomic elation. He wondered if this one was male or female. Our Lady of the Uncontrollable Chattering.

When he pulled the trigger the porcupine was blown back in a spray of juice and splinters of bone. The body did a flip and long skid through the slippery needles.

That night in a rock bowl among the larches, Troyer proceeded in an orderly fashion to build a fire, his first on this trip. Now that he was beyond most human habitation. Not all but most. For the fire he constructed a fine aspen spit, and he skinned and skewered and decapitated and cooked the carcass over red and soft grey coals, much as he had done on many occasions as a young man on hunting trips in woods not twenty miles from where he sat tonight. But he did not feast on the meat, did not cut it away in narrow strips as once he would have, delicately sucking the grease from his charcoal-black fingers, thinking, Now, this is the life. And, I should do this more often. Instead he allowed the meat to continue to cook until it was in flames and continued to burn until nothing remained but the charred mass of it. And this he took on its stick and walked some distance into the woods and tossed it away.

The head he had already removed and placed away from the fire, to watch over this ceremony of abstinence perhaps, from the crotch of a double cedar.

The night was clear, but in the morning there was once more no sun, just low dark clouds. After less than an hour of walking, he came to a bush road that according to his instrument would at least for a short time convey him roughly southeast. A turkey vulture swept across the channel of grey overhead, and as Troyer watched, another zoomed in from nowhere to join it.

Watch those quills, boys.

Hope you like yours well done.

If the road had been maintained recently, it must have been by a snowmobile club. Its surface insufficiently graded for the logging trucks and unsuitable for passage by car. But a four-wheel drive with a high wheelbase would have little trouble. In winter a snowmobile. The road was also good for walking, and it felt like freedom to be moving upright, the ground level underfoot. Now and then the road traversed a swale of sedgegrass and scorched stumps primary in size, and he congratulated himself on being spared the tedium of those detours necessary in bush hostile to those who number themselves among the wingless bipeds.

He walked three hours, lulled by the speed and ease of his trek now, for it seemed to him afterward that he heard the engines only seconds before he saw the plane. As soon as he did he sprinted for the forest margin, not far. It was a twin-engine Otter, and it passed directly over him, quite low, not twenty feet above the canopy, and then, as if it knew him, it swung round. Before it did, and several seconds before he was to any degree aware of what he was doing, perhaps out of a need to compensate for that initial lapse of attention or perhaps out of some older need or reflex more arcane, he had slipped the rifle from its case and gone down on one knee. Had lifted and in rapid succession released three blasts into the underside of the forward section of the plane.

After which there followed an interval, not a pause exactly but something more like a recurrence, or echo, of that original lapse, and in the space of that repetition, time ceased. But no sooner had it ceased, no sooner had it laid itself down upon the black glass of eternity and stretched out fully and breathed its last, than it was back, in full force, effect rushing upon cause with clamorous urgency. And like a toy on a cord of India rubber, the flimsy vehicle of air snapped left and rocketed into the forest. A gatling commotion of splintered branches and shearing metal. And that was all.

Except for the silence.

No screams. No jolt of impact. No crackle of flames. Not fifty yards away. Not fifty yards of trunks and green. Invisible. Nothing. No squirrel. No cicada. No bird. In five seconds a sudden nuisance cancelled out of all existence, like a mosquito by an immediate slap. But even a mosquito will leave a trace. A blood-burst cool on the skin.

But cancelled by whom? By what authority? By what issue of what place?

He sat back on his haunches, looking over his shoulder, scrutinizing the viridescent barrier of forest in the direction of that utter silence. He was like a man searching for absolute assurance that what had just happened had indeed happened as thoroughly and completely and in its own way as perfectly as it had appeared to. Either that or for evidence that what had happened had happened at all.

With the rifle across his forearm, the butt pressed up under his armpit, he continued in that same attitude for a long time, eventually with his head fallen forward as if in prayer. Lips moving. Mouth forming silence.

And then he was using the rifle as one of those hoary wilderness prophets might once have leaned upon his staff after prolonged communion on failing knees, to push himself back to the trek, to the impatient suffering of his people.

What people? He looked about him. Dazed. Where was he? What road was this? What godless green corridor? With one hand he raised the rifle level in front of his eyes. It was trembling. He lowered it. The nylon case was twisted at his feet.

He fell to reflection. The hand goes in when it goes in. This will have been something like that. What in other circumstances, a bearded age, a fierce age of prophets, has been called the Wrath of God. Vengeance, saith the Lord, is mine. Whatsoever things may be imagined. Boils, locusts, it's my call. So hit the dirt, you miserable sons of bitches. As the biggest lizard said, There's only one monitor showing. No slack-jawed bastard winged or otherwise has licence to hound a man on foot. For the Lord saith, Has he who walks a bush road accountless offered himself for study? Is he some mangy threatened species fastened with a transmitter collar to have his movements charted by every slaphead bush jockey?

These thoughts and questions, grim as jokes, as they entered his mind conveyed little assurance. No more than formulas the mind will resort to at a time of distress, or than idiot lyrics enter it, or anxious fingers worry the contents of a pocket (or poke into the gaping seams of the ragged bear they find there). All he was getting from such thoughts was the solace of thinking them. Of thinking *Wrath of God*, of thinking *slack-jawed bastard*. The dumb solace of thinking somebody else's thoughts, which was no solace at all.

Time to step back to the road, a few feet only. Move on. Except the guncase had wrapped itself around his ankles and his right foot had caught and he was fallen to one knee in the gravel. Two knees. Curled into himself. (The bear pressed to his face, burst stuffing chafing the skin unfelt.) Collapsed onto his left shoulder. Unseeing. That trembling now at a pitch of convulsion like slow flinchings. Jolting forth the voice, small and old. A boy's. Breathless, tear-choked. Dislodged from the greater body. *Daddy, no.*

Wakelin was standing in the kitchen of his cabin, rinsing his mug at the sink. He had just got the pump primed. Another satisfying task, and useful. When he had made eggs yesterday for himself and Caroline Troyer, he did not need to unscrew the cap on the vegetable oil because the deer mice had chewed it off. Like the many trees around here beaver-felled too far from water, this had struck Wakelin as a good example of pointless animal labour, satisfying to the animal in the doing but quite useless, the neck of the bottle too narrow even for the first knuckle of his index finger. But last night, intending to cork it, he had noticed that the oil had a tinge of pink to it. An optical illusion? The back of the label reflecting through? They use a red glue? He held it up to a candle. Five deer mice asleep at the bottom. Intricately stacked, like art.

Wakelin fumbled the bottle back onto the shelf and retched into the sink.

By morning there were nine deer mice asleep in the oil, which was now the colour of crushed raspberries. He corked the bottle and lowered the perfect mousetrap gently into the garbage can.

This time he cooked their eggs using butter.

They ate them sitting in aluminum chairs woven with frayed and faded nylon stripping on the floating dock under a low iron sky. The aluminum chairs were impossibly light, but with two people on the dock at the same time, the weight was enough to cause the water to come creeping over the end of it. Wakelin considered that he would know when a bear stepped onto the dock behind them by the advance of water toward their feet. The rain had stopped, temporarily at least. The bay was a stirless private space of dead air. An owl flew overhead in a passage of deeper silence, a feathered cat. The water was mottled and viscous, like jellied savoury half-set. It reflected the near-shore cedars in laddered jade.

Wakelin was saying they really should try to find out if her father was being held or not, or where he was, if only because—

Caroline Troyer put her fingers in front of his mouth.

"What?" Wakelin said, jerking his head away, already everything he'd just been saying jigging before him, a tinkling cymbal.

She didn't answer; she was listening. Her head was cocked.

Watching her, he realized that very distantly, from somewhere far down the power line, he himself had been hearing the sound of a small-engine plane. Then, just now, faint but distant, shots. Two, or three.

"Hunters, right?" he said.

"Shh."

"What?"

"Can you hear the plane?"

"Not any more."

She was listening.

"It must have gone over a hill," Wakelin said finally.

"No," she said. "It stopped suddenly."

"Somebody shot it down? Is that what you think?"

She was shaking her head, not *No* but to make him stop talking. She was still listening.

At lunch, on the dock again, Caroline Troyer in her cabin all morning, Wakelin on the little porch, staring out at the water. Thinking about Jane. No. Thinking about himself. As ever: his failure to get the picture. The loving remove that had made it all possible, that made everything so much worse. A regular sleep of desire.

Now, on the dock with Caroline Troyer, he was back on the subject of getting out of here until they knew what was what. He asked her if she thought she'd be strong enough to go through the woods. Or should he paddle her to the landing and walk up the hill for the car and come down and get her? But then what to do with the canoe? Hide it in the woods? Strap it on the roof?

She was nodding yes to these questions, not hearing. Gazing at him watching the movement of his mouth instead of listening to what he was saying.

Did he notice? He must have, in some way, for he switched to talking about her. No. About himself. And then, after a pause, in a voice of one being realistic and coming to the point, he said, "Caroline, I'm falling in love." But these words hung in the air, and when he uttered a wild little laugh it joined them, and just to top off the folly he added, "With you," and these words too hung between them, and everything together—the words, the laugh—hung as well in the eye of a small twister of confusion inside his head. He couldn't believe he'd say something like this at a time like now. Unless he needed her to accept him as an infelicitous fool or not at all. Was that it?

When she asked the question it came out softly. As she asked it she placed a hand at the centre of his breastbone, something the way, at breakfast, she had put her hand in front of his mouth.

Wakelin was still looking down at her hand when she said, "Did you know you'd lose her?"

Employing great care, Wakelin set his plate on the dock by his chair. He didn't know what was happening.

"You don't have to tell me," she said.

"Hey, aren't I the one who gets to ask the—" but it didn't work. He could hardly breathe. Her gentle question was like a blow to the chest. He tried to collect himself. Could only nod. *Yes, yes, I knew. From the first moment I saw her I knew. How else could I have loved her so much?*

And he went on trying to breathe.

Finally, after a long time, lungs, heart, aching, he whispered, "What's going on, Caroline?" He was twisted in his chair, clutching her hand, pressing it to his breast, his head bowed. "I'm way over my head here. Help me, please."

"I am helping you," she said.

When exactly it had been that Ross Troyer resumed his trek he did not know later. He had no more memory of resuming it than he did of the old terror upon him once more, when he was down. All he knew he would have preferred also to forget but could not: that the contumacy of former circumstance may at any time cause a man to stumble and fall. Make of him a casualty of events that by their nature, or by the nature of their recording, have defied the assimilation of ordinary knowing and are therefore unavailable to memory. And so when he had recovered or at least was capable of standing, he had only the old imperative of moving on, the rifle as he eventually noticed naked in his hand, its nylon case gone. This was not as it should have been, and yet he did not go back to find it but continued, one foot in front of the other, until the former rhythm returned, listening closely now at all times for planes, and by mid-afternoon that road delivered him, as he had all along hoped that it would, to another: to the one built to service the power line, maintenance more lately performed by snowmobile, or helicopter.

Uneasily he glanced up.

Electrical wires in angry buzzing against the grey sky.

He was sitting on an elevation of land, more particularly on a shelf of quartz where sometime the previous winter it must have been a wolf that had left a beaver tail that now after three hot dry months lay in his hands lightweight and rigid, the recent rains having done nothing to restore its living heft and flex.

From here he could see why no pickups from Coppice had been down to visit the washout at the Pardee bridge. Below him the power-line road passed along the margin of a sea of cattails, or would have had the culvert once intended to carry the overflow from that marsh not been lying skinny and exposed, a shining corrugated cylinder at the bottom of a gully with radical banks. Another washout. The water trickling now.

He was gazing at that culvert, the look of something toylike about it, familiar in a way that he was trying to place, when a dull-black pickup rose silent over the crest of the road and came down the grade to pull up short, having no choice, at the washout. Troyer was a good distance away, but he slipped down behind his seat of quartz to watch the driver climb out and stand and survey the damage, his cap in his hand, scratching his head. Without a grader along, there was not a lot a man could do except look. Nobody could get a truck around this. The man climbed in and turned around and drove back over the rise.

Troyer walked down to the culvert. The road was steep and proceeded by cutback, and it took him nearly fifteen minutes in full view of the next truck that might descend that grade. He wondered what he thought he was doing. Other trucks would be down here, he knew that. The black one would not be the last. The boys from the mill would be wanting to see for themselves.

He Frisbee'd the beaver tail out over the bulrushes. In weariness he lifted his eyes to the wall of forest.

At the top of the hill along the north edge of the cut he went back in. After the Pardee it was not bad going. He took it easy. It was hardwood on the high ground, conifer in the low, the low sodden. Seasonal marsh. Most of the time he had sight of the road and was satisfied to see four or five pickups come down it. Qualifying to witness.

As soon as it was thoroughly dark he returned to the power-line road. If he heard a truck now, he could always lie down in the ditch. He heard no truck. The car when he saw it was two miles away. What he saw first was the cones of its headlights in the night mist, in sporadic slow ascent and as slow descent. So slow he had to wonder if what they sought was him. He crouched in the darkness by an alder shrub, but at that very spot the car pulled off the road. A hacksaw convertible. In the driver's seat a kid possibly seventeen, stretched out with his neck pressed against the top of the seat, moaning.

Troyer's immediate surmise: lover's nuts. The next moment in the light of the dash he caught sight of a blonde head, pigtailed, bobbing in the kid's lap. Preventive treatment under way.

He raised his sights.

Here comes the topper, boys and girls. Blow you both a good one.

Then again.

He lowered the gun.

The hand goes in when it goes in. There is no sense otherwise. This is not some berserker rampage. Start shooting slapheads for the mere reason they're slapheads pursuing slaphead concerns, and the next thing you know you'll be tearing at them with your teeth, while they're still hot.

Bolting them down like a ravening ghoul.

Best put away your weapon, Ross, my good man. Lest darker impulses succeed.

From the grunts and caterwauling the pleasure was over soon enough, for both of them. Her fulfilment complete in the happiness of her lad. His discharge, her duty. Either that or she was one of those who'd been issued a clitoris at the epiglottis wicket. The old mix-up. Or was as happy it was thought so.

After they had driven away, which was as slowly as they had arrived, as slowly as the lovers he supposed they were, he walked back into the forest and fell asleep under a maple.

Long before the sun rose, he—who knew this much: his dreams this night had been savage, unkind, not to be borne—was walking again. When the road left the power line and reentered the woods he understood that he had come too far north, too far towards Coppice. Still he did not turn around, and for a reason, because when he reached a narrower lane that returned nearly parallel to the direction he had come, he took it, climbing upward, then down almost back to the edge of the power line. Reaching a junction of paths, he chose the left hand, because he knew where it led: to where he used to bring her to camp in the early days, when her light was upon him.

The site was more or less as he remembered it. A yellow birch and balsam that as saplings had grown side by side now each sported a trunk nearly a foot across, the balsam a little thicker. How time flies rings round us all. He hiked up to the level patch of turf where he used to pitch the tent. Gazed down at the water. This was the first time he had ever seen it torrential, pouring green and yellow and black-green satin over the lip of concrete. Pluming out and boiling up white around the grey rocks below.

Newborn, he reflected, perhaps we're all forest gods. Severe in our majesty. And the energy of parents whether loving or hateful is directed toward the diminishment of that glory. The coochie-coos and the rest of the adoring flummery. The baby talk, the regimens and their lapses, the rewards, the punishments, the corruption of character palpable in adult inflections, the fulsome buffoonery, the clownish grimaces looming and hovering before startled infant eyes. All to diminish. All to take away.

And so you break them even as you love them, you split them into pieces and you leave your mark on each piece.

And when they grow older you watch them like stunned casualties of a thousand hit-and-runs struggle to put themselves together again, work to assemble wholeness out of bits of you and their mother, the way their bodies are assemblies, genetic assemblies, the look in their eyes, how they hold their cup, their mouth, assuming expressions, attitudes, tones of voice, and you think, That little trick isn't going to get you very far, why don't you just take my word for it, and you think, Did you really have to latch on to that one? and you think, How observant, how bloody dare you. And you do not need to ask yourself where the rule came from that in order to feel at home in this new fabrication they will be wanting to call *I*, they must first do battle against their progenitor. One day their arms are locked around your neck, they are swinging off you as if you were the kitchen door, and the next thing you know you are the enemy that just walked through it. And then nothing you can say or do is right. Your life with them it would seem has been from the outset a fabric of lies and abuse, and the symptoms of this fact they find in every gesture and word from you: you have become the living sign of all that must be rejected if life—the life of *I*—is to be lived.

Little do they know. That it is not so easy. That the terms were set long ago. That No might as well be Yes when the question remains the same. That no one can love herself more than she can love her greatest enemy.

Reflecting, he had turned from the water pouring over the dam to the longer grass among the aspens that ringed the cropped slope, and he was poking around in there the way he used to do when they were tired of each other, while she waded or napped or played with her dolls. He knew of course what he was after: the sweet garbage of love. The stained underpants, yellowed condoms, pink pages torn from magazines (sun-faded, rain-puckered, losing their surfaces in furred white strips and splotches when separated), empty mickeys of Kahlua (sedative of choice among the fair), crusted tissues, weather-blackened tampons, laddered nylons, all of it. And as he scuffed and poked he knew that what he sought here was the stuff itself of youth, the raw material and the effluence together of that perplexed manufacture of *I*, and as he searched, the whole array of it came back fondly to mind.

The carnal litter. Squalor in the grass.

Now, some have warned that a man's religion is what he does when he is alone, while others, less concerned for his soul than his genius for venereal contagion, have encouraged him at such times to be as nasty as he pleases. And yet on this occasion it was a little like the preacher who speaks gravely of all lost for a single night of passion, who does not understand that it was hardly passion, that passion, though in his imagination it may be common as dirt, in the real world is rarer than diamonds. Because no one was thinking of this. No one imagined shit-smeared newspaper, crumpled beer cans, disposed diapers heavy with their load, syringes, small broken-tined white plastic forks with moss in their hollows, cigarette packs, algaed rye bottles, Blizzard cups—

Nights of passion at the old Coppice Dam no more, it would seem. Unless of course memory had consolidated infrequent and disparate tokens misleadingly, as men will combine former glimpses of a hundred women to create a single stirring paragon. Or was it the case—and those blonde pigtails rose again, slow-pistoning—that for the man of true understanding it is more than the rubbing and the mouthing, it is romance itself that must be surrendered to the slapheads? Not their brainpans but that whole pleasing illusion exploded? And this absence of love-refuse here this summer morning was simply a further sign. As was the extraordinary softness of the weight in his hand.

It did seem so. And yet this too was surely important to know. Useful information for the traveller, and as he went stiff-legged to tuck himself in he lifted and turned his head at last to look about him, for he also did now know where he was. Knew perfectly. And he took the rising path that opened eventually into the power-line cut, which he followed to where the road reentered it, staying from that point just inside the woods, retracing his own steps from the predawn, when he had missed Cardinalis, should have crossed earlier to the other side, since of course the lake was south of the cut, not north, as he had known. And what was this but more twisting and darkness, and he wondered if all along he had intended unwittingly to visit the old dam, and what other hidden determinations, memories, and fears infected his actions even now? And what if the mind's eye, however trenchant, could not see where it was that it could not see? What if absence of information failed to be information, and yet what was not known could operate no less? Or for that reason all the more? How then could a man know with any certainty what he was doing or about to do? And did this mean his life might be little more than an ignorant participation in some unknown bastard's march to Hell?

When he saw the car parked at the far side of the cut at the top of the hill he knew it from the courthouse parking lot, as remarked by Crooked Hand, who had seen it first arrive in town last month. He himself last night had only missed it on account of darkness. He crossed the cut in open view. As he passed the car he glanced briefly through the dusty windows into the back seat, strewn with books and papers. Now, who but a reporter would drive a car full of books and papers? And then he was reentering the woods on that side, starting down the hill through the maple saplings that grew there at the edge of the cut as a result of recent logging through the area.

RECLAIMED

Timothy Wakelin wandered out dream-tossed into the grey light of four a.m. At least up here he had his unconscious back, ready or not. Nights, anyway. A sound from the woods like a time signal was not what had kept him awake most of this one, but once it started it kept him awake the rest of it. Half asleep, he was walking down the edge of the dock when he lost his balance and fell in. The water was not cold, but it turned his clothes against him: tremendous weights, intent on the bottom. He fought their drag and hauled himself out, tottering until he got his balance. Stripped off and went to find a towel.

Later he took a mug of coffee down to the dock, this time naked, this time stepping carefully. Alone again. Caroline had gone to visit her mother. Refused to let him go along. Declined the use of his car.

It was overcast, a gunmetal drop-ceiling not there in the night. Overcast and very still. Who knew the time? Where beyond that iron roof was the sun? He sat in one of the chairs and drank coffee. Occasionally he slapped a mosquito or blackfly, the towel draped over his shoulders. Was Caroline Troyer coming back? That would probably depend on what she found when she got to Grant. But maybe it wouldn't. She hadn't actually said. Maybe it was understood, and he was a fool even to doubt it. Maybe she assumed she was but didn't want him disappointed in case for some unforeseeable reason she couldn't, and that was why she hadn't said.

Or maybe it was out of the question, more of his old solipsism.

Out in the bay two loons were engaged in a diving demonstration for the benefit of their fledgling, an improbable dirt-coloured fuzzball with a marginal attention span. No wonder that nervous scissoring of the loon-parent beaks with terrific ululations of anxiety and spooked horror like the cries of human souls gone mad with terror and crazed grieving. By mid-November this little guy had to be ready to fly out to the Eastern seaboard.

How could Caroline Troyer have become the touchstone of his world? No. That wasn't the question. The question was, Why couldn't he simply open up his heart to the light of her? Why against all understanding this compulsion to abash himself trying to possess?

After a while it came to Wakelin that he truly was alone here. This whole bay could have been his own room.

He left the dock. A few minutes later he was back, crouched naked over the denim bag of Jane's things, and whether this was in a spirit of devotion or prurience, it would have been difficult, at first anyway, for the casual viewer to say.

Caroline Troyer in her own bed once again. From the street, familiar sounds in familiar sequence. Most of the pickups she knew by the tenor of their engines and so knew the hour. Half past midnight. The lull before the hotel exodus. On the walls and ceiling of her room the coloured shadows of the traffic lights in double, in overlap. In eternal sequence changing, unchanging.

She couldn't sleep. She listened to the street, to the rasp of the curtains. To her mother climbing unsteadily to bed.

Watched her thoughts return again and again to her mother in her sightlessness, to Wakelin lost, to her father unbounded. Watched them all, each as it came up, each anxious thought. Watched each rise clear of the falling husk of its origination and in the moment of seeing it released all claim upon it to watch it too fall away. In the same way she watched the next and did not enter into and go with those serial fabrications of how things ought to have been and so might one day be, with her mother, with Wakelin, with her father, and so with herself. She did not place her faith in these solutions, which would have been to behave as if what happened were by its nature a problem and nothing more. Instead she watched them come up, all thoughts afterthoughts after all, and her mind instead of seeking deliverance in those mechanical hopes stayed with them in their recurrence and attended instead to the structures made by the repetitions themselves, complex machines running in old channels of fear and desire, attended to those structures as to the fact of the matter. And so, as the mind attended, thought quieted, and as it quieted it slowed, the way the body of an animal will slow as it watches something new.

Quieted and intervaled, the intervals widening. Stately fissures of light in the body of thinking.

Eventually she slept. Still watching. At four a.m. by the bedside clock, awoke. A dream of the eye, the pupil dilating, no retraction, the light increasing.

Sat up to radiance. To illumination of faculties.

In a ragged T-shirt, wrists on her knees.

For two hours, ecstatic fire.

Wakelin did not see Ross Troyer standing on the dock until he was pulling himself out of the water and the top of his head made contact with the rubber camouflage trousers above the black boots scuffed like battle boots planted next to the denim bag amidst the scatter of sheer nylon and black silk. In his amazement Wakelin fell back in to tread water, looking up at Troyer who held a rifle in his right hand and was outfitted entirely in that camouflage gear, rubber, it did seem to be rubber, the jacket open on a green wool shirt. High against the grey sky he looked ten years older than Wakelin remembered him, the great round face tipped querying above the narrow frame, the long hair greasy, tucked behind the ears. Davy Crockett from an alien solar system. The face stubbled and scarred and soiled, the left cheek and temple a welter of fine scratches, the skin sunk to darkness around the eyes. A lost eerie presence as of a wraith's or other scarcely material entity's. A certain bloodlessness. His facial expression in the gaunt composure of a saint's, but out of what faith? Those eyes, those pale green death-rods, at the same time raging and dead, dubious sowers of devotion. God preserve us from the followers of this one.

"You really startled me," gasped Wakelin, familiar with shock. He hauled himself out of the water and snatched a towel from the back of a dock chair. On automatic, here. Just brazening through.

"Did I catch you at a bad time?" Troyer said.

"She died," Wakelin replied, touching the bag with a toe. "My wife." As if she were inside. As if this were information with extenuating force.

Troyer looked at the bag and then at Wakelin, who continued towelling vigorously, the guy at the next locker.

"Listen," Wakelin said. "Would you like some breakfast?" And he thought, This is the price of brazening. Impetuous hospitality. Panic largesse.

There was nothing in Troyer's eyes appropriate to Wakelin's or any other civilized invitation. But he seemed to nod.

"Great!" Wakelin cried, and like a man with a key in his back he scooped the underwear into the denim bag and sprinted the dock and up to the cabin, where he threw the bag under the bed and put his own clothes on and was in the kitchen making fresh coffee and cooking bacon and eggs and toasting bread on the stove top before, from the other room, he heard the scrape of a chair.

After a couple of minutes his guest said, "What happened to your windows?"

"A bear got in. I haven't had a chance to—" Why don't I just run? Wakelin wondered. Is it because I'll get my head blown off?

"Here you go," he said, setting down a mug of coffee on the table in front of his guest. "Milk?"

"No milk." Troyer's large hand closed around the mug.

Wakelin looked at Troyer's rifle, which was leaning against the wall by his chair. He saw now too the hunting knife on Troyer's belt. A serious knife. The handle worn from use. When Wakelin stepped back into the kitchen, he held his hands before his face and they were shaking.

A few minutes later he had finished setting Troyer's breakfast in front of him. He stood looking to see if he had forgotten anything.

Troyer tipped a filthy palm toward the chair opposite.

"I ate," Wakelin said quickly, though he hadn't. Could not imagine it now. Not with his stomach in his throat. But he sat down. Jumped up to get himself a coffee and came back and sat down again.

Methodically Troyer was slitting the yolks and spreading them across the surfaces of the whites. He did this without looking at Wakelin. The face tipped over the plate seemed as large as the plate, the wolf eyes emptied to nothing. He went on spreading the yolks. Molten amber. Wakelin kept looking away, then sneaking glances. He wondered if Troyer's were also wolf ears. If they could hear the pounding of his heart. And he understood how easy it must have been for the ancient Greeks to place the mind in the breast. Because at this moment his head was nothing but a clearing house for his eyes, whereas in his breast he was completely out of control.

"How's the story coming?" Troyer asked, still spreading yolks. A man keeping alive a conversation as he prepared to eat.

"What story?"

The eyes came up. "I thought you were a journalist. Writing a story."

"Not me."

The eyes stayed with Wakelin's face.

"Honest," Wakelin said and shrugged.

The eyes returned to the spreading of the yolks.

"What'd she show you?" Troyer said. He was cutting bacon into squares.

Wakelin told him about the barn of a place with the view of Grant but no water and about the home for hydrocephalics next to the gravel pit. He couldn't remember names or locations, but Troyer nodded in a way that indicated he was familiar with these properties and that Wakelin may or may not have been wise to put them behind him.

"What'd you pay for this place?" he said.

Wakelin told him.

Troyer made no response.

"Too much, was it?" Wakelin said.

"It'll be worth what it's worth to you. I wouldn't waste time on regrets."

"Or trips to the bank machine," Wakelin said. "I have no idea what it's worth to me. But whether or not I could ever get what I paid for it is probably going to affect how I feel about what I paid."

Again Troyer did not reply. He was using his knife and fork to slice his toast.

Wakelin watched this curious operation.

"That's your car up the hill?" Troyer said, reaching for his mug.

Wakelin said it was. He told Troyer he was sorry about his truck.

The mug stopped on its way to Troyer's mouth. "Right," he said. "What happened there?" He set down the mug.

Wakelin was starting to explain when Troyer said, "You know, her mother and I haven't seen her since she drove off with you."

Wakelin sat back in his chair. "But why not?"

"She's an impressionable girl."

"I don't think I made much of an impression," Wakelin said. He indicated Troyer's rifle. "You were out hunting and just dropped in, or you came straight here for her?"

Troyer's eyes passed down the length of Wakelin's gaze. They seemed surprised to reach a rifle at the end of it.

"We—I heard some shots," Wakelin said. "Yesterday morning—"

"Wouldn't be me. Nothing left to shoot around here since they took the bounty off the wolves." Saying this, Troyer reached over and lifted the rifle into the air and laid it on the table between them, a shocking act. "She hasn't been through, then?"

Wakelin could see the black circle at the tip of the barrel, though from where he sat it was more an ellipse. The smallness of it was astonishing to him. And then he noticed that the hand he had left lying casually on the table was trembling, badly. He dropped it into his lap.

He told Troyer his daughter had stayed three nights.

Troyer's eyes went to his plate. There with his knife he straightened a piece of bacon. When his eyes came up he said, "How's she doing?"

"Fine."

"Why'd she come here?"

"That's an awkward question."

"You're not going to tell me sex."

"No—not sex. Refuge."

"From what?"

"You."

"Ah." Troyer laid down his knife and fork, side by side, to the right of his plate. "What do you make of her?"

"I've never met anybody like her."

238

"How's that?"

"I can't express it. It's like finally here's somebody using her mind for what minds must have been designed for. I don't know what that is. Perception? You know what it feels like? Weather. Spiritual weather."

"Do you believe she can heal?"

"I wouldn't be surprised. Amazed but not surprised. And you? Do you believe?"

Troyer leaned forward. "She's my daughter. I don't need to believe. You people should leave her alone."

Wakelin raised his hands, disclaiming.

Still leaning forward in his chair, Troyer brought his right hand up out of a side pocket of his jacket and placed on the table between them a wreck or lump of cloth, like something shaped from a brown rag or old hand towel. But it wasn't that, it was a small stuffed animal. A bear.

When Wakelin looked from this to Troyer, the man was watching him, his hand on the bear.

For her scent, Wakelin thought. "Where's your tracker dog?"

Troyer just stared at him. And then he said, "Where is she?"

"At home, as far as I know. Seeing her mother."

"She didn't take your car."

"No. She's not eager to drive again so soon after what happened. And she wouldn't let me take her."

"What are you talking about?"

Now Wakelin told the story of her seizure while driving the truck. As he did so Troyer nodded sleepily, as if it were the most predictable thing in the world that someone like this would tell him something so preposterous. He seemed ready to doze off from the overpowering predictableness of such behaviour on Wakelin's part. Either doze off or explode.

"She's coming back?" he said when Wakelin had finished.

"I honestly don't know. I guess we left it open."

"Maybe I'll wait."

"Make yourself at home," Wakelin said quickly. And then he said, "She's twenty years old."

"Twenty-one in October," Troyer replied. He was stroking the bear. "Twenty-one years, almost, I've known her. How long for you?"

Wakelin shook his head. He indicated Troyer's plate. "Your food's getting cold. I'm not trying to poison you."

"Why would you want to do that?"

"Let me get you some hot coffee."

"Don't worry about the coffee," Troyer said, and he took his hand from the bear to push away his plate. "I never was a big coffee drinker."

There were voices in the register and had been since early morning, unidentifiable voices, the male voice familiar although out of place and for that reason unrecognizable, but what finally woke her was something accompanying the voices and becoming stronger: a grim, swampy odour, with a fungal undersmell.

In the kitchen, sunshine was streaming through the door open on the fire escape. After the gloom of the stairs and hall and living room, the brightness continued blinding as she approached her mother, who sat at the table facing into the sun, and even as she touched her fingers to her mother's shoulder, startling her, she could barely make out who it was there talking to her as he stood at the stove, stirring a pot.

"What the *hell* are you doing sneaking up like that?" Ardis cried. "I nearly dropped my cigarette!"

"What's he doing?"

"Ask him." Ardis half-turned to the one at the stove. "Tell her what you're cooking up, there, Medicine Man."

Bachelor Crooked Hand looked around at Caroline and nodded. He turned back to the stove.

"Eye remedy," Ardis said.

Caroline opened the fridge and saw that her mother had not been exaggerating last night about local sympathy. Shelves groaning condolence.

"You'd think somebody'd died," Ardis said. "Why don't *you* have a go at my peepers some time? Not that I can't see perfectly. Just not what's in front of me, only inside. Eye cells, brain cells, nerve cells, bone cells, some kind of cells. One minute they're blue, the next they're green. Beetle armies, all marching one way. Every once in a while they change their minds and march off in a different direction. Ginger ale's top rear left."

"I found it."

"Then close the goddamn door. We're not air-conditioning the kitchen. They're brightest in the morning. The most beautiful thing you ever saw. You've got one of your headaches again."

Caroline was pouring a glass of ginger ale. Now she stopped and looked at her mother. "How did you know?"

"Vibes!" Ardis crowed. "The old second sight's kicked back in! You lose the one, bingo!" Again she half-turned to Crooked Hand. "Hey, Medicine Man! Hold the cure!" To her daughter she said, "You're not the only member of this family with powers, you know. Some of us just never had all the advantages."

Ardis's right hand was sweeping the air in front of her. When it closed upon the bottle, she waggled it at Caroline.

Caroline refilled her mother's glass. Bright's President vermouth. She carried her ginger ale into the living room. There she lay on the chester-field and closed her eyes.

Last night such tremendous energy, tremendous intelligence, using this body. Intricate immensity of joy. No limit. Now, this morning, from the base of the spine to the skull and spreading over the brain like a cap and down the forehead and into the eyes, pain like cherry embers in a powder of ash. The brain, spine, nervous system, every vertebra and fibre and nerve an incandescent filigree of agony.

"How's the stomach?" Ardis called from the kitchen.

"Not very good."

"Did it start as soon as you laid down last night?"

"No."

"You know this is the price to be paid, don't you."

"For what?"

"For your powers. What are we talking about?"

"They're not my powers."

"Well, they're not mine. I traded mine down to a mess of pottage thirty years ago. What the hell is that, anyways? This mess you're cooking up wouldn't be pottage, would it, Medicine Man?"

A few minutes later Caroline heard her mother say more quietly. "Hon, when you get that under control, do you think you could pick me up a pack of fags?"

"Okay," Caroline said.

There was a pause.

"Not you, Dimbulb," Ardis said.

You could straighten the furniture until you made yourself crazy. Nothing you could do would make the windows fly open. You were there in the event, that was all. Awake. Not waiting, only watching. When others happened to be asleep or doing something else. Stoking the flames. Scattering their energy. Searching for beauty in other places.

"Before you go, now she's laying down," Ardis said. "Why don't you tell her how you lost your hair.

"Caroline, you don't remember his hair. He used to wear it down past his arse. He was a braided beauty in those days.

"Come on, tell her the legend. How the Brave Lost His Hair."

Footsteps descended the fire escape.

Ardis said, "It's not just him, everybody's been so sweet. People I haven't said a word to in years stop me and say hi on the street. How are you doing?"

There was no answer.

"I'm addressing my bug troops," Ardis said.

"What?"

"I said, 'How are you doing?'"

"Better."

"You don't mean all better."

"No."

After a pause Ardis said, "Just think about it. There's money in it."

"I won't do it," Caroline said.

There was a silence. A marshalling of hostility.

"Well, your evangelical phase didn't last long, did it? Two months, was it? Three? So what are we into now? A brand new hide-my-light-under-a-bushel phase? Or is it a let's-get-all-the-family-garbage-out-into-the-sun-so-it-can-really-stink-up-the-place phase? And what am I supposed to tell people? 'Oh sure, she can still heal fine, Mrs. Coopersmith, she just doesn't feel like it any more. By the way, she said to tell you little Danny can stick his heart condition up his rectal pore for all she cares. Oh, yes, she's still talking to God. No, she'd rather not tell anybody what He says. It might save a few lives around here.'

"Who knows, it could even save this family. I don't know what else is supposed to do it. Whatever your father'll be up to when he's not being hounded through the bush by packs of trigger-happy yokels hiding behind badges, it won't be selling houses. And when was the last time you saw a white-caner wait on a table? No way in hell can we expect to be back to normal soon. You know why they're giving us all this food, don't you? It's cheaper than money. We're going down fast, in pieces, just like the Titanic, and you know what we hit? You."

"Did you drop the charges?"

"The going gets tough, what does our little Queen of Heaven do? Shacks up in the woods with some cub reporter. Too bad you didn't run into your father out there. He'd have kicked your ass home fast enough. If I dropped the charges, they wouldn't be looking for him, would they?"

"What about when they find him?"

"We'll see."

"He's dangerous."

"Your father? Your father hasn't changed. Your father wouldn't hurt a fly."

"He'd shoot Keeper."

A silence.

"You don't have to get nasty," Ardis said quietly. "That was about you. He didn't intend this, any of it. This was nobody's fault except yours. Disappearing without a trace, no phone call, nothing. You know how he gets. And rightly so, as it turns out. Who trashed the truck? One thing leads to another, whatever it looks like when the shit's still in the air. This isn't the first time your father and I ever whipped ourselves over the edge, believe me. Not that you'd understand passion."

The starlings were making a racket under the eaves.

"Listen," Ardis said. "If this is about him and you back somewhere in the mists of time, I'm going to say it again: grow up. Either it happened—"

"It happened."

"Fine. It happened. The point is you survived. Hale and healthy enough to spend the rest of your life mooning around here with a chip on your shoulder the size of Labrador."

Ardis paused only briefly. "So who'd your reporter get the story from? The little girl who didn't have the wit to say no or the teen saint on a mainline to God? Stop, don't answer that. Something tells me either way there's nothing in it for anybody except you-know-who. And when I think how these perfumed magazines were ready to pay good money. Back, anyways, when you were flavour of the month.

"Aw, hell, who am I kidding. Do what you want. It's worked pretty slick for you so far. And while you're at it, why not drag everybody's name through the gutter? It's only the next logical step. You know this was your father's main concern, don't you? He couldn't have cared less about the healing, or whatever it is you claim you do. He's always said people do what they want to do and believe what they want to believe. For him, it was purely a matter of pride. He hated all this going public. Just another kick in the teeth is all it comes down to. A kick in the teeth for the people who brought you into the world and put a roof over your head and clothes on your back and a hot meal in front of you three times a day for twenty years. That's all it is."

Caroline didn't say anything.

Ardis was pouring a drink. "Shit," she said. Her chair scraped.

After a few minutes she said, "If you're wondering what I was doing just then, I was licking the table." She snorted.

Caroline heard the snap of the lighter.

"Anyways," Ardis resumed on the exhale. "I wanted him to tell you how he lost his hair. Are you still there?"

"Yes."

"You're ready for this? You're laying down?

"One day your father, who wasn't your father at the time, this was when we first started going out, he walks into my place uninvited and unannounced and comes upon me and Bachelor in a compromising position. I can't remember which one. At this distance of time I seem to recall that nothing had actually happened yet, but you don't have to believe that. I don't.

"So your father sneaks into my room and he slips the hunting knife out of Bachelor's belt, which is in his jeans on the floor alongside the bed. I hear the rustle of denim and your father's standing there with a knife in his hand. I scream.

"So there we are. The Three Stooges. Bachelor and me in the bed with the sheet pulled to our chins. Your father with Bachelor's knife.

"Bachelor, he doesn't say anything. He's watching the knife.

"Your father doesn't say anything either. He starts to unfasten his pants.

"Ross, I say, what the hell are you doing?

"He doesn't answer. It takes him forever to get them open. He's only got the one hand, the knife's in the other.

"Now, I know you don't appreciate this kind of talk, but it's material to the story. Your father takes out his cock, penis to you. It isn't hard, and it's not shrunk to a bathtub plug, with the balls pulled away up to hell and gone, the way they get when they're ready to fight. It's perfectly relaxed. I can't tell you how much that's just like your father. Anyways, the balls are hanging down twice as long as it is. Sorry to be graphic here, honey, but this is one moment that will be forever imprinted on my mind. One of the few. With his left wrist, your father pushes his cock back out of the way and with the fingers of that same hand—are you following this?—he grips the balls, he's got big balls, your father, if you haven't noticed, balls like a horse, and he pulls them downward and he holds the blade at the neck of the sac there, and he asks Bachelor if he wants them. Because they're his if he does. All Bachelor has to do is say yes. A simple nod will suffice.

"Well, no, Bachelor doesn't want them. He leaps out of bed, hair all loose—you should have seen his hair, it was like those shampoo commercials

where the model lets it fall and waggles her head and the hair ripples like oil—
and he asks your father to give him back the knife. Your father shakes his
head, very sober. He's sorry, no. He sets the knife on the dresser behind him,
and he starts to do up his pants. Bachelor takes this opportunity to jump into
his jeans. He whips the belt out of the loops and holds out it and the leather
whatchamacallit—"

"Sheath."

"Sheath, to your father, who accepts them, in a formal way. The presen-
tation of the belt and the sheath is a real little ceremony. You can see it
means a lot to both of them. You have to hate that about men. You didn't
know that knife used to be Bachelor's, did you?"

"No."

"Well, that's it. Bachelor hightails it home. Your father, he takes it out
on me a certain amount, takes the belt out, you could say, but I got used
to that. Used to it, hell. And look where that's got me. But never mind."

"What about Bachelor's hair?" Caroline said.

"Bachelor's hair." Ardis took a drink. "Next morning Bachelor wakes up
and it's pretty well gone. He can hardly see the sheets. By the end of the week
there's nothing left. Eyelashes, eyebrows, the works. All lost. Because of me.

"I felt like Delilah. You can't tell me a woman doesn't owe a man after
something like that. And, you know, if this eye brew of his works, I'm going
to owe Bachelor Crooked Hand until the day I die. I won't have enough
years left to pay back what I'm going to owe that red bastard."

"Bachelor loves you," Caroline said.

"Maybe Bachelor loves me. Or maybe he got stuck. But let's say he does
owe me—whups, my foolish tongue. Love me. Or let's say everybody in
love is stuck. . . . What am I trying to—? I'm trying to say I just wish for
once I could believe I deserved a whole lifetime of somebody's love. It's like
a truckload of chocolate backed up to your mouth. It's too weird. It's too
much. In the old days I'd be dead twenty years ago in childbirth and this
situation would never have come up. Your father could have bagged some
little airhead homebody to look out for you, and we'd all have been a good
ways better off."

"Everybody deserves as much love as there is in the world," Caroline said.

A silence followed this observation. Very quietly then, Ardis said, "No, everybody does not deserve as much love as there is in the world. Whatever the hell that idiot pronouncement is supposed to mean. Most people don't know how the hell to deal with the scraps that do come their way. For most people, love is the one thing that makes them ready to kill. Trying and failing, trying and failing, to believe how it could have anything to do with them and not be just a piece of dangerous insanity from some worthless fool."

"Bachelor's not a fool," Caroline said.

"No, but he's an Indian."

"You don't mean that."

"Oh, I don't mean that! You know what I mean now! Well, thank the Christ! Finally! Even when to anybody else on the face of the earth what I just said is perfectly clear, you know what I mean! Of course, I keep forgetting you're fresh back from fine-tuning your sensitivity skills in spill-all sessions around the campfire with your cub reporter. 'Yes, uh-huh. Oh, my gosh, Caroline. And what did he do next to your little rosebud?' You didn't happen to notice by any chance what the hand in his pants was up to?"

This question being met with no response, Ardis seemed to reflect. Finally, in a voice of weary disappointment, she said, "Ah Christ, I must be crazy trying to talk to you about anything halfways important. It's like trying to carry on an intelligent conversation with a five-year-old. What'd your father really do? Freeze you in time? When the hell are you going to grow up? When are you going to pull your head out of your ass long enough to look at the world for once? And while you're at it—here's an idea—why don't you take a few good big cocks up there? More important, why don't you learn to want them up there again, I mean, want them up there so bad you can't see straight? Then maybe you'd have some clue what real people are talking about when they talk about deserving and not deserving and about love and not love. Christ, you make me want to puke sometimes—"

Here Ardis lapsed into quiet weeping.

Caroline took a drink of ginger ale.

"God," Ardis sobbed. "I knew you were vicious, but I can't believe you'd taunt me about poor Keeper."

The weeping continued. When it grew clamorous, Caroline started to get up to go to her mother, but Ardis must have heard the creak of the chester-field because like a wolf at its kill she snarled, "Don't you fucking dare."

Wakelin locked the door and the window and took off his clothes and slipped into the narrow bed. He was still shaking.

What was he doing? He put his clothes on again. Opened the window opposite the one he had boarded up the other day to keep the mosquitoes from Caroline Troyer, in her state. What a long time ago that now seemed. Could this be the same space? What a lost unfinished little fellow he was back then. How moving, how disconcerting, how strange, how unlikely, to have been witness to something like that. It was not to be believed, was it?

Who—or what—was Caroline Troyer?

When she left to see her mother yesterday he'd gone with her through the woods to the power line, where, as she was walking away, he said, "Some time I'd like to know what it would be like to have just a tiny fraction of your faith."

She stopped and looked around at him. She shook her head.

"You had faith in me," he said.

"That wasn't faith."

"What was it?"

But she declined that one, and all he could do was stand and watch until the road took her back into the trees.

Now he shifted the table away from the window and set up the chair directly under it, his ear to the screen. Listened.

For footsteps. For snoring. For anything. Heard silence. Bullfrogs kept starting up, loath. Reluctant croakers. Every once in a while, from the water, a plop. From the woods, random snaps of twigs. Suddenly, yards away, among the boulders of the shore, a long, phlegmy hiss, very threatening. And another.

Mink? Marten? Raccoon? Who knew? Not Wakelin.

No further sound. It was hardly past two. Night of ink.

He waited.

At three he eased out of the cabin. No moon, no stars. Crept around the front and started west along the shore. A soft night, air pitchy. Darkness swelling to fill the eye. Along here the path was old growth, broad and moose-travelled. In daylight a lakeshore forest thoroughfare, tonight uncertain. Vistas truncate and shifting. Half imagination. When he reached the deeper shadow of a great hemlock brought down by the recent winds—utter black in that darkness, a horizontal band, like a wall—a second, vertical shadow, to the left, the shadow of the jagged stump of it, seemed to shift, and nervous Wakelin went tripping over a rock and collapsed into the branches of the uprooted tree, the soft undead needles. Lay there, breathing hard. Trembling.

He should have eaten more today. Troyer wasn't stopping him. All Troyer did was sit on the dock. At lunchtime Wakelin took him out a sandwich, but Troyer after gazing at it too long put the plate by his chair. Later Wakelin took it away. Troyer was still sitting on the dock. He was facing the channel to the main lake, a man watching a door. When the light began to fade and the bugs grew bad he came up to the main cabin, to sit at his former place, with his rifle against the wall as before, the stuffed bear on the table, his hand on the bear.

For Wakelin, there was no question of cooking his guest an evening meal. He did not even rouse himself to light the lamps. He himself had no appetite, was too unnerved by having spent a whole day alone in the man's company. Two or three times, in an attempt to break the silence, he had said something, and as soon as the eyes located him in the gloom Troyer seemed to need to remember who or what was this latest source of annoyance, and when he had done so he felt around behind him for his rifle, and though he didn't lift it onto the table, only seemed to assure himself it was there, Wakelin, on the bed pretending to read, would brace himself to die. Until the eyes, the mouth having given no response, moved away. He was not exactly a demanding guest, Ross Troyer, but neither was he an easy one. That conversation at breakfast now seemed the tip of a fresh-calved ice-chunk of will to communication on Troyer's part, an ice-chunk dissolved since, in darker, hotter seas of concern.

At one point Wakelin—after rehearsing the words so long before they left his mouth that when they did they sounded like something in a foreign tongue—at one point he said, "Did you find that on your walk here?"

"Find what?" Troyer said, after a long time.

"The thing under your hand."

Troyer lifted his hand and looked at the bear. Then at Wakelin.

"No," Troyer said.

"It's hers, then."

"Hers."

"Caroline's."

Again for a good while Troyer made no response. And then, soft as a church counsellor, he said, "If I ever hear you say my daughter's name again, I don't care if it's in your sleep, I'll kill you."

These words froze Wakelin in terror where he lay.

At nightfall, without a glance in Wakelin's direction, Troyer rose from the table and went back down to the dock. An opportunity Wakelin took to pretend to go to bed. Shut himself up in the plywood cabin where he understood as soon as he had put his clothes back on that already he had no idea where Troyer was. Maybe on the dock, maybe up at the other cabin, maybe standing with his right ear pressed to the wall alongside the window screen that Wakelin had his left ear pressed to.

Wakelin snuck out, shaking, at three a.m.

The click of a flashlight.

Oh Jesus I'll be shot and Wakelin threw himself off the hemlock, which lit up. Clambered to go staggering through saplings chest-high, grazing trees. The light swung away. Swung back. Forearms upraised, Wakelin, crouching now, went on staggering blind. A sway of shadows, then stumbling darkness. A fallen trunk slammed the front of his thighs and flipped him into a criss-cross of boles, dead branches stabbing upward in a commotion of ascent, and he was spiked in air, blood in his eyes. Light sweeping back and forth behind him. Below, a gully or ravine he had not known was here. And just around the corner from his own place, too. When he shifted he suffered a fall, not long but bruising. Scrambled steeply downward, to a stream. Not the one he usually followed on his way down the hill but a lesser he'd been crossing closer to his property as he came along the shore from the west. A vein of rocks stone-dry until the recent rains. He ran stooped, pursuing its course upward, through bouldered ground. What a scuffling racket he was making. When the rocks of the streambed before him lit up, he sank down among ferns.

No light now. The rasp of his own breath. Periodic crack of branches. Higher up and behind, in a hunter's circumspection of advance.

Ross Troyer returned to the window of the plywood cabin and looked inside. He tried the door. It opened. He played the beam of the flashlight in there. When he stepped in he could smell her. He could smell naphthalene, and he could smell the reporter, his fear, but mainly he could smell her, a scent of blood and ozone. He sat on the edge of the bed and pressed the heels of his hands against his eyes.

He sat like that for a long time.

When he stood up it was morning. He descended the cabin stairs and looked again down the grey path west along the shore, the path the yahoo had taken before he crashed off into the bush. So much for his word.

Troyer circled behind the main cabin and down onto its open porch, the roof of which was so low it was necessary to stoop.

Back in front of the cabins again he drew his fingers through the dew beaded heavy on the bottom of the upturned canoe, then walked out onto the dock and surveyed the wall of whiteness the bay was now, the water invisible, so richly steaming. He looked down when he heard the strange sound. The water had crept over the surface of the dock and was kissing at the soles of his boots.

Wakelin ate berries he picked in patches flush with bears. Enormous rustlings. As he picked, his peripheral vision was a rush hour in black and cinnamon. When he lifted his eyes from picking he continued to see small suns of blue or red floating and jerking in the trees. He ate berries in a dull ache of fear and bug-slapping until his shit was wet and purple and seed-filled and could have been a bear's. Wiped himself with a leaf and trudged on.

The first day he heard gunshots, quite a few. They seemed to come from the direction of his cabins, though he could not be certain of this, being no more certain of the direction he had come than of the one he was headed. He did not turn around and walk toward the shots. He did not want to see Ross Troyer again. Not out here. He also did not want to be shot for a deer by a party of drunken hunters. But it wasn't deer season, was it? For a bear, then. He did not want to be shot for a bear. He imagined he was looping around from the southeast, heading north to meet the power-line road, which he would walk to his car. Taking care that Troyer was not waiting at it. Or had some of those shots been him blowing out the tires? He kept on looping. It seemed to be an awful long way to the road.

On the second day he might have heard shots again but was no longer all that sure what he was hearing.

Both days were warm, the nights cool. There was no more rain. Not too many bugs.

He was pleased he'd worn his wool jacket. Hiking boots. What more did he want?

Starch. Protein. Matches. Knife. Blankets. Tent. Compass.

Any human sign. Jets overhead weren't enough. Something here below.

Jets overhead said this could be a walk in the woods. A walk out. It didn't seem to be. But any time now. Surely.

Wakelin moved slowly through days on the far side now of the cobalt poise of high summer. No longer cicadas ratcheting heat and repose. The rock still held the warmth, but time was in motion again. The breezes died only in the depths of the night and at the changeovers, at dawn and dusk. Time was in motion, but in fits and starts, without pretence of uniform flow. It wasn't long at all before Wakelin had no idea when exactly it was he had spent that first night quaking inside a spittoon of rock, where in every twig-snap had been the fatal approach.

Wakelin moved slowly, but sometimes recklessness took over. One moment he'd be trudging along, the next—sweating, mouth dry—crashing and floundering like a fly-maddened moose. The right way doesn't seem to be working, so let's do everything wrong. Lunge and bolt until we're squelching into bog or corralled by rock or pierced to a halt by dead grey branches of cedar. Until we're forced to backtrack and lean on something and get our breath back. Check for fresh cuts. New rips in our clothing.

On the third day, as Wakelin slumped against a boulder the colour of modelling clay, a young fox walked into his leg and fell back amazed. Various moose and deer, in states of unobservance as profound as his own and the fox's, had been similarly shocked to come upon him. He was downwind or there was no wind and these were creatures of scent, but were they nearsighted and deaf? Their minds on something else, obviously. Narratives olfactory? He wondered. The raccoons and foxes in particular but even the weasels speed-limping past appeared more bemused than anything. Even the deer, and certainly the moose, forest locomotives, seemed abstracted from life. Animal attention fleeting, despite the hype, which had minimally to do with its subject and everything to do with human guilt, human arrogance.

Another day, as Wakelin was passing under a porcupine hanging slothlike from the lower branch of a young maple, the creature lowered a gummy red eye to regard him, upside down. Raised it to resume its thorny reflexion.

Wakelin kept walking. No sense of where. But a good long way yet from club-
bing down a porcupine and drinking its blood. A good long way yet from
abjuring all foolish hope. For four days Wakelin peered to the canopy for any
thinning of its crown beyond the high ring of non-horizon, imagining that
next time he would emerge into the power line. Ah, so this is where it's been
all the time! Imagining wires. Again and again he came to deadfall, beaver
meadow, pond, swamp. A lake would promise canoeists, but in this land of
lakes he could not find a lake. Understood how rash it is to head for every
imagined goal in no constant direction and kept doing it. When he came to
streams he hiked up them away from Cardinalis Bay, or so he imagined,
toward the higher ground of the power line, except that the power line was
never there. For one whole day he expected at any moment to come upon
the former logging road that ran along the south end of the lake, a new goal
decided unnoticed by some interior vane whipped from north to south by
pure desire. That night he bolted up drenched in terror from shivering sleep,
scattering boughs. Gasped squatting in the black air to shit berry juice. He
would fail in his own way, was that the arrangement? If not himself alone the
saviour of himself, then he would not be saved?

A static dawn. Sky the blue-watery grey of skim milk. Was he feverish? All
directions now one to Wakelin. According to the moss on the trees, north
lay in a proliferation of 270 degrees. Through certain tracts of this forest,
moss was as scarce as cactus or palm. Otherwise, reading the green stain
was like reading a clockface from a state of mental blindness. Brain of
Teflon. He kept walking.

Suddenly, at last, Wakelin found himself in a place he seemed to know.
A former log-sort clearing at the southeast corner of Cardinalis. He had
seen it in the aerial photographs. Half a mile he had travelled in four days.
Probably walking fifteen or twenty. The scenic route. Still, that initial fine
weather early in the day—what day? yesterday?—must have been a sign.
With all evidence to the contrary, the world was, finally, a benign propo-
sition. The old hope, the one behind them all.

He sank down on a mild shale slope, triggering a slide. A chain of small reprises. Domino-clattering. He would rest a moment at the bottom here and then he would step along to the shore, as any weekend hiker might. From where he sat he could see the milky silver gleam through the trees. Reflected light off the water. He would follow the shore westward and later he would follow it north. A hard trek, for the west shore was rock bluffs, he knew that, and where it was not bluffs it was muck and brush, but he would know where he was, for the lake would be at his right hand. He would come to the power-line road before nightfall and two or three hours later he would be in Coppice. If a truck stopped for him, which it would, he could be in Coppice in twenty minutes.

And he could hear the hollow throttle of that imaginary truck now, the rattle of heavy equipment in its bed. Suspension bottoming in the potholes. He turned his ear the better to hear it, the beautiful imaginary sound, and that was how he came to notice the cairn, behind and above him, on a summit of grey-white rock, brown- and orange-lichened and motley with archipelagoes of thick-piled, viridescent moss. He waded the shale slope he had just slid down. Climbed diagonally to that firmer surface. Reached the cairn and knelt in the deep moss on the lower side of it. The moss was flecked yellow and scarlet with flowers like micro-snapdragons. His hands moved out to cup the space of the cairn—slate chunks in a small cone— as they would a fire. The warmth of a human sign.

It was while he was in that posture that Wakelin's mind rose clear of its recent dream state of famished trudging, and as his mind came up it opened out into perception, and below it like a landscape seen from a prospect was the commotion that passed with him for thought out here, this frightened and regretful head-noise as inexorable in its march as these tracts of forest passing under his boots, as insistent and unvanquishable as these endless implacable trees. And the commotion that was not about Caroline Troyer was about Jane, and maybe it was Caroline Troyer's refusal to be assimilated by his understanding, but at this moment he knew that Jane was as intimate to himself as this head-noise, and yet it had never been her. In life she had been, as surely as Caroline Troyer, someone other than him (incredible as that had always seemed), and this commotion was really only himself, now in his loss. Formerly in his desire. And he had never really got it. That all Jane's unhappy behaviour was grounded in a reality beyond what it meant or did not mean to his own happiness. And this did not mean that his willingness endlessly to absolve, in loving solidarity to be unhappy too, to cherish her, was above it all, nor was it enough, nor was it in any way innocent or unrelated to the problem of her suffering. And if he wanted to know her in the only way that was now possible, the way she now existed, which was in his memory and in his behaviour, then he would need to keep in view the fact that beyond this commotion there really had been another. An actual, separate person. As actual and separate as Caroline Troyer, or as anyone else. Even if she had been the bride of his life. Whom he had loved. And lusted after. And feared. And hated. And walked out on a thousand times in his heart. While staying grimly at her side. And served an ignorant blind part in the destruction of. And all the rest of it. All the hellish misery of the rest of it.

A woman once as real as this forest. Still as real as this commotion. With him, a part of him, until he died. But not her. She was gone.

Shakily—how long had he been sitting here?—Wakelin rose to his pins. Stepped sinking and sliding back down the spill of shale into raspberry bushes. Held his arms high and pushed through their multiple small catches. Reentered the trees under a giant ironwood, thinking, Awful big for an ironwood, although, as he next thought, he had no idea how big ironwoods grow, nor did he know what kind of tree that actually was, an ancient white cedar, to judge from the trunk alone, and then he was down among balsams—he thought they were balsams—and the balsams gave way to other cedars, red cedars, that he had not remembered. He kept walking. Why was it so dark? His answer came at a quartz vein possibly eight feet high. Still trying so hard to see that field of dull whiteness as dead-calm water under a grey sky that in order to know what he actually saw he found it necessary to reach out and touch his fingers to the hard white facets. And then he sank onto his haunches to rock heel to toe there, to rock and moan.

On Wednesday Clarice Heinrichs got in late from showing a property and missed her husband's call.

He left a message: "Hi, it's me. I'll call tomorrow. No. Back tomorrow. Love ya. Bye."

When he arrived at eight the next night she told him she'd seen Caroline Troyer at the property she'd sold on Cardinalis.

"When was this?" he asked quickly.

"Monday," she lied, to avoid another lie about why she hadn't told him sooner.

"What were you doing out there on Monday?"

"Taking him the counteroffer."

"How'd you get in?"

"Through the woods—Why?" Oh, what tangled webs. Now she couldn't tell him about the canoe until the next time he wandered out to the shed and came back pale and trembly.

"What's he doing in there already?"

"I gave him the keys."

"It's not his place yet."

"I know that. It will be."

Walter Heinrichs shook his head. And then he said, "I can't interfere."

"What? Walter, the man is charged with resisting arrest! It was your warrant!"

"That's why I can't interfere. You tell them. You saw her. I don't know why you didn't tell them Monday."

And so it was Clarice who got on the phone to the police and told them that if they were still looking for Ross Troyer, they might want to check the cabins over on Cardinalis Bay because she'd seen the daughter there.

"When was this?" Elvin Hryniuk asked her.

"Today," Clarice said. And then she looked up and saw her husband watching her from across the room. "Oh, *see* her?" she said. "Monday. I saw her Monday."

"Well, I saw her today," Elvin said. "At the 7-Eleven, there. She's back at her mother's. On the main street—you know where they live."

"Today?" Clarice said dumbly.

"If she was in at Cardinalis," Elvin said, "she's back now."

"Elvin, could you talk to her? Could you ask her if she thinks you should check out those cabins?"

"Sure, I guess," he said. "If you want, Mrs. Heinrichs. I could ask her tonight. If she says check them out, we'll check them out. The sarge could send a couple of the boys in there tomorrow."

"Thank you," Clarice said. "She won't lie to you."

"I know that," Elvin said.

The next morning two officers left their cruiser parked on the power line and set out into the woods in the direction of Wakelin's cabins on Cardinalis Bay but got lost. Two hours later they reemerged into the cut and walked back to the cruiser. While eating their sandwiches they radioed the desk, which gave them hell. After lunch they tried again, this time did not get lost, exactly. After some difficulty they found Cardinalis but failed to locate Wakelin's cabins. Then they drove back to town.

Five hours later the next shift coasted down off the power-line road and came to rest in the centre of the clearing at the Cardinalis landing, the lake somewhere in the darkness ahead. A gleamless night. Low talk from the cruiser, eventually soft snores.

The next morning the young trapper whose section included Upper and Lower Cardinalis led the same two officers who twice the day previous had failed to find them, directly to Wakelin's cabins. No sign of Troyer, who had fled on foot, or so it was reported. Of Wakelin, no trace.

The afternoon of the next day the sergeant at the station south of Coppice on Highway 63 refused to allow Caroline Troyer to visit Wakelin's cabins. Later when a police clerk called back to request a piece of footwear recently worn by her father, she said that the reason it had taken her so long to come to the phone was that she had been out back helping Bachelor Crooked Hand keep an eye on a bonfire her mother had wanted made of her father's personal effects. The sergeant arranged to have her picked up in Grant and taken in to Wakelin's cabins by boat, a wingtip of her father's in an IGA bag on her lap. As she stepped onto the dock she handed the bag to a man holding tight to the collar of a German shepherd wagging wildly to see her and turned to the beef-fed young officer standing looking at her to inform him that there had been a canoe, which she described.

Later that afternoon the dog located a scent at a portage site at the south end of the lake. A logging road had once run along there. An officer followed the tracker and the German shepherd west on the level grass path that the road had become, while back on the bay the officer who had taken Caroline Troyer in to the cabins by boat walked with her the route she believed Wakelin would have followed to the top of the hill had he tried to reach his car (now iron-booted). They found nothing.

Neither was Troyer overtaken by his pursuers. But three-quarters of a mile down Cardinalis Creek, where the going became more difficult, the men entered a space of dire stench a minute or so before they came upon an extraordinary sight: a parliament of turkey vultures neck deep in the carcass of some great animal. As the men approached, the vultures lifted their featherless gore-gobbed heads like a single creature adjusting multiple profiles, blinking blood from its eyes. The only sound then, beyond growlings and hissings from a couple of the larger birds, was the buzzing of a thousand flies, until, from two hundred feet away, on the other side of the creek, the dog started to bark, and in one movement the vultures gave a great flex, hauling upward their enormous wings, which with replay slowness they thrust downward, lifting themselves into the air in a uniform silver-black fabric of feathers, which separated to large birds rising upward to the high canopy, where heavily they settled to watch.

"Would you look at that," the officer said, dropping his eyes to the blood-ribbed carcass but not approaching closer for reason of the stench. "The bastards chewed the whole damn head off. You know, they start with the eyes and work from there."

By the size as indicated by what remained of the carcass, it had to be a moose.

The tracker went to the dog. She was barking at a pile of recently cut alders close to the last of the long rapids before Lower Cardinalis. Under the alders, which were sticky with blood, the men found a canoe fitting the description that had been provided by Caroline Troyer, a lightweight ruby fibreglass model, scraped and battered. Bloodstained. A paddle and a short coil of yellow rope were stored underneath it. When the tracker looked to the dog, which had continued to bark at something high above, he saw, overhead, suspended on a length of that same yellow rope tied to its antlers and slung over the branch of a red spruce, the head of a deer. The tracker used the rope in the canoe to climb the tree to where the rope attached to the antlers had been fastened. He lowered it.

The path taken from that point by the wanted man the dog was not able to determine. Almost certainly into the creek, but where or if he had emerged to make his way by land—an almost equally difficult passage of boulder and slash—remained a mystery, and a good while before the dog would lead them as far as Lower Cardinalis, the men, by this time maddened by deerflies, turned back to meet the boat scheduled to pick them up at sunset at the south end of the upper lake.

As they made their way upstream, the officer, in his relief perhaps to be getting out of that terrain, could not stop talking. About the unusual size of the deer, which in life, he said, must have weighed four hundred pounds. The rack alone at least three feet across. The officer said that he had never seen more than two vultures in one place at the same time, let alone five. He complimented the tracker on the dog's training, that even with an aroma like that in the air she would stick to her last. Mostly, however, the officer talked about the decapitation of the deer, which he characterized as a different order of crime from what a man might commit against the person of his wife in the privacy of his own home. And he said that the only surprising thing about domestic violence is that it should issue so rarely in homicide, whereas hacking the head off a deer and hanging it from a tree by its antlers with nylon rope is a senseless and unnatural outrage committed against all God-fearing people.

In the night Wakelin slept half under an overhang of horizontally fissured granite, awoke in the predawn to serial leathery flittings in the air at his face. Awoke to scrabblings. To one after the other pointed rump in caped silhouette, entering the black profile of rock. After a while he turned his head to the side and that was when he saw, also watching the bats' return, a far more astonishing sight in this place: a cat. Silent, colourless, unmoving. The cat returned Wakelin's gaze for a short time, then swung away without sound and stepped among bracken into shadow.

Not a bobcat, too small. Wild, then? House? In Wakelin's mind's eye, there flashed a saucer of milk on a woodside back porch. *Oh, yes!* And then he thought, A hundred and fifty million years our mammal forebearers spent no bigger than house cats.

Wonder what he thought of me. The shape of things to come.

When Wakelin woke again, it was to a small puff at his chest, a nervous movement. Ochre fox-snout, black-masked eyes intent. Needle bat-teeth bared in minuscule squalling. Wet, scarlet mouth. Wakelin's body, with a mind of its own, jerked to toss the creature, which however clung to the woolly fibre of his jacket, swung round on one claw. Glanced over its winged shoulder at the flesh planet of Wakelin's face. A sober, harlequin regard. Disappointment, not unmiffed. Crawled off on legs and wing-knobs. Scuttled through the parched slippery needles and climbed the rock by Wakelin's elbow to cross the ceiling of it. The caped rump in silhouette. A clamour of mewlings. More scrabbling. The scrabbling ended. The creature recreviced against the dawn.

Later Wakelin thought, That bat. Cardinals, nuthatches, orioles, waxwings, raccoons. Why do so many in these woods go masked?

In daylight he trudged mature hardwood forest, skirted a high swale, and when the ground rose steeply he climbed, one foot in front of the other, watching the toes of his boots, imagining prospects. Pylons in majestic sweep through the trees. A particular white pine, towering in his hopes. A lake he would recognize from the aerial photographs—purchased in his first enthusiasm for forest living, and how long ago was that?—photographs whose edges he had scotch-taped at overlapping angles for the larger picture. See? he'd told Caroline Troyer, who already knew. This here's Cardinalis, over here. And we're right . . . uh—

"Here." Her finger already on the spot.

I am too weak for this, Wakelin thought, but he was not too weak, not yet. The boots kept moving. One in front of the other.

The high ground when he reached it was that other forest world. Softer and darker, in spruce and hemlock, mammoth pick-up-stick deadfall. A greenish light. An interior space of silence, dim and cool as a church, lit by luminous moss on grey-blue boulders, by ferns pale lime against the black peat soil, low and springy in a bowl of rock.

Somewhere something was screaming. Periodic in the silence as a car alarm. Periodic like that time-signal kind of sound he had heard from the woods once, at his cabin. But not electronic. And not human. Mammal or bird, Wakelin had no idea, until he was squatting before it, and it was neither: the head of a green frog staring up at him from out of the stretched jaws of a gartersnake. A gartersnake with two heads, nested heads, both dedicated to watching Wakelin, the foremost, in addition, to intermittent screaming.

Beyond the grove of conifers was a pond, the near lip of its shore a feldspar-pink swell in a glare of sun. Before he reached the light, still in shade, Wakelin came upon a circle of blackened stones. Spectral within the charred ring, a clutch of devil's pipe. A stooped cluster. Roundabout, crushed beer cans, broken glass, rusty bottle caps, faded red plastic cases of shotgun cartridges. Human traces. Nothing recent. But that cairn the other day could have been a century old.

Well, now. Finally we're getting somewhere, and about time. I've been start-ing to hope Ross Troyer would show up. He'd get us out of here pretty quick.

Wakelin entered the sun. Across the pond a blue heron lifted away over the trees on slow-motion wings. *Crawnk. Crawnk.*

Wakelin lay on his back on the pink rock, an arm over his eyes against the pain of the light. The rock was warm.

Silence. The zoom and growl of a hummingbird. Here. There. There. Here. There. Gone.

Silence. From out of the silence a slow distant rending of roots or limbs, branches slashing and raking all the way into the tremendous crash.

Stop moving and pay attention for one second around here and life rushes in. Followed by the question, Where was I before? Don't tell me trudging that narrow tunnel of commotion again? The one you trudge and trudge and nothing changes? Where you're comfortable enough, you suppose. More or less uneasy. More or less grieving. Caught in those former grooves. A creature of your own history, just like the next animal. Harking back, thought like a tongue visiting and revisiting in that obsessive tongue way sites of oral disturbance, or let's say thought for reasons of its own assumes the past is a string of knots in need of untying, except with every pass the knots are pulled tighter, and really the only way to do the job is to loop back through each knot with an end of the string, meaning your own birth or death, one or the other, well, hey, no problem. . . .

Wakelin sat up, opened his eyes. The day was dark with brightness. He edged down the rock on his heels and palms. To be closer to the water, which was very clear. A bottom of muck and rock and woodland debris. Gaunt soft poles in eidetic parallel like a gathering of fallen masts. Scum-green bottlenecks and glints of broken glass. Humanity with its sad message.

Wakelin came onto his knees and leaned forward, the water a mirror. Narcissus lost.

Skull and grizzle, hair matted. No beauty here. He sat back, eyes closed. Narcissus saved.

Heard next, though at first in the form of a more palpitant and interior order of event than actual sound, a hollowing roar, wide and distant at first, and then everywhere. He looked up. A jet. A moving glint of silver that plumed fat vapour against the blue sky, like aerosol foam from a tiny moving slit in luminous bristol board, the soundtrack of its own roar lagging. Watched it until the reflection of glint and vapour in the glassy pond drew his eye downward, and exactly there, in perfect intersection with that moving slit, as if it knew, the head of a snapping turtle broke the surface. First the bevelled wedge of skull, then the green-black hump, rocking a little, sending out ripples. A buoyant stone. The water so lucid that Wakelin, when the snapper swam in closer to check him out, could see the red-spotted leeches rippling like pennants from its shell, and when it ducked its head for the bottom he could see the clawed stout forelegs part the water before it, first one and then the other, like the paws of a strongman.

A solitary vireo projected its slurry song onto the silence. And did it again.

Wakelin rose to his feet, emptied and sun-heated. Stretched deliciously.

Two hours later, in a cold sweat, night fallen, the forest darkness high against the sky all around, black tar sloshing slow in a bucket, he had lost the trail in every direction, come to a swaying stop, whispering, Help me, Caroline, please, I'm lost. I'm serious. July or not. I could die out here.

"Walter, Wakelin should have been back at his cabins by now," Clarice Heinrichs said. "Wherever he went." She was in her shift, at her dressing table. Smoking again, after six years.

Her husband lay in bed, the sheets around one leg in such a way as to secure his genitals tightly. Walter Heinrichs never slept in more than a T-shirt. A resister of reading glasses now for some time, he was squinting at his magazine. "That's right. And when you thought the Troyer girl was at Wakelin's cabins she was safe and sound in Grant with her mother, sworn to secrecy by Wakelin, who will probably be back in the city by now, filing his story on her."

"She doesn't lie, Walter."

"So I've heard you say. Veracity's an important quality for you in people, Clarice, I wonder why."

"Oh, give it a rest." She butted out her cigarette. "What's next?"

He shrugged.

"Walter, they've got to find Wakelin and they've got to find Troyer. Escalate their search. Something."

He glanced at her. "So tell them. Tell them to escalate their search. While you're at it, you can tell them how it came to be my canoe that got trashed."

Clarice closed her eyes and said in the affectless voice of one saying something she has been required to say too many times, "Because I lent it out to sweeten a sale."

"With my full knowledge and consent."

"If you like. And you could tell them the same."

"Good. I will. Except, Clarice, I can't tell you how sick I am at the thought I should come to lie to those fuckheads."

"So don't. We won't lie."

"And tell them what?"

"We'll tell them I thought it would be a couple of days. We'll tell them I thought you'd never notice. We'll tell them you haven't used it for five years."

"Oh, they'll like that. Wonder what else old Walter hasn't used for five years? Wonder what else she thought he'd never notice? And what has starting smoking usually meant for you in the past, Mrs. Heinrichs? Something been tickling your—conscience?"

"Why are you persisting in being weird about this, Walter? The only way I screwed the guy was by selling him a property worth approximately half what he paid. I've been worried about them both. I don't want to be the one who organized the warrant that turned a wacko wife-beater into a homicidal fugitive. I don't want to be the one who's going to have to live with the guilt if anybody gets hurt. And if I told you the mess Wakelin's head was in when I left those two alone there, you'd think worse of me than if I told you I blew him on his dock with her and ten fishermen watching."

Clarice went into the bathroom.

"That wasn't funny," he called.

"I know," she said to her face in the mirror through the foam of her toothbrush.

When she got into bed he was reading again.

"Walter, please stop dragging your feet on this."

"Who's dragging? What can I do? It's police business. I'm not a cop."

"No, but you can talk to them. They'll listen to you. You're practically their boss."

"I'm not their boss, I'm their worst enemy."

"Walter, they have to find Wakelin, and they have to find Troyer. I'm telling you the truth."

"About this."

"Just stop it right now! This is getting stupid!"

He turned a page. "Yeah."

Clarice climbed out of bed and crossed the room for her cigarettes and lighter. Climbed back into bed and lit one. "Christ," she said quietly, exhaling. "Six years. How many times do I have to apologize? One fucking lapse."

"One lapse of fucking. Clarice, I don't care about the canoe. It's the going behind my back. It stirs it all up for me."

"Well, I'm sorry you're all stirred up. But this is something different. You don't play with other people's lives to get back at your wife for a mistake she's been apologizing for, for six years."

He smiled sadly. "Sure you do. Six years is nothing. It's a blink of the eye."

The doors of the cabins were padlocked and cordoned with strips of yellow plastic, but there were no police on the site when Caroline Troyer came in through the woods in early morning with a small pack on her back in which she carried, along with a little food, a hacksaw of her father's. With this she cut the padlocks on three doors—the doors of the shed and both cabins—and searched each structure and the surrounding area for a sign of Wakelin. Found nothing in the main cabin beyond unwashed breakfast dishes. In the plywood cabin the table had been moved away from the window and the chair placed next to it. This would be him trying to hear what her father would do in the night.

Again she started to trace the path out she considered he would have followed, assuming there had been an opportunity and he had taken it. This time, in the grounded branches of a fallen hemlock, she saw the disturbance, and beyond there, perhaps fifty yards, a few blood-drops on the pale carpet of leaves. Tracked a stumbling progress to a place of erosion beneath brittle deadfall at the edge of a small ravine. Saw where someone had dropped through to more deadfall. Saw further commotion in the gravel beyond there.

Leapt down. Saw moss-skidded rocks in the streambed. Saw crushed bracken. Tracked a path that moved generally southwest, in great circles away from the lake and the power line both, and she understood that he had started out floundering, terrified in the night, and when daylight came he had stumbled on, able to see now but hardly less blind, with no idea where he was or in what direction he was going. And she understood that he was not hurt, not badly. Only, by the time full daylight came, utterly lost.

And she remembered that for some out here it is all just trees.

Wakelin was eating almost-ripe blueberries that grew around a green saucer of meadow, anxiously scanning the perimeter until at last he knew why: just across the way, watching him, was Ross Troyer. Tall and grey as a column of smoke. But Wakelin must have been madder than he knew, because no sooner did he understand it was Troyer than he set out across the clearing toward him, thinking, I'll just brazen my way through, like last time.

Except, the ground went immediately springy, and Wakelin thought this must be himself, collapsing with joy and terror, his legs gone to rubber, and then there was nothing underfoot at all, and he was in ice water, flailing at a ragged mat of sphagnum, sensation and motor control together sucking away to cryogenic nothing, to doomed meat, numb and thrashing, instantly weary as death, already sinking, sinking, until his fingers brushed, and subsequently boot struck, a thick-furred bulk of flank, and he kicked, a slow yield, an initiation of rocking or toppling of far more substantial meat than himself, and it propelled him upward to crawl out, arm over de-sensationed arm, clutching somehow at moss yielding under his numb hands as he hauled himself and hauled himself, to clutch at moss that at last did not so readily give way. And crawled out senseless and aching and pulled off his clothes and wrung them with every ounce of his shuddering strength.

The air at first was incredibly warm. Then it cooled fast. And Wakelin was shivering before a swollen red sun, shivering and rubbing his arms until no part of that empty radiance showed. Ross Troyer did not so much slip soundless back into the woods as in the changing light stand revealed as a hollow grey trunk of cedar. Christ, what a fool I am, Wakelin thought. And as he moved from foot to foot, he wondered what you are supposed to do, anyway, in the sinking chill of dusk with soaked clothes and no fire, short of develop hypothermia. Short of hug yourself, rock and moan, teeth chattering, while the wolves gather to lounge in the slow regard of their animal patience, muzzles on paws, eyes glowing yellow in the moon-slatted shadows as you grow warm and die on a bright summer night with your pants around your ankles. O for a blanket! O for the skin of a deer! What else was it people used to cobble for warmth in this pitiless land? Moss? Bark? Feathers? And why when such a question was asked was there always a First Nations, just at your shoulder, who knew exactly what to do right down to the last herb and cross-hitch?

In the dusk, bugs gathering, Wakelin held his wet clothes away from his body and carried them to higher ground. There among mainly hardwoods he dug a burrow, which he lined with moss and covered with branches from a new-fallen balsam. On top of the branches he laid his wrung-out clothes for a roof and curled up under there wondering from what distance of ambient air clothes as they dry will extract warmth, knowing that an Indian would know, daring to wonder if his own humble jerry-rig here would win that Indian's approval, knowing that Indian approval was the last thing it would win. Of course, an Indian would know how to start a fire. That would make a big difference right there. All Wakelin knew was the joke about rubbing two boy scouts together.

And so, as Wakelin in his burrow shivered himself into a fever of unconsciousness, the dreamer set out to interview, for a desktop publication of few subscribers, a shining lashless Indian said to have the q.t. on Caroline Troyer (the true towerer over Wakelin's trudge, the saint in the sky towards whose shrine the pious pilgrim plods, a towerer taller even than his Indian), but from the Shining One could be elicited only oblique tales, banal and preposterous, accounts of men changing into women and women into men, both sexes into animals, animals into rocks, old rocks into new rocks, all rocks into gods, gods into animals. A regular hail of transformation.

Shaggy boundary stories. Land of water, land of dreams. To hear this fellow talk, you would think reality was nothing but energy in a constant state of flux. You would think people had nothing better to do than roam endless forests half naked and completely lost. Out there only the animals seemed to have any idea where they were, but except on the rare occasions something startled them into vigilance the animals were all hopelessly bemused, and of course their identities kept changing as much as everybody else's. The only one crazy enough to think he might be able to nail something down around here was the dreamer, except that he had forgotten his pen, and most of the night he spent standing around with his eyes popping out of his head and his hands patting at his pockets. But when the dream-dawn broke and still nothing had been settled, he tore a piece of charcoal off a lightninged oak and went looking for a writing surface, which he found in the form of a large flat rock resembling a pallet for a god. By this time those eyes were spinning like pinwheels. Whose eyes, he was no longer sure. Nor whose shaking, blackened digits these were gripping the charcoal. Still, to give him credit, he tried to get something down. Tried until the tears brimmed and burned. By then of course he couldn't see anything at all, was working from pure memory, a faculty never pure.

In the darkness, meanwhile, the sound of rain, just starting.

In the morning the sun rose bright through the trees. Wakelin was curled in his burrow, clutching his feet. When he imagined the air had warmed a little he crawled out. The air was not warm at all. He carried his clothes back to the spruce bog, where he saw the rend in the moss, the slit of black water, and he wondered what creature had saved him. A moose, preserved fifteen years in the gelid acid tea? A woolly mammoth, preserved ten thousand? Performing from its watery grave every few thousand years a dolphin-worthy good turn for a fellow mammal?

Wakelin put on the shirt and boots. The jacket and jeans were too wet and cold, not that the shirt and boots were not. His underpants he had left behind somewhere, just as well, a stinking itching rag. There was now no doubt in his mind he had a bug of some kind, this was not mere exposure; he was exposed all right, but it was more than that, beaver fever probably, and he saw himself drinking from a stream below one dam too many. Today a temperature and the runs, tomorrow uncontrollable gnawing and ground-slapping. Or maybe it was too many insect bites, a touch of encephalitis. You could tell by the late incredible tightness of the circles he now wandered. Also the way the biggest of them had lost their symmetry, like the webs of spiders fed LSD. Or maybe it was more than one thing. Bush, beaver, and brain fever in virulent collusion. Whatever exactly his problem, he was not well, but he knew it, he knew he was not well. Not well. Not well.

He was headed what might have been northwest, or possibly east, carrying his jacket and jeans, still heavy with water. More of that life-giving, life-taking substance squished in his boots with the ominous warmth of a near-zero liquid scarcely warmer than the limb immersed in it.

He had come to a stream. He stood a stick in it to determine the direction of flow, his perceptions were now that unaccountable. Upstream would be marshland, he decided on no evidence, downstream a large inland waterway dotted with pleasure craft. From his forty-foot sloop a kindly silver-haired tycoon with a talent for the big picture would dispatch a native guide in a small outrigger to pick up Wakelin (collapsed among the rocks at the shore, so much turtle food), so that his petulant bombshell daughter (who bore a striking resemblance to Clarice Heinrichs), on holiday with the folks after an ugly divorce, might have a chance to feel not so much like a complete failure by nursing back to health, civilization, and storybook romance this otherwise doomed feral journalist.

Wakelin followed the flow, which seemed to be southward. His choices were pure now, free of fact. He was extremely tired, lassitudinous almost. Giddy. The land on either side of the stream was more chaos of brush and slash. Where the water ran shallow he staggered rock to rock or waded, boots soaked anyway. And then the terrain levelled out, the stream ran deeper, and he crawled up its banks to stumble its winding course, which were he to lose he could no longer trust himself not to head off in a completely different direction from, oblivious to any shift of intention. This was why he kept saying, over and over, to the beat of his trudge, If you can't be alert, be a slave. Soon these words had lost more than all meaning, they had lost recognizability as sounds within the competence of an English speaker.

Still, again, third time lucky, Wakelin was once more pretty well home. On this morning because he was hearing that time signal, the sound from the forest that had kept him sleepless one early morning at his cabins, now so long ago. On this morning here, Wakelin wasn't remembering the time signal from that other morning, he was hearing it. He knew that. He had come to a low flat rock in brighter light, under a gap in the trees, a great birch recently fallen. It was the pallet for a god from his dream, the one the dreamer had found it so difficult to get anything down on, the tears burning, though Wakelin's memory of this dream was limited to a mild pang at the emptiness of the rock and a faint sting along the lower eyelids. He sat on the rock, cool and sticky on his bare stinking ass, a prime hemorrhoid candidate as he waited for the time signal to sound again, but it did not, and he had forgotten it completely, was sunk in the old commotion, and then it did, practically inside his head, and that was when he saw it, perched in a variety of bush unfamiliar, burgundy-leaved, two feet in front of his face: an earless owl so tiny it was like something at the wrong depth of perspective. Six inches from foot to crown. Yellow eyes blazing. The lids slowly falling. With equal slowness lifting.

Wakelin made no move lest the creature fly. How long the two of them continued face to face he could not have said. Quite a while. Mad Tim Wakelin and the tiniest owl that ever lived, gripped in a terminal headlock. Either they were mutually hypnotized or, more likely, the bird was sound asleep and it was Wakelin hypnotized, by the rhythm of those lids lifting and lowering against those giant black pools ringed by such intensity of yellow glowing.

In the end, innocent of choice, Wakelin rose and stepped toward the creature, which continued to sit even as Wakelin's left forefinger came up to stroke the delicate bones of its head. An activity that like a great airship swung slowly round and started outward to infinity. The owl gave every appearance of enjoying the experience, in any case made no objection. It was unbelievable. Connection at last. Like rising blest from slumber. Like emerging from the endless conflict of dreaming into a wakeful calm. And Wakelin went on stroking the tiny head.

And then, somewhere on the horizon of this unbroken expanse of time, there dawned a presence, from behind. Wakelin told himself that this would be his imagination, as had been Ross Troyer, as was surely this owl, and yet how could even an encephalitic hallucination achieve such zeal of ocular flame, such subtlety of shading and intricate arrangement of feathers to make a coat, such exquisite silkiness against the knuckle of so beautiful, so gentle-feathered an avian head? No, it wasn't his imagination. Not this owl, anyway. This owl was real. And just because he himself was the only one in a position to judge in this matter did not mean that no judgement was possible. Did it?

And then Wakelin was turning, and long before his brain was able to compose itself to let him know what it was he saw next, his body wobbled in a kind of bliss.

The owl conveyed its weight from one foot to the other and lifted off.

"I scared the bird," Wakelin gasped in a voice of amazed apology or complaint, it was not clear which, clutching at his chest like a coronary victim. He did not know if she was real or a vision. But he knew that he did not know.

Caroline Troyer had turned her head to watch the owl pass through the trees. She looked at Wakelin. "Saw-whet," she said, and smiled. "At night he'd as soon kill you."

"Look, I'm sorry about the no-pants thing again," Wakelin told her. He held up his hands, gazed at them unseeing. Strangely, they were empty. "Where are they?" he wondered. But even as he cast his head round to have a look he was falling in darkness.

Bachelor Crooked Hand's fingers scooped the congealed mud from the pot, which he had set on the floor next to his boots.

Ardis was stretched out on the chesterfield. Her eyelids quivering. Crooked Hand's left buttock was on the edge of the chesterfield, his hip pressed against hers.

Gently he spread the substance over her left eye. When he had also covered the right eye he said, "How does that feel?"

"Warm. The little marchers are slowing down. Or maybe everything just got darker."

Ardis's right hand groped in air for his knee. Settled a moment on the warm chino. Moved from there to his left hand now cupped over the mud on her right eye. With her hand she cupped his hand that cupped her eye.

"Bachelor," she said. "If it doesn't work, it doesn't matter."

"If it doesn't work, you're not going to be able to see."

"I'll have you."

"Me? You don't even remember my fucking name."

There was a pause. "Bachelard," she said slowly, with a touch of amazement. "It's Bachelard. I knew that. When the hell did I stop calling you Bachelard?"

"Twenty-some years ago. Because Bachelor's what he started to call me. One of his jokes, that's me."

"But that's awful. I switched and I never even noticed."

"No, you didn't notice."

Her breath began to catch.

"No tears. You'll upset the pH."

She laughed.

A few minutes later she said, "Don't you think Keeper would've made a terrific seeing-eye dog?"

"You don't have to worry about that. You're not going to need any seeing-eye dog."

"Bachelard, you'll forgive me, won't you?"

"You don't need any forgiveness. Not from me."

Ardis squeezed his knee. "Even if I told her how you lost your hair?"

"You did, eh," he murmured as he continued to hold both hands over the mud on her eyes. "She like that story, did she?"

"I need to know—" Wakelin said. "You have to tell me—"

They had reached the road that followed the power line. It had taken almost five hours. Now it was late afternoon. Wakelin had not understood how little strength was left to him until he had to keep up with her. Again and again, if she wanted them to move forward—which she did—it was necessary for her to support him. He could walk, but his legs were not steady. The ground was by no means always flat or unobstructed. He kept falling. Every time he fell he was less able to get up without her help. He could feel his own weight on her, heavy and growing heavier. She bore up, she was not sinking under, but this was not an easy thing she was trying to do. Her strength was not limitless. How long she herself had been out here he did not know. If she told him, he failed to take in this information or else to retain it. The support of her arm, of her shoulder, was a blessing, and he wanted it to be infinite. He could feel his own interior insistence that it be so, and when she herself stumbled or when, after a time, gently, she gave back to him his own weight, or most of it, he could feel the strange, ruthless force of his complaint, of his childish resentment.

But they had made it as far as the power-line road, and now they were stretched out below it, near the base of a great pylon, wires overhead, in the long rain- or deer-flattened grass that grew on that rocky ground, half under raspberry bushes, waiting for a truck to come along. If no truck or ATV came soon—which seemed likely, likely that is one would not, there had been only four sets of ATV tracks, two coming, two going, since the rains, which had been when?—they would walk the road, and maybe, though this was no more likely, one would appear as they walked. She had said they were two or three miles down the line from the height of land above his cabins. They would not reach there before nightfall.

She was touching the swollen glands behind his ears, his mind adhering to that interface, his body slumped larval.

Later she was cradling his head in her hands, the warmth from her palms penetrating the back of his skull to illuminate, along with the linings of his eye sockets and nose and mouth, the multifold surface of his brain, and he could feel the heat of that simmering, swollen walnut, how crazed it was, and he could feel that other order of warmth assessing the fever there, something the way a different quality of intelligence simply by entering a room will reduce the confusion, will harmonize a good proportion of the noise.

"What is it?" she said.

"These experiences of yours," Wakelin said, and the syllables were a stream of sound, like a snake descending from his brain and flowing out his mouth. "What is it about them guarantees a better person at the other end? Forget the healing. What's the next person supposed to take from this? Okay, so there's no story. Let's say the next person can live with no story. How about a moral?" He looked at her. "Your hands feel great. Who says you stopped healing? Please don't ever let go of my head."

She was looking down into his face. Hers was dark against the bright blue of the sky, but there was light in it too. He could not return her gaze for long. Dropping his eyes, he saw his foreshortened body, jagged-ribbed and bony-hipped and angry with bites, and he saw how it was sprawled in her lap, the two of them making a grunge Pietà, him with his filthy flannel shirt twisted nipple-high, no loincloth. His cock, foreshortened too (he just knew), was invisible from here, shrunk amidst a wisp of black hair like armpit hair. His knees were scarred knobs, his bruised, sun-burned shanks criss-crossed and purpled with cuts and contusions. Both feet, in big scuffed sodden hiking boots, had flopped to the right.

He was still talking. That snake. "Bliss doesn't get great press," he was saying, as if she didn't know this, over the past year hadn't learned it very well. "Except for endorphins, or romance. Everything else is suspect. Fitness and procreation, right? The most brain-dead rationalist is going to get behind those two. But not this. This has got to be sex gone oceanic. Some kind of super-sublimation jackpot. Right?"

"We have to walk," she said.

"Why you? What happened?"

She shook her head.

"Sorry," he said quickly. "Head wants to know. Causes. Science, religion, it's all let's-get-some-purchase-here."

"So put it aside."

"Uh-huh. But—"

"Please. We have to—"

"Caroline, I'm just trying to make sense of this."

"For the next person."

"All right. For me."

"You could make sense of it forever. It's not the same as what it is. You're standing on the bank. Now dive in."

"To what?"

With her eyes she indicated the grassy bouldered terrain of the clearing that fell away before them to the wall of trees, and above the trees the sky.

"I thought I just did. You had to rescue me."

She smiled. "I guess the next person led you astray."

Wakelin sniffed, and then he said, "You know what they think it is? Dissociation by trauma. They think if you could remember half what your father's done to you, you wouldn't ever come within a thousand light years of experiences like the one I was there for. And you wouldn't be such a terrific healer, either. That's what they think. But it's not enough, is it? It doesn't account for what even I could feel in that cabin, and I'm not exactly a sensitive. And it doesn't explain how those experiences could heal you, if that's what they've done, I mean make you whole. Whole? What am I saying? What do I know about whole? Exemplar. Ideal of my life. What's going on, Caroline? Is this me doing this, making me feel this way, or you? Am I a devotee? You put a spell on me? *It* put a spell on me?"

She was looking at him.

"What is this, witchcraft? God, what am I saying?"

She did a strange thing then. She leaned over and kissed his forehead, a cooling touch. A chilled ice-cream scoop into the brain, a cold-drink headache between the eyes, except ice-stillness, not ice-pain. She raised her head away from his own and looked at him again.

"I never forgot what happened," she said. "I wanted it all. He knew what he was doing. He didn't hurt me. I was a child. I thought the physical part was how it was. I loved him. He was the one I trusted."

Wakelin closed his eyes, twisting his head in her hands. "No," he said. "No, no, *no*—"

"That's enough," she said. She slid her hands down under his shoulders and lifted with surprising strength until he was in a sitting position, starbursts in front of his eyes.

"Now stand and walk."

When Caroline Troyer saw her father he was half a mile ahead, coming down a long grade steep enough for the road to switch back twice before it disappeared into the woods. Even at that distance she could see it was him. The tallness, the gait. And then she saw him stumble, and it seemed to her that by the time they reached him he would be fallen in the road. She said nothing to Wakelin, lest he be thrown off the small pace he'd been able to maintain. As a result he did not see her father until he was almost upon them. When he did see him, his head swung in her direction like a sign on rusted hinges.

"Devil Daddy," he said.

Her father was carrying his deer rifle over his right forearm and a denim sack in his left hand. He was not stumbling now. He could not have seen them from the hill, because the late sun must have been in his eyes, but he had seen them before Wakelin saw him. His clothes, his old hunting rain gear, were stiff with dried mud and luminous with pollen. He looked as though he had been wading through swamp to his neck. His head he held boldly, like something ornamental. There was jubilance in his bearing, his movements galvanic, and about his eyes as their gaze entered her with fanatic calm was the cauterized and smoking aspect of the wasteland prophet.

Suddenly Wakelin lurched and cried out, "You bastard! That's my wife's gear!"

She staggered to hold him.

When she looked again, her father had stopped to lift the denim bag and hold it away from his face. It might have been something he had picked up in the road and was only now taking time to examine. Its bottom was stained dark. Methodically he set it down and laid the rifle against it and straightened up once more alongside these effects, arms hanging, swaying a little.

She halted in front of him, not too close, Wakelin still with her, leaning hard on her arm.

"Why'd you steal my stuff?" Wakelin said.

"Help me," she told her father. "He's sick."

Her father tried to speak, could not. His tongue passed over his lips. "So heal him," he said. His voice was scarcely audible.

"Have you got any food or water on you?" she said.

His left hand was fumbling at his jacket pocket. And then he was holding something out to her, something draped over his hand.

She looked at it. A half-unstuffed bear. "I said food."

"I want you to . . . have this."

"Whose is it? Where'd you get it?"

Wakelin seemed to look at her.

Her father shook his head.

"I don't want it," she said. "He needs food and water."

At first her father didn't seem to understand. And then, with some difficulty, he put the bear back into his pocket.

"I need to get him to Coppice," she said.

"Bachelor at the house?"

She nodded. "Help us. Turn yourself in. You know she'll drop the charges. Or don't. Just help us."

Her father took a step forward. He reached out and tugged the matted hair at Wakelin's temple. "Look at all the grey," he said. He looked down. She had tied her jacket around Wakelin's waist. "Has he still got his little clay pipe?" He pulled at the front of the jacket, which fell to the ground at Wakelin's feet.

They all looked at his nakedness.

"Why'd you steal my stuff?" Wakelin said, continuing to gaze downward, still searching perhaps.

The other had lost interest. He was reaching around behind him to pick up his rifle and the bag. And then he was coming forward to pass her on her left side, the side opposite Wakelin. As he did so, he said quietly, "Nobody will ever know how much I loved you. Don't let them pretend." As he said this he seemed to stumble, and though there was little she could do with Wakelin hanging on to her so heavily, she made a move, all but involuntary, to reach around a hand to slow her father's fall, but his arm was already coming up swinging the barrel of the rifle, and it struck her hard across the side of the face, and it was she who went down, Wakelin with her.

Casually, though taking aim, Ross Troyer tossed the bag in such a way that it landed in front of Wakelin's nose in the dirt of the road. And then he walked back and as casually, holding the rifle in one hand only, his arm outstretched, placed the tip of the barrel at the back of Wakelin's head and pulled the trigger. But the cylinder was empty, and it only clicked. Troyer looked at the rifle as if it had suddenly flown into his hand for a purpose unknown. Impatiently he threw it into the ditch and reeled round.

He staggered on.

Wakelin's hand was in the air, coming for her face. It was shaking. There was dirt at his mouth and a paler path of tears horizontal across the bridge of his nose and in a splay of streaks from the corner of his right eye and through the grime at his temples to his hairline.

She had been thinking it was him who was hit. She had been trying to push herself up to see to him. She kept thinking it was him long after she knew it must have been herself. She stayed his wrist.

"Are you all right?" he whispered. He was sobbing again. "I'm so sorry, I—I—couldn't—"

"It just hurts," she said, or tried to say. That was when she knew it was broken. Something. Her jaw, her cheekbone. She tried to sit up, fell back sideways. Succeeded at last.

When she looked around, Wakelin was fumbling like an old man at the drawstring of the bag. She looked away as from an intimate act. Finally he got it open. "Aw jeez," he whispered and slowly lay down once more in the road.

She pulled the bag towards her. It stank. Inside were heads. Squirrel, chipmunk, raccoon, rabbit, groundhog, weasel, skunk, mink, snake. There must have been two dozen heads, eyes glazed. Not a great bulk of heads, considering how many. Considering how many had died.

She turned where she sat and looked back down the road to the west, in the direction that she and Wakelin had come from, the direction her father had gone. For some reason she anticipated that he would be difficult to see for the glare of the sun on the horizon, but the sun had set some time ago, there was now only a silver paleness in the west, and her father was not in sight. She no longer knew how long ago it was now when Wakelin—no, when she—had been hit. Still, it surprised her how rapidly, in all, the night had come on.

In the darkness Ross Troyer slept by a rock. In the night the rock was black, a darker shadow, but in the morning sun it became a presence eroded and decomposed, layered pink and black and red in collapsed and sagging pleats, some granular, some platey. Others fibrous. Some seams choked massive with white crystals, others dwindling to agonized scribbles of darkness. A nightmare of striped and rotting complexity.

With relief he left the rock and stepped back to the road.

That same morning he came to the lone standing pile that remained of the bridge at the Pardee. The fact that reconstruction had not been begun here would account for why there had been no traffic up from the west. Normally pickup trucks would be down from Coppice, to view the damage. As it was there had been only the two ATVs. The washout at the swamp he had crossed last week could not have been repaired yet either. The graders would still be busy elsewhere, their first priority the town-owned roads. The hunt-camp boys would be taking a collection to hire the first to become available. Either it was not available yet or this time round the boys had been slow to organize.

There were no tracks at all through the smoothness of the mud on the lane that ran along the river on this side. It surprised him that the ATVs would not have checked on her. It must have been a couple of fourteen-year-olds. He took that lane. Soon he came to the stand of birch, where the old truck was still on its nose. He descended to have a look.

The driver's door stood open like a platform. The mud on it had been

291

disturbed, and the drowned were no longer inside. He crouched to examine the disruption in the mud on the steering wheel and on the driver's seat and along the dash. The stink of the mud.

He sat on the edge of the open door with his boots planted in the deeper mud of the grove floor. He lowered his face into his hands. He knew that if he were to weep now, it would be as much for the youth of this birch tree as for the ones now gone from this truck or from anywhere else. If he were to weep now, it would be for himself, and he knew that once those gates were open it would not be in his power to close them. When the body ran out of tears it would stumble down to the river to drink, and the water it took in it would salt and extrude as more tears, and when it had no more salt it would go forth like a porcupine to gnaw bark, and from that bitter cud it would create more tears, and it would create them for as long as the body was able to drink and to gnaw, and yet how could there ever be enough? And what would the body be at the end of such an insufficiency of tears but the carcass of an animal wrung and discarded by sorrow?

He did not weep. Why start now? What had changed that had not changed too long since?

Instead he followed her footsteps where she had carried the child, and he could see the second trail where she returned to drag the boot heels of the other through the mud, closer to the lane. And sure enough, on a saddle of grass above the road as he drew nearer to the house he saw two crosses, straight and white, assembled out of scrap lumber, the one smaller.

Now, there was something he liked to see from a woman: the proper observances.

Meriting perhaps a little something in marble. Here's an area it happens I might just be able to help you out. You know they deserve the best.

From his pocket he took the now slack bear and looked at it and it at him, a bituminous gaze. Full circle, he whispered. A home-fire-burner like this one, she'll have some thread around the place. Get you restuffed, little friend.

Wildflowers grew on the slope up to that narrow cemetery shelf: cinquefoil, loosestrife, knapweed, musk mallow, and he picked a bouquet there, lighter than his bag of soul palaces and of more conventional delight to the fair, and this was what he was holding in his left hand, the bear in his right, as he skirted the foundations of the former barn, now a rock enclosure for a stench of rotting meat, for the buzzing of a million blowflies, to pass among the relics of ancient machinery, the mud on it dry now and falling away in wafers, on his way toward the porch, where he could see from the pattern of darkness and light from behind the screen that the main door stood open, and only the screen door—the last time he had seen which was flung smashed and mud-silted and half torn from its hinges against the clapboard aluminum wall—was closed.

He stopped. He raised his bouquet high. The small bear pressed now to the side of his face. He tried to speak, could not. For those, he considered, who do not see. Neither do they know what they do. He was not weeping that he could tell, but that screen door kept blurring. Otherwise it was vivid indeed. Of ancient rough-hewn construction, with its sagging rusted screening and its battered and misshapen wood frame and crosspiece, scored and glossy grey with age.

A gate of beauty.

And then he saw that the screen in its two sections, one above and one below, was breathing. Moving in and out. Panting, as it were. The lungs of this house.

"Grief shared is grief halved," he said, more loudly. His voice rough with disuse.

That screening in its two sections was grief halved. Somewhere an oven-bird sang.

He started forward once more. How good is arrival when at last. What man could guess at every moment where his true destination must lie? And to think he had almost waited too long. Why, he could hardly walk!

He thought he saw movement in the light from beyond the screen of the screen door.

Again he stopped, swaying. "Darling!" he whispered. "I'm home!"

He was climbing now with difficulty the same steps, he realized, that he had watched her cows stumble against in the darkness of the flood, and now he could see the section of the porch where she had repaired the damage made by the one that had gone through. And as he came up onto the level of the porch he studied, from that distance, the fit she had engineered between unpainted boards of a different gauge—the same boards, he noticed, that she had used for the crosses, one-by-four spruce—and those of the original porch floor, and everywhere the new joints, which were not tongue and groove, met the old, which were tongue and groove, cleanly. And as he admired that unpainted patch in its unity, it seemed to him the image of his own soul returning to the palace of his own head, imperfect and yet a job ever carefully and sorrowfully done, as it was for him the image of herself at home here on this humble woodland estate. And no sooner had these resemblances arisen to mind than from the corner of his eye, which is to say from directly in front of his chest, exactly as he was taking his first step across the surface of that porch, he saw something from within the ancient living screen of the screen door, and it was not light but, in an area not far above the midpoint crosspiece, a kind of roiling or stir, initially without shape but immediately forming to a bloom of black and iron-brown, a mighty trumpet-blast of buckshot and rust, moving outward in rebuke (he imagined at first) to this bouquet, and yet instead of their blooms from their stems, blowing deep into the very centre of his own chest, and his first thought as he experienced his entire body lift up and away like dust raised by the wind, a creature unworthy to compete, possessing no longer the requisite strength or skill to remain in the game and so fed with iron, blasted from the field, with the breathing house and the rustling and now darkened treeline descending on all sides, the sky lowering like a blue bowl in the grip of an invisible hand—his first thought: There must be some mistake.

And from his vantage as he was lifted in air he could see the cows, nine in all, scattered along the river, one engrossed in nosing mud from a clump of weeds, two fooled by the echo, looking the wrong way (though one, already realizing its mistake, seemed about to turn back), and finally the six others more intelligent, or perhaps only older, more experienced, their sombre eyes upon him, a bovine regard, until a shift in the gaze of two of them directed his own reflection—not attention, his attention was everywhere, at all times—directed his reflection beyond the hands, which were far out at the very ends of the arms, completely empty, trailing the body, useless appendages, and beyond the ends of the fingers of the left hand he saw a fan of wildflowers, while drifting free of the side of his face was the bear, somersaulting in air. Released perhaps, at last. But not these hands, which looked in their emptiness as though they might be clutching upward for that lowering sky, a child's hands upreaching, saying *Take me back!* And for that second, or that eternity, as he continued to rise, he knew that he was rising home.

And as soon had arrived.

And with arrival the descent.

Home as of ripeness between unripe and rotting, a point on a line only, another empty abstraction, as he had always known. A brazen commodity. Best blasted and brought down. For already he was falling, and falling he understood that home was behind him now, perhaps had only ever been behind him, had only ever been a vain and foolish hope, spun out of some lost memory of lost time.

And hard upon this hard knowledge came a second concussion, equal and opposite to the first, this time from behind, and it was more iron, for what is the ultimate invariable product of stellar evolution but iron? and what is Earth at her core but iron, slow moving, like something remembered? There was no sensation, only the knowledge of a terrific blow from the Earth, an iron paw clapped across the shoulders and the back of the head, saying, *Heads up, camper!* And yet he was no longer intended or expected to lift up his head. The Earth had already brushed him like ash from her sleeve. His last chance had already passed. The way that home had passed. The way everything had always seemed to pass. The way everything he had ever done had been done too late, always with a quality of regret. Remorse the only medium of his life, it now seemed to him. And he remembered a former perception, a perception undead after all, a light from far away, the cradle perhaps, removed from him thereafter, until now. And he knew it must have been the fact of having once enjoyed that light and then enjoying it no longer that had made refusal of it so automatic when she had tried to tell him. And one with the light was the knowledge that there is what a man has the power to convince himself concerning the world and there is what he has the power to do there. And then there is the world, the whole scene of it as it is spread before and within his eye, a site of wonder, a universe of energy where iron and flesh and will and desire are no more than what they are, which is nothing, a shadow, in the light of that.

And what he would not give for a glimpse of that light now.

When the screen door opened it was neither in haste nor timidity, nor even caution, but rather in the methodical manner of a mechanism being appraised for repair, and when the woman, once she had stepped out onto her porch, closed the door behind her, she continued to look back at it, judging what might be required and what she might have on hand for the purpose. And then, the shotgun over her arm, she crossed the porch, stepping through the scatter of wildflowers, to pick up her boy's lank stuffed animal, which lay on its face at the edge of the porch, and this too she appraised, turning it this way and that, judging it too for repair, and then she stepped carefully down the steps, because although the rapist had been blown from the porch to lie in the dried mud like a turtled and flabbergasted hunter, hands clutching at nothing, the feet in their boots had not altogether cleared the steps, which should have been built wider. Something she had always felt. She squatted beside him, the bear tucked at her belly, to check the neck for a pulse—nothing—and close the eyes and the mouth. The rubber jacket he wore lying spread to reveal a sheathed knife on the belt. The well of blood at the chest already crawling and buzzing with flies that had stopped off on their way to the barn site.

She rose up and went back into the house. A few minutes later she came out, again examining the door, carrying no unstuffed bear and no shotgun and wearing workgloves, and with these she grasped the rapist by the ankles and dragged him around the house to behind a low scrapboard shed there. From inside the shed she emerged carrying a shovel and walked back up to the higher ground behind the house, continuing deeper into the woods to a spot at some distance from the crosses on the ridge above the road to the house that marked the resting place of her two.

From the woods, the sound of digging.

After forty-five minutes the woman returned to the shed for a hatchet; she had come to a tree root too slow with the knife, was doing this properly. Of course, in a few days, with the heat and the bears and the wolves, you would have a sorry mess if you didn't. Three hours later she came back for the body, which with difficulty—for she was tired now, and it was a long body, though narrower and lighter than her husband's and easier to drag by the ankles than his had been under the arms—she laboured up the hill and among the trees to the grave site, and after removing the belt from the trousers for the sake of the sheath she rolled the body in and covered it and worked for some time to obscure the place with leaves and branches and then, the belt and knife over her shoulder, walked back down to the house obscuring the drag-trail as she went. By that time half the herd was waiting for her at the bottom of the slope. She pushed through them and went and got a broom and swept the now-wilting wildflowers off the porch.

And then she went back inside the house to find a needle and thread and also clean ragging in order to restore her boy's bear to a semblance of itself, as well as to find, if she could, a scrap of screening, for it seemed to her that she had recently seen a small section of such material folded and tucked up somewhere, and though it was not metal but nylon (she believed), it would do. Perhaps in the attic or out back in the shed. She only hoped that she had not seen it in the crawl space under the house, in a cubbyhole between joists, something like that, for she was reluctant to descend there on account of the muck from the flood but also on account of a horror of those of God's creatures He had relegated to creep, with a particular loathing of serpents, in their alarming and insinuate shame.

Even lying here on the cold ground, Caroline Troyer thought, we wonder when heaven will come. Not understanding that it does not come by waiting any more than by going out and throwing yourself at life, or at death. Or holding on to this or that person, or religion, or endeavour, or conviction. One thing you don't say about heaven is, Here it is. Or, There it is. Another thing you don't say about heaven is, It's not here yet, where is it?

"You have to walk," Caroline Troyer said.

She cradled Wakelin's head in her hands. He was shaking all over.

"I'm freezing," he said. "Why is everything so wet?"

"It's just dew. The fire went out. I'll help you up. It's not far."

"The hell it's not. Where are we? Why haven't you healed me?"

"You're too weak. The fever's down a little, I think."

"I thought you did miracles."

"Just get to your feet. Hold on to me."

What did my father do? Caroline Troyer asked herself. He betrayed what was right and so undid me. He disordered my hope and there was no escape. Only stories, the ones the doctors and the priests are trained to tell. And the writers, according to their imaginations. And no one knows anything. And you are supposed to embrace that whole world of distraction, those lies. You are supposed to assent to stories that say, You will not be harmed. And this is social morality.

But how can you discover heaven's secret if you refuse what you already know perfectly: There is no escape, not really? If you provide yourself with no opportunity at every moment to know heaven's secret, which is just this: There is no escape.

She was feeding Wakelin berries. He had lost control of his bowels. Dehydration, she knew, was the most serious thing now. She had half carried him into the woods, for shelter from the dew, and there she had lit a fire and held him in her arms, but after midnight the air had turned cold, and by morning it was wet in there too. Now she did not know how she could get him any distance at all. But she believed that she could get him back to the road, and surely today another vehicle would be down it, or a plane would see them. This was not exactly the middle of nowhere.

"What's wrong with your face?" Wakelin said. "I can hardly understand you."

When her father died she knew it. The gunshot sounded very distantly, but even Wakelin heard it. He halted and looked at her and said with surprising quickness, "What's that?"

She collapsed to her knees. Wakelin had no choice and fell with her.

It was blue sky she saw, treeline and some kind of house, all sinking. A child's arms outreaching. The terrible innocence.

The grief that struck her down was her own. For the damage done to him, for the havoc created by the course of his life, for the loss of the man she had loved and trusted and who in his ruined, ruthless way had destroyed her.

"What's wrong?" Wakelin said.

Clarice Heinrichs got out of her Corvette on the Coppice side of the washout at the cattail swamp. The man with the electronic voice at the Shell station had told her the washout was here. That it had not yet been repaired. She didn't disbelieve him, she just needed to be going somewhere, doing something.

She skidded down into the mud of the gully to the culvert. Climbed over it and struggled, slipping, up the other side. When she was on gravel again she scraped the great boots of mud off her shoes and started to walk.

She came upon them an hour later, at a point where the road cut back hard into the woods. They were on a rain-ravaged hill of loose gravel and protruding bedrock. They had fallen on the steep slope. The sun here was perpendicular to the angle of the slope and it was very hot. Wakelin was motionless, face down, but Caroline Troyer was still struggling, a creature autonomic, struggling to pull him up and to keep on, but there was not enough strength in her body, and her movements were only digging her deeper into the gravel.

As Clarice knelt to hook her hands under Caroline Troyer's arms and pull her to her knees she caught the stench of Wakelin, who for some reason was still half-naked, a swarm of flies. And then Caroline Troyer's face lolled up on Clarice's arm, and it was monstrously swollen blue-black. Had she fallen? Caroline Troyer's eyes had rolled back in her head, but now they came forward, and when she saw who it was she said slowly, hardly audible, "Thanks . . . knew you'd . . . come."

Wakelin was alive, Caroline Troyer nodded that he was.

Clarice left Caroline Troyer's head resting on Wakelin's back. She couldn't move them, she couldn't comfort them. She had no water with her. She couldn't do anything for them here at all.

But she could run for help.

When Clarice Heinrichs came to the door of Timothy Wakelin's room in the Grant Memorial Hospital, Gail Poot and Elvin Hryniuk were sitting outside it on a bench in the corridor. Elvin was not in uniform but wearing tan cotton pants and a mauve shirt with pearled buttons.

"We already visited the dork," Gail said. "We're waiting for Caroline."

"Caroline?" Wakelin said when Clarice entered the room.

"Not Caroline. Just me."

"Just? Hell. Listen—Thanks."

It hurt her to see how emaciated he was, how small and broken against the pillows.

"I believe," he said, "I owe your husband a canoe."

"It's replaced. Don't think about it. I sold a car dealership last week."

"Do the cars go with it? I always wondered."

"You wouldn't want to pay the kind of money these custom canoes cost."

"Do they cost as much as I overpaid on my place?"

She smiled. "Almost. I'm serious."

"I didn't mean it. It's what it's worth to me, right?"

"Did an agent tell you that?"

They talked. He could only talk about Caroline Troyer.

Finally Clarice told him, "You're both out of your heads, you know that, don't you?"

Wakelin closed his eyes. "She is," he whispered. "I just wish."

Gail and Elvin were still in the hallway when Clarice left Wakelin's room. This time Gail was holding the back of her left hand alongside her face, waggling the fingers. An engagement ring.

"Gail, Elvin—congratulations!" Clarice cried. "That's wonderful! I'm really happy for you."

"I know," Gail said. "It was last night. I thought he'd never fucking ask."

Elvin just went scarlet.

"You can live at my cabins," Wakelin told Caroline Troyer, who sat by his bed in the hospital room, her hands in her lap. Her face was still bruised, but the swelling was nearly gone, the bone mending. "No strings. I don't need the place any more. I've had it with nature. It's back to the city as soon as I'm strong enough to crawl to my car."

After a few minutes he took her hands from her lap and held them, hard. "I'm serious, Caroline. It's all yours. For as long as you want it."

The next day he said, "But if you let me visit, I will. I could sit at your feet."

I don't know what this energy is, Caroline Troyer thought, this intelligence. Obviously it's impossible. All I know is what I remember at any moment, which is only a shadow. All I know is that no one should pretend to understand what has been happening to this body. No one. All I know is that there is no way to know when or if it will ever come again. All I know is that it is always here a little bit and that it is real. That you care for the body, you keep the senses open and clear, and you keep an eye on the injured one, myself, who thinks this all must be for her. You watch her as you'd watch a strange animal. You do this, and there is nowhere to be for this but here. And this is virtue. And this is life.

"You're my saviour," Wakelin said.

"No," she said. "I'm human. I exist. Don't forget that."

"Again, you mean," he said.

"I didn't say that."

"Yeah, well—"

"So where is he?" Wakelin said, meaning her father.

"Buried in the woods."

"You don't know that."

She didn't say anything.

"Have you been to the place?"

"Not yet."

"Will you take me when you go?"

"No."

"What will you do there?"

For a moment she looked at him, and then she said, "I'll remember."

Wakelin seemed to know Caroline Troyer was in the room without opening his eyes. "The first time I come and visit you," he said, "I'm going to sit you down and tell you all the things I learned out there. I swear I could write five books."

"That's because you write," she said.

While Wakelin was in hospital in Grant he started to keep a journal. The first entry:

> With Caroline Troyer I didn't know what I was getting into. I didn't understand that for some people there is no looking away. Most of us are like this only with some things, and these are the things we narrow down on, we specialize. Most of us don't have a lot of love for the world. Maybe we can sense it in others, but we don't have it. We have only so much attention to give, and after that we draw the line. We forge alliances, we man the barricades. And no wonder, when otherwise there are some things you will learn that you can put aside only at your own mortal risk. Either you look away and these things kill you slowly or you face them and they blow you wide open. And who will understand you then? And who will be your guide?

Another entry, when he was back in the city:

> I know that I don't know how to love anyone without, in some way, wanting them, or needing something from them. With Caroline Troyer I want everything. When I told her this she said, Find it in yourself. There's no shortage.
> But what if I've already found it in you?
> Then you found the wrong thing in the wrong place.

307

When Caroline Troyer left the power line she came out of the woods at the top of the garden, now mostly gone to seed, and she moved down through the rank growth slowly, with her penknife cutting wildflowers—monkshood, joe-pye weed, fireweed, late hollyhocks—and these, after she had dropped her knapsack, she carried down between the cabins to step out onto the dock. The breeze was light from the west, and the clouds were white like batting stretched thin, and they moved in stately silence across the blue sky.

After a few minutes, the flowers still in her hand, she stretched out on her stomach and cupped her face and looked over the side of the dock at the trout minnows resting lucid in its shadow and below them, half buried in muck, liquor empties, spirals of fishing line, rotted cans. Wakelin's aluminum chairs were down there too, a gust must have sent them to the bottom, and they had settled upright, side by side, waiting to be used. Now she got to her feet and taking aim at the sun she threw the flowers high, and they scattered and fell upon the water as white and faded litter, and immediately the little waves went to work to hustle everything toward the eastern shore. And early one morning, after she had got herself moved in, and Wakelin, benighted searcher, had paid his mid-September visit and was gone back to the city and the frost had put an end to the bugs, she would walk down the power line to her father's grave, and there perhaps if flowers would not be appropriate, then tears might.

And she thought, There is no story. You do not, like a dreamer waking from a dream, insensibly provide the connections that will make sense of the pieces as if they were a series of events in the world. Thought is physical like the world, but it comes from the past. Its connections are not here and now, they are vertical. You do not string them, you stack them. Memory is a story I tell myself. This is not memory. This is stacking. Like rock. Like earth and seeds. Like atomic fuel.

Other books by Greg Hollingshead

Famous Players (stories)
White Buick (stories)
Spin Dry (novel)
The Roaring Girl (stories)